Al Basha

Al Basha

Our Stories

Franco Minasian

All writers of confessions from Augustine on down have
always remained a little in love with their sins.

- Anatole France

© 2018 Franco Minasian
All rights reserved.
ISBN-13: 9780692857137
ISBN-10: 0692857133
Library of Congress Control Number: 2017903690
JD Enterprises, Homewood, IL

CHAPTER I

UMAIR

Great achievement is usually born of great sacrifice,
and is never the result of selfishness.

—NAPOLEON HILL

U mair, whom I had dubbed "the Arab Woody Allen," invited me to lunch. I could not refuse. He was my most endearing and likeable client; intelligent and kind yet self-deprecating and almost deliberately, calculatingly timid. Every little thing Umair spoke of, every small matter he brought to me, and with every menial decision he made, he would either overbuild or drown out in such sappy accolades. I got a real kick out of this way of him. Umair was curious about me and my life; the guarded sound bites that I shared resonated with him and left him wanting more. Yet as to his divorce and the serious legal issues it demanded - those that warranted decisiveness and conviction- Umair was quick to table them, preferring to let them go stale, even rot, rather than take them on.

When it came to Loona, Umair's horrible wife, matters that were cut and dried and required very little consideration, even those with nothing at issue or at stake, drew out a deep fear. It became apparent that

1

Loona possessed some great power over Umair to make him feel that he was deservedly unloved and properly powerless. The combination of insecurity and despair that Loona set upon Umair left him adrift; he was submissive, uneasy, and overwhelmed with an unworthiness and great sadness. Umair was an emotional train wreck. He tipped his hand every time and therefore was a sure mark for the barrage of the abuses that this wretched wife threw at him. All I could do is lug him along, make our time together enjoyable, and never needlessly push him.

That Umair adored his children so dearly gave Loona—to whom they were but pawns - precious and well-played for dominance and leverage. As to their divorce case, she was the overwhelming favorite. Umair lived by the domestic violence victim's checklist: powerlessness, desperation, and uncertainty. As for his abuser, she was unyielding, wicked, and cruel. Loona was an aggressive, torturous wife. She could run hot or cold whenever, whichever, was best suited to hurt Umair. While Umair and I both feared Loona, he knew that I could not back down from her or her formidable attorney and would not undercut the good standing I had with the Judge presiding over this sour case.

Umair was unusually firm about our lunch date, more so after he learned that over my four years in private practice, I had never, ever broken bread with any of my firm's clients. He demanded that I meet him at Al Basha, a quaint, tucked-away Middle Eastern restaurant located in the Southwest Suburbs of Chicago. This hole-in-the-wall featured Friday night belly dancing and a deluge Mahleb-scented bread, baked with a hearty roasted quality. This bread was therapeutic, almost medicinal.

> *It's nice to just be a kid and hang out*
> *with your friends at lunch.*
>
> —KARLIE KLOSS

CHAPTER II

IN-FIRM

You never see further than your headlights,
but you can make the whole trip that way.

—*L. Doctorow*

During my last of twelve years with the Cook County State's Attorney's office, an insecure boss ordered my transfer out of my cherished courthouse, from my position as supervising prosecuting attorney over every incoming felony case the crime-ridden areas of Chicago's far southern suburbs. I would have to abandon the three young and eager-to-learn prosecutors who looked to me to teach them how to wield power with discretion and exercise discretion from a position of power. These crackerjacks knew that I had their backs and that I was committed to nurturing, guiding, and teaching them both the art and science of prosecutorial decision-making.

They had eagerly signed up and instantly bought into my methodology. As a result, our courtroom had a smooth rhythm over a solid direction. Our battle plan was to work up, lock in, deal away or toss out cases - as they so warranted. It was file-by-file, dynamic decision-making. Granted, this was the first time I had officially held the title of "supervisor" over anyone, yet it did not take long for me to see that the best way for me to ensure our collective success was not by ordering, but by teaching, supporting and performing and supporting. With that, we became a super-tight, highly productive, intense, steadfast and never-doubted section of "the Office".

When I got the word that I was being pulled, it was all I could do not to tender my resignation and walk away from a job I had held, for all intents and purposes, since the spring of my last year of law school.

But now I had family. My four-year-old son, Rory, the apple of my eye, was my companion - my running buddy; we hung on each other's every word. He was my toddler prince. My second, impending child, who I had always sensed would be a girl, was only a handful of days shy of coming into the world to be my cherished daughter, Mollie.

I had recently joined my village's fire department with the intention of becoming a part-time paramedic, only to learn that I would first have to become a trained, state-certified firefighter. True to my nature, my upbringing, I was intrigued and from the first day jumped right in.

This endeavor gave me respite, a chance to spend my nights away from my wife, Erin. Our marriage was on a steep downturn; the beginnings of its end were camouflaged by all the positive things around me. With Rory's blessing, I took the oath to protect the people and the property of our village then signed for my gear.

Knowing that rank ruled and my being a lowly recruit, I kept my mouth shut and my eyes and ears open, as I had when a ten-year-old third mate aboard a party fishing boat. The Miss Rye Harbor was a sturdy wood-framed double-screw boat captained by Mindy Ritter, a weathered, opinionated skipper, who I could sense was intrigued by me.

I talked my way into the job - cleaning fish and toilets, scrubbing Miss Rye's hull to a barnacle-free sheen, and swabbing her deck from stem to stern; until she smelled like a sushi bar. All around me were gritty, no-nonsense New England fishermen and lobstermen, in it to make a living from the Gulf of Maine and beyond. I knew to bust my ass, keep my mouth shut, and take up the perspective of these seasoned veterans.

That I knew it then, I knew it now, some thirty-three years later-ocean or not.

The paid-on-call firefighters and paramedics were quintessential Midwesterners, who smoked cigarettes and remained unfazed either by sweltering heat or bitter cold. They rode the running board of their mighty Mack fire engine (pre-OSHA) into the wind, ready to take on that formidable land element: Fire. These men and women were in it not to make a living; they were in it to save lives and protect their village from "the beast" whenever the alarm sounded.

My fellow recruit classmates, most of whom were at least twenty years younger than me, well-mannered, and respectful, were all business at the station. When it came to the fire service, they were serious and passionate; this was their lives' calling. Every one of them had grown up in the culture of firefighter families, raised mostly by moms and always subject to their dads' schedules; shift, overtime, being "bubbled in" for duty, answering an "all call" or doing a side-job, either for wages, cash or barter.

The Homewood Fire Department, which operated by the Midwest version of New England mechanical aptitude, teamwork, and commitment - how my Ma and Dad had raised me – would became family.

In only good ways, I was thrown back and felt like my pudgy-kid self, heading out from the Rye Harbor jetty to the Atlantic; just as eager as thirty-three years before, but I was now in tip-top physical shape. While the fire service was unfamiliar territory for me, beyond arson cases I had prosecuted, the construction skills I learned from my Dad and Ma, and the vague memory as a young child in the town of my birth, in which my Dad and every other able-bodied male was a volunteer firefighter gave me something to work with.

This never-before-experienced training, especially the fire-ground work, called into play every other job, task, and chore that I had ever loved or hated. Fire training demanded something new of me: to come to terms with fire; by entering into a love-hate relationship.

My young family time and this new calling were now being placed in jeopardy by a supervisor, with sites on becoming a Judge. Somehow for his benefit in a way I never figured out, I would have a tortuously longer commute for the next eight months to and from a file drawer jammed with red-flagged murder cases; those that had been sidestepped and left to rot by a team of slacker, hack, worthless prosecutors, who had the collective work ethic of dust. In typical Office fashion, their reward for flopping was a transfer to an easier, cushier assignments.

Their mess was now to be placed into the hands of a 'hand-picked' three-man team consisting of Joe Gamati - an unassuming, hardworking, straight-shooter, low-key, company man – in the very best sense; Sam Sorsanno - a tough-nosed Italian, bold-fronted prosecutor –a modest but very clever drummer - purely coincidentally, the very first fellow student I firmly shook hands with in my first day of law school some twenty-two years before; and me.

Joe was destined to rise, Sam wanted to rise yet would never be given his due and me. I just could not buy into this.

Word got out and began to bounce throughout my courthouse that I was ready to uncork. While everyone else kept me contained or avoided me saying very little, one old-school prosecutor, whose heavy gait never snuck up on anyone finally barged into my office. He was tastefully boisterous; a gum chewer, even when in jury trials - never unwilling to speak his made-up mind. Fond of mapping out plays for young prosecutors to run during trials, he was known as "Pops" or "Coach" or the occasional "Ara".

Assistant State Attorney Billy Quill softly knocked, pro forma ala insult, then entered like a father into his 'you are busted' son's bedroom…

He asked if we could have a "friendly chat". When I looked at him with "As if you'd take no for an answer?" he pointed his finger at me and said,

"Now's not the time for your clever…f…Listen, now's the time for you to …Please, I just said please…just listen, Franco."

Billy held a genuine interest in the well-being of those around him and his ability to make the most out of any situation. This attitude, coupled with his cagey "game-on" trial skills, made Billy Quill a prosecutor's prosecutor. While South Side Irish, he had a soulful, black man from the Mississippi Delta way with jurors, witnesses, and victims for whom he cried out for justice. Violent criminals and their attorneys never stood a chance against Billy Quill. Willing to litigate any case and work up any file, Billy cut fair deals and gave considerate breaks when appropriate. But unlike me, perhaps given his Catholic upbringing, he would never, ever buck the higher-ups or bad mouth the flaws in the system, which is why he was respected by everyone and never questioned by anyone. Billy Quill did not ride the fence; he had built and continued to maintain the fence - and mend it when needed.

After mouthing to the crowd gathering outside my office to hit the bricks, Billy gingerly closed the door, double pointed at me, then lowered his hands- as if displaying that he was unarmed – and said:

"Franco, always remember, change is good; change is fucking good— it has been good for me and will be even better for you. So. Get your ass down to *26th 'n Cal* and do what you have to do to find a way to make it all work. My kid's a fireman; I know what that side job means to you. I know that your son and your other kid on the way mean everything to you. I know you hitched yourself to an Irish drunk. But all of that doesn't mean jack-shit to the Office. Does it, Franco Minasian? I have never, ever said anything to a boss that I might later regret. And neither will you. Not on my watch. And check that wise guy Eye-talian tone and your Garo Yepremian arrogance and your *'Baah-stin spoahtz teamz'* and all of *'Yoah eye-dears'* [your ideas] and listen, but freakin' good."

"Franco. You are one hell of a lawyer. You have never come close to – let alone cross any bad lines, ever. You clearly see - with a microscope in one hand and a telescope in the other what all of us – including these idiots standing right outside of the door -eavesdropping- will never grasp. And yes, I do pride myself on my chess game way of things; but your Mr. Spock-stacked-three-high shit is brilliant – it blows all of us away."

"So please, Franco. Stick it out; see this through, for the good of the company. There are two guys who can't wait to work with you. Don't let the brass use who you are against you."

"You can leave on your terms- but do not leave on your anger's. So. What do you say you and I start packing your shit?"

Sam, Joe, and I knocked that call down and took it out in eight months, as ordered. We tried case after case after case—violent crimes, dealt a deserved blow to wrongdoers, and dispensed justice for grieving families on both sides of the courtroom to grapple with. When our work was all done, both Sam and Joe were promoted. I was given two choices: 'continue to prove myself' or take a demotion and go back to my old assignment.

By that time, I could change my dear princess Mollie's diapers in my sleep—with Rory always waking up and weighing in while I wiped her clean. I had just earned my firefighter certification and was enrolled in EMT-B school with paramedic training on the hori-zon. It was an easy decision. I went back. I wanted home. I missed my courthouse. I wanted to work close to the firehouse.

Having litigated a mass of murder cases – each a senseless act of violence - over the three coldest seasons – and with mission accomplished, I packed up and bid "26' n Cal" a bitter-sweet good-bye. Billy was right; it had been a great run, and Sam, Joe and I had done what Joe called "God's work" and Sam boasted as "kicking ass and taking numbers."

My supervisor was gone. He was appointed to the Bench. I picked up right where I left off, supervising a new group of eager young prosecutors.

I was now off God's clock and the only asses left to kick was fire's and whatever was ailing my any given patient.

For ten years as a firefighter/paramedic, I served with humble pride. At one point, contemplating an outright career change, I began to test for full-time openings in Suburban Chicago Fire Departments. After finishing second on the hire list of a progressive fire department, the Chief called me into his office, made me an offer, and then told me point-blank that I should turn it down.

"I know where your head's at. I had this guy like you a few years back; a brilliant violinist. This kid – much younger, but so much like you- he was one hell of a boxer. He nailed the test just like you did. Franco, you are in a crappy marriage and think that you have found a replacement wife. I put some feelers out and found out that you are a very gifted lawyer. And while I could sorely use you, I don't need your service or talent more than the people you serve and those you serve with do.

You would let us mold you, for your love of the job, but I wouldn't, in a million years, think to do that to you. You operate with my nephew's energy and my grandpa's smarts. Stay being a lawyer. Stick with your part-time job with Homewood. It's a great Department. You have been well-trained. It will be good for you and them. Take care of your children. Keep practicing Law. As for your marriage; I can't help you. But if you take my advice, I am confident that you will get to where you need to be. But that's not here."

He offered his hand, and I accepted it. "Probie, our loss, not yours. You are dismissed."

My would-be chief was right. I had already been welcomed into an unconditionally loyal family. And no matter where I would go or might find myself, I could always count on and call upon those in the fire service. I loved the job, in many ways because I was much better operating in police stations and courtrooms. I was not a natural at putting out alchemy fire and had to work very hard at it. That was a good thing.

And so, I would answer both bells- one by day and the other by night. Over my decade in the fire service that I began while in the office and ended after my solo practice was in full swing, as my children came into their second decade of life, many lives had been saved; some were lost. In the company of such decent, committed men and women, we battled fire and provided tip-top patient care.

It was in the midst of this when I was offered a position with a small law firm, to work as an associate attorney. Before I had told anyone in the office, let alone make my decision, the sound of Billy Quill, who "came-a-knocking", offered his congratulations. "It's a great move for you; it's a better one for Matt and Dirk. Let's pack your shit, Franco. Christ your fucking hair smells like my kid's... That nasty smoke; that shit never gets out."

I was full-bore raising my children and honing my firefighter/ paramedic skills, but now defending, rather than prosecuting the accused.

To those charged with crimes - "in the system." I held the reigns. Now they - and not the "People of the State of Illinois" - were my clients. Greater expectations and a new set of obligations were now before me.

Thankfully, this side-switching transition had been such a huge part of my collegiate debate years. Once again, such things came easy. Having criminal law, procedure, and "the system" firmly tucked under my belt, why not continue to practice law as a fair-minded, reasonable prosecutor? After all, no matter what side of the pleadings I was on, my only foes were those who saw themselves as above the law and viewed criminal justice as their sword to wield rather than a shared shield.

Change is the law of life. And those who look only to the past or present are certain to miss the future.

—John F. Kennedy

My new bosses, Matt and Dirk, with whom I had developed a wonderful working relationship when I was their "adversary," appreciated to how I managed my caseload, recognized the way I connected with the Judge and enjoyed how I operated in courtroom and with all of its players.

Yet instead of being dispatched into this familiar territory, I was delegated with our handful of domestic relations cases and charged with building up that area of the firm's practice. I was being thrusted into an area of the law I avoided – the area of the courthouse that I had stayed clear of - and with which I had no familiarity. I had not taken one domestic relations class in law school. The only thing domestic I knew was its insidious violence.

I now had to survey an uncharted ugly landscape of divorce, child custody, and support. I was thrown into the fray and told to get the "lay of the land" so that the firm could keep domestic relations cases and not lose sizable revenue by referring them out. I had to master a different type of case management, focused on meticulous, assertive billing. This was precisely how I was to earn my keep. What made things crueler was that my own marriage was now failing.

To me, this was neither healthy nor fruitful. Just about every day, I would come close to reducing thoughts to words – by advising certain clients either to kill their antagonistic spouses or kill their pestering, needling, whining selves. Had I been at liberty to bill out the time I spent on mentally playing out these lethal, yet somehow soothing, thoughts, the firm's gross revenue would have spiked.

I hated almost every moment of my assumed law practice. I loathed the trashy grudgingness and clumsy impracticability, almost unheard of in the criminal law world, that characterized almost every case. Take, for instance, the insecure salesman whose hobby was African safari hunts. He filed for divorce in order to be able to legally bang his bimbo whenever he pleased. It all started the morning after his inaugural cheat – when he cut a check to his very sweet and gentle wife. Professing his change of heart, he apologized for having belittled her ideas; that he had now "changed" now wanted to support her start-up business plan and give her the "space" to pursue it - the very one he had relentlessly mocked, shamelessly reducing his wife to tears. Within three months after he offered her "seed" money, she was making a killing.

But now, he wanted every nickel she had turned from it.

In the end, this case settled in typical fashion; the decent party getting less than deserved and the party with unclean hands getting more than merited. So many cases, with a settlement so close at hand, featured a last-second blow-up, tritely over some low-value issue or item – always with a story to it - the billable hours expended haggling over it always cannibalized away whatever it may have been worth.

More unsettling for me than litigants and their antics were the seasoned domestic practitioners whose expertise I sought out, to whom my nature told me to defer - many of whose former clients I had either prosecuted or advocated – in the storm of domestic violence.

Unimpressed with my inside track or proactive view of the case, it meant not a hill of beans either if their clients had suffered or had inflicted unwarranted pain. Taking no real stock in their cases seemed to be an essential part of the job. As one chain-smoking, seasoned domestic relations practitioner waxed: "You actually can fight city hall, but you don't stand a chance against bad emotions like these – coming at you from all sides. If you are not careful, Mr. Minasian, you will be drawn into their hatred-fueled stupidity. And the children will eat you alive- even the dumb ones always know how to out-game their parents…"

I resented the billable hour system, that I earned a living by surrendering my time and ear to my clients' unchangeable dysfunction; that my bosses were appreciative and very generous could not make it right. But when it came to our criminal law practice, I was included in case analysis. This was the part of my employment I most cherished. We drew our very best from each other; my moxie - their legacy; in the form of a likable, formidable firm; it worked - and we performed miracles.

Matthew Patrick Walsh, born on Pearl Harbor Day, had been raised to always show savvy and never, ever surrender his resolve. Matt was a prosecutor's prosecutor, who could have been – should have been - the State's Attorney of Cook County – if not Illinois Attorney General. Instead, he formed an instantly well-known, rightfully feared and highly respected small firm, focused on criminal defense. Matt's partner, Dirk Vagalis, liked to joke and tease others when bouncing around Courthouse hallways and if Court was in recess. But as to any traffic or driver's license matter, either in Court of before the Illinois Secretary of State, as to any nuance or interpretation of the law, Dirk was ferocious and could snipe away at the government's case - with calm, and that disarming smile of his. Dirk was measured and tight, with an arrogance and swag akin to his baseball pitching game. While I never saw Dirk operate from the mound, just having finished our discussion inside the rear entrance to the Bridgeview courthouse, he looked outside and 'called' the spot on a light pole some 150 feet away he claimed he could peg with a snowball. With a wind tunnel whipping up the single digit air, Dirk- scoffing at my suggestion that he shed his overcoat and scarf - fired a hand-crafted orb, etched with icy laces to boot- and hit his spot. The face of that light pole was indelibly marked with snow – weeks later ice, three months later a water stain; one that remains to this day.

Matt, Dirk and I – as a unit - truly missed out, as did the Criminal Justice system. Given what we were able to accomplish, it is regrettable that we never worked together in the trenches of the Office. What a team of prosecutors we would have been and what irreproachable justice we would have dispended.

On 9/11, our nation twisting with outrage and flailing with uncertainty in the face of terror, needed hope, from the steadfast valor and selfless virtue of so many – including 343 from the rank and file of FDNY- helped reset and inspire the rest of us. They and the many others who forged forward - in the air, one the water and on land - so honorably in such self-sacrifice- are America's heroes, in almost mythological proportion; and deservedly so.

Our Department turned dark with frustration and grew sick from its utter powerlessness – this was a survivor's guilt that every firefighter across America will forever bear.

With the country in a chaotic state, everyone who could, went home. Two days later, Matt called me and told me to meet him at the office at sunrise. No sooner did I sit when he came right out with it. He told me that he had always had a huge problem with me because, although I pulled more than my weight, I seemed to show more passion – and with half the talent- for the fire service than practicing law. Matt then extended an earnest, warming sympathy; the first person to help me through what I was feeling. He let me cry.

Then in his quintessential "keeping you off-balance/by reading your mind" way – of which he was the master – Matt tersely forbade me to go to New York. "Your ass stays right here, to take care of your town and tend to our clients. Your department needs you. Well. Don't kid yourself - they don't need you at all; but they like having you there. And I pay you for your work here – to ply your craft here - for what you produce here - for our clients who need us. And by paying you for your work, you can afford to play fireman over there. I know it and you know it."

"But just in case you thought to get cute, I already called your Chief, and he has ordered you – he has ordered me to order you - to stand down."

"I'm telling you right now; you stay the fuck here; don't you dare think about heading to that horrible scene; or I will fire you, and so will your Chief. And your Chief - he's a straight shooter. I represented his uncle. And he will put anything in writing I ask him to. Franco. Please. I get it. But, you don't need to go there."

Those who marched to Ground Zero are saints of courage and pillars of honor. Corroded by toxins, they were valiant and remained steadfast. Those who toiled there at Ground Zero are the heroes' heroes, who suffered dearly. Matt spared me from their scars.

The fire service saved my life. It became my second family to Rory, Mollie and me during my doomed first marriage. All my good that followed, it celebrated; all my pain that ensued, it shared.

While working as an Associate, my undivided attention - at a snap of a finger - was Matt's and Dirk's to rightfully demand. In fire service parlance, they were 'white shirts'. And however invigorating running down and strategizing over criminal cases was, when the dreaded divorce billable hours clock compulsorily started up, misery would always kick in.

Unbeknown either to Matt or Dirk, I felt completely owned by them - their pimped, albeit high-priced, whore. I pretended to take an earnest interest in what to me was broken and beyond repair – bad marriages and worse divorces, riddled with toxicity and idiocy. That it hit all too close to my home-made matters worse. Unendingly biting my tongue, I constantly played company man, in the form of either a flat sounding board or eager beaver. With our clients, I shallowly sympathized, endorsed – rather than rebuke - their over-emphasized claims. I acquiesced to their unreasonableness, unfairness, or maliciousness- after all, "You can't fight city hall."

The reality that most criminal defendants wanted and needed to hear was totally off limits in the divorce milieu.

And so, the firm's client base grew, and from every maligned spouse, attorney's fees were paid. I was earning a handsome living as a sucked-in, spite-driven, sounding board. Hardly satisfied with anything or anyone, my clients were quick to blame me for their circumstances.

In order to balance this out, I would meticulously bill every call, every letter, every call about every letter, and every letter about every call. It was not long before this bean-counting folly began to wear me down. It did not ease my suffering that my opposing counsel seemed so better equipped than me to handle all of this. When it came to settling the cases, I learned the hard way that it was never about winning, losing, or even finding a "win-win." The goal was always to load up and dump dissatisfaction onto two piles; so as to leave both litigants as equally miserable as possible. If the attorneys could achieve that kind of parity, it was a success! In time, I shamefully succumbed to this way of things; as others put it, "the arrangement."

I would go along with the shtick and faux-clash with my adversaries in order to play out the pre-scripted performance. We were litigation imitations of professional wrestlers, who also made a handsome living feigning conflict and playing to the paying audience. Laudably, the match generally kept the peace between the litigants. I did get along well with opposing counsel who, along with me, cleverly pulled their punches and even given the blurred lines of our respective roles in all of this, honored certain boundaries.

But how I loathed those lawyers who made all of this personal, selfish on all levels, who were fueled by sheer ego and unimaginable greed. These wretched lawyers wanted to humiliate me more than to humiliate my client. Their personalities, whether genuine or concocted, were indecent and accomplished nothing more than string cases out and make me ill.

When I took their bait, foolishly too often, I wound up validating - even inflating- their egos and their professional worth. There is a term for this dynamic in professional wrestling - "shooting" - when one wrestler goes off-script and – forgetting the premise -becomes overly, even dangerously, competitive.

The lawyers who operated this way and developed reputations were shamelessly proud. Private dialogue and letters were one thing; but these types abandoned all sense of decorum and fair play in the courtroom –

even when on the record. It was seedy and shameful beyond the worst of any criminal defense attorney I had ever encountered.

In the world of professional wrestling, 'shooting', albeit avertable, was excused as overly spirited, misplaced battle-mindedness. In the legal profession, it amounted to unnecessary, utterly frivolous pleadings - annoy-ing motions and ridiculous -turned frustrating hearings.

Such domestic relations practitioners were bogus; pleased to kink things up, clutter the record, all without any scintilla of dignity. The worst of them were so overtly greedy that in order to wring out more billable time, they would object to anything under the sun, including the very time of day. They would object to the Court after it sustained my objection or overruled theirs. Reputation meant nothing. Billable time was the prime mover, with their duped clients fueling the jejune and unnecessary slog. What sustained their practices was that primary component of their business model: over-billing, over-charging and demanding then securing a huge down-stroke to devour.

From the very beginning, I took to Umair. He would always ques-tion my billing statement, having calculated to the penny by how much I had under-billed. So different from the majority of my divorce clients (certainly from every male client), Umair never blamed me for the system's flaws or Loona's unpunished misdeeds. He earnestly appreciated our professional relationship and our time together, which was more like a friendship, albeit with pre-set parameters.

When I uttered anything mean-spirited toward Loona, Umair would put me in check. He had neither the heart nor the stomach for ven-geance. And early on I learned never to joke about violence in Umair's presence. I did for the first and last time – after Umair asked me about the trial I had just concluded before our meeting. He scolded me then got up to leave. I asked him if he knew either my client or his victim. He shook his head in disgust and left. I didn't hear from him for over a week.

Umair was otherwise an unassertive type, lacking any of that desert-forged fierceness that those in his bloodline surely possessed. He had a great business sense and certainly was no slouch when it came to ana-lyzing deals, but when it came to backbone or repelling aggression, he displayed unease and great discomfort.

Loona carried on as if she and her attorney, Themis Kronas, were sleeping together. Shrewdly risqué, Loona displayed just enough body language and uttered sultry innuendo that planted this seed. Delicately displaying herself as having been sexually conquered by Kronas, his Greek-American bravado could not help but play into her hand. Loona fed his libido, with touchy-feely flirtatiousness that any man's man would have otherwise found irresistible. She wanted Umair to think it and me to react to it.

I knew this was all ploy – Kronas was much too grounded; bedding a cli-ent was beneath him. Into her hand, I played the frigid type – uncomfortable with this display of sexuality and lacking carnal self-confidence. Completely misinterpreting my move, Umair was now certain they were romping in the sack. And yet it did not seem to faze him.

CHAPTER III

AL BASHA

PEACE is the foundation of Happiness,
for where there is Anxiety, Tension, and
Turmoil, Joy cannot exist.

—UNKNOWN

When I arrived at Al Basha, fifteen minutes early, Umair was waiting outside the front door. Before dropping his bombshell, Umair made a point to tell me why he had chosen this little gem for lunch. He explained that 'Al Basha' was a title of respect with Turkish origins, which translated to "The Prince."

Seated at the restaurant's center table, just us and the staff (all family) to serve us, Umair grabbed my right hand with both of his and demanded that I listen to him. He acknowledged that much of what had come from his mouth was never worth listening to, but what he was about to say was; he had made up his mind to be strong with what he was about to lay on the table.

Umair's words; they made no sense. he started begging me - to take up his torch and finish what he could not.

"You want me to marry Loona and then file for divorce against her?" We laughed.

"Franco, listen to me. I demand that you put my case down. You can send me a bill, and I'll pay. But you have to promise me that in turn you will do something for both of us: That you will tell our story—yours and mine. You and I, we are 'Al Bashawat'. We are Princes, who have suffered; and you need to write about this. I'm not asking you to defend me, but if you write about my life and yours, you can save yourself. Honey (his word for 'Dude' or 'Brother-My-Brother'), I know you have told very little to me about you, but you have shared enough for me to know that you can do for yourself what I can't and never will for myself."

"If you promise to write our story- and call it "*Al Basha*"- it will save you and keep me alive. You will find your very special place; just like Morgantown, West Virginia, was for me…"

"…If you do what I ask, you will make me a hero…"

"…I want you to have what I almost had—peace and happiness – for you to be where you belong – and to share every moment of it with the true love of your life. Honey, promise me that you will write and I promise that you will be rewarded. That hesitation in your eyes is ours: 'Al Bashawat'. We are our own worst enemies, no?

"Write our stories: Yours, like your children, your music, your career, the Fire Department all depend upon it; Mine – in the same way that you have always cared about me. If you do promise to do this great thing, I will rejoice in having convinced you to do this; this great thing."

"I want no part of my divorce for either of us any longer. For the sake of my children, for me, and for you, I want to drop it. And after things settle down, I will decide what to do…For the first time in a long time, I am being a true friend to myself, so you need to be a true friend to me…and to yourself."

Before I could say a word, Umair belted out, in a tone I had never heard: "Read my lips: Franco Minasian. You're fired!"

Over the hours and plates of delectable food that followed, my now-former client told me his story, at times, stopping to pray aloud in Arabic/English, that by doing so it would empower me to honor his wish.

Amidst this mystic haze, hearty, cleverly presented, delicately spiced, earthy, slow-paced lunch at Al Basha, I began to open up - and Umair's story-telling concept started to take form.

We re-discovered how at a very young age, each of us by choice, insurmountable external forces or internal reactions, assumed formidable roles. As the youngest sons, Umair and I took on a persona of wise old men and timid little boys, by which we were treated as the Princes of our respective families. I had never talked about any of this ever before.

The more Umair shared his life story with me, the more I discovered just how burdened we were by this "special" status and how driven we were to hang on to our "Al Basha" privilege within our respective family units. Through Umair's story, I saw how I too had surrendered to my fate and then arduously trudged through my younger years.

To make up for our lack of toughness, Umair and I were always intellectually sharp and rhetorically aggressive. We wanted to be known by or even referred to behind our backs as "smart" - by our intellectual superiors and inferiors alike. We craved the moniker of "intelligent" or "gifted" from our elders, educated family friends and relatives. We carved and served up adult-like wit, cheerful references and cerebral quips; "Groucho Marx" sense of humor, that schmoozed or insulated, depending upon our mark.

Most importantly, we loved food.

We absolutely fancied, foraged for, cleverly helped prepare, cook and plate, gawked at, guarded, secreted, laid claim to, and meticulously stockpiled food. Our burning quest for higher knowledge and its intellectual payload parleyed nicely with our capacity to procure and put away a second or even a third helping. Enlightenment was one thing; but food was our trusted companion; in excess, it was our dominatrix.

For the most part, I had no trouble gorging myself. On rare occasions, I ate too much, even by my well over-the-top standards.

After holiday feasts, having been surrounded by family, with a bounty laid out over the tablecloth, I maneuvered for the center seat from which my spoken word would be heard and my gluttonous gullet could be fed from two sides. Eventually, while everyone else was glued to a television movie or football game, I started to get a sick stomach. Then, the physical attack of puking came; it was like getting punched out of a deep sleep. I dreaded the panicked sensation of losing control of my physical faculties in a way that rendered my smarts useless. When it was finally over, I caught my breath and washed my nose and mouth; nothing tasted better right then than a slice or two of pie- hold the whipped cream- or/and a salad bowl full of pilaf.

Holiday gatherings continued to provide an abundant reminder that when it came to food and family gatherings, my body tended to overreact; when I would try to blame my regurgitation on whichever family member may have caused trouble at the gathering, the bathroom mirror would reject my pitch. Years later, I would be reminded that when it came to food and extremes, my body had the last word, would not be fooled by my rhetoric and could take me down, intelligence and all, if I pushed things too far.

Umair and I were the attention-getters, because we were the attention-makers. We would release our jaws whenever we saw a rhetorical or culinary opening. We had an appetite for the gift of gab and a hearty, healthy measure of talent to back it up. But for all of that, we were plainly definable by one word: "fat." That we were flatly obese and roundly blubbery was an ominous, dark cloud that dampened our otherwise predestined, purely self-created, paradise.

During our respective childhoods, bad weather was a gift. It meant not having to do anything athletic outdoors, especially anything swimming-related. Umair and I cringed while recounting gym class, outdoor recess, and the dreaded, yearly field day, at which we were so exposed and could in no way hold our own. Failures at athletic competition of any kind, we could never talk our ways out of the clocked times, final scores or mitigate the humiliation of finishing, by our own calculations, well below last place in every athletic contest. The only exception was the tug-of-war, in which I was chosen as the human bollard.

We had no place to hide and generally could not stand up to a fight. The only exception was on a rare occasion when the gym teacher made up some pagan contest; hand-to-hand, free-for-all. That crooked smile on his face brought me to sheer panic from which I summoned up a hippopotamus-like rage; blind forward momentum, flailing arms, some respectable blows; when I was inevitably ganged upon, I would rotate to face my mark, close my eyes and force myself to fall over. The screams made my ears ring for days; about as long as I would suffer paybacks from whomever I had squashed.

For the most part, holding our own employed the same technique: transmuting panic and fear into a lot of screaming and yelling, usually reciting famous literary passages (for Umair, the Koran), hoping, even if only subconsciously, to get an elder's attention to rescue us or, appealing to vengeance, for our older brothers to bail us out and clean house.

And for all of our likable, admirable qualities, during most of our school years, Umair and I, simply put, were egg-head, chicken-shit fatsos.

CHAPTER IV

THE UNEXPECTED

Violence is the last refuge of the incompetent.

—*Isaac Asimov*

My turmoil-laden journey, with its struggles and heartaches, paled in comparison to Umair's; menacing pain and unconquerable anguish - the oppression pinning him down. Next to Umair's, my trek was a cakewalk. His was a forced-labor march. "Al Bashawat" of our respective families, with our place at the table served the good and the bad, all of which seemed pre-destined and unchangeable. Yet no matter how much despair and self-pity I felt, what Umair suffered landed more cruelly and cut so much deeper. What he endured probably would have killed me (or driven me to kill someone); it certainly should have killed him.

Over that succulent meal at Al Basha, Umair would tell his story. In so many ways, it was no wonder that he fired me - and so fitting that he would issue me a mandate that I tell our stories.

Umair never recovered from having lost his one and only true love. His demise came not because he had failed to commit. Umair had not cheesed out by claiming that the two of them were 'not meant to be'.

Umair was blameless; cruelly left so utterly hopeless. Goodness had been inhumanly ripped away from Umair, leaving him chronically septic and forever vulnerable.

Raised up in a traditional Muslim American family, Umair was much my double; the capricious, portly, and articulate propped-up, young intellectual. But, unlike me, Umair never got his hands dirty growing up; he knew nothing of the trials and tribulations of physical labor. He was rather effeminate, about whom my Dad would likely say, "Someone who can't swing a hammer."

In contrast, his older brothers were, from the moment they came from the womb, unruly, brawny thugs; completely underhanded in their ways. They were dirty in every sense.

Umair always clung to his warm mother. He gravitated to her kitchen, where she would encourage him to read to her. On rare occasions, while ever mindful of where her husband and sons might be lurking, she would whisper her abundant and highly profound thoughts. Her arranged marriage to Umair's father had long since crusted over. The younger, male-dominance-driven man to whom she was given had degraded into a wretched and resentful, malodorous old fart. To him, Umair's mother's only attribute was that she had spawned no daughter.

At a very young age, Umair became enamored - then obsessed - with numbers and returns. By the age of eight, he aspired to be the "top dog" who would work at the numbers and pump life into any worthy business; his spreadsheets always came with a guarantee.

Umair was offered part-time apprenticeships during his junior high years - then accepted full-time jobs with a fortune 500 company dur-ing his high school years. Executives praised him; his collogues – many twenty years older - tapped into his beyond-his-years insight into how growth and stability were "alternating rungs up the ladder of business success". His female co-workers were like the sisters he never had. They could feel his honesty, appreciated his respectability, and took to his gen-tility. To them, Umair was everything manly. To the Corporate Officers, Umair was a first-round draft pick.

After finishing at the very top of his high-school class, Umair secured a full academic scholarship to the University of West Virginia. The executive vice president of a company that owed his bosses a favor closed the deal, even before Umair aced the ACT test.

Although sights were set on their younger brother enrolling in a local community college, living at home and indentured to them, Umair's brothers acquiesced to their father's "dollar signs in his eyes" scheme. Umair was allowed to attend that "far-away school" so that he could refine his business acumen- the key to their master plan. In four years, the three vultures would be in the money. And so, Umair was told to return home with a business degree – summa cum laude- or face very harsh consequences.

From an early age, Umair's two older brothers were unchallenged and unchecked. They never earned anything the hard way; from an early age, they joined sordid ventures and associated with miscreants.

To their credit, they were somehow able to put resentment and ridiculing aside, realizing that without Umair's brains, they were doomed. The one-sided bargain his father and brothers had struck and was now set in motion. Umair would study hard, secure his degree, return home, remain under their parents' roof and make his father and brothers rich men. In order to save face with their circle of cronies, triumvirate agreed to go in equal shares on the purchase a suitable bride for Umair.

In reality, their future sister-in-law would be paid for with Umair's funds. His selected bride would be his to accept, sight unseen - haggled for and contractually bound to them alone. If his brothers could somehow manage to chisel down the dowry, they would pocket the savings.

It is greed to do all the taking, but not to want to listen at all.

—*Democritus*

Umair's brothers had not a smidgeon of savvy to put any such deal together. So for a paltry price, they sought the counsel of their greasy lawyer pal, Lamese Shaykum. He was a hack attorney, a hair away from being disbarred. Lamese had squandered large sums of client funds and blown just about every filing deadline. Long since rumored to have bartered his bum pleadings and bogus claims for sexual favors, a low-grade escort on the ropes for a prostitution charge turned Jane Doe/Informant, and set him up. Unbeknown to him, a Federal RICO Indictment was looming over him like the sword of Damocles.

This deal was right up Lamese's alley. While he and Umair's brothers devised their flimsy scheme, Umair was settling in to new surroundings; finally free from his dysfunctional past.

No sooner did Umair land upon this clean and academically invigorating, yet quaintly paced part of America, then he met unencumbered students from all over the country and all over the globe. For the very first time in his life, Umair walked tall, could feel his back straighten and his abdomen pull tight. Umair formed a wide smile and developed a hearty laugh. He was capable of anything and would embrace anyone; everyone.

He landed a summer job with a venture capital firm that paid a lucrative salary. The new and improved Umair pitched a "risk-free, but {*whispering*} very - highly - illegal" plan to his brothers: If they let him spend his summers in West Virginia, he could "rig" an insider trading deal that would yield five-figure profits. In reality, Umair would simply sign over his salary to them and deposit it into a "front account."

They could not resist the summertime fun-money and were impressed with Umair's miscreance. And so, they were in; and so was Umair.

In his junior year, Umair met Kristin, a fiery, cleverly opinionated, redheaded spitfire from the rural mountains of West Virginia. Kristin was a self-proclaimed feminist, with a passion for wholesome food, hard work, and frugality. She had a gymnast's body, lush green eyes and a sexy, silky, perky torso. Jeans and a baseball T-shirt became Kristin in a way that put the tastiest runway designs to shame.

Umair and Kristin had a circle of friends. They and those about its periphery could feel their energy and were drawn in by their growing love for one another. It was as if the campus itself knew that Umair and Kristin were meant to be.

One day. Kristin invited Umair to hike with her. He held his own. After that hike, their destiny flowed like the majestic mountain waters. They fell in love. The couple that everyone adored celebrated art, science, culture, nature, and the spirit of the West Virginia landscape. Their energy flowed to those around them- beaming laugher and the sense of hope.

Certain that he had outgrown his past, Umair reckoned that he had perhaps exaggerated his younger years and unfairly vilified his brothers. When recounting his childhood to Kristin, Umair self-censored its emotional turmoil, and faulted himself for having misunderstood his brothers.

And so together, Umair and Kristin celebrated everything about each other, including the contrasting worlds in which they were raised. Their souls were so warmly kindled by the storybook tale of having found one another continued to write.

Kristin was passionate about honoring open spaces by creating small, intimate, and convivial living places. Aglow, she talked up the tiny home where she and Umair would share each other, amid the beauty of nature and raise a family. Ahead of her time, Kristin designed colorful, ornate and architecturally-precise plans for their home; relenting to Umair, by increasing its square footage from 500 feet to a whopping 720 square feet – yet still keeping it "16 on center", explaining to Umair what that meant.

Umair was standing tall and was more self-assured than ever before. With his frame squared-up and firm, his head pronounced and leveled, Umair would have been all but unrecognizable by those from his past. He would do right by Kristin and himself.

Determined to keep his voice and speak of his desires, Umair had arrived at his true destiny and would finally achieve happiness. He said his good-byes to those unsavory yesterdays and totally shed this former, weaker self. Umair needed only to make one last visit to Chicago then return forever - to West Virginia – and live out his life with Kristin.

When Kristin became pregnant, Umair fell to his knees; his voice quivered as he offered praise to his God, curled up and cried out in song. His unmusical croon was a heavenly psalm for his future, which laid his past to rest and called up his rebirth.

Now supremely confident in his manhood, Umair's marriage to Kristin would bind them to the sacred tenets of his faith - that honored the father's obligation to his wife and child. He would bring joy to his mother and be embraced in a manly way by his father- and finally be at peace with the soon-to-be uncles.

The morning mountain air encouraged Umair that Kristin and their child would be wholly accepted by his brothers. After all, even his troubled brothers could not defy their faith's tenet that his precious child, sinless and pure, was to hold an adored place in this world. His child was destined to warm their hearts.

Umair, soon-to-be father, was certain that the gift of life that he and Kristin offered to his family would be enough. Umair was now a man off-the-hook, with the high cards and an irrefutable, final say in the matter.

With that, Umair readied himself then made his journey back to Chicago to be with his family. The first few hours back home were gauchely cordial. Self-disciplined and composed, Umair attributed the uneasiness to his surroundings; what was left-behind, and unchanged.

The reunion awkwardly settled into trite pleasantries and forced small talk, until Umair took a deep breath from which both his mother and father flinched. Unfazed, he forged ahead, self-confidently proclaiming to his mother and his father his unconditional love for Kristin, their betrothal, a sacred commitment to his faith, and the unyielding will to fulfill his fatherly destiny.

Just then, his brothers barged in, cursed, spit and screamed demanding that "...your white slut get an abortion!" His father and mother seized up, as his brothers forbade him to marry "a white slut." True to his ways, Umair's father deferred to his older sons, drooling out the feeblest suggestion that they temper their tone and lower their volume.

Through the brutal yelling and unholy insults, Umair looked to his mother – to no avail. She collapsed from the couch and onto the floor, turned her head - and without uttering a word - shivered and sobbed. Umair's father ignored her, instead he shook his head at Umair with a look of revulsion. His transformation into manhood clearly under open attack, Umair stepped back and regrouped; realizing that his quest for happiness would leave his beloved mother in a wake of hopeless despair. Umair had found his new world. Yet in order to live in it, his mother would be stuck in her empty one. He had to make a choice.

But for the very first time in his life, Umair did not reel from the madness around him. That was his past and not to be his future. Unlike then, when he would succumb to his brothers' "pledge" - a cruel ritual they used to torment him throughout his youth – this time he would neither give in nor surrender. But he knew better than to challenge them. Instead, he disengaged, calmly stepped away – not turning his back - took a knee and placed his hands onto his broken mother. She curled around his legs, defeated – weeping in fear.

Umair was in his world. But his calm resolve, with his broken mother at his feet, knocked his brothers back. They were no fools, finally coming to terms that they no longer held title to Umair. They neither said nor did anything more; accepting their fate, they walked out.

Only then did Umair's father come to his mother's side. Umair attempted to embrace the two of them. He could feel their anguish. Somehow sensing his reaction, they pulled away from him. For the first time in his life, Umair's father accused him of having done wrong.

All of this was so converse to life in West Virginia. Its mountains had given Umair the strength to hold his ground and accept what was unchangeable; and were now calling him back.

1. Dear Mother

Family dysfunction – in any form – was good for my business.

I was before the Court, my in-custody client by my side.

Out of nowhere, a raving, mad woman started to berate the Judge, my client, and me. The Judge pushed the red button next to his dog-eared, annotated jury instruction two-volume set.

My client and I were bum-rushed by a lunatic. She was elfin, yet with fists of fury and piercing voice, seven deputy sheriffs poured into the courtroom.

In the face of this elderly woman's tirade of ver-minous, vile threats, armed personnel eventually took her down to courtroom floor; finally secured her then dragged her away. All the while, my client laughed.

The detained spitfire was his mother, whom he had neither seen nor with whom he had spoken in over a year.

I called my client's brother to let him know what had just gone down. He said, "I knew when I sent her she was gonna' do that."

I asked him why he didn't inform me that he was sending her my way.

"Sorry, man. I didn't mean to fuck with your shit, but I was hoping my bro's white nigga' [the clean and neat – in every way– Irish-American Judge presiding over the case] would lock her ass up. Listen here. Don't be givin' up your number. That bitch is crazy. I know I should have told you. I *pre-dictated* she would start slammin' hard on white nigga'z ass."

When I reminded him that this was his mother and that his brother was her son, he replied, "Look, man, I'm banking you. You ain't gotta give her sad, sorry ass no motha-fuckin' mind. Look. Listen man. That skank, she ain't put not one dime on his shit. So look - fuck that crazy bitch. Come on man … is you Superman or ain't you?"

Everything happens to everybody sooner
or later if there is time enough.

—GEORGE BERNARD SHAW

Now that Umair was out of his brothers' lives, they had finally lost interest in tormenting him. Their smiles and nods, however, did not fool Umair. He knew that his brothers were celebrating their new destiny; sponging off of his mother and father. That they seemed content to live out this less-lucrative, larcenous existence pained him, but did not deter him. Umair walked out of his birth home forever, without even saying good-bye.

Liberated and soundly reinvented, Umair closed out his past, prayed for his mother and father and forgave his brothers. With that, he readied himself for his special day and a lifetime of special days to follow. Retreating from his ordeal and back into Kristin's arms, surrounded by the comfort of their awaiting entourage of close and loyal friends to whom she sent word of his return, was all that he needed.

By local standards, their wedding plans had been made in haste. How Kristin's family so adored Umair and cherished his love for her. This was to be a celebration of their unbridled love and of gratitude for how Umair unconditionally honored Kristin.

Alongside their wide circle of their entourage, other college friends, intrigued fellow students, faculty, and employees, so remarkably diverse and full of vivacity, Kristin's large family could not wait to come together and witness their special moment.

This early May afternoon was unseasonably warm and sunny. With anticipation filling the country air, an occasional cool exhale blew over the mountainside. Under this comforting canopy, Umair and Kristin sounded their wedding day fanfare. The giddy buzz from this small and tight, vibrant community was back-dropped by Mother Nature's bosom.

Cradled by the foothills of Morgantown stood a rock-solid church, the lighthouse for both the townsfolk and their University neighbors. Seamus Ferrous, philosophy professor emeritus, campus chaplain and Kristin's trusted confidant, took his place upon its weathered altar.

This wedding was, quite literally, the talk of the town. When the winds whistled through the foothills, the congregation knew it was time to come together.

Hand-in-hand, they entered the church – then as if on cue - turned to one another and embraced. Only after they filled the pews did Kristin's parents walk down the aisle, followed by their Kristin and her Umair. Once at the pew, then turned to the congregation and took in warm greetings of all kinds.

Kristin's parents were profoundly moved by the love Kristin and Umair gave and received from others. A young bubbly couple promenaded toward the altar, beckoning all others to circle in and around Kristin and Umair. All the while, Seamus was deep in prayer, rejoicing in what God was bestowing upon his congregation. What he was about to consecrate was nothing short of a miracle.

The pronouncement of "Let us pray" delivered reverent silence. Then, as if on scripted cue, Umair's brothers - donned in ghoulish street clothes - stampeded onto the alter, out from the chancel.

This was vulgar, overblown with sick braggadocio. At first, this display seemed an odd Avant-garde prank. Misperception gave way to shock when the duo charged like bulls took over the altar - built by parishioners in 1853 -then kicked it apart.

Umair fainted, headed face-first to the floor when he was grabbed by the neck and yanked up. As always, his brothers applied mean, cruel hands. True to their ways, Emad clamped the nape of Umair's neck as Sadiq joy-sticked whichever arm was closest.

Emad, the eldest and strongest brother, fished around with his other hand for the shirt under the jacket's collar in order to complete the choke. Once he found it, he jammed his forearm into Umair's throat while clawing the nape of his neck.

Familiar fears set in, this time magnified a thousand times - and Emad knew it. Meanwhile Sadiq, middle child and family unrestrainable bully, was salivating at his role as gangster thug. He twisted Umair's arm while breaking apart the desecrated altar. When Seamus tried to cradle it, he was kicked into it then stomped and spat upon. This hallowed place of peaceful worship and service now wreaked of alcohol and cheap cologne – the air stifled from a collective fear. In a state of utter shock, Kristin had wet herself, collapsed to the wood floor, curled up and froze. Her parents fared no better.

For Emad, winning any fight was synonymous with maiming some body part, orifice, or organ. He was typically partial to setting his victim up for an unsuspected sucker punch. With this, his go-to move- thanks to the many times he practiced it on Umair - he gave it his all, without shame or any self-restraint. Emad was always willing to injure himself in a miss, rather than measure his blows. In those rare moments over his childhood, when Umair flinched, sending Emad's haymaker astray, a high price would be exacted from the targeted spot.

Umair finally succumbed to the electrocuting torque in his elbow and the fire in his wrist that Sadiq was unleashing, now desperately trying to pass out. This viciousness brought back old -now fresh - childhood memories away from which Umair could not escape.

In the blink of an eye, Emad and Sadiq had Umair outside on the crushed flagstone graveled parking lot. Completely exposed and virtu- ally paralyzed, between Emad's late-model pimp-tricked BMW and the powerfully hinged rustic door to the church, Umair was now splayed out, rendered completely defenseless. Right where they wanted him, their flesh and blood, Emad and Sadiq began to mercilessly beat Umair, using their fists, elbows, knees and feet.

Deafened and unable to move, Umair received his brothers' fury. He was being raped. Not content to just beat and break him, Emad and Sadiq were hell-bent on violating him. They loudly spit on him and slapped his face, mocking him as they wiped their wet and bloody, grimy hands around his neck, into his eyes and onto his hair. When they finally ran out of breath, they pulled Umair up by his hair and ears, manhandled him over to their car, and jabbed him with their thumbs, elbows, and knees into his exposed ear, eyes, rectum, and groin. After taking a breather, they kicked him into the back seat then whipped him with the rear shoulder strap fortified with the meaty backseat buckle. It cracked his left cheekbone and his right forearm.

Sadiq started up his pride and joy, gunning and spinning the tricked-out tires into the earth, spraying crushed flagstone and a choking dust at those few who dared to venture near to this butchery.

Emad, who had now caught his second wind, began waylaying Umair with all of his might, unphased as to how or where his punches landed. Umair finally surrendered his bladder then his bowels. Slipping out of consciousness, he now prayed for his death. On his last beseech to his God, he threw up. Emad rubbed the vomit into Umair's face while repeatedly sending measured jabs into Umair's stomach, as if to pump up more. When Emad drove his thumb into the golf-ball hematoma that his work had formed just below Umair's eye, Umair let out a whimper- the best scream he could muster.

Over the months that followed, Umair was held captive. After his reprogramming, he rejected the decrepit Morgantown, demonic Kristin and her dirty, unforgivable spawn. Umair's spirit was finally excised and cured.

As far as Umair was concerned, none of this happened to him. He was back home for good and where he had always belonged.

Umair would never see West Virginia, his friends, his true love or his child ever again. Never to embrace, talk with or take part in the lives of those who meant something. He would not be Kristin's husband or father to their child.

No wonder that all these years later the Umair who I represented was kindhearted, and yet pre-defeated by any given act of unkindness. Umair took to total surrender. As to Loona, Umair was for all intent and purpose, her virtual almost-housebroken pet.

Ask yourself whether you are happy, and you cease to be so.

—JOHN STUART MILL

Umair had lost forever any sense of life's willingness to give and please. The best that could be said for Umair was that he was still alive. And however listless, his broken, defeated heart still had a beat - slight and irregular – weakened by chronic fear and malfunctioning under a backflow of despair.

That Umair had been done in by his own flesh and blood, in and of itself did not shock me. Yet way atop the list of adult victim domestic violence cases I had seen over twenty-plus years of criminal practice was his. The only slight 'upside' to his victimization was that Umair was alive - and not left permanently physically disfigured or horribly visibly maimed.

Learning of Umair's past, I pledged to honor his mandate and tell his story; and was suddenly overcome with an obligation to tell mine. How strange that the first person who came to mind was Joey Lark.

CHAPTER V

JOEY LARK

*Avoiding danger is no safer in the long
run than outright exposure.
The fearful are caught as often as the bold.*

—*Helen Keller*

O ne of my first wife's drinking buddies was her fellow courtroom
partner, veteran Deputy Sheriff Joey Lark. I was just hired by
the Office and this, my very first courtroom assignment, where we all
worked, was a highly prized one for me.

Joey was an old-school, "Back of the (Stock) Yards" - South Sider.
He was born and raised in gritty working-class Chicago and, but for his
stint in the Army, never left the neighborhood where he was born.
Once a place where outsiders would never dare set foot or even drive
through, Joey was now a noticeable minority. The old folks who watched
him grow up and the newer arrivals, Mexican and African-
Americans, all loved him. He was known as "Sheriff Joey."

I would years later meet his kindred spirit in the form of an 'ex-
pat', Milan, who like Joey had a big heart and was Army/tough as nails.

Sheriff Joey would walk his dog and chitchat with his newest neighbors, those who were able to get out from the scourge of public housing.

They adored him and felt safe knowing that he was their neighbor. When on the job, Joey would treat the inmates, young and old, with respect; but when it came to keeping them in line, he would not spare the rod. Joey's Army MOS was medic/orderly. After having set straight an unruly inmate, he recounted to me the matter of a disrespectful lieutenant who was to have sutures removed after he had injured himself during a training exercise demonstration. *'Dat Lou had no class and didn't know nut'in about nut'in'. He should not have tried let me know who was boss. I respect da rank and all dat, but not some jag-bag pointing his finger at dat one freekin bar of his... Yes, Lieutenant! So, I removed his sutures, all right."* Joey explained. *"Ya see, what I did was I doused his mitt wit' al-key-hall, den' yanked dat' udder' end - wit da frickin' sailor knot; one – by-one. Right tru' dat jag-off."*

Joey had a set-in-stone drinking night; he would start early Wednesday afternoon and wrap it up early Thursday. Every Thursday morning, reeking of Old Style, Joey was snap-to-it throughout the entire Court call. He always answered the bell and was on-the-ball; attentive to the Court, considerate and dependable. Joey had seen it all in the courtroom. He had a pulse on every Judge and attorney, understood the law, and could ferret out the genuine from phony, the competent from hacks. Joey could have run the entire courtroom by himself, yet he was so humble - earnestly oblivious as to how keen a man he was and how highly others respected him.

Drinking was hardly Joey's Achilles' heel. It was his youngest son who was the rock in his shoe; a lowlife wannabe. He was a moocher, a liar and a thief. The first time I met him, I was unimpressed, to say the least. His lame attempt to intimidate me left me more unamused than offended. Out of respect for Joey, I checked my tone and tenor and let him get over on me. It was obvious that his game was to use his father however he could and otherwise make nothing of himself.

Two years later, on a particularly cool, late Friday autumn night, now a rising star in the office, I was paying dues, just ready to begin the first of three-night shifts on "felony review," As of 1:30am, I was next up, having just missed a midnight 'armed robbery gone bad'. I got called out a South Side Chicago Police District for a person in custody for an on-the-street shooting. As part of my job, I would reach out to the violent crimes detectives, "dics", who had been assigned to investigate the case – they would usually call in their cases when they were ready to be reviewed, but I liked to jump in while the investigation was still underway. They gave me the heads up that the dead-to-rights suspect was the son of a deputy sheriff.

Mind you, there were over seven thousand deputy sheriffs. Even if they had mentioned that he was assigned to Court Services, there were over 170 Courtrooms in the Circuit Court of Cook County. By the time I was transferred to felony review, I had practiced in a dozen courtrooms, stretched all over Chicago. Why would I think to ask the offender's name? I grabbed my files, brief case and bag phone then made my way through the city to the 8th District, known as Chicago Lawn.

When I rolled up to the station, there sat on the stairs Joey Lark, half in the bag. Once he saw that it was me, he started to cry; he begged me to help his son. There was no time to make small talk about coincidence and such; this was as real as it would ever get. This was the hand I was dealt, and I had to play it - and its heat - just right. I promised Joey that I would do whatever I could. The detectives immediately sized me up to make sure I could be trusted. Once they knew what I was all about, they tried to apologize for doubting me. I shook it off and said, "Gentlemen. Let's get to work." They briefed me with straight talk - leaving out the bullshit, after which we agreed to felony review this shooting by "the" book.

Joey's derelict son had been out on the street, acting the loudmouth fool. It was no surprise that he had done very little with his life since I met him four years before and was known around the neighborhood for taking out his sad state in life on his neighbors of color, without any discretion or judgment. Only later did I find out that everyone kept this from Sheriff Joey, not wanting to embarrass him.

On this fateful night, Joey's kid had gotten into a shouting match with some of the neighborhood's young, gangbanger street dealers, whose quiet, after-dark "work" the neighborhood ignored.

Joey's kid got drunk then got high on borrowed coke. Overplaying a dead hand, he started getting real mouthy with the crew on the corner.

They called him out on his jawing and then one of them - who didn't know Sheriff Joey – stupidly raised him for not being man enough to 'back up his play'. Things broke bad. Lacking any sense, let alone decency, Joey's nitwit son went into the house and retrieved Joey's service revolver, which had been tucked away for 'drinking night' some eight hours earlier. Joey had never converted to a semiautomatic.

When, years before this colossal cluster fuck, I had asked Joey why he stuck with the six-shooter, he had replied in his ever-clever role-playing way: *"Pardon me, sir, my Kraut -or Deigo - heater here has just jammed; could you stop shooting until I fuck wid' it for a freakin' spell? When you're all alone, you want six rounds from a Smith and Wesson that you can count on to fire, not a clip full of sardines, that grab you by your freakin' giblets and get ya nothing but dead. I'll take my barrel full of torpedoes and my trusty speed loader – times 2 - six more fish each - over some overseas paperweight bullshit. And I would say dis very same 'ting' to my udder friend."*

Joey's son, wielding his father's service-six, came out of the front door and opened fire, unloading without aim - every which way- hitting a young man. As the street law of averages always adds up, when an idiot hothead fires a gun, a random round will invariably find the innocent— in this case a "neutron with privilege" (a non-gang member, trustworthy and designated as 'off-limits'), who just happened to be walking home in the same direction - and could not resist but see the verbal thrashing he could hear from around the corner as he was headed away and home for the night. A stand-up comedian in the making, he just could not resist the material-potential from the barrage of clever insults and profane buffoonery.

Hearing this, I slumped into a dry-rotted chair and dropped my head onto the ratty, sticky, metal desk. That could have been me.

"Well, Counselor, what's our play?" one of the dics asked.

That some clever kid had been horribly wounded and that I had known Joey for so long, I was ready to bury his son. But, before I could even finish telling them about my year of service with Joey, working elbow to elbow in the presiding Judge's courtroom, my very first prestigious assignment in the office, the lead detective put me in check with:

"Ya, ya. Blah, blah, blah. We get it counselor. Listen here Mr. Prosecutor. We all know Joey Lark; everybody knows him - and has a connection to him. Most of us have thrown back with him on more than a handful or two of Wednesdays over the years. Out here, in his territory, all the old folks love him, and the real gangbangers give him respect. Hell, half fear him, but not one of them would dare fuck with him. He's like the last of the freakin' Mohicans."

His partner quipped: "Except he's the paleface, fer' cry-sakes."

"Now he's the paleface with this piece of shit for a paleface son who is our collar. Kimosabe."

It was time, we decided, to stop thinking too much and trying too hard and just take things as they came. One thing Joey's kid had going for him was that the best witnesses, hardly choir boys, couldn't seem to keep the truth straight. Preprogramed to lie to the police, even when I convinced them to tell truth, to them even undisputed facts to which they had personal knowledge seemed like lies.

Meanwhile, a decent kid was fighting for his life at Cook County Hospital, trauma medicine's hallowed grounds. Cook County (later 'Stroger') Hospital, a peacetime MASH, treated volumes of menacing injuries, providing the very highest quality of patient care. If this kid had a chance, he was almost certain to recover. Anyone who "caught one" anywhere in the Chicagoland area prayed to be run to Cook County Hospital.

Meanwhile, Joey continued to pray the rosary for him. He had walked to St. Galls' rectory, banged on the Father's door, asked to borrow a rosary, returned to the district, praying it along the way.

Officially, Joey's son approached the boys on the corner then started talking smack - for no reason. When they verbally outclassed him then mocked him, he reacted without regard, impetuously retrieved Joey's off-limits, secreted service revolver and discharged it in every direction but his own. An innocent bystander was non-fatally struck by an errant round. By the time I had arrived at the station, the "comedian apprentice" was recovering from surgery.

I re-interviewed each witness's parents as to their take on Joey. Each and every one of them said the same thing, a version of the following: "*That crazy white-ass motherfucker, Sheriff Joey, he is a real trip, but he is righteous people. He watches over the old folks; we tell the young guys, don't fuck with them or him or his puppy. Sherriff Joey is our friend. But we all hate that hype, punk-ass son, racist son of his.*"

The victim's parents, even amidst their warranted outrage, expressed sorrow for Sheriff Joey's paralleled pain.

Before the dics and I went in to formally interview Joey's son, I reiterated our play, emphasizing that he had been identified. The weapon was recovered. If he lawyered-up we could charge it and be done. Had he not been Joey's kid, I would have helped this chatterbox walk himself into saying the magic words and becoming eligible for an extended sentence of thirty to sixty years in the joint.

> ***Once you make a decision, the universe
> conspires to make it happen.***
>
> —*Ralph Waldo Emerson*

Without another word, we made our way to our interviewee; the reprehensible cause of this. I shook my head in disgust when I saw him, thinking to myself: 'I should have snapped his jaw then stomped on one of his knees the first time I met him'.

So as to keep it short and wrap it up, with no desire to 'buddy' with him, I stood on the other side of the lockup bars and obstructed my face. He was greasy and twitchy and could not have recognized Vice President Dan Quayle if he were in my shoes. Before I could utter a peep, he started spouting off about who his Dad was and how it was self-defense because he tried to stop an armed robbery.

This cokehead yammer could have easily buried him. I moved closer and tried to talk over him, vociferously advising him of his rights. He would not let up. I raised my voice to my Dad's level, blasting him with his constitutional rights, rattling the lockup bars. But he was so hyped up on coke and oblivious, or as my Dad would say, "high as a kite an as numb as they come," he was not receiving me.

Our voices continued to climb over each other; as if insisting upon talking himself into up to three decades in the penitentiary, Joey's son mocked my reference to him invoking his right to remain silent, now determined to further embellish his twisted-around account.

The quiet detective had heard enough. He reached through the bars, cup-headed then pulled Joey's son into the bars - as if they were about to make out. The Detective said not a word. The heavy breathing lasted from the other side of freedom for a second or two; then the room went pleasantly dead silent.

"Shhhhhhhhh…listen to me."

After spooning - so to describe - with Joey's son's ear, and saying whatever was said, Joey's son took it down and finally started listening and repeating:

"I revoke my right to remain silent. Did I say it right?"

"You meant invoke, right? You invoke, right?"

"Right. Invote. I promise not to say another word. I revote."

With that, I said to him: "I wish you all the best, sir. I bid you good morning and only pleasant days to follow."

This was one for the books. Before I left the station, the detective pulled me aside and said: "We all feel bad about all of this. Joey's outside. He's been waitin' on you. And he thinks the world of you. He's been praying for that poor kid who got shot and so has the whole district and all the families out there and our families too.

Beyond that, not so much of this is good - but at least you were good - and that counts big time. Go be with Joey. We will cover you with review. And if you need some beer, let us know."

42

2. Post-Miranda Acting up

The only other interrogation that came close to the bizarre nature of this one was one during which, in an effort to throw off a belligerent know-it-all suspect, I summoned up my best fake cry, that one suppressed for decades since I had summoned it up when faced with a high-school bully and his ultimatum.

This time it carried no personal stake. I was at work and bored. On a whim, I chalked it up as what I can only describe as an experimental interrogation technique.

Unfortunately, I laid it on too thick. Just as my hook was set to throw the perp' off his game, the preoccupied detective - who clearly missed the whole bit-assuming that the suspect had somehow caught me with a quick punch - started to tear for him. Thankfully I blocked the cop's path, by fake-keeling over while salvaging this now dangerous melodramatic, interrogative ploy by yelling out, "I'm crying because I believe this man! Please, let us be. Let me talk with him some more."

After the clearly perplexed detective left the room, I confessed, telling the suspect exactly what I had done. Without missing a beat, he said, "Man, I like your play. You actually got in front with your shit to stop him justifiably kicking my ass? Yes. You did do that. I appreciate you. I ain't gonna give it up, but I want you to know that you're cool with me. You know what? When I finish doin' my time for this fuck-up, I'm gonna use that cry baby shit of yours to either make me some coin or keep my ass out of jail."

When I stepped out of the lock up with the arrestee's written invocation of rights, the detective knocked it out of my hand and laid into me. Conferring with his colleagues who filled him in on my unorthodox interrogation methods did not bail me out. "In

the future, you need to let me know when you're playing your apparently well-known by everyone but me,
frickin' mind-fuck games. I almost cuffed him one for
you, Chrissakes! I should cuff you, Counselor.

"You are a frickin' different son of a bitch. And
you are good at this shit. Some guys call you "the
Martian", because they claim you come from 'out-of-
space', beam down here and clear our cases. But for
that one back in there, I should still cuff you one.
Finish your paperwork, get on your spaceship and
blast the fuck off owda' here...before I give you what I
was too freekin' close to giving him."

It was three in the morning by time I limped out of the district. There
was Joey, clutching his rosary. His eyes were puffy and bloodshot. I told
him that his son was going to branch court in the morning, charged with
the felony, but I made sure that we had not make bad things worse, which
was the very best I could do. Joey slumped over and began to sob. Joey
eventually dozed off on the stoop, long after he had finished saying whatever he had say about the matter and neither of us had nothing more to
offer. I stayed with him, calling off other cases with "personal business"
until sunrise. The rest of my team already gotten the word and covered
for me. Only the roar of the mornings first run of CTA Bus #63 startled
me out of my sleep. It was a deep sleep, under which replayed the story of
Joey's life, his children's upbringing, the bad turns and the deaf ear of
his son. I gave him a ride home then went back to 26th & Cal and fell
asleep in the car.

Working nights meant getting dragging my fanny home against the
rush hour traffic, settling down, and then sleeping from around 11:00
a.m. to 4:00 p.m., with the television on. That is because, years before, I
had discovered that I could get deeper sleep and better rest during day-
time hours with the television playing in the background. Throughout
my youth, Ma and my Dad slept the very same way. My Dad needed
the noise; Ma tolerated it. The lingering effect of my Dad's service aboard

the *USS Midway*, when he embraced sleep under clamor. I recall their snores drowning out the sounds of lost signal 'snow' or the one-note soundtrack to test pattern image.

To live is the rarest thing in the world.
Most people exist, that is all.

—Oscar Wilde

On a Friday afternoon, before the last night of my "three on/three off" shift, I was awaked to the name "Joel Seamus Lake" and Joey's picture on the bedroom television tube. I had to be dreaming. Yet once awake and having shaken it all off, I heard and saw it again. Joey Lark, an off-duty deputy sheriff, had been shot and killed.

According to witnesses, Joey was shot in the back while he was walking his dog down the middle of a quiet street. He crawled until he finally died, all the while gasping, holding on to his dog's leash, desperate to get the two of them back home. I fell to the floor and began to weep. I banged my head to the floor knowing that this was an act of dumb-ass revenge. By the time I got to the office, the case was already stacked under two other murders. By sheer coincidence, however cruel or poetic, I was up and this homicide was mine to review.

When I made my reluctant way to Area Three Violent Crimes, the lockups were bursting with witnesses and suspects. The Cook County Sheriff himself had dispatched bigwigs with huge clout to oversee things. One big-brass type, a spit-polished commander, a rank I had yet to encounter, approached me and started to barf out some company line then began to meddle. The Martian having landed, I communicated, "Let me stop you right there, Commander. I - more than anyone except you - appreciate the gravity of what is before me. I give you my word that I will work this case seam-less-ly."

I then I offered him my hand and non-verbally ushered him to the exit door. He left the Area without fanfare, acknowledgment or escort.

He just scampered away.

According to the dics put on the case, everybody was talking. The slew of witnesses— eyewitnesses, occurrence witnesses, and "third-party admission" witnesses—were telling versions of one story. The 'perps' all knew about Joey's drinking-night routine; no matter his condition or even the weather's, his night did not end until he took his dog for a walk. Only one time, the night his son fucked up, did his routine get disrupted.

They were waiting for him. Once they faced him he did not look for an out. Joey just stood there, but he would not take sides against his son's bonehead move. He defended his son's dishonor – they knew he would. After all, whenever anyone would dare approach him about his son's disruptive antics, Joey would reply, "*Listen here, my friend. Blood is 'ticker' den wahdder.*"

Knowing Joey's reputation for never backing down, his attackers had no courage to go fist-a-cuffs with him, even with the four-to-one advantage, never mind any of them, one-on-one. Joey's ambushers had the numbers, yet they had not one iota of his honor or loyalty .

As soon as the first one drew, Joey charged at them from fifteen feet. They shot him multiple times without any regard, horribly mortally wounding him. Yet not even their strikes could take him down before they ran off; in utter fear of him, still standing until they were gone.

Neighbors poured out and held him until the ambulance and police arrived. His last words were about getting his dog back home.

As the investigation turned up, the four gunmen were hardly a hard-core, violent pack. They were just knuckleheads, who lacked the where-withal to check their Super Nintendo video game impulsiveness. Like so many, they had not the skill set to contemplate how their decisions would turn on them. This shooting was all about 'street cred'.

I forced myself to take poor Joey out of my thoughts. Instead, I focused on his derelict son, laying all blame on him. Everyone else saw it the very same way – including Joey's neighbors - and even the accused.

Each of them confessed to me, proud of what they had accom-plished, even though not one of them was a witness to Joey's idiot son's shooting. Through a grueling and painful calm, I kept my composure. When I could not hold back any longer, I told his killers that they had killed a good man, who was good to people. Each one of them took my words as praise for what they had done.

If you risk nothing, then you risk everything.

—GEENA DAVIS

In the end, I accepted, or at least convinced myself, that if it hadn't been this, something even worse was bound to result from Joey's circumstances.

My supervisors were not pleased that I memorialized so much of Joey's son's wrongdoing into the defendants' statements. I told them that this case was all about two innocent people being shot, the real cause of which was the very same person. Out of respect for Joey, I made a decision and I would not back down to obtuse second-guessing. My supervisors blinked; and with that the case that I saw through from its bad beginning to its sad ending was now closed.

I attended Joey's wake. He was barely recognizable. While alive, Joey had a striking resemblance of a combination of the young Sean Connery and LBJ. Lying in state, Joey looked like Khrushchev in his hard, late years. It was as if Joey had been embalmed through a fire hose. I could feel my then-wife's embarrassment when I began to cry. Erin had no sense of or empathy for what I had gone through. Instead she joined in on the small talk around the casket about how booze makes the postmortem face bloat and actually looks respectful, like a millionaire. This tavern factoid was received and passed around like some heartfelt eulogy –or a bottle.

Joey Lark's murder was the by-product of that too common combination of impulsivity and firearms; with bad aim and lack of foresight significant contributing factors. His murder was set into motion, as with so many bad outcomes I handled, by an adrift son or daughter. Working up these cases - a victim done in by someone close - even the "slam dunks" would ultimately compel me to delve into and splay what a dear old Irish soul, June Butler referred to as "the story under the roof" – I seemed to want to find ways to complicate matters.

Then a prosecutor, and as of twelve years later, a criminal defense attorney, I had encountered hundreds of young men who were the offspring of former defendants or clients. In time a mother or father whom years before I had either prosecuted or defended was now footing the bill for a new generation's wrongdoer. Recidivism was one thing; but a sense of tradition was now feeding the criminal justice system. And yet I never bought into that common courthouse mantra, that this sad reality was just another form of "job security".

"Worry does not empty tomorrow of its sorrow,
it empties today of its strength."

—*Corrie ten Boom*

No matter how hard I worked - either as a prosecutor or a defense attorney - to dispense justice for those victimized, the innocent and the accused by applying the rule of law in sound ways - my feelings remained unsettled. When I talked about this with my Dad, he aptly noted, "That's what happens when you try shoveling shit against the tide."

Even more disconcerting was that by the time I became a sole practitioner – focusing exclusively on criminal defense - learning about my clients' lives and family dynamics – bad choices galore - was becoming a welcome distraction from the worsening troubles and unmanageable struggles I was facing in my own personal life.

That I saw it as a perk of my line of work, these places to burrow, was an unnoticed indicator that something was terribly wrong under my own roof.

Two kinds of blindness are easily combined,
so that those who do not see really appear to see what is not.

—*Tertullian*

CHAPTER VI

FRANCESCA AND SARKIS

*Our parents were our first gods. If parents are loving,
nurturing, and kind, this becomes the child's definition
of the creator. If parents were controlling, angry, and
manipulative, then this becomes their definition.*

—DAVID W. EARLE

Throughout my younger years, my Ma, Francesca, supercharged with a maternal instinct to protect and demand greatness, was the sturdiest person of all. Through her toughness I ended up either placed in the forefront or knocked on my ass. Even to this day, my Ma remains the most fiercely loyal, blatantly in-your-face honest person I have ever known. Whatever my immediate need was, Ma would always deliver. Our house was stocked with music and art and books and quite a cache of kosher treats and yummy Middle Eastern delights of all kinds.

While stocking up our kitchen, she once sent me, all of six years old, down the aisle of the New Hampshire State Liquor store to grab a jug of Mogen David wine. One of the middle-aged cashiers, donning a smock with an official state emblem, attempted to chastise me. I knew he had me, hand in the cookie jar, but I would not put up with his mouth.

"What do I 'think' I'm doing? I know what I'm doing. I'm filling an order - One! Jug! Of! Mogen! David! Maaaaa!!! Just wait...."

Ma rounded the aisle and squared up with him. She intimidated him and cut him down; it was like something out of a gangster flick. He dared not open his mouth, and I knew it. I could feel his fear and saw it in the familiar way he swallowed. I added a contemptuous gaze, swinging the jug of wine mockingly as I turned my back on him. Ma grabbed me by the neck and scolded me for yelling in the store. I kept my mouth shut, and we went about our business.

On one occasion, Ma brained a clearly mentally deranged but dangerous woman, wielding a cast-iron frying pan. The woman had come onto our property, charged at my siblings and me, and even tried to injure our defending puppy. Ma pinged the frying pan off her head, flicking it like a high priest issuing holy water. This whacked out trespasser learned what my siblings and I knew: When it came to corporal punishment, the kitchen was Ma's arsenal.

Ma would go toe-to-toe with any outsider and would not think in the slightest to back down. Beyond all the praise and inspiration, she provided me her most precious gift; the one that all have received it have celebrated and always remembered: Ma's food. Ma remains hands-down the best cook ever; I could and would eat everything she cooked. When at family gatherings on my Dad's side, my Ma would always find herself in the kitchen with my Grandma Anoush, taking mental notes and learning the old country nuances in Armenian cuisine; in no time she was held high with Gramma Anoush and my Auntie Betty as one of the best cooks in the Minasian family.

I shall never forget when one day at the age of seven, I was helping Ma in the kitchen. She let me take over, playing sous chef to me. When we finished, just before Ma would whistle then announce or have one of us announce "Time to eat," she looked me in the eye, with a wooden spoon fixed as her conductor's baton, locked me in, eye-to-eye, and began to issue a stern admonishment. Ma forewarned me that I would never, ever find a woman who could cook like her and so my only options were either to "eat swill" or learn to cook like her. I needed to learn every technique, note every antic, and master every nuance; otherwise I would come to regret, later in life, that I would never eat such succulence. I took it all in, and from that moment on, I made sure to learn how to cook it all. Knowing that it was unfair to expect the unachievable, I would not count on or hold any woman to cook in my Ma's way; it was on one hand a priceless gift yet on the other became yet another way to pit myself against others.

3. The junkie detainee—Stuck in between a rock and a hard place

Jake, my twenty-two-year-old client, got arrested; he had passed out in his car after shooting heroin. The needle was dangling from the back of his hand when the cops arrived. Jake's mother was outraged that he got high, explaining how he was supposed to pay his dealer, and that with his drug debt wiped clean, her wedding ring - her grandmother's wedding ring- collateral to secure repayment and spare Jake from a severe beating - would be returned. Instead, Jake paid up, then traded the ring back; he could boot up and have ample credit.

The ring went gone forever.

For two weeks, Jake was in compliance with the conditions of his bond, then got nabbed trying to "cuff in a clean drop" - substitute purchased clean urine for his. The Federal Court Judge, a no-nonsense Coastal-Italian type, ordered Jake to produce his own sample, knowing that his urine was "hot". Against my advice, Jake's parents dropped a lot of money to have

him immediately placed in a posh private rehab facil-
ity, bumping the next person on the waiting list. The
Judge shook his head at Jake's parents, then asked,
"Counsel?"

"Your Honor, in light of the effort my client's
parents have made, would the Court consider giving my
client just one more last chance? They really want
him to get clean."

The sarcasm worked.
Before Jake was released, in what little time with him
at the lockup, I read him the riot act – demanding
that he make a choice between beating his addiction,
a life in prison or an agonizing death. "You obviously don't give a shit about your parents. You need
to decide is whether you give a shit about yourself."

Later that night, Jake sent the following text
message:

*"For what it's worth, I was looking at my original
bond conditions, and there was nothing checked off
for tampering with the drug test."* He added, *"By now, I
should be almost crystal clean, which, by the way,
something I am proud of."*

Two days later, he skipped out of the rehab clinic.
US Marshals nabbed him at a dope house where he was
"working for his fix". The Judge revoked his bond and
held the case over for three days, ordering the Clerk
to "Get ahold of Attorney 'One More Last Chance'."

Before getting the word, Jake's Dad, who had just
landed in LA from a business trip to Taiwan, sent me
a very mixed text message:

*"According to Jake's mother, Jake did not complete
his treatment. The Judge wants you in Court. She said
Jake is doing really well and made a friend with some
guy, and they seem to be "taking care of each other",*

whatever that means... As usual, none of this making much sense to me. I'll mail you a check as soon as I get home."

I feared my Ma's hand or anything else that she grabbed up and fastened as a bludgeon, especially her dreaded wooden cooking spoon. With no quarter for disrespect or laziness, my Ma would address infractions with mighty blows, which were clearly intended to be smart and redirect me to the straight and narrow.

Throughout my preteens, my Ma would grow heavy when she asked if I was being picked on at school. I did not have the heart to tell her about what I was unable to fend off with words; I did not want her to repel, crossing the line. Sensing what I would not confess, on more than one occasion, my Ma would tearfully recount the story of one particular grade-school classmate:

'Teli was a gentle and educated boy, who my Ma, then a young girl, sensed was gripped by primal fear. He seemed purposely quiet and became painfully startled by the slightest of anything loud. When his new classmates smelled fresh meat, and began to circle in on him, my Ma stepped in to protect him, declaring him as hands-off with both words and fists, yet not even her protection could ease his anxiety. On his first day of school, Teli's impeccable, very sweet English was heard. When his classmates, including my Ma and his teacher froze, Teli got scared and thereafter intentionally dumbed himself down.

The only other time he opened up and spoke in his pristine English was when he waited for my Ma after school on a Friday afternoon. Seeing a troubled look in his eyes, my Ma told him to meet her by the single apple tree, surrounded by oak trees on the edge of her family's land. As if begging for his family's life, he told my Ma that his father was a "factotum" and was not a political or hateful man.

My Ma had no idea what he was talking about but assured him that she would look out for him. Doing the only thing she knew to, my Ma climbed the apple tree, in her dress that had been handed across once and down twice and picked four of its best ones for Teli to bring home.

"You can eat them, slice them and put sugar on them. Your mother can bake them with dough or fry them in butter and cinnamon."

Teli did not make it to school on the rainy Monday that followed. When he did not show up on the clear Tuesday, my Ma rode her bike after school to his tenement home. She never saw Teli again.

Eventually, my Ma found out that Teli found his way there after his family fled from Turkey. By doing so, Teli's father ended up putting his family in grave danger. The Armenians from Watertown had misidentified Aydin, Teli's father - who was a writer, with Aslan, his estranged, distant cousin, a Talaat Bey henchman.

Teli's attempt to correct the misidentification was futile. It was either stay and suffer or pack up and get the hell out of Methuen.

My Ma felt for this kid. After all, he had nothing to do with anything for which his uncle, let alone his country, had done. Seventy plus years later my Ma's take on it was, as with most everything, direct:

"Either bump the father off and then shut up about it, or leave all of them the hell alone. Teli was a good kid; he was sweet and was so very smart."

When it came to my Dad, my Ma bit down her tongue and rarely stood her ground. Instead, she endured playing his inferior. In this relationship, my Ma was all about keeping the peace. Even in those instances in which she could take it no more, got in my Dad's face and he backed down by walking away or storming out of the house, my Ma knew that it was a losing, defeating situation from which a more lasting unease than desirable good was sure to linger.

My Dad was the only son with two doting sisters, while my Ma was the youngest of thirteen. I gained no insight from either of their sibling experiences when it came to my upbringing, especially with regard to my relationship with my younger sister. Unlike the tone of my Dad's brother-to-sisters reference point, I was so self-absorbed and emotionally confrontational, I gleaned nothing from that; instead I took to rugged ways, turning away from his brotherly goodness. Looking back, as to my younger sister's upbringing, I was too unloving and callous. I should have treated my younger sister the way my Dad always has.

My Dad, Sarkis Vartan, is the son of my Grampa Vartan, Vartan Sarkis, a highly revered man who escaped death at least twice. At the age of fifteen, he was sent packing from his village of Khok, Armenia (now renamed, located in eastern Turkey). While he was over the Atlantic, Grampa Vartan's parents and sister were butchered by Ottoman henchman. He scarcely survived his rough journey to America aboard the SS *La Savoie*, only to be turned away from Ellis Island, because of a debilitating ear infection, which spiked a blistering fever.

A weed is a plant that has mastered every survival skill except for learning how to grow in rows.

—Doug Larson

Swept up from American soil, Grampa Vartan was directed back to his last port of call, Marseilles, on the southern coast of France, where *SS La Savoie* had taken perishable provisions and contraband. Although he spoke not a lick of French, Grampa Vartan, experiencing a horrible journey, somehow recovered there, regained his heath then put together the funds, in French Francs, to return to America. This time, aboard the SS Venezia (sunk decades later during an air raid at the Port of Messina), by the nurturing of his fellow third-class passengers, mostly Portuguese and Moroccan, he was granted passage through the port of Providence, Rhode Island.

That Grampa Vartan survived the genocide, endured denial of admission, restored his health in the South of France then returned to America for good, standing in line with Prussian and Ottoman dignitaries - at the age of fifteen – remained mind-boggling.

The stories of Armenians always seem to fall into categories: those who made it out to some distant land; or who were viciously killed—quickly or slowly—at the hands of the Ottomans; and those who were somehow spared, only to be left with so little of their ancient land and the beauty of what would never again be.

CHAPTER VII

HOT AND COLD WAR

One can assume a subservient persona,
which can serve as subversive,
albeit through subterfuge.

—Redatteur Roode Bloede

The USS *Midway* was America's resilient, water-bound mighty beast that flexed her huge, steel-forged muscles and darted rumbling heavily-armed birds of prey over the Mediterranean Sea. An ocean warrior, through sheer intimidation and her display of precision operations, would take on every enemy throughout the often on-the-brink, postwar, Cold War era and into every conflict that followed.

My Dad's crew vigilantly manned the fail-safe, auxiliary diesel room, where full power was reliably supplied at a moment's notice to the US Navy's symbol of post–World War II might. He and the equally rugged men at his side stood ever-ready.

When called into action they answered only to the *Midway*'s savvy engineer, who answered only to the Midway's deep-south factory-built engines.

Fixed into the very thorax of this paranoid world on the edge of self-destruction, my Dad's crew was positioned, aside the aft galley, to ensure that emergency power was the Midway's in a snap. Her galley chef was a combination of French cuisine and Canadian quick temper. My Dad gradually made friends with him and won him over. The result was quality chow, worthy of command staff, delivered under wraps – without the asking. This impeccable flavor was paid for with bottles of European wine that my Dad secreted onboard when returning from his prized shore patrol details. Like any black-market operation, this was kept quiet from pickup to cleanup.

On those few occasions while policing distant shores, when my Dad couldn't reason or coax the drunken or talk down the unruly rabble-rousers, his massive arms, and his square build, displaying – and as a last resort well-placing - his white billy club, would set any sailors or marines shipshape. On one occasion, my Dad crack-whipped his neckerchief, taking down four and sending those ready to jump in scampering. The scuttlebutt from this event created a rippling deterrent effect and ensured that his crew's *cuisine de jour* would not be interfered with by scallywags on liberty or local thugs looking for trouble.

> *We ourselves feel that what we are doing*
> *is just a drop in the ocean.*
> *But the ocean would be less because of that missing drop.*

> —MOTHER TERESA

During his tour of duty, my Dad met a Lebanese-American who hailed from Lawrence, Massachusetts. Peter, known as 'Rocky', had worked his way into the inner circle of the *Midway*'s affairs. He was the Midway's very best radioman, who spun LPs heard from stem to stern. At the snap of a finger, Rocky could raise the smaller ships of the Sixth Fleet, including the USS *Albany* and USS *D'Amato* (Anthony Peter D'Amato sacrificed his own life to save two foxhole companions, two years after having survived harrowing combat in Northern Africa). I heard my Dad recounting his service with Rocky, of some twenty plus years before, when I nosed in on his time with his old running buddies. It was no wonder that his story would take on life of its own.

Rocky had a direct line to both the *Midway*'s big brass and the seem-ingly more powerful communications and business contractors. He and his men answered every message, maintained vigilant radio contact, and coordinated every onshore microwave and upstart satellite operation. They ensured that lines, signals, and security were top-grade and in an instant, were operational. For Rocky's reliability, discretion and his crew's like effort and ship-tight lips, he was given the go-ahead to work a side line as a would-be travel agent. As part of Rocky's business model, he could allocate passage on and off the *Midway* and give priority – using a password system- to local dignitaries and their guests. Everyone else was subject to hard bartering and lop-sided negotiation.

Rocky lived by the only Latin phrase he knew: *quid pro quo*. It was not long before he put together junkets from the ship to distant shores and was given the authority to separate the Midway from her support -deploying destroyers and frigates to adjacent shores and commence so-called 'communication training exercises'. The "optimal atmospher-ic" locations were where his tourists could off-load to take in the prime local sites. The crown jewel of these Fleet Command ordered – clearly ahead-of-their-time cruises - was an elaborately coordinated "Parisian Supported Radio Relay Training".

Even though the *Midway* was docked off the breathtaking shores of Naples, somehow Rocky was able to sell the exercise, code-naming it with the cocky "Sightseeing in Paris".

After considering the geography and running the logistics, I pressed my Dad on the matter. He explained, *"All I know, or so the story was, that there were a lot of strings pulled and even more palms greased to pull off that Paris scam."*

Many years later, my Dad somehow ran into Rocky at Bishop's. To outsiders, it was a top-notch, succulent Syrian supper club. To insiders, it was the very best lamb joint/card room in the Boston area. My Dad was no insider, but not a threat. Rocky happened to be out with his brother, a man whose reputation - and nothing more -was well known. He went by the family name, "Katter". Only those who he chose could identify him by face. Even certain members of the Bonnano family, with whom his business dealings were rumored to be, wouldn't have known his face from Adam's. What they did know was that Katter could do some things and take care of various matters.

Katter and my Dad shook hands. For none to see and no one else to hear, Rocky acknowledged that my Dad was "Meano", the sailor who held things down when "jobbing" on shore patrol. "Meano's the one I told you about who could clean house and shanghai bottles of fine wine; a real asset to our European operation."

My Dad said nothing, but his body did. Katter could sense that for my Dad, what was then was then – and that was that. Out of respect for what my Dad had earned for him and now showed to him, Katter reciprocated by not asking my Dad to work.

"Meano. We thank you for your service."

This was the last time my Dad would step foot in Bishops. He never saw either Rocky or Katter again. Katter was horribly killed five years later. The word was that Katter was at the wrong place at the wrong time; that during an exchange of gunfire between some individuals - with no connection to him – he was accidentally shot and the engine to his 1953 Packard Caribbean Convertible was accidentally hit and exploded.

During the time, when my Dad kept the Midway's diesel engines emergency ready while multi-tasking using his brain and brawn, the stories of two other men were writing themselves.

Jo Bucci was an Italian American from the rough side of Buffalo; a Seventh Army soldier who had become every big brass's go-to Italian-French-English translator. Transferred from Germany to Naples, Jo Bucci decided to go exploring. After what came of him, a general order was issued denying any leave to a soldier's requesting trans-euro, mountain region travel. The big brass wanted no more Jo Bucci affairs.

On a whim, Bucci rode through the primitive mountainside, making his way to – of all places - my Grandmother Civita's namesake village, Civita Vecchia. In a state of pure fancy, Bucci pulled his Citroën to the edge of a flowery hillside. There, he took a skyward walk. Meandering through a mountainside, he met a slight - yet sturdy-girl, who was out of breath, walking with her bicycle, equipped with a handle-bar mounted, wicker basket, chock-full of greens. In that instant, Bucci fell in love. It wasn't her intriguing nose and dark almond eyes or her light olive skin that overcame him. It was Serafina's resplendent, indomitable spirit; that she could love him forever or kill him in an instant.

Bucci would never return to Buffalo again. This was a story of immigration in reverse.

Such was the lore of Glen Bougoir.

It isn't the mountains ahead to climb that wear you out;
it's the pebble in your shoe.

—*Muhammad Ali*

A fireplug from Queens, Glen Bougoir was mild-mannered, yet had the sturdy jaw and meaty fists - and too many reasons to pummel the deserving. Glen grew up in a house of utter turmoil, spilled over yelling, broken things, sickening fear, the *corpora delecti* of domestic violence amidst full-blown alcohol abuse. When given the opportunity to take an overseas job with ITT, Glen jumped at it, packed a clunky pawn-shop, bartered suitcase, which eventually was plastered with travel stickers, always marking the spot for the next one. In many respects, that suitcase was Glen's life's story.

His leap of faith landed him in northern Europe. While my Dad was busy tending to the Midway's primary emergency response operations, cruising about the waters that changed the history of its every shore - and Joe was following orders and settling into his new homeland - Glen was more fully engrossed. His hands and brain were figuring out for those who couldn't, elaborate communications and surveillance technology. My Dad's engine and Jo Bucci's translations were helping to protect Glen and his work from harm's way.

He was up to his elbows in equipment and paper- every item stamped "PRIORITY", the pieces to an elaborate state-of-the-art communication system that either over, on or under channels and bands of all kinds, could monitor allies and foes alike; from Scandinavia to the Middle East. One of many skilled "bricklayers", albeit the only one without at least some college, Glen worked tirelessly and was the first to put together a solid transceiver that could peep at communism and monitor the Kremlin's upper echelon, even when they traveled beyond Moscow.

All of this was sold with three main priorities: To stop a preemptive Soviet nuclear attack; to design a fail-safe protocol for a preemptive strike against the Soviets; and to prevent the first two priorities through distraction and subterfuge.

Upon Glen's reassignment from a reconstructed Germany to a still-in-shambles Italy, he took the common piece of advice from his both local and stationed friends and purchased a tight little speedster. With good wheels under him, he would cut his way over Europe with confidence and in style.

In Naples, atop Monte Somma, to be exact, Glen's work and pleasure brought him close to the true cradle of all things Italian. Once his ride was ferried, Glen could truly marvel at the centu-ries-old undisturbed Greece before him and would hold his breath rac-ing down unpaved suggestions of roadways over Turkey, under a sense that he landed back in time. Glen's travels beyond Turkey were rougher than he ever imagined, and, at times, they were too perilous for either him or his speedster to mess with.

Determined never to fold, Glen nonetheless fell hard for the daugh-ter of a highly protective - and highly decorated - Colonel.

Together, Glen and Judy set their path; they would travel the rest of their 'one world'. Along the way, they had formed firm bonds, particularly with those who shared their view. One couple in particular, Joe and Haydee, was quirk and curious, whose pioneer, come-as-it-may spirit tickled the safer Glen and Judy. Their paths would find mine decades later. I would fall in love their daughter, Melaura.

Joe and Haydee were a couple from New York City, atop and the most-loved of Glen and Judy's circle of abroad Americans. Destined to crisscross the globe with an adventurous spirit and a genuine adoration for its people, Joe and Haydee self-set no limits. They were the original cross-culturals; a couple whose children hung on and took the ride.

This nomadic family knew how to make its way to and stake its claim upon any place on the globe. While in Greece, Joe and Haydee gave birth to their second child, Jennifer. Glen would be her godfather.

Born in Catania, their third child/second daughter, Melaura -the family treasure - would always display that determination and those inquisitive ways. Only a stone's throw from the American military base, Melaura's delivery into the world was exclusively Sicilian, complete with a language barrier-turned poetry – with Joe manning Haydee's throne and Melaura's crown – as their de facto doctor/deliverer. Melaura came into the world into her father's hands, swatting at the swarming flies with his head, finally relaxing when he heard the sound her cries, underlined by flowing wine; only then could Joe take a deep breath and inhale the bouquet of roasted garlic and grilled bread and fired eggplant from the upwind *Grotto D'Gatto Cassanelli.*

> *If it hadn't been for the Cold War, neither Russia nor America would have been sending people into space.*
>
> *—JAMES LOVELOCK*

Years later, Glen's path took a turn and would never be the same. It would happen on a nondescript night over a nice stretch of Grecian roadway. Fallibility was about to have its reckoning.

Winding his way down a mountainside, three-lane stretch, rounding a good turn, in line with two cars side by side to his right, Glen was in his element. He respected the inner lane, divided from opposing traffic with a jagged, clunky, fortified ditch. As Glen coolly decelerated, ready to punch into the impending straightaway, his comrades to the right of him oddly locked their brakes, almost in unison. Hearing before thinking, Glen's instincts engaged his brakes. In hyper – focus, he scanned the entire road in front of him - seeing nothing.

Out of the corner of his eye, there was movement. Just as he reacted – running every equation through all of the outs and numbers- the perplexed Glen heard a dreaded, never-to-be-erased thump.

What his eyes saw was the scarecrow of some dark figure suddenly appearing, drifting across both cars to his right, illuminated by the bright beams thrown by headlights of the car right next to his. Glen could not factor this bizarre figure and the sound of screeching into his mental equation.

So, he downshifted on a dime, coaxed his brakes as best he could and braced himself for his only out—away from what he could not process- and onto that craggy band of demarcation. Desperately correcting his wheels, a jagged hump sheared his undercarriage, disemboweling his car. As if on cue with his, the other two cars came to a stop in unison. Each driver got out and froze.

The deceased had intentionally darted out in front of Glen's fellow travelers. Disoriented and adrift, this poor soul somehow threaded past their rapid reflexes. With just enough failed hesitation, this doomed pedestrian, instead of running in front of Glen's car, hesitated, stumbled then corrected by impaling herself into the rear quarter-panel of his trusty set of wheels. So trusty that its Austrian-forged replacement quarter-panel bounced the deceased's head back, torqueing her torso around. With her appendages spiraling, she landed into the pavement. The cacophony of tire screeches muffled her final, primal scream.

The deceased was a troubled woman in her early seventies; a Georgian Bedouin who had long since slipped into mental instability and chose this time and place to leave the world.

This event took hold of Glen and would never let him go. Despite the witnesses' accounts, Glen was brought in and held at the local jail, while a makeshift investigation ensued. Word quickly got back to Joe. Ever the man of action, Joe made calls, decked himself out in his authoritative best, dusted off some Maltese in-lieu-of-payment attaché case then stuffed it with documents and papers and credentials of all sorts.

Meanwhile Haydee rushed to Judy's side, prayed with her - then got her head on straight. Haydee has always been the very best at tempering the supple, gentle words of God with a terse, necessary dose of reality.

It was a miracle that the best two to stand a chance to get Glen and the love of his life out of Greece were squarely on it. This crisis threatened ominous consequences that required epic delivery. Joe dropped names, business cards and money to broker an in with the gatekeeper and then set his workable wedge into the police chain of command. This was a foreign negotiation with the highest of stakes. Pulling all the stops, Joe staged his very best New York G-Man/Wise Guy, knowing that in order to spring Glen from that wretched jail and hustle him out of Greece, he had to be indomitable to a T.

The plan worked. But once at the airport the play caught a snag. The next flight out to Glen's company's Rome corporate office was not until the next morning. Joe knew that getting out meant "now or never". So, he dropped the names of those he had just duped and "ordered/national security" first class accommodations for Glen on the very next flight out of Greece. It was either one an hour later for Paris/ pre-boarding or the one ready to taxi for a nonstop flight to Cairo.

Glen departed Greece to Cairo, with nothing but what Joe handed him and his gaminess from his rough time behind foreign bars. Courtesy of Joe was his passport and a fistful of money, the equivalent of $310, in at least five different currencies. Joe had passed the hat, to anyone and everyone. Before he let go of Glen, he administered a double dose from a nip bottle and a few pumps from a spray bottle of good cologne that Haydee had given to an oblivious Joe, for what were now obvious, reasons.

Haydee had used her own connections to secure Judy's safe passage, without a hitch. With portable, essential belongings in tow - that Haydee had meticulously packed – Judy had lifted off to a clandestine fight to Rome well before Glen's Cairo flight was ready to pre-board.

Once Glen and Judy reunited in Rome, Judy told Glen that she wanted to leave Europe and make a life where she and Glen had dreamed of since their honeymoon: Guam.

The higher-ups, however, both military and private contractors, had other ideas.

The people in those places decided, for the sake of corporate and state interests, that Glen must return to Greece, waiving his right to counsel, and close the matter out. When Joe came at the 'big brass' hard, Glen insisted that he "back the hell off". Glen knew what was good for the both of them and their families. He would do what he was told.

The moment Glen cleared customs, he was seized and was hurried to Athens National Prison, where he was thrown in with highly violent criminals from all over the world. His body language said that he was a New Yorker, not to be tested without severe impunity. After a day in a holding area, Glen found only one welcome sight among all of the bad seeds. Clean-cut and outwardly peaceful, this one man, inwardly troubled, on the edge of instability, ready to explode – he was Joe's oasis. After all, he had an affluent air; his nails were manicured and he too was worlds away way from his element. These tells/contradictions, coupled with his flat/intense demeanor told the other detainees to leave the man be.

Glen would not let him be.

*As a matter of self-preservation, a man needs
good friends or ardent enemies, for the former
instruct him and the latter take him to task.*

—Diogenes of Sinope

4. Jailhouse paralegal— Chaste of Characters

The mother of a mousy, needy, twenty-two-year-old client of mine, Jerry, begged me to go see him – and make sure that I tell him that "I love him more than anyone." She was an educated and attractive ICU nurse. Yet all of that good stuff was negated by her obsessive hovering and constant poking into the attorney-client domain. Jerry's Dad was a nuts-and-bolts type, a pipefitter by trade, who cut my check then decorously left Jerry's demise to me and his doting mother. She couldn't stop jibber-jabbering about Jerry's circle of fools – a bunch of goofy bust-outs, half her age – she was so proud to tell me, were her cherished Facebook friends.

Once I cleared the jail gates and was set up in a conference room, Jerry was escorted in. Although a first semester college dropout, he was bright and a very quick learner- which is why it seemed odd that he wanted to go over what we had already painstak-ingly covered. Attributing it to equal parts stress and denial, I complied with Jerry's request and took it from the top – hitting on every piece of evidence.

As I ran his case down, it became obvious that Jerry was trying to pin me to various conclusions I could not draw. Sensing it was time for one of us leave, I started to gather my things. Jerry launched into a bizarre, frenetic monologue; one measuring his case against a catalog of other crimes – a litany of dissimilar fact patterns- a salvo of incongruous scenarios. His engine was staring to overheat.

Granted, many of my incarcerated clients would preach the gospel of jailhouse lawyers, to which I would always psalm:

"If you were in the hospital and your life were on the line, would you take medical advice from a patient?"

But Jerry was not coming at me like that; he wasn't questioning my advice. He was flick-jabbing me with a barrage fact-based legal questions — hooking them with obvious elements of his case.

It was clever, but the cinder-block room, poor lighting, bad ventilation and over a dozen what-ifs were wearing me out.

"Jerry, what the fuck is going on here? Are you ghostwriting for *Law and Order*? Have you just recently discovered the hypothetical?"

Jerry came clean.

He had ignored my first piece of "while in custody" advice and talked about his case and me. His fellow inmates were apparently impressed by the both of us.

None of these Joliet-area detainees knew the legend of "Superman", but thanks to Jerry's big mouth, they may as well have. They wanted Superman. "Jimmy Olson" would squeeze me for legal analysis and advice, in exchange for which he would be left "untouched".

"So that would make me the turnkey to your chastity belt, no?"

Jerry laughed through his tears and quivering lip. We spent over two hours briefing out every case on his list. When the guards, called "Time's up, Counselor - Way up - Like an hour and fifteen ago.", I was mentally exhausted.

"Jerry, I'll be back in a week. Keep 'em coming... the detailed fact patterns, that is."

The only way for Glen to survive was to maintain his wits, size up his surroundings and create some movement.

Just the right amount of information was circled around that Glen was mechanically adept. Some feared that he was connected, given his "safecracking" and "car-bomb rigging" exploits. He also heard rumors that he was a clandestine American.

Glen was certain that Joe was working the angles on the outside. He was determined to work his own angle from the inside.

As luck would have it, an electrical problem was developing. Glen could hear and smell that a generator was about to seize. He got the guard's attention, threw big words at him, pointed in the direction of the equipment and then said one word – in five languages - everyone could hear and everyone knew: "Fire".

Glen was pulled out of his holding cell and ordered, "You Feex!" Without hesitation, he called over the guard's watch commander and explained that in order to get the job done, he would need a skilled assistant. He pointed to the prisoner with clean hands and good feet and said, "I need him. This guy studied under Linus Pauling."

In order sell it, Glen shouted across the room to his mark then spouted out a deluge of mechanical gibberish, topped with "*The two-stroke four-phase, not the four-stroke two-phase*" and a gesture to which any response would have worked. The man, got up from the floor slowly, dusted himself off and walked toward Glen, nodding.

With that, the two of them were relocated to a utility room. Guards were standing about, chatting and one-upping. The pungent smoky odor of an arced electrical circuit had been apparent to Glen from twenty feet away. But instead of getting right to it, he looked at, but did not touch each and every connection, intake, and switch. After conferring with his partner, he called for tools.

After a barrage of Keystone Cop-like radio transmissions, a burlap tool bag, inscribed in both Arabic and French, was produced, Glen shoved it at his work crew of one and gestured as if to say, "Fiddle around with whatever is in there, and make it look good."

With their concocted assignments in place, the tandem began its "work". Even an arduously detailed inspection was made (akin to a pre-assembly check of edges and thickness of each factory cut jigsaw puzzle piece), Glen needed to eat up more time. He hammed it up, meticulously sounding the metallurgy to this rattletrap machine and every piece of equipment and electrical switch and plug within five feet of it.

Before beginning each phase of this non-work, Glen re-sized and re-calibrated every tool in the bag, overly dramatically handing each one over to his second, to double check his imaginary computations.

Well before making the obvious and simple repair, Glen built it up as being complicated and highly risky. When it was time for the grand finale, Glen conferred with his assistant in order to reach a consensus as to which of the two trouble spots they should begin the tricky repair.

Prior to wrapping up the essentially completed job, Glen built in some extra work, by looking over anything he could find that moved – "Check the balance to those wires," he ordered – handing his sidekick a mini level – outright mocking safety inspections and proper tool selection.

His assistant, apparently finally catching on, went rogue; he began to square up the slots of every sheet metal screw- without flinching, Glen concurred, noting to the guards how doing so, "...*would allow for maximum residual condensation drainage and keep all of you safe from danger.*"

As compensation for their great work, these master mechanics were issued separate quarters - away from the other inmates, with clean bedding and plenty to eat.

Once settled in and left alone, Glen introduced himself to his shill, Giv - an Iranian citizen -whose first words - in fluent English were "*You were like Groucho Marx out there.*"

Giv had been living in Greece, earning a handsome salary as a very capable commercial pilot. His second wife was a Greek girl.

Two years prior - to the day, married to his first wife, Giv had returned to their home in Tehran – after a very long trip. As he arrived, his six-year-old son ran out to the street to greet him. Without warning, and with his wife's back oddly turned to the two of them, a sports car raced by and struck Giv's son. The driver did not stop and was never identified. Giv's son was left dead and horribly mangled. After the boy was buried, Giv's wife left him and passed into permanent anonymity.

Adrift, Giv somehow settled in Greece. He found comfort in a Greek girl who sensed his inner pain. In time, they fell in love. Giv had finally healed, thanks to his wife, who restored his sense of hope and helped him say goodbye to his son in a healing way.

On his last day of freedom, Giv came home to his wife - earlier than expected. He snuck into the apartment, intent upon playfully surprising her. He found her in bed with another man. She began to shout and accused him of barging in on and embarrassing her. As her lover tried to scamper away, she shrieked at him – demanding that he not leave her. The painful noise would not subside. Giv cupped his ears to no avail then retrieved his handgun.

All Giv wanted was for the man to be gone - and for his wife to be silent. Yet all he could hear and see was the screams and look of disgust that his first wife had shot at him, turning away from her son's broken body while declaring how having mothered the dead would bring shame to her.

That flashback was being pushed in by his second wife's lover, begging for Giv's mercy. After proclaiming his sorrow for what he had done a third time, Giv shot them both to death; alternate rounds – three each.

His son's murder had finally been avenged.

Giv was Iranian. The murdered were Greek. The story of the remainder of his life would begin with "Incarcerated..." His hopes, but also those hurtful dreams, were gone forever.

Giv began to pray to his God above for Glen's liberation; that he would return to the world where his hopes and dreams ensue.

"I pray that you will be freed so that you will have children and celebrate their lives and tell them what a great machinist's mate, Linus Pauling's favorite student, Giv, was to you, Glen..."

The first step toward change is awareness.
The second step is acceptance.

—Nathaniel Branden

While this con was being played out, Judy had cut through red tape and reached her father, who was at a secure location in Rome, in a high-level command meeting - critiquing various failsafe scenarios.

The Colonel excused himself, summoned his attaché and ordered that he draw up and execute an extrication plan. The attaché issued coded messages - with orders to priority ready the Colonel's prototype Lockheed C-130H Hercules and man it as directed. After take-off, Hercules ripped across the heel of southern Italy's boot. The Soviets got nervous and began to track this lone blazing bird, partially deciphering what appeared to be oddly coded messages. From its operatives, the Soviets learned that every airport in Greece had simultaneously cleared its runways and diverted all air traffic. Through deep sources, called up from the very nervous KGB-Kiev, the unwritten word was that this was "family business". With that, the Soviet air command – extremely armed and dangerous - and all intelligence operatives – were ordered, out of respect, to shut down and stand down and make no record of any of this.

Once the turbo-prop, multipurpose bird powered down, the Colonel, still in dress uniform, but now side-armed, took charge of a cache of fully armed air-force security forces plus two men dressed in pressed, crisp, black suits - stepped onto a remote section of Ellinikon International Airport and into transport vehicles.

Once at the gates of the prison they were given immediate entry.

This was a totally improvised, semi-covert personal matter. On paper, it was designated a joint American-Greek training exercise. Yet from a sovereignty standpoint, this was an American invasion, carried out by armed airmen and intelligence operatives, determined to secure and remove one package, by whatever means necessary. Glen was hustled through the prison gate; he was surrounded, packaged and loaded. A suitcase was left on the very last ground his feet touched. With all personnel accounted for "plus one", the convoy blazed back to the still powered up Hercules. This was "load and go". The Colonel gave the order to push off. His son-in-law could never again step foot on Greek soil.

Once reunited in Rome, Glen and Judy were dispatched back to the States. From there, they relocated in Southern California, where Glen would work as a civilian consultant at Vandenberg Air Force Base. Glen would go on to work on NASA's most delicate missions, living a kindhearted life with gentility. When faced with any problem, the unfazed Glen would solve it in a thoughtful way; always calling for an assistant, whom he would nickname 'Giv' —and solve it. This problem-solving way defined him when he and Judy relocated to Guam, where she worked as a teacher and Glen opened an appliance repair shop called "*Giv's Place*".

"Limits" is a relative term.
Like beauty, it is often in the eye of the beholder.

—CHRIS BURDEN, ARTIST

My Grampa Vartan thrived in America as a self-taught, highly-gifted gardener. He was a survivor with a Native American like spirit. When I cajoled a job, creating the rank of third mate, aboard the Miss Rye Harbor, Grampa Vartan - who came to live with us after my Grandma Anooshigah passed away - gave me marching orders to bring back fish or fish parts – as much as I could lift. Tossing whatever I could into a doubled-up paper bag – I secured the load to my girl's Schwinn three-speed and wobbled my way back to dump my slippery load. Grampa Vartan had great patience when it came to nature, from which he grew first-rate fruits and vegetables – and from a lush garden situated on the edge of a salt marsh that he painstakingly blossomed out of a briny, salty, slimy, rocky, crusted-over sand section of earth. Such a feat was unheard of before Grampa Vartan.

Grampa Vartan was a clever writer and a delicate thinker; strong and stoic and very sweet. He and Ma shared hot, spicy food, which my Dad could not stand. In many ways Grampa Vartan harbored impatience toward my Dad, his only son. This always struck me as inexplicably out-of-character and rather unfair. I could not make sense of their strained father-son dynamic.

In his last year, Ma nursed Grampa Vartan. The day he died began with a morning amazingly full of light and hope. Throughout that day, he was unusually chatty, intoxicatingly so, as if he had smoked -as he called it – "*the veed.*"

That sobering, somber early October evening, was the first time I saw my Dad powerless and crying; it scared me.

At both Grampa Vartan's wake and funeral, waves of people paid their respects; those who marveled at his beautiful flowers and juicy vegetables, including many jockeys from the Rockingham Race Track where he had shined as the gardener, but most notably Ma's side of our family- Italians, young and old, newborns and the very frail, many of whom were very distantly related - poured in – in droves - to offer their warmth and kindness. That they honored my legacy, by mourning Grampa Vartan as theirs, I have never ever forgotten.

My Dad is my idol; Bruno Sammartino his distant second. My Dad taught the importance of greased mechanics and tight connections in anything that runs on power and in any social settings – particularly at the card table. With keen aptitude to make things work, my Dad demonstrated the power of charm. His truest gift, not tapped to its potential, is his ability to mediate – while holding others to keeping their word, perform quality work and be kind to those in need. From my Dad's example, I learned the art of the bargain, the diplomacy of the deal and the proper way to give someone a break.

A man's man, my Dad has a negotiator's stealth and to this day – now in his late eighties- he can dig out a tree stump by hand and certainly handle himself in a fistfight. During my teen years, his fuse was tightly bound but arguably short; it took a lot of heat to set it, but once ignited, it exploded with fury.

My Dad taught me at an early age and has ever since the value in knowing how to do everything, being willing to take anything on and helping out anyone needing it. Turning down work was contrary to his nature and so became contrary to mine.

Bravado may stir the crowd, but courage needs no audience.

—*T. F. HODGE*

On a late fall afternoon, with the leaves blowing and ground shivering, I, at the age of three, decided to climb the wooden, hemp-roped/pulley - raised extension ladder thrown against my birth home on Angle Pond, Sandown, New Hampshire.

My Dad was on the roof, leak-checking the cricket he had shored up from the roofline and against the flagstone chimney that he and Ma had painstakingly built, piece by piece.

My Dad has recalled that before he could say anything, I made my move and unabashedly began to climb. When Ma, in a rare moment of abandoning her toughness, likely due to my age, rushed in a panic to get me down, my Dad yelled, "Hang on, Fanny [his nickname for Ma]. He's already on and climbing. He's made up his mind to head up here; he'll make it, and I will show him how to get his ass down. I think you had better get used to this."

> *But 'tis a common proof that lowliness is a young*
> *ambition's ladder, whereto the climber upward turns*
> *his face; But when he once attains the upmost round,*
> *he then unto the ladder turns his back, looks to the clouds,*
> *scorning the base degrees by which he did ascend.*

—WILLIAM SHAKESPEARE, *JULIUS CAESAR*

Looking back, my Dad missed his calling. In my view, he would have made a most fine and highly successful attorney. I never felt that he took as much pride in his work and what he accomplished, as much as he did in not having turned down the job. For my Dad, much of everything has seemed tedious. Proficient because of what he knows, he has at times appeared to lack the inspiration to see things through in a way worthy of his talent; which in his case is a tall order.

For me, it has been from what my Dad knows and how he articulates it, rather than what he does and how he approaches his work that I have learned the most. Over the years, I have commented on how my Dad and I seemed to have been "*switched at profession*". Career-wise, he would have been happier in – and better suited for- mine; and I might have been more fulfilled by a hands-on, trade-skilled means to earn a living and build a reputation.

The only enduring bond that Ma and my Dad seemed to be able to fully celebrate was their tough, unresolved upbringings and those values that their parents demonstrated and demanded. My parents grew up in a world of first-generation self-determination on small, rural American farms, close to the city as the crow flies but geographically bound and isolated. They grew up north of Boston and were raised in the world of farming, one that drew upon the old-country ways for sustenance, if not outright survival. They raised and slaughtered animals, canned their homegrown vegetables, and saw their parents go off to their jobs in choking, tedious, dangerous mills and factories.

Unlike my older brother, younger sister, Endzanoush, and me, Ma and my Dad had grown up dirt poor. Traditionally chained to the old country through language, customs, memories, poverty and many forms of overt discrimination, they sought out and swore unquestioned allegiance to - and assimilated with – the American way. They developed strong bonds with Americanized friends, who recognized Ma's and my Dad's family values, character, unbridled loyalty, and unmatched toughness. My grandparents and parents earned respect of those from the other, more affluent ethnic groups with their delivered goods and services, and, above all, their irreproachable character.

My siblings and I were taught that there was something special about the Italian-Armenians - that set them apart from any other ethnic clone (RIP- Sib Hashian). It was with this ethnicity-aware, "chip on the shoulder" way of living our lives that we experienced our parents' closest affection with each other; one second only to their devotion to us.

CHAPTER VIII

HYE-RED ASSASSINS

When the belly dancer dies, often her waist is still moving.

—*Arabic proverb*

Lawrence, Massachusetts, a textile-mill driven, hardly gentile, North Shore Immigrant city was in many ways much grittier than Boston. Its southern edge bordered the rugged Merrimac River, which at Newburyport flowed into the Gulf of Maine. So many of my older relatives, both Armenian and Italian, had earned a living in Lawrence, making shoes and coats in its huge factories.

A formidable Irish power base took hold of its riverside, while Italians settled and planted it its fertile north. Scores of other ethnicities, including Armenians, filled up the remaining pockets of this once Native American, sprawling stronghold.

All but one of the numerous European and Middle Eastern immigrant communities could form there. All but one could erect its churches and build social clubs. Turks were not allowed in Lawrence.

Not one Turkish family could be found anywhere near Lawrence. While many Turkish nationals and immigrants disavowed their former government's inhumanity, the stench of a genocide became them. Most Turks generally admired the qualities of Armenians; proud of and driven by their quality goods and services; their fullness in trade, their faith and kindness to everyone - especially those in need.

It is globally noteworthy that in 301A.D. Armenia became the first Christian nation, yet would never endeavor to conquer land or convert non-Christians. Locally relevant was that in 1964, the year of my birth, two Armenian assassins had settled in Lawrence. Their presence certainly provided an additional explanation as to why Turks still dared not to move to Lawrence.

This was not spun from the Armenian community's rumor mill; it was known to be so - in the whispers of Lawrence's connected Italians - which made it fact.

Never openly spoken about, especially when non-Armenians were in the room, two Armenian professionals were on call for powerful North Shore Italians. Known by the Capos as "Medigan" was the Medavjian brothers - street-named "the Injuns," by younger Italians. They were protected even more than many of those who benefited from their services. That they were ghastly assassins was all well and good; that they were traceless was what all but "made" them.

Situated to Lawrence's southeast was the older town of Andover, settled in 1642. Andover's soil produced the lushest corn, heartiest carrots, richest turnips and meatiest rutabagas. One of the earliest Armenian men to stake a claim for his family there was Ashaa Medavjian.

Known as "Ace", Ashaa was a wiry, fun-loving, hard-drinking soul who hand built an irrigation system that rivaled the Dutch, which quenched his swath of land in the Merrimac Valley. Ace coaxed the best vegetables from the soil; those destined for Boston's high-class restaurants either on fine china or in a fine snifter. After years of precision farming and quality bootlegging, Ashaa wanted off his feet and so he landed a job as Crown Supercoach school bus driver. Over his route, he would sing to the children and when necessary, would grab an unruly one by the ear.

The parents were overjoyed by this wide-smiling, precious-cargo carrying, highly trusted man.

Ashaa and his wife, Ani, had deep roots in their happy valley adjacent to the Merrimac River. Their two sons inherited the strongest quality of each parent, respectively so. Their oldest inherited his father's no-nonsense, right-and-wrong drive; their youngest, his mother's guilt-ridden, turmoil, from which only the kitchen could provide solace.

The Medavjian brothers, tighter than a Dutch lap joint, were nonetheless paradoxical. Shahe and Khajag were warm and gentle souls, yet as cold-blooded killers were staggering. Shahe was clean and deliberate, like some "to-the-penny" auditor. Khajag did not believe in efficiency and rebuked cleaning up. The way he saw it, scrubbing down the kill zone was like white-washing Picasso's *Guernica*.

Together, the "Injuns" were unstoppable.

Shahe's careful, formidable and measured ways - and Khajag's harshness and relentlessness- somehow resolved. It showed in their work. Shahe was a clean, sure-shot from any range or angle. Khajag viewed a long rifle as clunky and impersonal, preferring the intimacy of the edged weapon. He would poke at his brother for "always hiding."

Shahe kept to himself emerging feelings of shame and remorse; while still willing to snipe away, he desperately wanted out of this line of work. Khajag rebuffed his feelings by seeking out and taking on even more work.

The Medavjian brothers continued to work seamlessly, their trail always swept away. They never deviated from or even joked about "the five elements": planning, execution, concealment, escape, anonymity.

By this time, Armenians – displaced from their homeland, ravaged by genocide and carved out - were scattered all over the world. When it came to political thought, they fell into competing schools: One bold, brazen and indignant - like Malcom X; the other more moderate, temperate and forgiving - like Martin Luther King Jr. Shahe and Khajag could kill two bottles of Ararat brandy while going round and around, with point/counterpoint pondering the "hows" and "whys" and "whens" and "by whoms." This would lead to screaming, followed by heavier drinking, finally ending in the silence of hearty eating.

While handsomely paid to do what the Italians hired them to do, it was their "pro bono" work that proved to be Shahe and Khajag's signature pieces. In tight tandem, covering each other's every breath, this seamless team took down culpable Turkish diplomats and complacent Ottoman business executives. Assassinations were carried out over a stretch of ten months on American soil (California and Massachusetts). When the time was right – they trekked a little over three hundred miles to northeast of Boston, into Ottawa, Canada. At that time, anyone not on the FBI's most wanted list could skip the light fandango over the Northeastern American/ Canadian border.

What Shahe fondly remembered was how Khajag's request for an improvised five-course dinner and the very finest French wine was honored. The Chef and Sommelier, the Le Russe brothers, personally served the exquisite bounty.

I have never killed a man,
but I have read many obituaries with great pleasure.

—CLARENCE DARROW

After this killing spree, Shahe and Khajag agreed - no more. By Armenian body clock standards, they were spring chickens; but by American standards, they were getting up in age. Over those last ten months hunting Turks, they turned noticeably old, especially to each other.

The Medavjian brothers had accrued a king's ransom. On many occasions, instead of cancelling the debtor, they recovered the money due and owed plus compounded interest, granted by subtracting their fee. Such unauthorized negotiations with a condemned mark – initiated - by a hired gun, no less - would have been met with sanctions. Yet the Italians never ever judged the "Injuns" and could not deny the bottom line. As Rosario Rossi - who turned government informant – testified before a Federal Grand Jury, some three decades later: "*We weren't in New York, and we sure as hell weren't the Irish. So, we were okay with it—but only under certain circumstances. And by "certain circumstances", I mean whenever the Injuns saw fit to work things out another way – other than the one way. After all, they would do it for free…*"

Yet now all Shahe and Khajag wanted was an out; and to be free from this world of retribution and carnage it commanded.

I'm for truth, no matter who tells it.
I'm for justice, no matter who it's for or against.

—MALCOLM X

5. The oldest profession—Justice on the nightstand

My prosecutorial mission often took unorthodox turns, as when I ripped into three in-custody Catholic high-school punks, screaming, "Repeat after me: I will never not pay a prostitute ever again!"

Pulling no punches with their parents – how I had handled them and what I thought of their cruel and arrogant game, I assured them that their sons would not be charged with "rape" and thrown, head first, into "the system".

At first, they scowled at me - certain that that this was all some trick. Yet once I knew that they saw me as genuine, I placed the second to the last part of my one-sided, non-negotiable deal on the table: Each individual parent would have to address their respective son, first individually then together, as a group.

"Your sons need to hear it from all of you - what a gentleman is - and how a prostitute is supposed to be treated. I found what your sons have done to be abhorrent."

I then pulled one of the parents aside—the one who had early on flashed his "Streets and Sans" identification. He was placed in charge of the last part; he would pass the hat to the other parents and return it - and square up with, "Cat Eyes", the so-endearing hooker they had tried to swindle. I said, "Unless it's over two hundred dollars, you had best keep passing it around. And under no circumstances is anyone allowed to make change…"

"…If You Make Change, Me Change Mind!"

Once they had it, I ordered their sons' release, rejecting even the compromise misdemeanor charge, "theft of services", that the B-team detectives begged for.

As for Cat Eyes, I issued a no-limit, free pass, a get-out-of-jail-free card, good for one year. I wrote it all out on the back of my business card and signed it. I pled with her to be careful and then handed her the collection.

"Thanks for getting me my money and for setting their punk-asses straight and for being so good to me, baby."

Cat Eyes touched my cheek and said:

"You looked out for me because I know that you respect me, which is like you loving me; and that means the world to me. I won't call you unless I really need to. Don't worry; I won't be stalking on you...unless you really want me to...You think of me whenever you want to – and I, sure as my gramma's sweat potato pie, will be doing the same..."

Perhaps the world's second-worst crime is boredom;
the first is being a bore.

—CEPHAS BEATON

6. Seattle – The City of Goodwill

Rather than blindly sign off on a child abduction arrest warrant as ordered, I demanded – over the phone- that the out-of-line father either grab the next flight from Seattle with his child – or see his child taken by State of Washington's CPS {Child Protective Services} and held in protective custody pending his extradition back to Chicago.

I assured him that if he complied with my directive, I would see to it that once the two of them arrived, the matter would be put to rest. How much easier to approve the arrest warrant, given the dozen long distance phone calls and clunky slow dial-tone faxes and teletype messages that that followed. Once I received verification that father and child – under SPD escort were moved through Tacoma International Airport security to gates and pre-boarded into their seats for the direct flight to Chicago/Midway, I formally rejected the arrest warrant and felony charges.

After creatively writing up my file and just about to call my supervisors and clear out of the

Station, SPD Watch Commander Tom Nguen paged me. The Chicago Juvenile Crimes Detectives, still livid that I rejected their pitiful case, would not let me use their landline. After three tries, I finally got through on my clunky [early nineties] "bag phone".

"You did the right thing on that one, Counselor. Huge call. FYI, my lieutenant and Captain caught wind that you were about to catch some major league heat from this one, so we ran it up to Chief of Police, who - believe it or not, already put in an 'atta-boy' call to your boss— and I mean your Big Boss. Talk about Karma, the two of them rode together on the West Side, when your boss was going to night law school and ours was cranking out his application for SPD. You're actually in very good shape on this one. My Chief and the State's Attorney of Cook County are placing a joint letter of an accommodation in your personnel file."

Every evil is a sickness of soul, but virtue
offers the cause of its health.

—SAINT BASIL

More bountiful than the handsome sums Shahe and Khajag earned and recovered was Shahe's appetite that he had developed, one bordering on the hypnotic, for Italian pastries and confectionaries. Eventually, putting his money where his mouth was, Shahe bank-rolled his every last dime into an old country *Napolese* bakery, which he christened "*Italina*".

Despite Khajag's irresistible passion for food - especially the spicy, garlic-driven dishes, even as he aged, he was somehow able to maintain his fighting weight. As if not to be outdone by Shahe, he built from the ground a fabulous supper club; filled with live music

– American and traditional Armenian. Its Italian-Armenian cuisine culminated with "*Dolci Di Mia Fratello*" and the silkiest espresso.

In tragedy, it's hard to find a good resolution; it's not black and white: it's a big fog of gray.

—PAUL DANO

7. Fashion Statement of Law — per Order of Court

Waiting for my case to be called, I watched as a Public Defender pitched, at the insistence of her high-maintenance client, an overly drafted motion requesting the Court to Order that the clothing pro- vided to him from the Public Defender's Office's donated wardrobe for his Jury Trial be dry cleaned.

All eyes and ears in the Courtroom perked up, in anticipation of the Honorable Leandro Panelli rul- ing/explosion. Ever a no-nonsense jurist, the spiffy Italian-American from Chicago Heights {Da' Heights}, with a criminal defense attorney pedigree – whose attorney son and daughter shared his sharp and engag- ing, endearing and charming ways, snapped, "Your Motion Is Denied! …But here is what I will do for you, sir..."

Judge Panelli pulled out his broccoli rubber-band bound wallet and said:

"I will personally take your clothes to my dry cleaner for overnight service, pick them up tomorrow morning on my way here and deliver them to you myself in the lockup; and depending upon how long the trial lasts; I will do it as necessary - - so they don't get 'troppo puzza'. And that's my ruling. Counsel, you draft your client's order. Indicate light starch on the shirt. And underline that."

The Medavjian brothers would remain lifelong bachelors who sparingly dated – exclusively Italian women. Carrying an impressive look and swagger, they were Italian-classy and Armenian-thoughtful. Everybody stayed clear of their territory, let them be and never patronized. When the Medavjian brothers and their dates entered the room, it snapped silent– then quickly unsnapped – this was a scene that went over most everyone's head. Those who knew anything, acknowledged nothing.

The Medavjian brothers would grow old together, live out their lives in a culinary way and die on the same day. Even long after they both passed, not one incriminating iota of their work ever surfaced; not the slightest scintilla of evidence ever tied back to them. Even Rosario Rossi recanted his Federal Grand Jury testimony, claiming it was just a story about two Sicilians, he had heard about, *"…whose food – everything they made- all the 'Napule' guys – they 'was jealous'…"*

And so, the Injuns, Shahe and Khajag Medavjian, honorary Italian-Armenian Americans, remained all legend.

Never allow the fear of striking out keep
you from playing the game!

—*Babe Ruth*

CHAPTER IX

NEW ENGLAND HOCKEY

I'm a terrible dancer! Oh, I'm an awful dancer!

—*BOBBY ORR*

For me, a New England seacoast boy, winter months were all about hockey and Bobby Orr, who was a class by himself. From Parry Sound, Ontario, Canada, Number 4 -Bobby Orr [pronounced 'Numb-bah Foe-ah Baw-bee Oh-ah'] was the most talented, gifted, and creative player of them all. The very toughest of men, his fans on both sides of the border, his teammates and all of his opponents melted and at times could not help but gush over him as if he were an unapproachable "hottie". They would react acceptably effeminately at his moves. Orr was cunningly powerful and disarmingly manipulative and could coax the ice; like some bladed poetry, he proffered so endearingly pure and seductively sharp; a majestic, guile beast on blades. I loved hockey only because I loved Bobby Orr; I cherished his brilliance, self-confidence, concepts ahead of his contemporaries' time and how he so dearly loved the game of ice hockey. And how the game loved him back. Yet for all that skill and poise I witnessed, internalized, processed and actually understood, I could not skate. This blubbery sea cow, when forced to, had no choice but to sloppily lace up the very lowest of skates: Double-Runners.

And it was during my early, chubby/overweight, cherished Bobby Orr years that I was dispatched to spend tortuous winter months on frozen-over salt marshes clinging to the edge of this makeshift rink, while real skaters warmed up, gliding around and sizing up danger spots near the perimeter; where jagged ice met marsh hay -matted down with a fishy muck. I stood around simply trying not to fall. I clumsily foraged about, hoping to find something out there. Perhaps I was optimistically - desperately - looking for anything that would call the game off: an artifact, a bag of money, top-secret documents, a gun, or even a dead body.

Once ordered to the dreaded ice, I tried to play it cool, pretending to be careful, not to ruin my double-runner specials, as if they were a rare and valuable antique. I sized up the rink, searching for the closest point on which to enter the slippery mine field, all the while knowing that I was preordained – doomed, that is - to play goalie. My long list of hopeful scenarios was crumbled up once the others declared it game time.

At first, I stood there, vainly hoping that some other unluckier kid would arrive. Next, I left the ice, meticulously retracing my steps, pretending that there was something important to do or that I had left some mysterious valuable behind. I used the briny edges for balance, mindful not to stay in one spot too long, lest I sink too deep into the mucky, putrid collar. I knew that if I fell down (a fate worse than death), I could not get up; worse yet, I would have to crawl to the marsh's version of land- which had the bouquet and texture of gone anchovies mortared and pestled with the clammy nub of a spent cheap cigar.

Thus weakly armed, I moved about in a tippy-toe trudge, pathetically resembling a little girl walking in her mother's high-heeled shoes. When there were no other options or pretended matters of importance remaining, the skaters now yelling at me, I wobbled onto the ice, hopefully unnoticed - spared, at least in this moment, any ridicule.

Death is a delightful hiding place for weary men.

—HERODOTUS

Barely able to inch my way to the goal through the nippy winds, as a last resort, I pretended that something was wrong with my skates. Of course, my teammates had seen these slippery gymnastics before; they could smell blood. While they may have enjoyed my performance or perhaps were impressed by my persistence, the truth of the matter was that all of my futile survival mode, which seemed like slow motion to me, lasted about a minute and a half. My final hope was that Mother Nature might put her foot down and that the ice would crack so I could fall in and die from a less painful combination of marsh-water poisoning and hypothermia than from the blood-thirsty marauders swirling around me.

Better that than the impending blunt force/penetrating trauma! I knew that once I squared up at the net (a goal composed of two broken, discarded stinking, rusty nails-exposed lobster traps), it would be open season, fire (and slash) at will. I could not hide, shift, or cut; I was unable to protect my goal or myself. Furthermore, I was cold and hungry. All my movement was restricted. I could not lean over, bend, split, glide, or duck. I resorted to words - high-brow and guttural alike; then an otherwise profound appeal to humanity; and then outright begging. But nobody wanted to hear anything I was thinking or saying. Escape, at this point, was futile.

I did my best to obstruct my broken, lobster-trap goal, hoping that its owner might show up out of nowhere and claim it so that the game would be called and I might live. Now under attack from all around me - and way out of my element, I could not think clearly. In this circumstance where I was about to feel both physical pain and outright humiliation, I even tried to make myself throw up, but with my stomach even more afraid than the rest of me, I couldn't.

So cold and hungry, my only move in the goal was a feeble flinch. When the puck was at the other end, I sucked in my stomach, for some unknown reason, and play-acted that I was making saves. When the game turned at me, I prayed and then screamed out for "Offsides!" Nobody listened. Even I knew that, given the rink size, any offsides call was an absolute mathematical impossibility.

I closed my eyes, mustered up my marsh-water courage, and took the shots, which were dreadfully close-range and dead-center. I could only hope that my cardboard pads and the Little Tike's baseball glove (I didn't own a baseball glove), which some kind soul thought to bring, would somehow ease the pain. Blinded by fear, I kept telling myself—begging myself—not to fall. In such a moment – even if I made a save and lived - I was sure to be "snow-coned" with briny march ice from skaters and beaten to a pulp by their electrical taped sticks.

Next, out of sheer terror, I pulled up anything I was wearing below my neck to cover my quivering, burning face. With undeserved visions of the legendary Gerry Cheevers's battle-scarred, pagan-like face mask, my heart raced, and my throat went dry. I was sucking air, trying not to cry.

Sooner or later, it all comes crashing down.

—N. E. R. D.

The only pleasantry was that the uncontrollable shuddering that my inexorable fear produced kept my extremities warm. Only years later would I relive the frustration of being mocked by the sting of a blunt, bone-cracking, cold: From New England Atlantic's even meaner Midwest Lake Michigan cousin.

8. Disturbing the peace — Dismissed and into the cold

Worse than arriving at a locked South Side Branch Courthouse door on a bleak Chicago winter morning, amid dry, slashing, burning winds eddying – those

long ago named "the Hawk" by Native tribes— was finding one homeless man sleeping outside the door and a
more fortunate other one sleeping inside the door.
They had nestled together, having formed a pact—once
the latecomer arrived - to keep each other warm by
cuddling up on either side of the reinforced glass-
paned security door.

Even worse was being denied entry by the courthouse Deputy, who, in his "quiet voice", ordered me
to wait outside.

Even worse was when storming away, slipping on
urine-iced over [@23°F] steps, taking a toss onto my
ass, with files flying into the air, never to be seen
again -then being barked at by all three of them for
having disturbed their peace.

Before I could pull out my three layers deep handkerchief, I keeled over and began to dry heave. A frozen sheet of bile, like some slice of raw beef liver
slapped and stuck to my face matting itself onto the
leeward side of my barely effective earmuffs. I
wanted to die.

The slums are not a place of despair.
Its inhabitants are all working towards a better life.

—*Vikas Swarup*

My makeshift cloth mask revealed my stretch-marked belly, fully
exposed to the slicing wind. Worse yet, it became a tempting target for
mean-spirited or just ill-placed wrist shots. Anytime I somehow made a
save, usually by my blubber somehow flopping into the path of the puck,
the shooter would be mocked and shamed - even by my own teammates.

While, to my older brother, Bahred, and his hockey buddies, I was
nothing more than fresh meat when on the ice, I was always invited in

earnest when these self-proclaimed Boston Bruins made up their minds to form a line and throw snowballs at cars. They listened to me, as I set them up at great vantage points and gave foolproof strategies regarding both attacking and, more importantly, escaping. They took no inter-est in from what referenced epic historical battle my given strategy was derived; yet even they knew to follow my bold, Atlantic Ocean–wind fac-tored battle plan to the letter. Unlike them, I couldn't run or skate away. Unlike them, I didn't have to resort to fleeing the scene. My mouth could get all of us out of any accusation of wrongdoing, usually with the accuser offering an apology.

9. The Runner — Losing track

There is a trick—or an art—to appearing subservient while, in actuality, being subversive. It is the kind of finesse that my judo Sensei called, "baiting the sleeve." In my professional arena, it denoted legal analysis that both respected the rule of law while calculating how any given client might have avoided arrest, a.k.a. "How to deek out Po Po."

Such a familiar paradigm emerged during a meeting with Marquis Bobo, charged with selling dope on the corner, packing trouble —in the form of a rattle-trap, poorly defaced, .25-caliber handgun. When he began to explain exactly how he was caught by the police, I became increasingly frustrated.

Three squad cars had advanced on him: one from his south, one from his west, and one from his east. They closed in on him and his friends over one-way, decrepit, narrow streets.

The young and athletic Master Bobo so stupidly came to arrest himself. He took off running right into the open, away from where he was first spotted and into the clear path of a converging pack of squad cars. This wasn't even a decent foot chase; it was car versus idiot over the open road. Marquis sadly set the best course to his own capture.

Instead of chatting about the evidence, his statements to the police, and the rest of his old-hat file, I delved into the very essence of his demise: How could a lean and young, quick-footed dope dealer, holding a cache of drugs, a wad of cash- and while packing a mini loose-cannon not have found the way to escape the clunky, marked, out-of-synch, one-man squad cars while on his corner, i.e. his place of doing business...

I began to school him, mapping out on a legal pad how he had played into his pursuers' hands. I then scripted out a file-it-away pre-plan: If ever faced with three converging squad cars, he must fake surrender to one – wait – then break into a sprint, right past the faked-frozen; forcing the second and third to collapse into the duped first. Driving home the soundness of my strategy, I showed on paper how doubling back around then cross-cutting away would have set him free.

"Once you start running, run. Keep the chase going until you are either in the clear or and tanked and have to hide. The very worst thing that could happen is that you get shot. The odds are low. But once you give up the chase, you may as well be shot. So, in the future, you run this play – just like Walter Payton would- and get your sad sorry ass home. Otherwise, Marquis Bobo, you need to find a new line of work."

Who Waldo Pain?

"Walter Payton. Sweetness."

Who is them?

*"Marquis BOOB. You need to find
a new line of work."*

**I am the world's worst reporter.
I am apt to try too hard to help rather
than just document my subjects.**

—DAVID RAKOFF

As for either Umair and me, the only thing in our preteen-to-teen years that was even remotely macho was our sheer size. Vaster in weight, appearing older than our peers, we nonetheless were at a distinct disadvantage age-wise. Our protective defenses ranged from talking our way out of falling prey to rogue bullies - to the staged crying, our dignity-sacrificing move to ensure either a pain-free end to the torment - to the dreaded fear-fueled flight, displaying the blazing speed of a dying lobster.

Nothing ever allayed our servile timidity, not even knowing that neither of us rarely had to stick up for ourselves. It was not that we amply demonstrated that we ever could have. Yet despite our combination inability/unwillingness to put up our dukes, vengeance would still be ours. After all, Umair and I could summon up our tougher, stronger, leaner, taller, older brothers who would dare not deny us protection. They would, and so easily could, fight any of our fights. Even more emphatically, our fathers and mothers certainly seemed to demand it. That our families would offer us unconditional protection from those whose menace approached the line, may have saved our lives.

My older brother, Bahred, would not hesitate to scold - just like our Ma or Dad would, or, if necessary, thrash- just like our Ma or Da could -

those who lacked the capacity of self-restraint. He may not have loved this position, but he never turned down the work and always got the job done. My Dad praised him for using his fists to dispense justice. Ma, on the other hand, never said a word, leaving in the air a silent discontentment that I had not her fighting spirit and that my more gentle-souled brother, Bahred, had to resort to those rough ways that indelibly marked her youth.

Umair's brothers, he scornfully told me, had a clever knack for always being in a place, lying in wait, where the would-be predator would happen to walk by. The way Umair saw it, Bahred did not think in any way like those who wanted to hurt me; while his brothers where no better – in many cases much worse - than those who preyed upon him.

He was right.

Always starting with his calm yet formidable presence and then words, offering them an out, my brother, Bahred, only resorted to serious fists of fury when his reason and appeal to compromise were met with undignified, defiant, stubborn aggression. This turbulent aspect of my childhood, the feelings and reactions it created and suppressed, all that it provided and deprived, utterly confused me; which frustrated me in the worst of ways.

Umair and I retreated to our safe haven, as "Al Bashawat"; branding ourselves with this stature and self- scripting this junior regal role was ours and came to be our inescapable destinies. We convinced ourselves that those around us were the hamstrung ones; and that we held some prized place in the world; high atop realm of rhetoric and adorned with heaping helpings of majestic food.

This persona of mine, adult-society honed and well-fed to the edge of gluttonous excess, left whoever I really was lost - somewhere out there, beyond any recoupable reach. Completely disconnected from my peers, my overconsuming body and overdriven mind were my irrefutable destiny, no matter how short my life-span. In brief, courageous moments, I tried to become outright defiant, even deviant. But when I tried to fight back by acting out in unfamiliar ways, I fell back on my fat ass, flopping face first into destiny's path: The refrigerator.

Trapped in this mind-set, I chose to give up. I outright refused to find it within myself to lay an honest claim to what I should or could want and what I might strive for. I played inwardly stupid while outwardly cluttering my thoughts with complex data and logistical syllogisms and almanac-like knowledge. I needed the self-recognition from my high intellectual talent and the anticipation of my next heaping meal in order to convince myself that I was not living out a folly or playing out some sham. Reward and recognitions always did the trick; the right answer or a mountain of pasta padded my gastro-intestinal wallet.

What was this one thing, out of everything, that I seemed to not want to know? What was it that I was so utterly afraid to learn? These were the questions that crept into my solitary moments, fiercely so, late at night. Only after raiding the refrigerator and reading the next letter up in my bedside encyclopedia set from cover to cover would I fall asleep in my self-compromised version of peace.

Umair had confided in me that he too could not 'own up' to himself. So often, he would get out of bed, sneak into the bathroom, look himself in the mirror, and say, "I don't want to be you." Once back in bed, he would finally accept that he could not change who he was; he would give up on these inveterate thoughts- until the next pointless outbreak of pointless hope.

Love cannot save you from your own fate.

—Jim Morrison

CHAPTER X

ARROGANT CHILDHOOD

The hardest thing of all to find is a black cat in a dark room,
especially if there is no cat.

—*Confucius*

As a distraction from earnest self-examination, during my childhood I was my own and many others' worst enemy. I utilized—
often outright abused—my ability to shine in the world of my elders;
in a constant war of words against the educated or uneducated alike. I
was determined to dominate every adult conversation. It was the only
place where I wouldn't hesitate to be aggressive, often
indiscriminately and brazenly engaging the unsuspecting in the
intellectual ring. I could run clever, assertive circles amidst any adult
gathering. Even though I had yet not reached the proper age, Ma and
my Dad would never hesitate to let me roam free to stalk adult
discussions and move in on the issues. They misinterpreted,
understandably so, my successfully suppressed despair as shrewd
talent and scholarly self-confidence.

It is no wonder that, combined with the food it usually delivered, these
twin obsessions became my comfort zone. Eating to excess and brainy antag-
onism were my safe-haven for emotional solace. In no time, my rhetoric
was irrefutable. As to Vietnam, Civil Rights, Watergate, Energy

Independence, the Middle East and Women's Lib—I could define, refine and render unbreakable assertions, gilded with a full plate or heaping bowl and cloth napkin artfully tucked in under my double chin. When anyone dared rebut my word, I would sir-rebut the debate, easily win the round in between huge bites, my fork and knife underscoring my solid premises and game-winning conclusion.

The summer of the Watergate hearings, just after entering my second decade of life, was all mine. I would sneak away from my busboy and prep-cook duties at my job at the seasonal restaurant/ motel owned and run Ma and my Dad, and – grungy apron and all- I would enter into one of the checked-out rooms in the adjacent motel. Cruelly ignoring my younger, toddler sister, Endzanoush, I was glued to a grainy, black-and-white, wall-mounted television screen; I devoured every transcribed line of testimony. I always packed a to-go plate from leftovers on plates brought in from the dining room, staying clear of those to which a slip was attached, indicating "doggie bag up". Eating dubious uneaten food was referred to in restaurant jargon as "swillin". I made every effort to wait to feast until breaks in the action. Our chambermaid, a mid-fifties, salty, toothless woman, would piss and moan, because the soap operas that she was accustomed to taking in while cleaning rooms had been preempted by network coverage on all three channels.

With my picnic lunches comprised of pickings from customers' uneaten portions spread out on the bedspread of whatever unclean room I had commandeered, my "smorgasbord of swill" I made a brilliant case that this was a true soap opera lives unfolding – on the brink of destruction, stories abound with human weakness, especially power's narcotic effect. She gave a hoot about any of this, and I knew not to push. Instead, I resorted to charming her into keeping my little rendezvous our secret - my very best Cary Grant for her; after which I assured her that I would change and clean my viewing room, claiming to have always admired her work from afar, to a level that would make her beam with pride. With that, she and her cleaning cart moved on to the next checked-out room. In reality, all I did – in between witnesses- was doll the room up, place the clean sheets in the lower drawer and plop the clean terrycloth items on top of the toilet tank.

When John Dean finally was sworn in, I set my food aside and barricaded the door. Meanly ignoring three-year-old Endzanoush, who was marveling at her tricycle skills while motoring up and down the motel's sidewalk, I sat upright on the edge of the bed and shut out everything else. The television volume was all the way up; I couldn't even eat. Spinning with excitement, I found myself shaking and turning, pleasantly cynical with every word of Dean's prepared statement and his sweaty brow. I pon-dered the vast corruption depicted in the written words he was now crooning under oath. Here I was, pulling off my own little scam; unlike Nixon, I was getting away with it. That was a profound historical moment, replete with banging gavels and Dean's hot wife, who distracted me. This was the story of absolute power's power to corrupt absolutely and one's ability to fool or be fooled by just anyone - including one's own self – if the payoff were sufficiently attractive. However well-chosen his prose, the way I saw it at nine years old was that John Dean – unlike his proud-to-the-end partners in this devious criminal enterprise - was nothing but a two-bit snitch.

For the first time, I was earnestly considering running for President, placing atop my campaign promises to not surround myself with a cabinet filled with either the larcenous or the disloyal. By Halloween, just after Nixon's Saturday Night Massacre, I had secured seventy-six votes.

This endeavor gave me the chance to wedge my way in with anyone and find a way to appeal to any audience. Through rhetorical persuasion, the art of the word, touching on themes of honesty and integrity, I could find the soft spot in every listener. I lived for the predictable response; be it pleasant recognition or unrefined rebuke - against which I would still get that savored last word.

It was all about what I could extract from my audience; and it became rapturous, almost erotic. I was now the future hero, the big man in the making, to be admired by older women who missed JFK and with a tweak of my message, by older men who wanted an old-fashioned future; without hippies and their despised kind or bra-less women's lib.

Then, I pushed these things a little too far.

I kept hearing subtle messages; references to religion. I had to get on this. It was good - another way to separate me from my younger peers. Until this time, my understanding of religion had been more of an ethnic phenomenon or non-negotiable holiday obligation. Yet now, I saw potential – the challenge of learning the Holy Bible and its benefits - food for my ever-starving prepubescent ego. As the result, I willed myself to embrace religion: the liturgy, the proverbs, the songs, the letters, and the scripture—this entire narrative – arguably, the original rap.

Things would go from verse to worse after I got careless and unaccountably dropped my guard. I would invest my heart, yet end up losing my shirt.

Keep in mind that, by this time, at age eleven, I was a size 24/husky – headed to a men's XL, able to eat more than any man. I tried to break several Guinness world food records. At least I stood a chance and did pretty well for myself. I stood no chance when it came to my Uncle Leo - and his beer.

Uncle Leo was not technically my uncle, but he was unquestionably my uncle in spirit. The two of us loved to indulge and were praised for it. Older than my Dad and younger than my Grampa Vartan, Uncle Leo's Armenian-American wit was sharp and uncensored, he was so much smarter than he ever led on and he could push any envelope further than anyone else. Uncle Leo, so much like an Ernest Borgnine – but with dirty words, was married to and adored by Auntie Bettie, a gentle, saintly, disarmingly subtle woman who I cherished and whose cooking very closely matched Ma's.

Auntie Bettie played a sweet, adoring George Fenneman to the out-wardly gruff yet subtly prurient Uncle Leo and his Groucho-like antics. She never denied him or deprived him of his beer. Uncle Leo once drank a case of beer and then finished the six-pack of some nameless Syrian, a sucker who had wagered on his ability to slay the master of suds. To celebrate this Secretariat-like victory, Uncle Leo drank half as much more.

This runaway-train idea of mine started when Uncle Leo, on a rare visit to our home, said, "Hey, smarty-pants, go find me some beer." I said, "You mean, go find *us* some beer?" He replied, "You go and get it, and you and I will drink it together. Just don't tell Sarkis or Auntie Betty or we'll both have our asses in a sling."

For the first five I remember, I held my own. With the rest of the family in the house, feasting and replaying old stories – the cheerful and tragic, Uncle Leo and I were out in the garage, throwing bottles back. After needing two hands to choke down number nine, I staggered away, as Uncle Leo said, "You did well, kid. And I know you're going to be a fuckin' good lawyer. I could always tell…"

I had sloshed too deep into these fermented waters. I somehow floated to my Dad's side of the spinning bed, two o'clock on that Sunday afternoon, after drinking nearly a gallon of dusty bottles of Ballantine's Ale in fewer than ninety minutes. At some point, my Dad figured out where I was and came in to check on me. We locked eyes; mine pied. Without uttering a word, he shook his head and smiled, as if to acknowledge that the torch had been passed, and now a new branch of the Minasian family tree became a fresh notch in Uncle Leo's belt.

No disrespect to this icon, but I could have eaten both Uncle Leo and anyone he picked way under the table. When it came to the primitive, insidious consumption of food, I found pleasure; the inhalation of massive quantities of food had come to validate me, to offer me credibility and to grant me standing in the family - especially from Ma's Italian side. Finding, cajoling, and eating amazingly exceptional food—and lots of it—were the cornerstones of my duel ethnic identity. Showcasing myself with edibles became the center stage on which I took the leading center role. One early spring afternoon, I ate five Whoppers with Cheese in less than an hour, with a chaser of two large orders of French fries.

I had no respect for a small, single, or half orders - particularly anything fried or in the ice cream category. Inhaling a pound of pasta was easy, well before anyone else was hardly into a first helping. When eating out Italian style, it was a 'double order' of pasta. While two pounds was doable in one sitting, I preferred to finish off what was left from our family meal when everyone else slept; the pasta cooled to room temperature goodness, with the dew of condensation, dripping down from the plastic wrap's underside, which made it go down easily. I often stuffed it into pita bread or a baguette; a complex carbohydrate take on the turducken in my world of clandestine cuisine.

Al Basha

Love is whatever you can still betray...
betrayal can only happen if you love.

John Le Carre

Balanced against any childhood excesses was the firm hand and unconditional love from Ma and my Dad. They nurtured me with hard rules and kept hawk-like eyes on my comings and goings with those who befriended me. It took everything for me to successfully conceal anything. With warming comfort, solid shelter, and abundant sustenance, Ma and my Dad kept me both centered and strong. It was important to them that their children show respect and appreciation for our comforts; they drove this point home by exposing us to the hard truths of the world: the plight of poverty, the ugliness of discrimination, the rawness of dishonesty, the allure of addiction and the criminal element's undeniable, yet often fatal, attraction.

Against this bitterness, they bestowed upon my siblings and me life's sweeter bounty: every form of art and music, fine ethnic and traditional cuisine, theater and literature; nature and science. We were raised to stand up to prejudice and counter any such evil in whatever way we could; we were to treat any persecuted person like family.

Yet as much as Ma and my Dad saw eye to eye when it came to raising us, they remained at each other's throats for the balance of their married life. Their fifty-plus years as husband and wife were uncanny; of such a dichotomous nature. Being "Al Basha" of our family, my upbringing, vibrant and full of ethnicity, equally both toughened and softened me. My high place in our family both protected me yet left me exposed and vulnerable. Making good on my increasingly fattened form, I worked like a mule for my parents, and, in return, I ate well—extremely well too well. All the while, my mind was searching, and my stomach was stretching. I was always either hankering for food or the prowl for knowledge – often time simultaneously: book in one hand, food in the other. Distracted, I looked away from seeking answers to personal questions.

A barely pubescent walking contradiction, I was content with the distraction that engaging intellectually with others – almost always prevailing – had easily provided. In my self-instigated war of words, I battled and defeated both real and imaginary foes. My mental gymnastics would fly high and tightly twist- capable of taking on anyone—anyone, that is, but myself. I could analyze, problem-solve, analogize, and syllogize anything—anything, that is, but my inner pain.

At this very young age, I found myself firmly footed under my formidable self-created, self-rationalized lofty platform. I was wired for debate. Ever desperate, I tried to grab any ear then not let go. I learned how to emotionally move my audience by cleverly playing what I knew, against what I calculated it needed to hear. It mattered not whether I believed in what was coming out of my mouth. I never embraced anything that truly counted; instead I just used – as in "took advantage of" – big words and bigger ideas.

Like some frumpily-groomed, self-made politician, I operated by persona, tapping it at the right moments in order to verbally barge into then physically imposed myself upon targeted adult conversations. Exhibiting self-confident posturing through this version of me, one influenced by television's iconic Perry Mason, I dogmatically quoted everything from the scriptures to the best Yankee sayings for the benefit of those engrained by Watergate and our "…not a crook" President.

Wanting a larger cache, I read, wrote, watched, and grabbed everything remotely informative, persuasive, engrossing, or inflammatory. After having that one time been caught off guard by a cagy local dairy farmer, I self-demanded to get up at the crack of dawn to watch and study every fact and figure from "U.S. Farm Report", the first television show of the day. I needed this raw data, so I would crush that crusty rooster farmer – who I admittedly underestimated - should we ever cross paths again.

Years before, while manning the counter at our family-franchised Dairy Queen, after I had dropped out of kindergarten, I started to question Nixon's Vietnam War, follow certain stocks, and felt the outrage of Attica and the IRA. Even then, and for most of my childhood, I pushed the envelope, always asking those hard, Walter Cronkite–inspired questions, but I was afraid to explore his sincerity and consider his earnest depth of character.

> *There is something maddening about mediocrity*
> *that calls forth the worst in those who*
> *are forced to deal with it.*

> —Moss Hart

It was meant to impress; pure bravado. Once I made my way into dialog, I bided my time then without any real sense of it all, turned the tide on my drawn-in listener determined to take the wind out of his or her sails. I thrived when not backing down during a worthy debate. And in those instances when my overestimated opponent scampered away or capitulated, or worse yet disengaged, I felt all alone, cheap and used.

Getting a playable reaction or verbal kudos, even an underhanded compliment was all that mattered to me. Angling for the predictable desired result was what fed me, a troubled man-child. Others' cheap emotions were welcomed – in order to distract me from my own unsettled ones.

My outward self-confidence was but a front, with acrid arrogance and encyclopedic attacks, ignoring what was conquering me from within. Repeating the history I claimed to know oh so well, I, like so many other arrogant, was doomed to defeat from the flanks. Transformed into an otherwise easily electable textbook politician, I side-stepped the deep meaning of words, measuredly – shallowly - identified with the goings-on and plights of others and stuck to problem identifying - not solving. I played the game and played hard. This was my hockey game and I was no longer in the net.

In 1977, at the age of twelve, four years after my Executive Office interest sparked, I sought out and was pledged 274 votes from verified registered voters for Presidency in the 2004 general election, the earliest year in which I would be eligible by age to run.

How slick was I.

CHAPTER XI

EARLY TEENS—
THE STORMS

To succeed in life, you need two things:
ignorance and confidence.

—MARK TWAIN

A s I approached my early teenage years, rules of engagement were revised. The mystery of girls and the perplexity of puberty complicated things. My maiden voyage plotted a course, full steam ahead, toward a straight-haired, wide-eyed, full-lipped, would-be cowgirl, the girlfriend of my class bully. Mannie Terrill had long, straight-hair, big but squinty, beady eyes; a raw-boned frame, meaty fists and a primitive overbite. He found out that I had asked his girl, Susan, if I could kiss her and that she accepted my invitation. Mannie cornered me at the beach and demanded that I let him punch me in the face. His terms were, "…either you let me punch you in the face, or I'm going to beat you up." Guilty as charged and afraid to fight, I surrendered my face. I stood there, eyes wide open, and let Mannie Terrill issue a haymaker.

He wound up and delivered a right cross that caught me squarely in the face—racking my teeth, compressing my cheek, and causing my eyes to flash. Instinctively, I ran away – waiting to cry; then I became con-fused. Slowing to a walk, not even out of breath, I couldn't understand why I was not crying. After all, anything Mannie dished out was supposed to devastate his victim. I had to be missing something. Perhaps I was in neurological shock. No matter how much I tried, I couldn't pull up even the feeblest whimper.

I finally concluded that being punched in the face was just not what it was cooked up to be. With that, I stood there fidgeting; oddly not knowing what to do with myself. So, I watched two seagulls fight over some pizza crust. Over their heated battle for scavenger supremacy, I gave this more thought – overthought - and concluded that Mannie was owed satisfaction, albeit fraudulent. I felt better about the result – but rather stupid for letting him hit me in the first place. So I was a diplomat - I proudly self-proclaimed - as the seagulls divvied up the beach pizza scraps and flew away.

Kudos to Mannie Terrill for delivering a truism: While the solid punch to the face should be avoided, if taken and shaken off can be just as effec-tive as a counter-punch. In those rare, touchy situations later in my life, recalling Mannie Terrill and my time with those seagulls would factor into unavoidable physicality. His punch saved me three. Fifteen years later, while riding the CTA—wearing a suit – my mind elsewhere - I was marked as having money and found myself caught off guard. How fortunate that the would-be robber struck me in the exact spot as did Mannie Terrill.

This time I did not run - and I kept the pizza.

In my early teens, the fact that I was much younger yet much fatter than my classmates greatly complicated things; it was a convenient bless-ing to have both musical talent and an ability to make anyone laugh in an instant. I continued to inhale food and earth's other bounties…followed by more food. My persona morphed John Belushi, Morton Dean, and Curly Q Link onto which I sprinkled the very best of professional wrestling, Bugs Bunny, and Socrates. When on my clarinet (the precursor to my lifelong choice of the saxophone), I could glide, role-playing a young Bennie Goodman, albeit a much fatter one, on his licorice stick, playing Carnegie Hall, the women fawning.

Beyond my first kiss upon that ornery bunko's cowgirl's lips, every girl I had ever pursued shut me down. The only 'luck' I had was from charming older women, who made flirtatious play, amused by how I would get worked up and begin to fumble.

Being knocked down by females seemed to become me. After all, at the age of five, it was a girl who led me to drop out of kindergarten – leaving my kind and committed teacher, Miss Clark. I despised my classmates, who were idiotic simpletons.

On what would be my last day of kindergarten, I was all business, talking over the heads of my dimwitted classmates, which was my daily routine. From day one, I saw my classmates – as infantile - unread and unrefined. I put that aside when a fair-skinned, sprite blonde girl, sporting a bright yellow dress, looked right at me, grabbed my chin and gazed right into my eyes. I felt different – wobbly - all over. This moment lifted me up then set me down. I was strangely at ease, even in a better state of mind than when eating a second plate of Ma's rustic cuisine.

Not until I broke her trance and sized things up did I realize that she had pilfered my boring work and copied my perfect answers onto her messy, tattered paper.

When my Ma picked me up, I was heartbroken. I wanted to cry but didn't. Instead, I grew worse, accusing and indicting "those bums", one by one, proving my indefensible case. Like my model, Perry Mason, I lashed out, wide eyed and self-righteous, in a terse voice, leaving my audience-of-one silent.

Then, my thoughts turned to the girl who had played me while committing her 'Mata Hari-like' act of espionage. Angry and hurt, I summoned up every arrow in my quill and let them aimlessly fly. I could not accept my embarrassment, my vulnerability. Ma said not one word.

"I cannot, and I will not, ever go back to that classroom—I will not go back to them or Miss Clark even though she is a good person – and is actually quite bright."

Ma honored my demand. My Dad never had a say in the matter. What did she sense? What did she know? The effects of this event, becoming a kindergarten drop-out, followed me well into my teens and adult life. Why I did not let it go? What was I hanging onto?

I was kept home until Ma enrolled me in the first grade; my time there, amidst the truly dense, did not last long.

After my first (and last) day, when Ma asked me about my new frontier, I quipped back: "The letter 'S'. Sam the snake? The letter S: Stupid Students!" I put my foot down with "IQ. I quit." So long as my intellect could back my play, it seemed I could control my destiny and dictate my terms.

Two days later, I was moved up to the second grade. While this group was mentally flat, Ma would not let me quit. I was stuck with them. It was all I could do to keep my disgust in check. My mind wandered.

Even with classmates who were decidedly older, the classroom day was dreary; pathetically bureaucratic. It felt like a prisoner-of-war camp. The bullies knew I was two years younger, so nothing I said or did fit in. In order to survive, I found ways to play stupidity against stupidity, making sure that toughest and smartest of the slim pickings found the punchline or insult. The only reason I was not preyed upon was because of my much older brother, Bahred, although he was only a grade ahead of me.

Third grade was no place for someone my young age. While I was academically flawless, I was socially stunted among my peers. I stood out as a double-promoted freak. I made acquaintances and got along; and diligently worked a teacher's pet angle. Because I was unwilling to set aside my bounding questions and out-of-place thoughts, I couldn't either keep any friends or become my teacher's favorite. By the age of eight, I had become a defeated cynic. Despite this burden, my sincere and earnestly decent classmates - especially the bright ones, were friends in the best sense I could ever hope for. That they stood by me, but kept their distance, most off all did not taunt me – and made the effort to understand me was all that really mattered.

Over the summer after I turned ten years old, I had crushes galore on girls but continued to come up empty. I struck out with every girl I pursued. The summer help at our family restaurant and motel, situated on the New Hampshire seacoast, offered romantic disappointment of every variety. I made moves on waitresses and chambermaids, who were in high school or college. While we connected through our shared intellect, I knew that none of them would ever kiss me, let alone want me. With the drama of brainpower-fed libido, I condemned myself to the reality that none of them would ever love me.

None of those I yearned for during those summers working for my parents in our family business, despite my clout, would grant me any affection. I was trying way too hard, yet giving nothing of myself other than a high IQ chip from my fatty shoulder. I would continue to struggle to protect myself by lashing out, trying to overcome my self-perpetuated fears. I now know that the girls my age and older women I approached could sense my emotional frailty. They knew I was worthy in many ways, but only from afar and in the extrinsic.

The distance between insanity and genius
is measured only by success.

—*Bruce Feirstein*

During sixth grade, I gravitated to and befriended a kid who was tough as nails, had a wit about him, but suffered from mental illness. Russell protected me because, although I feared him, I was eager to offer him validation, which he sorely lacked, in the form of a voice. I became Russell's lawyer. I used my very best words against those who taunted him standing shoulder to shoulder with my client. In those who just would not back down, Russell could smell blood. Once revved up, he would clean house. Russell's restrained punches made Mannie Terrill's seem like a last flutter from some terminally diseased butterfly.

We were like a Professional Wrestler and his Manager: Russell was my leaner, and even meaner, *George "the Animal" Steele* and I was his younger, more polished *Grand Wizard of Professional Wrestling.*

One time (and only one time), I went to his house; it was dusty, dingy, and stank of urine. His decrepit mother, who looked like a man, was unkempt and noisy. For whatever reason, perhaps because Russell had invited me in, she beat him mercilessly right before my eyes. He got mad at me when I could not force a smile or join in with him pretending to laugh at what had happened. The fact that Russell allowed his mother to brutalize him, when he could have run away or laid her out, brought our partnership to an end. Still "his attorney", I maintained attorney-client privilege and safeguarded what I had witnessed. I remained loyal to Russell and respected his privacy. We stayed on good terms, but it was now a strained association. I made sure to stroke his wounded ego, as I started to fear that, at any moment, he might take out his inner rage out on me. Knowing how much we were alike, I would have stood there and just taken it. Not understanding what I should have, I failed to report what I had seen. I should have been disbarred at the age of eleven.

The next week, Russell was withdrawn from school. At my twenty-year high school reunion, the only one I unwisely attended, I learned that Russell had been committed to a state mental institution. The classmate who told me this referred to him as "That nut job you used to hang around with when you were really fat."

I corrected him. *"That 'nut job' was my friend and my client; when you weren't fat - and still had hair- and could get over on me..."*

I know that Russell ended up where I could have; in many ways where I justifiably should have.

Whether I was seeking out an earnest, intimate, personal connection to something -or just looking for some other way to legitimize, or at least excuse, my ongoing, ever-growing folly - for whatever reason, I gravitated to religion.

By now, I was in seventh grade, and I had quickly developed a peculiar shine to our local Baptist church, where, at this time, Ma and my Dad took us for weekly church services. After a month of attendance, I wanted to be in the limelight, resenting that on any given Sunday, I had to play second-fiddle to the third-rate Minister. Determined to rise above, I become a devout, passionate parishio-ner, immersing and well-versing myself in the holy scripture. I sought out and quickly earned praise from my pliable and playable Sunday school teacher, who finally saw me as her house-broken puppy. I quickly earned hash marks cut from sheets of colored felt and ceremoniously affixed them onto the cardboard cross -that looked more like some an industrial gasket-upon which she wrote my name. Seeing my future in the Church, she recommended me for the teenager youth group.

I had watched a lot of war movies growing up. Ignoring obvious historical realities, my imagination soared. I subscribed to historical factoid: Military service produced presidential candidate material. And so, still on the campaign trail, my plan was to follow in the footsteps of my Dad and John F. Kennedy; I would enlist in the Navy and serve as Navy Chaplain. I formed my plan to join up these two forces—religion and military might, seeing myself proudly shouldering bars under crosses, atop a crisp, white officer's dress uniform. Expanding this fantasy, I would be there to take charge during some sneak attack on the high seas, single-handedly man a .50-caliber deck gun, and, while gravely wounded, fend off some dastardly enemy, to save the life of a tougher and manlier, but dumber and meaner, enlisted man, whose girlfriend I loved…she would come see me, in the ward of the hospital ship after recovering from surgery – gunfire wounds – whisper me "thanks" and then kiss me on the lips...

Always emerging validated from this sheer escapade, I continued to anoint myself in the scriptures. At first, I utilized a handy, dandy in-vogue Good News Bible. Then, I asked for my own St. James Version of the Bible, complete with maps and indices. Trudging my way outward from the Passion Narratives and backing my way into the Old Testament; I embraced the Song of Solomon and Psalms and used them to entertain the old women who packed our church on Sunday. I imagined that this was one of JFK's tea parties and these were my new, fertile voter base. My Sunday school teacher praised me.

With THE Law on my side, I took a running tally of every command-ment those around me were disobeying. I cited the infraction to which I had borne witness, publicizing the indictment, but it was well under my breath and well out of earshot. I adapted a rather peculiar mental image of God as some tall, African, "Big Cat" Ernie Ladd/Frederick Douglass hybrid (with Idi Amin's props); I thanked God for having distracted me from other, disquieting thoughts and having offered what I considered to be my salvation.

Religion worked for me like a charm. I could bring joy to the clue-less, kindhearted women, intimidate most men, and even have a weapon of protection against bullies who knew, once I napalmed them with verses, to not mess with God's chosen messenger. For all of this blasphe-mous bravado, I was earnestly grateful to God for having finally granted me peace. I came to love God and formed a belief, however qualified, in the existence and power of God. I certainly could not deny the results.

All of that changed after a youth group visit to a rural, antiquated, parishioner-built church.

This house of the Lord was dank and swampy - the parishioners seemed throwbacks in time and place. Very little, if anything, pro-nounced by the pastor from the creaky altar was intelligible. Those in attendance uttered not a peep. The opening prayer was peppered with indecipherable tongues. Its theme was much like begging. The plot was that God would spare the right kind from eternal damnation and burn-ing-hot fire. As to all others...

The lights were cut off for the feature presentation, a reel-to-reel film played over a clunky Korean War–era projector onto a war-surplus screen. In other words, a supermassive sail, hoisted up and then tied down to the pulpit, high atop the grungy odoriferous congregation. This schooner sail of a screen eclipsed the massive, paint-by-number rendition of that classic, blue-eyed, fair-haired portrait of Jesus [ala Richard Harris - *"A Man Called Horse"*].

I was actually quite familiar with and, in the moment, oddly pleased to see this recognizable patchwork media production. This was the same setup as the one utilized by my junior high school's audiovisual crew on an impromptu, two-part extravaganza, just before our Christmas break. The traditional opening act was a screening of the movie *Zulu*.

After the last Zulu warrior was cut to pieces, the colonists emerged victorious and the final credits rolled to black, the second act ceremoniously unfolded. My principal and his teachers issued us free reign over the gymnasium/theater then tossed in every last piece of athletic equipment to our feet. They let us run wild. Screams of "Fire at will!" kicked off the mayhem. With art imitating life, the fifth through eighth grades took up sides and, in a worked-up, entranced state, acted out - with prodigious, *Zulu*-inspired passion.

Strikingly sequenced, the ensuing frenzy formed a clear line of demarcation. The darker-skinned Greek, Italian, Portuguese, and Lebanese children, along with the French-Canadians, special education kids, and all but the very prettiest girls, were cast as Zulus. So doomed, we too were about to be crushed. The school nurse and recruited teachers were soon up to their ears with patients in need of triage, ice packs, Band-Aids, and pledges of silence. Before this, I saw the Zulus as the Black Panthers, the Underground, the IRA, FALN, and, on the eve of the bicentennial 'Clamshell Alliance' Seabrook Post Office bombing - all rolled into one. That the fed-up underdogs went face-to face in the battlefield proved that conventional war was the sport of the establishment against which guerrillas stood no chance. I admittedly fought dirty during the gymnasium Christmas break war, using the shell-shocked around me as human shields.

In terms of impact, the political message of Zulu Christmas did not even come close to this interfaith gathering, let alone its feature film. Unlike the understandable, historically based *Zulu*, I was now gripped but confused by this grainy, end-of-the-world flick, which confounded then panicked me to my deepest core.

In this damnation documentary/drama, those who in some unclear way fell short of the glory of God were rightfully destined to be wiped off the face of the earth. Those who were "the saved" seemed so differ-ent from me, while those who were toast were people with whom I could identify. When the built-up, finishing, deserved blow was struck to the damned, the audience cheered with wild delight. The movie distinctly identified those in the "saved" category from those with a one-way ticket to Hell. Fair-skinned, bland stock families had the inside track and were almost always spared; so long as they didn't mingle with the mongrels.

In sharp, overplayed contrast, those who spoke broken English, were poor, took to the bottle - and even those who admirably toiled in manual labor and had dark skin - were plucked from earth, sometimes while in the midst of their daily tasks. They didn't stand a chance; after all, they were the damned ones. When one's number was up, the church organ soundtrack went silent until he or she was gone.

I had not the wherewithal to see this as propaganda. Surrounded by an adoring audience, overcome by numbers and confusion, I was too overtaken by the wave of Pro-Wrestling Arena-like blind faith to even be scared. For the first time in a very long time, I drew a blank.

The movie pulled no punches in declaring - without reservation or qualification-that damnation was all about class, ethnicity, and race. This film was worse than *Zulu*, because these nonwhites were portrayed as deficient, meek, defeated, and predestined to be forgotten. Powerless, incapable, and unwilling to rise up, they were hopeless, and they knew it. That it was embraced by the congregation left me numb – feeling for the first time in my life – quite stupid.

When the lights were turned on, I noticed that many eyes cast upon me. Their smiles were but wide scowls. I pretended not to be afraid, but I was now terrified. I could not hide, speak, eat, or run to anyone.

I could feel, and then see, my Sunday School teacher and my fellow youth group members disassociate themselves from me. I choked up. Panic plunged deep inside me, because I did not have an answer and could not conjure one up. I had no out. I went numb. On the silent ride home, I was praying that they kill me quickly and not make me suffer.

Over the days that followed, I desperately tried to rescue myself - rationalizing the movie and writing off my experience, certain that I had missed something or misinterpreted it all. After running the equation into the ground, I came to one conclusion: I was being punished for my dishonesty. Because I had engaged in a life of lies and selfish desires, Mexican landscapers and African children would burn in hell. I was a sinner and everyone in that church knew it. Having pushed my luck and displeased God, I was damaged goods and it was just a matter of time.

Not even Jesus Christ would cut me a break. And why should He? I had lived an insincere life. Yet somehow, I was content with my deserved fate. My life was no longer a mystery, and my hellish destiny could not be altered. I felt free as bird; albeit a turkey in mid-November...Ma became concerned when I started picking at my food and preaching damnation to her.

I took small bites, made stern reference to the book of Revelation and referred to the film. Any such unchecked transgressive tongue would be cracked open by Ma and my Dad, but amid this spiritual matter, I was spared the hand or wooden spoon. My Dad just looked away and then left the house. Ma sensed that something was not quite right. She decided to convene a meeting with the church minister, going around the chaperon of this cinematic revelation. When the minister came into our house, I was seated at the kitchen table. He sat across from me. Ma served him coffee then left the room. I was overcome with a need to trust him in earnest, drop my bold front and pour out my heart. I revealed my burning fear, brought about by my inability to reconcile the movie with the Bible's messages of hope and salvation for all, which Jesus lovingly bestowed. I earnestly confessed my sinfulness of constantly seeking high praise and protecting myself from my frailties at all cost. I told him how weary I was from my constant inner battle. I admitted that I had exploited faith and abused the Word of God – instead of embracing it and letting go of everything else. I then reached out to him.

He pulled back sharply, cut me off mid-sentence, and said, "It was only a movie. Don't think about it. I have no idea what you are talking about. You aren't making any sense. By the way, your Sunday School teacher told me that the youth group members and their parents would rather that you no longer participate."

He gulped the last of his coffee, stood up, yelled a good-bye to Ma, and after misbuttoning his stained overcoat, he waddled out the back door. I watched him from our kitchen window situated above the sink in which Ma had just washed dandelion greens. He was muttering to himself.

I wanted to grab Ma's garlic-imbued chef's knife from the cutting board, run outside and stigmatize him. I was enraged with a realized sucker's shame. How stupid was I; having pitiably surrendered all that was sacred; my ability to think, my desire to reason, and the power with which to articulate.

Thus ended my fantasy of serving both our nation as a Navy Chaplain and serving God as his top-dog messenger. I dropped the Supreme Being thing like a chained anchor axed loose and dispatched into the ocean depths during "General Quarters – Man Your Battle Stations!"

Now adrift, I formally rejected God and abandoned my foolish journey for inner peace- and would never again send out a distress call to anyone. Done with atoning, I no longer cared. Not tough enough to be a Satanist, I took up the safer tenets of atheism, which kept me afloat and a safe distance from further damage. Now, completely out of touch with my feelings and fantasies, I would not forgive myself for having compromised reason and intelligence, at first seeking rapture of personal gain then the warmth of emotional reward then foolishly believing that I would ever find salvation.

Childlike surrender and trust, I believe, is the defining spirit of authentic discipleship.

—Brennan Manning

CHAPTER XII

THE EGG AND I

There is nothing more romantic than self-destruction.

—*Kaya Carvajal*

From that moment forth, I worshipped food as my eternal savior. I ate like a so-called "Dead Man Walking"—one-third craving, one-third in need, and one-third as a death-row condemned, with every last-minute appeal cashed in at a loss.

By the time I was fifteen years old, in my junior year of high school, I weighed over 220 pounds and had a forty-two-inch waist; I put away as much food during any breakfast, lunch, or dinner as my other family members combined. Foraging for food in the middle of the night, I exhibited great stealth and precision. I devised ways to sneak food without being caught. I could surgically slide a wooden spoon under the handle of a cast-iron Dutch oven's lid and gently lift it without sounding a warning clang to my snoring parents. I knew to use my hand as a plate and lick it clean, so as not to leave any incriminating forensic evidence behind.

Leftover beef stew was never safe; I could fish into the pot with two fingers, troll for meat, and then return later for the second-class carrots and then potatoes. Pork chops and drumsticks were hidden in the bathroom, sometimes between towels or behind cleaning products. To my credit, I learned from my mistakes. After a first, ill-fated miscalculation, I never ever flushed bones—technically, bone portions down the toilet. As for other evidence - stems, plastic wrap, aluminum foil, empty boxes and cans – I would take them to school and stuff them in my homeroom trash receptacle.

The only place I showed restraint was at school. As much as I loved to eat, even I had scruples. The school lunch was served on Formica-like, dimpled trays that never seemed to dry, and the lunch ladies were like longshoremen, dumping the contents of cans and peanut butter-laced, drenched concoctions about the kitchen, invoking images of autopsies. I would have nothing to do with school so-called lunches.

It all would come to a close in the early spring of 1980 at two thirty in the morning. While spending the night at a friend's house, partying, watching Rodney Dangerfield host *Saturday Night Live* and listening to *Franz Zappa* albums, I woofed down three massive, perfectly griddled chocolate chip pancakes, artfully encased in butter and syrup and topped off with equal parts fluff and peanut butter, known as "a fluffernutter." With the others crashed, I tried to sleep, but could not.

I got up from the couch, climbed over bodies and went back to the kitchen, where I silently opened the refrigerator, gently retrieved an egg from its cardboard carton - then walked upstairs and into the master bathroom. As if in some hypnotic state, I locked the door, stood up to the sink, squared up to the mirror, looked myself in the eye and said, "The End." As egg and shell dripped from my face, down my neck, onto my shirt, and into the sink, I made a silent resolution. I was swirling with the anticipation of what this simple plan would be like. The chicken had come first. Now I had smashed the egg in my face with a firm resolve - to stop eating. I swabbed my face and neck with my hands then wiped them clean onto my shirt.

Subsequently, I did not eat anything. Not one morsel. For over three weeks, I did not chew – and I had no intentions whatsoever of tasting food ever again. Things went from bad to worse to grave. Realizing that this was not one of my many hypotheses, Ma finally put her foot down. When I put down the both of mine, she declared that I was no longer her son. My Dad tried everything from halfhearted threats of violence to outright pain compliance. Capable of serving up a fierce licking, with his massive arms and pronounced hands, my Dad never seemed to have had the stomach for spanking when it came to me (unlike with Bahred, on whom much less was spared). When I steadfastly refused to renounce the egg, my Dad gave up.

No matter what Ma and my Dad tried, nothing—absolutely nothing—would make me eat. I remember thinking that if they had somehow broken me and forced to eat anything, my stomach would have taken on the exact geometrical shape of whatever I ate. I envisioned a drumstick permanently protruding out from my now-shrunken abdominal cavity. This cartoon-like take on gastronomy really kept me going.

Before that egg, I couldn't fall asleep unless I was completely stuffed. Now it was hunger pangs that cradled me, comforted me and rocked me to sleep. It was a friend's "no bullshit" warning, followed by his sober appeal – peer pressure at its noblest - that convinced me either to seek help or continue to wither away.

On the day of my wake-up call, I was hanging out with Glen Hale, a diabetic, a great trombonist, and a self-proclaimed descendant of Nathan Hale. Glen begged me, for sheer shits and giggles, to pee on one of his keto-dye sticks. As he read it, I felt his fear and saw the color exude out from him. He said, "Dude, you're fucking dying." Without needing a second opinion, I got it. With no will to eat, erotically asphyxiated by the sensation of starvation and repulsed from the idea of sitting down for even a morsel. I was too intelligent to ignore the fact that I was slowly killing myself and seemed to enjoy the process.

Not good.

I will no longer mutilate and destroy myself in order to find a secret behind the ruins.

—*HERMANN HESSE*

My pediatrician was a gentle soul, the finest physician, whose hands diagnosed and comforted with great sensitivity. She was a brilliant doctor of medicine, whom the great ones aspired to be and against whom very few measured up. It had been two years since I last saw her. I was now two inches taller and sixty-eight pounds lighter.

Dr. Rose Sceduri examined me from head to toe—by the book—without saying a word. When she returned, she stood upright and tight. Before she said anything, I could see her nostrils flaring. Then, this mild-mannered saint slapped me in the face and landed a scathing verbal attack, full of irrefutable indignation – profanity laden. That I had violated her care, she called me out as mean, arrogant, ungrateful, and selfish.

Dr. Sceduri then set her terms: it would be her way or she would be done with me. I had nothing. She extended her hand and as I went to shake it she held my outstretched hand with her other and placed that one on my cheek. She told me that I was a beautiful man, with the possibility of a beautiful life before me. She begged me not to kill myself. I agreed to her terms and unconditionally surrendered.

She prescribed a fixed diet to replenish my mineral and vitamin loss and revitalize my starving body mass. My health had deteriorated from having gone from eating like two horses to two church mice. Self-willed starvation almost killed me. My gaunt frame was now minus one hundred pounds and a full shoe size.

So memorable from this episode was what one of my friends told me - before I went from trim to grim. He overheard from a girl for whom I had hopelessly longed for - "I would go out with him now." Her retraction took hold - and while it keep me on course and even though I was now in her desired weight class, I still felt fat.

Unable to navigate the hurt, I resorted to angry thoughts. For the first time in my life, certainly from high-school relationship standards, I was in the game. Yet all I could think to do was back away.

Never insult an alligator until after you have crossed the river.

—*CORDELL HULL*

For so many years, I imagined myself holding the highest Office in Washington, determined to de-Watergate, to respect *Roe v. Wade*, work with Ralph Nader and conduct myself like Daniel Webster. More than anything I would find some way to reconcile our nation's insufferable connection to the Vietnam War – and honor those who lost their lives and embrace those were hurting – see to it that we as nation atone for our mistakes and tend to our troubles. Political discussions with my Dad often crescendoed with him storming out of the house - while he cooled off from my heated rhetoric, I would tally all of the votes from his like-minded electorate that I would never receive.

In my senior year of High School, I traveled to our nation's capital, revved up by the prestige of having been selected to represent my home state of New Hampshire in a mock political process - the US Senate Symposium - sponsored by a consortium of colleges and universities. I considered myself highly politically wise and sharply hyper-critical, with cleverness - way beyond my barely pubescent body.

I had set out on this adventure, beaming with self-confidence. The experience ultimately broke whatever idealistic faith I had in the political process. At the opening of the program, I was recruited by other students (mostly from Arizona) to consider - then support- then help organize -and finally spearhead their stirring, spirited cause and enact their proposed resolution: One aimed at addressing the deplorable conditions young Native American women were facing at the hands of overpaid, hack doctors, whose shoddy, shameful practices were entirely Federally funded.

Amid a crowd of name-tag clad high-school kids, the soon-to-be first love of my life approached me. Miriam grabbed both of my hands and said, "I know that you have come here to help my new and old friends and most of all me -with our important and vital cause." The academic, preemptive retort of her request and her striking beauty left my heart pumping. I was hooked, intellectually and romantically.

The others gave us space.

In this perfect moment, I offered myself - rather than asserting myself. Only after listening to her and taking in what she had to say did

I ask questions, real ones; and share my thoughts, honest ones. Miriam and I seemed to not be able to get enough of each other.

She demanded that I frame the political platform and policy angles and that I propose our political action step - with her holding veto power. Every step of the way, Miriam engaged me, augmented my words and challenged my thoughts, with what seemed to be a genuine interest in me - who I was - not what I knew or what I could argue. Without my knowing it, she convinced her team to work from my draft of their resolution. Her mentors were watching and her friends were getting a real kick out of Miriam – working tight angles and making real decisions. Flying high and smitten, I found our chemistry to be invigorating and powerful.

How could I feel so out of control yet in control, all at the same time? I had no answer.

Gamble, cheat, lie, and steal. Let me explain: gamble for your best shot in life—dare to take risks. Cheat those who would have you be less than you are. Lie in the arms of those you love. And finally, steal every moment of happiness.

—CAITLYN JENNER

10. The questionable collar—

Reviewing a murder case that the dics had called in, I was faced with choosing between my instincts - telling me that an arrestee, looking at murder rap, was innocent; and my unbridled oath - to never defy Constitution.

When I caught the case, I was assured that given the multiple positive line-up identifications, this was a slam dunk approval. Their collar had lawyered up and refused to utter one word after being told of this.

All I had to do was interview the "eyeballs", document the refusal, write up my file, call in my approval then stand down until the rotation came back to me. It became clear, however, that the lineups were dubious – with number three from a group of five having been picked by each of the pitiful hoodlums, who could not keep straight what they had either made up or were spoonfed; that all of this had eluded the rather marginal detectives assigned to work this case was troubling.

None of what they ran down made any sense to me: There was no motive; the suspect had a clean rap sheet and was taken in by uniformed beat cops after he had made a right on red without signaling, in the vicinity of the shooting – over ten minutes after the initial 9-1-1 call came in. No weapon found. No nervous behavior.

Something was not right.

And so, for the first time in my career as an attorney, I violated the accused's constitutional rights, admittedly circumventing his sacred assertion to remain silent. Knowing that if I did not convince him to put his trust in me, not only would he be charged, but any realistic hope of him later proving his innocence would be forever lost.

I introduced myself.

"You know that you are not supposed to be talking to me."

"Tell me about it. But if I don't, and more importantly if you don't listen to what I am about to say, you will end up in more trouble than I'm putting myself into. You are your way to the County

and facing murder time. I just don't want you —
down the pike - to blame your Fifth Amendment Rights
or me for that matter…"

"…You see, the only person in this room who I am
certain has violated the law is me, by talking to
you…"

"…The case against you reeks; four bust-outs have
identified you as the shooter. And none of this
makes any sense. I am sorry to say this, but you
need to- correction, we need to prove your
innocence. Right here. Right now. Unless you talk, I
can't help you. My ass is hanging in the breeze,
so please, listen very closely to the question I
am about to ask:

Can you unquestionably account for your whereabouts for at least two hours prior and up to
when you were pulled over? If your answer is 'Yes' -
and I am quite certain that it is, then you need to
lay it all out. Every detail. I'm putting my faith
in you. If I can't clear you, then my law license,
never mind my career, is history."

"What if my answer is 'No'?"

"Only someone whose truthful answer is 'Yes'
would ask that question…"

He gave me every detail: The store where he made a
return, the old friend he ran into; the location of
the pay phone he used to call a girl he was on his
way to meet; her address written on his windshield
suction-cupped note pad.

I asked him if he saw any police, fire, or EMS
personnel while he was driving - ten miles from the
scene of the 'drive-by'.

"No, but there was that Illinois
Bell chick, up on a ladder; she
had a smokin' hot body and funky
hair."

But before I called the detectives in, it was my
turn to coach - He was to repeat what he told me - but
leaving out the details - and in their place, insert
false ones.

"*You need to sell it - but not oversell it- like
you know you are lying, but think they are too stupid to figure it out... This is the only way I can
get those detectives to run down your 'false alibi'.
When I mock you, play along and act like I
caught your hand on the edge of the cookie
jar- but make sure it goes no deeper. Do not
lie. When in doubt, tell the Detectives that
you are smarter than them.*"

"I don't know about all this. This
is crazy. Why should I trust you?"

"*For the same reason that I trust you.*"

He half- gave it all up to the detectives, for
them to break apart. I assured them that if we
worked together and locked out his 'lies', their
good case would become a great one - promotion
worthy.

"Let's go to work and really jam this guy up!
Then we'll see who is smart and who is stupid."

Within two hours the evidence piled up, proving that it was impossible for their collar to have
gunned down the low-level dealer who had been
sitting in the passenger side of a parked car
when it was riddled with bullets, killing him.

Yet even with a solid alibi now locked in, it was
an uphill battle. They still wanted him charged with

murder and after I formally rejected charges, they would not release him.

I went round and round with CPD big brass; it was as if they were trying to wear me down. I really pissed them of when I said: "Alright, I'll approve murder charges – against me. I did it."

These dead-beat dics were fuming that I had "wasted" their time "for nothing".

In order to secure access to relevant Bureau of Indian Affairs documents vital to Miriam's case, some of which were marked as classified, I enlisted my two fellow New Hampshire students (we were the smallest - and only completely unsupervised- delegation at the conference) to go to work on the staff of our US Senator and congressman. These upper-valley guys worked very hard and came through for me huge. By lunch time, with a grin and a "Good luck with the girl," they handed me a stack of BIA medical records and reports "One report in particular -we dog-eared it for you – Franco, this one will blow your mind".

After skimming through the stack and twice reading the "big one" my "homies" uncovered, I presented it to Miriam's team mentor, a late-thirties Native American with long hair and a pronounced, Italian look.

He wore patched-elbow, perfectly fitted corduroy sport jackets and bell-bottomed slacks. After thumbing through them from afar, he beckoned me and requested that I join his "team" for their scheduled visit with his senior Senator, Barry Goldwater. I graciously accepted then summoned up everything I knew about him and I mean everything.

When we arrived for our meeting via the clunky underground congressional monorail, The Senator's executive secretary first informed us that the Senator had been delayed with very sensitive business - then assured us in an obviously routine way that a meeting would take place, but in the waiting area of his Office.

As the others despaired, I loosened myself up, took a deep breath, and then mentioned that Senator D'Amours and US Representative Gordon Humphrey were expecting me to report back to them - and were anticipating my report to follow a formal meeting.

"...which would explain why I was entrusted with these."

Once she saw what I had in my possession, she and the Senator's entire staff escorted us into the inner office. Then and there, our team was formally introduced to the 1964 Republican Presidential Candidate, Senator Barry Goldwater.

Knowing that our window of time was small, I kept quiet and tried to keep my eyes off of Miriam.

With poise and depth, her team mentor shared the team's resolution, which called for an investigation into the plight of scores of Native American women who, under the guise of public health and medicine, had been sterilized. The research and data corroborated the raw accounts contained in affidavits and letters, which demonstrated that a pattern of young women being subjected to radical procedures- after having been bombarded with misinformation, all of which the Bureau of Indian Affairs funded had clearly occurred.

I took my very best written notes while sizing up the Senator Goldwater's reactions. As to every document and each piece of evidence – as to any claim or question, he chuckled.

When the Senator shot me of all people - a look of disgust, my switch flipped. I closed my eyes, took a deep breath, stood up from the aged-leather couch, feeling large again. But when Miriam's eyes wildly twinkled and she shifted to the edge of her seat and smiled, I knew that my moment had finally arrived.

I made the case – through the Bureau of Indian Affairs evidence. I wove into it the culmination of my fifteen years, drawing upon the values Ma and my Dad instilled, contrasting what I had just witnessed in a United States Senator – in stark contrast to the record of great eight in *Profiles in Courage*.

In presenting the solid data, I drew upon the poise of Howard Baker, I held back Perry Mason, Billy "Superstar" Graham, Monty Python and my beloved Italian-American version of a rough-and-tumble country bumpkin, Uncle Franco. Most importantly, I meticulously referred to the Senator in the third person and never looked completely directly at him when I made my case for the living – and spoke of him and those he was defending as if they were not.

For the first time in my life, my spoken word produced beads of sweat that rolled down from my temple and onto my check. This was the moment that my Dad had prepared me for, by always insisting that I never leave the house without a handkerchief.

Homage to Othello, I kept it in my hand as I expressed how dis-appointing that in the face of painstakingly compiled, irrefutable facts and proofs, any United States Senator – especially a Senior one - would even think to resort to platitudes and chuckles.

"The Senator's fellow gentlemen from the 'Granite State' who were good enough to provide this lowly constituent of theirs such compelling evidence of these questionable practices would likely be perplexed that the great Senator would not be moved. Any young person, particularly one who hails from old and sacred land - including Winnacunnet, "Place of the Beautiful Pines", where the Native American's legacy is revered, would be disappointed, to say the least."

"Out of respect for the Senator's constituents, who sit before him and have made their proper case, would not a pledge to conduct a Congressional investigation be fitting – to say the least?"

"After all, did not the Dutch hierarchy listen to – and act upon – Multatuli, who made this very kind of case – to say the least?"

Reigning in my growing passion, I placed my handkerchief back into my pocket, resettled into the leather couch then lowered my head. The chambers went silent. One of the Senator's zit-faced pages broke the hush with a feeble scorn: "Who do think you are, speaking to Senator Goldwater like th…"

To my surprise, Senator Goldwater said "Sh Sh…Sh!" and gestured for silence. His chambers went still.

For the very first time in my life, I did not bandy about and toy with - from afar- a matter of public policy. The issue at hand meant something on all levels. After all, not only was I in it, for real, I was in the presence of the girl with whom I was completely falling in love.

Breaking the silent tension, our mentor motioned to me to stand up and exit, followed by the rest of the delegation. Before closed the door, he looked back at the Senator Goldwater and intoned resolute words in his native language.

I had come alive. Never again would my words be set aside or ignored; never again would my heart be sad. I would never again be lost in lonely frustration - or all alone with lost hopes.

How naïve was I.

For all my seasoned poise, my epideictic recitation and the personal rebirth it heralded in, I would ultimately pay a high price. From that moment of earned self-assuredness, I was left cynical and leery of the politically powerful. The Watergate hearings had left me a suspicious, acrimonious nine-year-old kid, but even I could not deny that the rule of law prevailed.

That an esteemed member of the body politic seemed unphased by questionable public policy let alone personal accounts of his constituency - Native American women and girls – stupefied me. That a high school senior, not old enough to be issued a driver's license, could seize the rhe-torical high ground on a Senior United States Senator left me very bitter.

My pre-teen takes of unpleasant, historical events as being glitches or disheartening anomalies now surrendered to resolute, defeatist views. I would operate from a presumption that until proven otherwise, those in high office had some agenda - and at the very least were at the mercy of private power, capital and influence; and the that real enemy of the state was compromise and indifference, if not outright ignorance and malfeasance.

And so throughout my legal career - first as prosecutor later as defense counsel - I would summon up the lessons of my Senate Chamber oration. I would never take for granted that even the bumbling, tongue-tied may likely have the backing – and the power - to trump decent, hardworking, honest, family-rooted common folk.

But in the midst of the contemplative, however, more immediate, important matters began to surface. After all, I had true love to tend to:

Miriam. Not even a front row seat at Blues Alley to hear the great Dexter Gordon, whose "Confirmation" solo I had painstakingly memorized and whose sound I copied, that were gifted to me from some anonymous, politically connected benefactor, would bump me off track.

An inner voice that kept telling me that I had true love to tend to was all that I could hone in on. Miriam's sweet, confident voice and her clever, engaging retorts lingered in and over and across and into my mind. Once outside Senator Goldwater's Office, my thoughts and emotions were swirling; everything from pride and adulation to disappointment and disgust. I was looking downward, trying to account for what exactly had just happened, when the door opened. His startled staff saw that we had not yet left – and without saying a word, they unceremoniously closed the door on us. It really was quite the perfect finishing touch.

Miriam's mentor gathered us around him. He offered praise on behalf of his people then presented the poignant lesson of the exercise. He said that its success was achieved not through affecting change or making progress; rather it was in our having set the record straight, fighting for and taking the mountaintop - where the truth and sun meet. He then quoted Black Hawk Sauk:

"How smooth must be the language of the whites, when they can make right look like wrong, and wrong like right."

He then turned to me and said:

"You, Franco Minasian, are a great, Winnacunnet Warrior."

Stepping aside, he beckoned Miriam in to stand next to me. In that moment, everything was true; time stood still; the failures of my past suddenly became passed tests.

There we were, Miriam and I, encircled by the delegation. I looked into her eyes; I could feel that she believed in me and cared about me.

I finally felt someone loving me back, who did not doubt me. The acrid rejection or condescending backpedaling I was so used to receiving was gone forever. That I had joined Miriam's cause and shared her passion made this the moment my heart was so desperately hoping for – and it was happening – it was not one of those dreams I used to create while still awake. Miriam was genuinely interested in all of me.

That she had made sense of it all and made everything right, I had no doubt that we would be together for the rest of our lives.

Miriam asked me to play basketball with her. This would be our first date, which was to take place in the field house at the small Catholic College where we Trans-America High School students were all housed. Everything would all fall into place on the parquet floor; a new-found confidence was sure to carry me.

Before this, the last time I had felt such coolness prior to stepping onto a basketball court was when I persuaded Ma to play my "ringer" in a father-son, two-on-two basketball competition during a summer camp family night, some eight years prior. Ma, who was quite the hoopster in her younger days, was sporting high heels and a polyester, aqua-blue pantsuit for this big night out, after a hard day cranking out Dilly Bars and Banana Splits at our family owned and ran Dairy Queen.

During this round-robin slaughter, Ma completely carried me on the court. "We" single-handedly crushed each of our two-on-two opponents in games to eleven. In the championship game, I faced a skinny, bratty jock kid and his blatantly chauvinist, ex-jock father, who by the time we walked onto the concrete court was talking smack about "The broad and her fatso kid." After every jumper and lay up Ma nailed, the father would berate his stunned son. For game point, Ma cleared out the lane with her ass into the father's hip followed by a well-placed elbow to his floating rib then hit me with a can't miss/don't miss bounce pass.

Ma's game - plus my bunny point - skunked our opponents 11–0. With that look of hers – which meant 'keep your mouth quiet' - she gestured for me to shake their hands, leading the way by offering hers. The father slapped his son's extended hand down and turned his back on

Ma. I was certain that she was going to beat that worm to a bloody heap. Instead, Ma smiled at his son, put her hand to his cheek and said to him, "You're a good kid." Ma held out her hand to me; I grabbed it, feeling sorry for the kid - she then shot a very understood look at the father, as we walked off the court, victorious.

With that win under my belt, this was my turn. But this time it was me alone - going one-on-one with true love. This game was for all the marbles. I was pushing in jump shots, coaxing in layups. Miriam was an above-average athlete. Perhaps on any other day, she would've destroyed me, but not this day, April 14, 1980. I would not suffer President Lincoln's fate.

At some point during this life-altering, one-on-one game, I told myself to move closer to Miriam. At first, I just wanted to be sure I was hearing myself right - then I decided it was time to size up my courage. I was falling even deeper in love. Miriam drew me into her space. She then told me that she loved me. I felt out of control, and I was scared, or so my pounding heart suggested. For the first time, I chose fight over flight. I convinced myself that if I did not kiss her I would, in the words of Shakespeare – "die a thousand times". My hands were warm and alive with good energy - I wrapped my glowing arms around Miriam's firm frame. For a moment I felt possessed by Bruno Sammartino, Bobby Orr, John Kennedy, Maynard Ferguson and the virile others on that mental list of mine. I was finally the ladies' man that my Dad was in his day. Then I realized that it was just me, finally that physically self-confident man I had so long ago resigned myself to believe I could never be. As long as I had Miriam in my life and in my arms, I could breathe easy, be giddy and not look around to see who was watching or talking or listening or gawking. I felt lean and stood tall. Miriam was my forever. I was hers forever.

I knew, with the absolute certainty of a young teenager's first love, that we could not survive – and should not be without one another. Together, our individual lives would blend even better, and even more happiness and greater achievements would come our way. I had survived the all of the suffering and had now found my answers to all of the questions I had been so terrified to ask. Finally, all of the pieces fit. I no longer felt wrong or weak or lacking.

My gentle confidence and loving offerings were accepted by Miriam. She meant more to me than anyone or anything. In my mind, Miriam had saved my life. At last, I was at peace and so certain that I was meant to live, to be happy, and to never be afraid, ever again. After we re-broke our twice broken curfew, she said, "Good night. I love you." That night, I went sleepless, longing for the next morning and all those to follow with Miriam.

Out from an unusually bright sunrise, reality began to poke at me. Rapture, under unseasonable mid-Atlantic heat, turned into an unsettled fear. My inner voice started to nag at me and would not give me peace. Old feelings awakened, mocked me; determined to not let me stay happy, they prodded at my thoughts, bullied my hope and insulted my happiness. What was I thinking? I had thought out nothing at all. Once fear took hold, my past experiences twisted into me and once again – as always- shoved hope away. My good thoughts and my healthy feelings were under attack. All I had was a return ticket on a Greyhound Bus from DC to Boston. I was dead.

It was all I could do to muster up the courage to look for Miriam where we were to meet at 8:35am sharp. She found me, before I got there. She told me that it was time to say good-bye. I did not know what to do. I cried. She smiled. After I wiped my eyes, Miriam held out her hand. I handed her my handkerchief and she tied it around her wrist. She touched the lingering tears with her hands and kissed me on the cheek. The clarity of spending the rest of my life with Miriam turned to my ears ringing with pain and my throat turning dry and burning. Before I knew it, she was gone.

While Northbound on I-95, I ran every equation and came up incongruous. I could not solve this equation. I could not come to terms with what I had left behind. I was spinning and needed help.

While Ma and my Dad had taught me so much, encouraged me to no end, protected me unconditionally and raised me up to set me on a path to enlightenment and awareness, this time - this most crucial time

– they did not lift a finger or say one word. From the horrible bus ride to the cruel station wagon ride home from Boston's South Station and over the days and weeks that followed, nothing essential was offered up. I had been abandoned.

I needed someone; I needed my Dad, who had always showed me the "how," and Ma, who had always showed me the "why," to navigate me through the pain of having my heart broken - by my own doing. And yet neither salvation nor rescue nor comfort was to be delivered, let alone offered. it was as if I had actually done something wrong and were rightly being rebuked for it. I could not understand let alone explain away any of this. The best I could do to ease my pain, after crying myself dry amid sleep-deprivation was repeating my "Goldwater's revenge" and "and those native American girls think they got it bad?" flop one-liners, followed by a "bah-DUM-tsshhhhh!"

But I was too desperate- and I just could not yuk my pain away. I attempted a cheap counter-attack, attempting to blame Miriam. But the more I tried to deny my love for her, the weaker and more confused I became. I could not cry anymore, so frantic for an answer. I paced, pan-icked, but could not find it. So then, I concocted an out. I blamed love itself. Love became the scapegoat. I dubbed love the menace that tried to weaken and destroy me. I vowed that forevermore, love would be my enemy. It was so easy. Miriam was history. She was a mistake. I was disap-pointed in myself for having dropped my guard and embarrassed that she had made fool out of me.

Never again would I would open my heart, take a chance, be emo-tionally honest or vulnerable - let alone fall in love ever again. My world view would remain tight – even dark - I would push back on anyone who dared to disrupt it.

> *Losing your life is not the worst thing that can happen.*
> *The worst thing is to lose your reason for living.*

> Jo NESBØ

CHAPTER XIII

LOVE NEVERMORE

A sword never kills anybody; it is a tool in the killer's hand.

—*Lucius Annaeus Seneca*

Emotionally unequipped to push or pull myself through my innocently broken heart, I sank into a toxic, sludgy existence. It now became all too easy for me to lash out and take up the behaviors from my fat years. My untreated, festering wound caused me to relapse into despair and anger. I even rejected my go-to cynical acceptance of undesirable things. This was not some transitional growing pain.

In a cold, emotionally detached state, I transformed myself into a sordid architect with a blueprint of partitions - constructed with cold dividing walls, dolled up with showy fences, and set off with flower-adorned ledges. I walled off my mean heart and dressed up its replacement, a fake heart, which easily embraced the very best of my persuasive powers - with games of all sorts that were outwardly clever and sufficiently touching to get without giving.

With coldly staked and footed boundaries, I would now say or do whatever was necessary to feel acceptance and warmth from women, while honesty and any measure of depth squarely remained off-limits.

While offering my gentlemanly personality, with surface caring and kindness, deep down I was truly uncaring and unkind, meanly unwilling, and so cleverly cruel. Right around spring break of my junior year of college, my college roommate David aptly expressed his amazement with my unmitigated, precision ability to make a girl feel special about herself- "until the expiration date – on either her or your milk carton..."

I would shortchange women and sell my cheap wares. I could be admired, counted on, and appreciated, but I would not, under any circumstances, be loved, sending off any woman who trespassed. I relished the feeling of being wanted, as long as there were no strings attached; abruptly dissolving any alluring relationship – if it crept too close.

I took to cleverly pre-planning my case for an out, constantly taking inventory on any relationship, judging its beginning, determining if it was "moving along nicely" or should be liquidated. As if keeping a binder - containing each persuasive and irrefutable claim - I made sure to cook the books so that my inner despair and outward fraudulence would always balance. While gentlemanly and kindly, offering laughter and gifts, its underlying fraud, covering up deeper issues, played both the needy and gentile souls, whose attraction I drew for my own selfish reasons - and to meet my foolish ends.

When I first began college life in the Back Bay of Boston as a young freshman, I ingratiated myself unto those who seemed more out of place than me—not the alien out-of-staters or even the Yankee-bred New Englanders, cut from the same cloth as those hockey players who had picked on me during marsh hockey. Rather, I took to the so-called 'foreigners', those who had come to Boston from overseas. Given that our Back Bay dormitory residents fell into two segregated groups—the foreigners and the Americans— I was up for the challenge to reconcile and intermingle these two worlds: the non-English-speaking "undesirables" and "my" people.

I took great pleasure in assuming the role of dorm ambassador, bridging the gap between often divergent views. Knowing that I was the only one in this dormitory, a Victorian mansion that had been turned into student housing, who could play the diplomatic game, work the floor and land safely in the middle - every day and with everyone. My Armenian-Italian pedigree, combined with my pidgin Spanish and a Thai roommate, sealed my ambassadorship. It did not hurt that I knew what it felt like to be treated like a foreigner by my fellow Americans.

When I was growing up, living on the beach and not the pale uptown, our family was among those of Greek, Italian, Syrian, Lebanese, Jewish, French-Canadian, and Native American descent. All of us experienced the attitudes and prejudices of turn-of-the-century immigrant life. Zulu Christmas certainly reinforced this cultural reality. My Dad and Ma and their immediate and extended families had endured their Merrimac Valley version of this - and made sure that my siblings and I knew what they overcame. Discrimination was a common reality of my relatives, both Italian and Armenian. With this influence having tightened my outlook on the world and offering me a perspective as to how all of her people should be treated, I role-played "U Thant". Intrigued and engaged, my strategy was to bridge cultural riverbanks- I would be the bridge. I ate what the "Foreigners" often primitively cooked, certainly by even the lowest of dorm-room standards. I played what they played, backgammon and dominoes. I became *un futbolista*, lean and agile; in the process, I presented a willingness to learn. This was hockey off the ice and with warmth. Skateless and smooth, I addressed *el futbol* and learned where and how to correctly place it; how and when to move up and challenge; and when to lay back and hold strong. I wasn't great, but I knew the field and where I was best utilized. I could form foreign alliances, especially over the meeting room – the apex of which was intense dialog that crisscrossed from English to Spanish, Spanish to French, French to Arabic, and then back around again. By the time we ended the enlightening discussion and went to our rooms, we were all partially multilingual from that session, a rumor began that that I was a CIA operative – ala Johnny Depp - "21 Jump Street".

I made certain that nothing was literally "lost in translation". The Libyans claimed that I could not be an American, given my un-American, worldly view of things. I became tight and then good friends with my roommate, Thaviot Techavimol from Thailand. He was a gifted mechanical drawer, Pac-Man master, and pool shark. He was clever and sharp. Known as Moo ("Pig"), he coined my nickname, Fran-*Kway*, a crude variation of my birth name.

After a while, even most suspecting and uncomfortable Americans came around and joined in. It helped greatly that most everyone in the dorm respected John McEnroe's talent, but absolutely loathed him. Aiding my cause was the warm and clever rapport I built with a special member of a group of girls who were junior college students working toward their associates degree in business, who landed in Back Bay Dorms. Even though they would not date any foreign men, they were intrigued by it all.

Renna Boudreau, of French-Canadian descent, was deceptively gentle yet super tough. She grew up picking tobacco in the dusty, humid fields of late summer Connecticut. In undue course, we were a couple. Deliberately, I began to over-give of myself, to the exclusion of my friends, my saxophone - even my studies. In effect, I was taking a break from my detached regimen to once more commit and court. Over spring break, I hitchhiked over two interstates and 100 plus miles to Renna's home. I scraped up all of my money – even sold back required textbooks - to take her to a five-star, high-end Boston restaurant and manor that was out of many a price range.

We recklessly made heavy love everywhere, which included- on our first and last visits to our respective family homes - in the bed of my youth and on the bed of her Dad's ten-by-ten, low-rider trailer- each time with-out any regard for the involved parents. Even before we became reckless, I was certain that Renna's mother had me pegged. Her cold shoulder contrasted with Renna's father's big-hearted, submissive demeanor. Ma was sweet on Renna while ready to brain me – while my Dad's chest puffed both proud and ready to lash out at me for my lack of decorum. For the first time for each of us, we were declared unwelcome in our own homes.

Renna and I were both deliberately making irrational decisions, hedonistically omitting birth control; soaking up one another's passion. Renna was a young woman whose decency and caring - for a younger and however overly gentlemanly me - I did not properly respect.

Once Renna moved back to Connecticut, what we had and shared faded away. This time, my method fell short. Changes and logistics, rather than my standard, usually well-played pitch, is what brought this relationship to a close. Disappointed, as if having let myself down, I resented that I had no control over ending our affair. In fact, Renna had found someone else. It was Renna rather than me who had found the way out of what was never really meant to last.

> *In love, as in gluttony, pleasure is a matter of the utmost precision.*
>
> —*Italo Calvino*

As a corollary, during my four years of college I developed into a basketball gym rat- a quality ball player, eager to take it to the hole, with an arsenal of clever, look-away passes and a highly reliable outside jumper. More importantly, I excelled academically. Our University's debate team was nationally ranked, traveled the country to college campuses, and offered fertile ground upon which for me to roam and graze. Over my college days, I rarely slept, constantly laughed and was always poised to ponder and profess - engage in – and pass around deep thoughts, biting barbs and cleverly crafted retorts.

After graduation, I was primed to learn the law and eager to follow Michael Jordan to Chi-town, sight unseen - a city where I had never before been. Over the hard-driven three years of Law School that followed, I had an on-again, off-again relationship. It was my futile stab at commitment; realistically, it was tailored to fit with the frenetic, toiling pace of my studies. Fellow student, Jinny Sirrace had every desirable, positive quality one could imagine. Jinny's mother was sweet and protective, immensely proud; Jinny's rock-solid father was so nicely rough around the edges, a man's man. He loved airplanes and adored his local airport buddies. I enjoyed his company as much as he took to mine.

Our intense workload offered Jinny and me, more so me, a convenient "out". While law school was rugged and rendered me sleep-deprived, I could have and should have either given Jinny more of me or just left her alone. How easily and often I scurried behind reading assignments, briefs, cases, treatises, and hornbooks – my saxophone – and my array of Converse high-tops – so as to toy with her from an unfair, emotional distance.

I was clearly too unwilling and weak-hearted to earnestly give of myself or take a chance on a woman so much stronger than me. Emotional depth would remain my last desire and my greatest fear. Luckily, the anxiety over final exams was not imaginary and the sheer terror of that ever-looming, vulturous bar exam was dreadfully taxing. Our common goal offered me a way to move on, wean off and weasel away. How easy it was for me to blame a newly implemented computerized legal research system and the cutting-edge floppy disk technology for my absenteeism.

When those grueling law school days finally came to a conclusion - the heat wave during which I crammed for and took the bar exam, which killed more people than murderers, finally gave way to an early autumn and my career now having taken root - I no longer had pursuable, perusable women at my disposal. The on-again, off-again relationship with Jinny Sirrace piddled away, just as it had with Renna. Logistics and circumstances saved Jinny from the bitter end of me and offered me yet another cowardly out.

I regret how I treated Jinny and for having once again "on paper" delivered respectability with delight and cheer, but in reality, was improper, self-serving and insincere. Jinny was the woman who I let get away because I was still guarding myself, clinging to self-deception and unwilling to let her in. Instead, I was disingenuous, inwardly phony and insulted her with my trite rationalizations and excuses of all kinds.

It was on to my professional life as a rising, out of the gate, promising prosecutor. I built a reputation and grabbed the inside track, nudging to the outside even to those with huge clout. Displaying trial skills, working hard, feverishly researching and briefing, showing affinity for the Irish, a love of the drink, and a bravado laced with a snappy East Coast sarcasm, I was off and running in my prized first assignment. In a groove and able prevail over my adversaries – even seasoned attorneys, I buttressed my good name for being hardworking, no-nonsense, analytically quick, and showing poise under pressure. I would say or do nothing to correct any misperceptions that I got where I did from heavy clout and strong political backing. Many Daley cronies, some lucky to have a job, generated a rumor that I was Ara Parseghian's nephew. I milked this utterly ridiculous Notre Dame/Daley Machine connection rumor for all it was worth. Some of my fellow hirees expressed their resentment to my face with "Why don't you go back to Lake County [Waukegan, Illinois), where you belong?"

Both Ma and my Dad had always told me, "Don't shit where you eat." Growing up in our family restaurant business, I saw my fair share of employee romances turn sour. Hot pants always resulted in bad service, even worse food; sloppy romantic drinking on the job, flailing knives, lovers' spats under heat lamps witnessed by orders up and wholesale firings. One of our most gifted chefs, Lee Sorfino, a bona fide hippie, turned to mush over one of the summer help, a college-bound chambermaid, and his food did likewise.

I was there when Ma spit his fish chowder onto his apron. "Did you wash your hands before you made this? It tastes like dirty britches."

Ma gave the object of his distraction the boot then set Lee straight with a wake-up call, of sorts: "You're here to cook, not screw!" Ma always had a nose for anything that compromised cuisine or attempted to play her kitchen for the fool.

Given this backdrop, even I knew better than to allow my carnal desires to interfere with my on-course, fast-track, and rising-star professional development. For the first time in my life, I passed my time playing the field in singles hot spots. Flashing my badge for secured-door passage then biding my time while those who could not get women and, worse yet, those who were desperate to find true love, drifted away. I enjoyed watching the train wrecks all around me, often forgetting why I was there in the first place. The setting was blatantly phony; and yet for those around me, it was reality. Alcohol fueled and sex-driven, it was but a world of denial and my way of self-enabling.

I actually started to distrust women, inclined to turn down even the most casual of encounters. For longer than accustomed, I was without female companionship. One-night stands usually occurred when I was doing sideman saxophone gigs. The sex, much of it drunken and still revved up from my show, was often rather creepy. I typically slipped out of bed, got dressed, grabbed my horn, and snuck away. Only after out to the street, would I find my bearings. Often, benevolent beat cops, who I would flag down and show my credentials, would get me either to the nearest "L" stop- or even to my doorstep.

It's nice to have boundaries, because as long as
we have them, we can cross them a bit.

—*Pamela Anderson*

CHAPTER XIV

THE ARRANGEMENT

*When two people decide to get a divorce, it isn't
a sign that they don't understand one another,
but a sign that they have, at last begun to.*

—*HELEN ROWLAND*

Meanwhile, Umair had been forced into an arranged marriage. Umair's parents had no say in this matter. Quite literally, they were silent business partners. It was Sadiq and Emad who picked him a real winner. The selection process must have been file and obscene.

Loona was a pouty-lipped Saudi girl. Her tight, bold figure, bounced defiantly back after each of their five children, she had no qualms about outwardly displaying. Loona and Umair "made love" a total of five times during their thirteen years together. Sadiq and Emad would openly flirt with her and automatically take sides with her against Umair in otherwise personal, spousal matters.

Emad and Sadiq remained filthy, greedy thugs. They had not developed an ounce of class between them or a measurable inch of direction. While Ashaa and Khajag Medavjian were certainly capable of undeniable ruthlessness, they were otherwise peaceful souls, good neighbors – who lived in harmony and were generally warm. Their line of work could be clinically rationalized as the rippling effect from the inhumane crimes committed against their flesh and blood; and so, there was mitigation – even if not complete and total exemption - for at least some of what they did. However misplaced and violent their path may have been, the Medavjian brothers settled verifiably, "due and owed" debts and exacted decades overdue and rightfully exactable retribution.

Emad and Sadiq would not have lasted a minute in the shoes of Ashaa and Khajag. Their unearned arrogance, complete lack of self-discipline and wholly despicable natures rendered them of no real use to anyone who was worth anything at all, on any side of the tracks.

It was a decade later that Umair would hire the law firm I had joined after having left the Office. I would represent Umair and handle his Petition for Dissolution of Marriage. Over its mean-spirited lifespan, I got a clear sense of Loona's manipulating, intimidating nature. Umair ignored her sexual antics, abuse, and blatant infidelity. With impressive precision, Loona played the oppressed Muslim woman hand – she knew when to cover it, turn it up, and fold it - either with sheepish passive-aggression, fake sobs of woe or full-bore "I am woman" shallow bravado.

I had no doubt that Loona, unlike Umair, could handle herself in a donnybrook. She had the backbone of a high-stakes gambler and the self-confidence of a club fighter. I saw her as some modern-day embodiment of the eerie Hindi goddess Kali, occasionally referenced in blue-collar American male circles as "the mean brunette hag with all the arms - who Moe fought with over the crate of hand grenades."

I did not fear Emad and Sadiq one bit – and they knew it. In fact, they turned tail from me before we were formally introduced, referring to me in whispers as "*Pastapanu*", the Armenian word for attorney [touché to "pasta"]. As for Loona, who verbally humiliated them for having displayed cowardice, I was completely intimidated. Whenever I tried to conceal it, she would make a point to call me by my first name - in a seductively, sultry voice- her mouth always half open.

Even when I squared up against her in the courtroom, Loona could always counter me with a clever, tough and sinister foray, so often unpredictable. Her lawyer, whom Umair presumed had notched Loona into his belt, was a Greek-American with a wrestler's frame and a perpetual five o'clock shadow. Over my years in Chicago, I became quite familiar with Chicago Greek-American persona; fellow law school students and prosecutors with whom I toiled in the trenches. Unlike those warmer, East Coast Greeks I grew up with, this sect displayed a coarse, distinctively untrusting, bravado. As with my former classmates and Office colleagues, I found that the best way to get along with her attorney, Themis "Tim" Kronas, was to disengage. In many respects, he was sharper and wiser than me; totally unphased by Loona's uncouth innuendo. Moreover, he had an astute command of domestic-relations procedure and the ability to cleverly paper any adversary down. To his credit and I would like to think mine, he never went for an unfair advantage against me. Out of earnest respect, I never called him "Tim". I always addressed him as "Themis".

It is always dangerous to underestimate anybody.

—ABDALLAH II OF JORDAN

When it came to Loona, Themis did not attempt to control her; instead, he would allow her to get riled up then step aside. With disastrous effect, Loona ran the show. Even the Judge presiding over the case, the Honorable James Patrick O'Rourke, a very kind and wise Irishman who resembled one of Santa's elderly elves, reeled from Loona's chill. From any ruling, whether favorable or unfavorable, Umair would suffer Loona's wrath. The local police in the town where they resided were well aware of this, having responded to countless anonymous "loud disturbance – female" calls from their neighbors. That Loona was self-confident, attractive, and ruthless created fear in anyone who encountered her, even law enforcement.

Loona made a point made to simultaneously overplay the role as prude, while cleverly coming on to any man. Much like the stuff of *Penthouse Forum,* she masterfully projected herself as some unloved, forbidden fruit, whose suppressed desires were ready to be - and needed to be - exploded. Loona imitated a misunderstood woman, whose pain and suffering cried out for the lust, craving the drive and touch, loving man. She was the epitome of sinister. Without a doubt, Loona was way more than I could ever handle – either in the courtroom or in the sack.

I had to remind myself to always measure my words and control my breathing, take a guarded stance and never, ever mention any personal matters of my own. Loona would have made minced meat of my marital troubles and would have gladly stabbed me with the dysfunction in my personal life - then twist it in.

By this time, I hated my work and loathed my wife. Whether Loona sensed this or not, she was clearly able to outmaneuver Umair and me. He and I were no match for her. Loona dominated Umair's affairs, thoughts and finances. She could even coax him to reveal what he and I had discussed in the strictest of confidence. I learned of this from her mocking words, which quoted me verbatim. It gave me goose bumps and made me dizzy.

Loona totally degraded her children, especially her daughters. Watching Umair whimper, curl up, surrender then beg her to spare them gave her great pleasure. Umair's children pleaded with him to stand up to their mother. Compared to Umair, his children were mighty. Over time, I came to understand that their strong-mindedness was born from the bold front they constructed in order to survive their hopeless family dynamic. To protect their dear father, they sacrificed their own feelings.

Two hard, long years later, Loona offered, through Themis, a pathetic and woefully lopsided divorce settlement. During our only pretrial, lawyers/clients meeting, so-called "four-way conference", Loona took and held the floor. The proposal was seedy and sinister, yet bold and brilliant. In addition to laying claim everything and conceding nothing,

Loona laid out the numbers – beyond the standard/routine attorney's fee language – a separate clause demanding payment for "exceptional billable hours", earned on "certain dates", at times that demanded "special times"; and "non-routine" attorney's fees.

Umair looked at me deadpan. I, however, took the bait and threw a look of disgust at Themis, who – clearly on cue - lowered his head and played hand in the cookie jar. So clever in his bluff, Themis's telegraphed reaction convinced Umair that he was sleeping with Loona - while simultaneously proving to me that he clearly had not. It was a textbook "Kansas City Hustle" – and I fell for it. Themis was cleverly playing along with Loona's predictable mind games and acting out a bit part in her seedy show, one negligently exposing himself as lost control of his client, as if she had conquered him in every way.

Umair took this innuendo to heart. He was not jealous, but the depravity of this display, even though he would bet into it so perfectly, deeply cut into him.

A woman is like a tea bag; you never know
how strong it is until it's in hot water.

—Elenor Roosevelt

Loona keenly observed her three marks' intended reactions, trying not to overplay what she thought was the high hand. In so many ways, this four-way conference was quasi pornographic; with Themis playing the stud, me the timid/curious and Umair the cowering, unwilling odd-man-out.

But in reality, both Loona and Themis had completely underestimated Umair. He neither justifiably lashed out nor predictably caved in. At least on this day, Umair not only raised Loona, but went all-in. He single-handedly and so tastefully matter-of-factly cut down her folly, by overdramatically groping for then pulling out his checkbook. Without the slightest hint of hurt, Umair made out the check, using exaggerated pen strokes, muttering under his breath to himself, "Eh. Throw in an extra fifty dollars." With swagger never before seen, Umair pitched that priceless check across the table to Themis then -with eyes only- looked up at him and said, "I'm sure you earned every penny of this." With pen still in hand, he winked at Loona then quadruple clicked it, with his mouth mockingly half open. Loona folded her arms in defeat and when she was just about ready to burst, stormed out of the room.

Marveling at Umair's play, I gestured to Themis, as if to say "Not bad, eh?" Ever the clever one, Themis spoke to Umair directly for the first and only time. "That, sir, was very well-played. It was brutally good."

This bold, assertiveness was the closest Umair would ever come to a triumph over Loona's cruel capers. Their children would have been proud to know that at least once their father had repelled their mother's outrageousness. Yet for Umair it felt cheap and shameful. He called me the next morning, expressing his regret for having "played Loona's game."

Avoiding humiliation is the core of tragedy and comedy.

—JOHN GUARE

11. Cold Judge—Surrendering to the Fire

Years later, I faced another Loona - this one donning a robe and wielding a gavel - Judge Shelly Pimmits.

As a matter of first impression, Judge Pimmits was squared away, quite the task master and likable. It was not long, however, before I noticed that there was more form than substance in Her Honor's ways and decisions.

I was still inclined to extend Her Honor every benefit of the doubt and make sure that I modify my approach to suit Her Honor's quirk-laden way of doing business.

My approach failed. With each appearance before Her Honor with my pending client and with two new ones somehow assigned to Her Honor, Judge Pimmits became increasingly impatient with my apparent inability to do anything – particularly knowing the law – in any correct way.

It confused and disappointed me more than it bothered me. After all, Judge Pimmits was hardly the first person to don the robe who was "All Show – No Go."

Then Judge Pimmits crossed the line.

Her Honor had blatantly misread the holding in a case upon which I correctly relied in my client's defense. There was no delicate way to set Her Honor straight, given how even the state refused to do anything. When I did, as gingerly as possible, Judge Pimmits lashed out from the bench, in a manner so cruel that it brought me to tears.

I finally accepted that neither precedent nor reason nor fairness nor graces nor I meant anything to Judge Pimmits.

I regathered myself, gestured to the choked up court reporter, as if to reassure her with, "Don't worry. I'm fine. Please limber up." I made my record:

"Mark the date and time. Let the record reflect that I am moving to withdraw my appearance – not just from this case, but from this Courtroom. I shall never, ever practice law before Your Honor again. Should this Courthouse that I cherish catch on fire while Your Honor's placard hangs outside this Courtroom – and if this Courtroom should be my only escape route- I will chose to burn to death, as a fate much less

painful than even the thought of ever returning to Your Honor's Courtroom."

> *"What about your client? Are you going to walk out on him? I'm not giving him probation. He is going to the penitentiary."*

"Yes I am. But before I do, the record should further reflect that as he stands, he is NOT getting probation and he is NOT facing penitentiary time. The presumption of innocence has not yet been overcome. He has neither pled nor has been found guilty."

> *"As usual, Mr. Minasian, now you are just...splitting hairs."*

"Silly me. Silly hairs. Silly Constitution..."

Just then, two lawyers who had entered into the courtroom during "Franco's Inferno" approached the bench and on the spot moved to substitute in, pro-bono. When Judge Pimmits pressed them as to which one, they looked at each other and said, "Both of us, Your Honor; as co-counsel."

With that agape, I walked out of Judge Pimmits' courtroom for good. Yet not wanting to ever eat my words, I checked every fire extinguisher, emergency exit and the fire alarm panel in the Courthouse before I left for the day.

In the end, the ever-conflicted Umair chose to withdraw his petition and abandon his claims. He could not bring himself to break up his family and lose precious watch over his cherished children. Umair would stay married to Loona, employing that so-dreaded buzz phrase "for the sake of the children." He chose to endure Loona's torment and would live out his life as her hated husband. This way, as a matter of principle – however questionable- Umair could focus on being father and just take the hits.

He profusely apologized to me. I begged him, as attorney and friend, to hold the line and push forward with that very same bravado with which he cut that that priceless check. To me, that proved that Umair had what it took to prevail over Loona, even with Themis.

Umair seemed to know this and was touched that I saw this in him. But when it came to Loona, Umair was no gamer. He demanded that I honor his decision. And so, against the advice of counsel - as it is said - and for the sake of our friendship, I relented and honored his edict - so that he could - for the sake of his children - resume his horrid marriage. It was like renewing vows in shotgun wedding ceremony.

Umair settled to a life of self-created suffering, lawyerless – yet having made a friend in me. Were it not for Umair, I would have likely shared his fate. Over our life-changing meal, Umair all but begged me to write *"Al Basha"*. "I promise to survive - if you promise to write our story. Deal?"

"…and this time, Franco, you will not back down…"

Like a master poker player who had missed his calling, Umair had me playing into his tell - that it was his survival at stake; when it was obvious from the deal that it was my survival, not his, that was on the line.

And so, it was not merely my promise to Umair that I was duty-bound to keep; it was a promise to myself.

Your soul knows the geography of your destiny and the map of your future.

—JOHN DONOHUE

CHAPTER XV

SURRENDER

Every act of creation is first an act of destruction.

—*Pablo Picasso*

From Umair's twice failed marriages and his mandate that I write our stories, I felt compelled to open up and earnestly share what brought me my marital despair. It was time for me to tell my story.

While hardly its beginning, a good place to start was that time in my life, freshly adorned with a law degree, when I was caught up in that reckless single life. Functioning like a heroin addict, I was fixed on a course, pretending I had it under control, yet all the while I was unhealthy and adrift. No longer able to handle the frenetic, bumper-car like, one-night stand merry-go-round, I got off and sought out steady ground. I took up new personal strategies, employing a different set of clichés and decided to settle down. Having substituted one self-destructive lifestyle for another, my *qua* methadone took the form of courting then marrying Erin.

Our surface affections, adored by all, lacking depth or honesty, almost guaranteed that we would be husband and wife. Just beneath its shallow glee and enjoyable fare festered unspoken fraud, constant uncertainly and cycle of side-stepped sadness.

A compromise is the art of dividing a cake
in such a way that everyone believes he has the biggest piece.

—LUDWIG ERHARD

Erin and I were convincingly satisfying our common needs; focusing on having fun and making a cozy home. Unable to see through my rationalizing, I was acting like a collared suspect - stubbornly hitching to a flimsy, breakable alibi. With Erin, I embraced the constant distraction of living in denial; our life of deception was stringing both us along.

Having met my match in the milieu of sham relationships, I succumbed to true fraud, gravitating to the convenience of guile and celebrating each successful sidestep from reality. Over well-delivered excuses of all kinds, our marriage grew; it bloomed from disingenuous apologies - shamelessly issued and shallowly accepted – to necessary lies – to effecvtive silence.

I was living out my wedding vows in folly and denial. Erin was an alcoholic, no longer capable of concealing it; suffering from repressed turmoil, which was either a symptom of her uncontrolled drinking or its byproduct.

Yet it was only after looking back, from a story-teller's perspective that I could see my own unacknowledged pain and resulting chronic state of denial. I took comfort in what felt like unconditional love by Erin's family, not realizing that I was being stroked for taking on the role of savior - more accurately, their permanent relief. With the exception of her much younger brothers and her sage Gramma Jude, who quietly read every nuance of the family circus like a book, the rest of Erin's family banked on me to draw her away from the bottle and cut them lose from any future disruptions, excuses, revolving apologies and dreaded 4:00a.m. drama. I bought into being idolized as some Messiah and all but promised that I, the smartest of the bunch, could make up for their decades of dashed hopes. They put their faith in the noble me, certain that my skill set would turn Erin away from her reckless behaviors and get her to "settle into married life."

In stark contrast to Erin's family's praise was Ma's feelings. Only years later I learned how she cursed my letter to her, in which I made my blatantly qualifying case for marrying Erin. Although Ma was outraged, she said not one word; uttered not one adjective. Ma let me climb up this ladder. During my courtship of Erin, I constantly acted the fool. That Ma refused to knock me on my ass, grab me by the neck or shove me away from the doomed path was a stark deviation from how I had been raised.

Consider when Endzanoush was born and I demanded "special treatment, just like her...", Ma grabbed me by the neck, threw me on the bed, powdered my dungarees then threw a diaper over them. "If you try and take it off, I'll brain you."

Somehow Ma knew that this was mine alone to own. Similarly, my Dad did not put his foot down; yet many years later, he waxed:

"...at your brother's wedding Ma and I danced - on your wedding day we cried..."

> *A bad marriage has the power to suppress true feelings.*
> *Only when enough time has passed*
> *and the convenient distractions are used*
> *up, will the tension snap it.*
> *Then the farce will unravel – and tangle.*
> *That's when things really start to bind up and get ugly...*

> —*Jason F. Danielian, criminal prosecutor*
> *and defense attorney*

While my marriage was accurately predicted to fail by many, it was hardly a loveless one. Erin and I realized unconditional love from one another, through our precious children - Rory and Mollie. To them I would dedicate my heart and extend every loving gesture from within me. As if transferring my wedding vows, I unconditionally lived for them. Eventually I would run routine interference between their mother's drunken antics and them, determined - foolishly so - to spare them. I self-spun the rationalization that since we were there for each other, keeping their mother's turmoil checked was not only the right thing to do for the ones I so loved, it was my fatherly duty.

When growing up, both my parents' afflicted contemporaries and my friends' similarly-situated parents operated in this similar "hush-hush", "life is good", "all is well" way. And so, when in the company of Erin's family and her circle of running buddies, I flaunted my unconventional parenting groove - augmented by my always-appreciated cooking skills, a bounty of tasty delights and helping out in the host's kitchen or the hired caterer's domain. Wanting no part of my life-of-the-party wife's antics, whose hollow leg the not-my-type husbands praised, I instead cozied up to the other similarly unhappy and unloved spouses, responding to their smitten "lucky catch" talk gallantly; to their 'innocent' repressed passion, I responded gentlemanly, yet with much less than innocent thoughts.

As to my children, notwithstanding my unconditional love and emotional closeness, our relationship would ultimately prove to be my fatherly blunder. No matter how much I filled their upbringing with laughter and beauty and charm, with fun and quips of all kinds, there was a somber footnote. For all the loving embraces and nurturing, there was this corresponding compromise that was always lurking.

It was "Water under the bridge." - as my Dad would say - when teen-aged Rory and Mollie – confided in me that I had not shielded them from anything. Rather, that I had burdened them and that my tumultuous reactions and wordy responses to their mother's hard-hitting alcoholism - not her frailty - is what hit them the hardest and hurt the most.

To now know that my display, however well-intentioned, was ignoble, worse than even their mother's most dreadful behavior, left me both blameful and shameful.

After all, how could my children not unconditionally love their mother - in even her darkest moments? My reaction to their mother, pejorative and self-centered, portraying them as victims, even though they didn't feel victimized, confused them - which was patently unfair.

While I had wanted nothing more than to spare my children the memories of their mother's alcoholism, it was my harsh reactions, irrational – technically hyper-rational - responses that left permanent bruises and readily recallable, very unhappy events. I should have understood that no matter how diseased, broken, or destructive - their mother would always hold title to their hearts – one rightly superior to mine.

In the end, Erin's dastardly alcoholism brought out the worst in and got the best of me.

> *Dusting is a good example of the futility of trying to put things right. As soon as you dust, the fact of your next dusting has already been established.*
>
> —GEORGE CARLIN

CHAPTER XVI

THE FATHER, DEFEATED; THE DISEASE, VICTORIOUS

You can't make everybody love you.
It's an exercise in futility, and it's probably
not even a good idea to try.

—*ROBERT CRUMB*

My powerless response to their mother's dreaded disease, delegitimized my claim to being my children's great sage, safety net or source of sanctuary. It raised questions as to whether I was ever truly fit to be a father in the first place. Oh, how I loved them so dearly, feverishly nurturing their minds, drawing out thoughts and creating laughter and allegiance - seemingly shielding them from their mother's demon. Yet over time, shielding turned to covering up; and covering up turned into dolling up. As much as I had set out to protect them from alcoholism's ugliness, I ultimately became its safe-house. In fact, I began to manifest alcoholism's ugly, turbulent behaviors.

I had failed to conquer Erin's alcoholism. It had proven itself more ominous and powerful than anything I could throw at it. Incapable of taking it down, I failed to live up to what I had propped myself up to be. I was liable for having baited and switched on my own children and as the terrible result, I shortchanged their feelings – often times denying them. Looking back, I was like some neophyte, exposed double-agent, whose miscalculations resulted in grave consequences.

Your tongue can make you deaf.

—*Native American saying*

How tragic - and telling – that I had even abandoned my prized, professional skill set; cohesion, common sense, discretion, and balance - resulting in a total disregard for my children's right to balance their mother's frailty and failing to allow them to weigh in all of this. Denying them, undeniably oppressed them. I had failed to heed the African proverb that holds that "if you want to go fast, go alone; if you want to go far, go together."

And so, I foolishly scuttled around in wide circles, reducing my beloved children to silenced spectators, forced to watch me drift further and further away – along with what they truly needed from their father.

It is no wonder that I confused Rory and Mollie. They had every right to pull away from me. I broke my promise to protect them from a disease; the more I vilified it, the more I made it mine. The more I made it mine, the more it sapped from me.

I became a sour spectacle of stubbornness. I failed to draw from the lessons I learned at the age of six from the nightly news reports from Vietnam. Instead, I arrogantly promised to control the uncontrollable and foolishly laid claim to actually knowing what I was doing. I fought an unwinnable war and produced innocent casualties; making promises to Rory and Mollie that I could never keep, leaving them to fend for themselves and to come to its terms on their own, while I kept fighting the stupid fight...

Just vengeance does not call for punishment.

—*Pierre Corneille*

The story of any comic book superhero, including Superman, recounts the self-destructive nature of vengeance, especially when employed against the nemesis who can lay an equally legitimate claim to it. That is why however awesome a superhero's arsenal, formidable his powers and mighty his earth-shattering might, his inner torment that renders him vulnerable.

On my path to tell Umair's story and mine, I began to question and ultimately resent my reactive behaviors. Having accepted my failures, it no longer felt right to calibrate the misdeeds or wrongdoings of others. I was no longer comfortable with the law's world of clash and conflict. I wanted out of the stress, bitterness and division. I was finding to it to be too arrogant in nature - and of so very little value.

Once I started to recount Umair's story - side by side with an honest recording of mine - I was determined not to be assailed by events or needlessly pit myself against those who allowed themselves or even chose to be so assailed. Umair's mandate willed me to check my thoughts and find a more balanced viewpoint; so that I could see hope and possibility in my world, beyond merely triaging conflicts and troubleshooting crises.

There are people who are excitable by nature and allow themselves to become angry for the most trivial of reasons. Judo can help such people learn to control themselves.

—*Jigoro Kano, educator, athlete, and founder of judo*

CHAPTER XVII

ESCAPE TO AMSTERDAM

All journeys have secret destinations of
which the traveler is unaware.

—*Martin Buber*

Just after the New Year rang in, fellow firefighter Syd Jefferson
and I worked an attack line against a pesky house fire, playing
to "empty house", as the entire block's residents - including the unfortu-
nate homeowners who had left an empty sauté pan on a heated stove -
were still out celebrating.

I had always viewed Syd – who I called "Shawnee' - as a man whose
USMC toughness was tempered with a puzzling, engrossing spiritual-
ity. Shawnee had two hearts: One of a lion, which fed his righteous,
raging black man's indignation; the other of a giraffe- serene and able
to see beyond – each which displayed his inner, African love of community. Shawnee's ever-yearning quest to make spiritual connections
would have made many uncomfortable were it not for his redneck
USMC bulldog tattoo bulging atop his beefy bicep and persona to
back it up.

In ways that reminded me of Ma, Shawnee was restless and unsettled; yet when it came to others, he left his worries behind, offered his might, gave an ear and would bear his soul. Like Joey Lark, Shawnee always found the best trail over which to walk the walk; always no-nonsense, assiduous and avoiding confrontation.

While we appreciatively, meticulously cleaned and gingerly hung our weaponry then scrubbed the soot and cooked, matted fibers from our gear – which brought our adrenaline back down and into service, Shawnee somehow asked the right questions for me to talk about writing *"Al Basha"*, Umair's mandate; he knew something was on my mind.

Having engaged me, I told him how Umair conscripted me as our story teller, offered me both a new view and a fresh voice; and that something was telling me to detach myself from my toxic professional world, my coexistent marriage and even the fire department's paramedic underworld; patient-created emergencies, poor health and appalling facility care, prescription drug abuse and untreated mental illness in the form of our frustrating "frequent flier" patients.

"Counselor, here's what you really need to do. You need to travel abroad, with your tenor saxophone in tow. Even if it means being away from your children and putting your clients on hold and taking a leave from here, you need to hit the road…then you will find the real shit that my man Umair needs you to find. And I know just the place."

Well into the pre-dawn of a new calendar year, while the rest of the crew collapsed into lazyboys and a consensus movie channel, Shawnee and I sat on the diamond-plated, rough-edged running board of old Mighty Mack Engine 536, with a hanging waft of wet soot. We reached up and grabbed onto her meaty overhead essential hose bar. "Five Three Six" creaked and she tended to leak, but her engine had balls and her pump was always reliable.

The way Shawnee figured, Amsterdam was the one and only place for me. A city *"so considerate to cats like you"*, it was rife with fresh possibilities and the best chance for me to connect *"two important stories- Umair's and yours...*" to words, share my music with a wider community and make my connection with the Dutch soul.

"*Once you step in to Amsterdam, they will want to keep you. You can clean out all your clutter, toss the depressing shit – the stupid shit - aside. Amsterdam will square you away so you can really get with this 'Al Basha' joint of yours. You know, I've heard that title before... yes...from the Kuwaiti soldiers I fought with over in Iraq. They had this commander who took care of them - and had his shit together on the battlefield. Who they called- 'Al Basha'.*"

"*Funny how once I start thinking about that war so much comes back to me...A lot of good shit...strange shit...I used to hang with Dutch soldiers over there too.... And that's how I know that Amsterdam will do it for you; playing your sax and doing right by your boy, Umair. And you may not look Dutch, but the way you talk about Umair and how it all went down in Al Basha; hell, you actually remind me of them Dutch cats; some real thinkers.*

"*Look man. You may not want to come back. But you will – and as a better man, 'Al Basha'.*"

"*Go to Amsterdam, where you will see and feel good things, as my aunt who makes the best sweet-potato pie says, 'through the proper perspective.' Put your pen to paper and let Umair's thing do right by you. I know that's what you want, and I am certain that Amsterdam is where you need to be. It will give you your kind of proper perspective.*"

"*Franco, you really have no choice but to get your ass over there and connect the dots and play your sax; take it all in, and tell your stories – and you damned well better call it "Al Basha.*"

Just then we got a full-arrest medical call. Shawnee pointed up to the clunky communications speaker, yelling over the dispatcher's call and tones, he said: "*You want to end up like this sad, sorry ass, with some serious fubar shit, spinning around, in your head, thinking about "Al Basha"—the promise I broke because I fucked up by not listening to Shawnee? Counselor, you're going. So now that I have saved your ass, let's go and try save his.*"

I radioed us in and put us en route.

We ran a total of five calls into the sunrise. I got home and fell back asleep, to Rory and Mollie kissing me and wishing me a Happy New

Year's Day. About four hours later, over a dial-up world wide web in-and-out connection, I discovered Expedia; then almost magically booked my Amsterdam trip, over Casimir Pulaski Day, a Cook County exclusive – first Monday in March- Holiday.

My next order of business was letting Matt and Dirk know of my travel plans. After the weed and hooker barbs, they relented. They sensed I was ready to make some serious changes; to finally stop playing fireman and devote my time to building the firm's divorce client base.

Matt added, "Didn't you just loose that sad-sack A-Rab guy; Uhura something or other?"

"His name is Umair."

Then Dirk said those magic words. "Franco, this is good. It's time for you to change."

Billy Quill's words sounded like a box alarm.

"You're right, Dirk. I can't work here any longer. I want things between us to be the way they were before you started paying me good money to work for you. Consider this my notice. I will stay for as long as you'd like - up to the day of my flight to Amsterdam."

Dirk's jaw dropped. Matt just walked away, grabbed his coat and left.

I immediately called my Dad. He chuckled then told me for the first time when he left his well-paying job with the phone company. "One day, I made up my mind that I would never work for someone else ever again."

I next called Ma, who said "If that's how you feel, then leave; but you have a family to support; once you're done with them and their paychecks, you had better start busting your ass so you can earn a living."

Rory and Mollie were excited and began making window signs and offering some of their extra items for my new home office. Erin said very little. As soon as the word got out that I was going out on my own, cops from all over called me and assured me how now that I was on my own, that they would steer collars with money my way.

My day of departure finally arrived. After checking through O'Hare's security, I proceeded to the gate, two hours preflight, where I encountered others who seemed to share in my anticipation. Our big blue KLM bird, taxied past the lounge across from our gate. Fellow travelers to other destinations were envious of us.

> *In tragedy, it's hard to find a good resolution; it's*
> *not black and white: it's a big fog of gray.*

—*Paul Dano*

CHAPTER XVIII

AMSTERDAM

He who eats alone chokes alone.

—*Arabic proverb*

The moment I arrived at *Centraal Station* and onto what felt like the bole of the city of Amsterdam's trunk to the massive cobblestone/ canal tree beyond it, I heard a resonant voice careening off of the walls to this majestic palace: "In each day and in every moment, it is the path before you that marks your story yet to be told."

"I rest my case," I nervously quipped as I journeyed into the city of Amsterdam, still holding on to doubts, pondering if my being there was a whim—an irrational overreaction to what was nothing more than a random convergence of events. Had I read too much into lunch at Al Basha with Umair and overreacted to my spirited conversation with Shawnee?

There was only one way to find out and so I embarked upon my journey into the city of Amsterdam, at this point, merely hoping to make the most of it.

After being warmly welcomed and checked into the Hotel Amsterdam, as if I were a returning, well-liked regular, I deviated from my usual travel routine of unpacking and then showering. I felt the need to return to Centraal Station and re-set my attitude. Perhaps that soapbox preacher with Orson Welles's pipes was onto something. He was gone, but the echo of his words was not: "In each day and in every moment, it is the path before you that marks your story yet to be told."

I sat looking over the water and took in the late-morning activity. With the sun now over the city, my eye was drawn to an oddly sunlit, uneven, cobblestoned opening from the *Prins Hendrikkade*, a main street now bustling with a crazy crisscross of cars, trams, bicycles, and pedestrians. Beckoning me in was the spot-lit mouth of *Zeedijk* (Sea Dike), where *Sint Olofspoort* (Saint Olof's Gate) connects it to Warmoesstraat (Street of Chard). The street sweepers had just finished wetting it down and then sweeping it clean; the path glistened, like some illuminated, must-take trail.

Amsterdam seemed determined.

Cats know how to obtain food without labor,
shelter without confinement, and love without penalties.

—*W. L. George*

No sooner did I pass through and onto *Warmoesstraat*, when the sun slipped behind the clouds. The door to Café Internationaal was open and it beckoned me in. I was greeted by the tavern keeper, sat down at the bar, and marveled at this Café's wood finish, leather-upholstered upper walls, ageless, weathered tile floor; the rich sound quality of the tasteful music being played. Its confident, oversized windows showcased a hypnotic crossroads - the septum to Amsterdam's heart.

Before I could introduce myself, "That's on me," said the tall, cool-vibed Dutchman, a perfectly sized beer was set before me. After I took a sip of heaven, we made eye contact. "I'm Franco."

"Franco, everything is going to fall into place for you," Casper said, as we shook hands. Over the rest of my trip, Café Internationaal would be my satellite office, my work desk; my makeshift breakfast nook and lunch counter; home base and sanctuary in which I could imbibe water, coffee, beer, and spirits; chased with deep discussion, good cheer, soulful music, playful barbs and powerful silence.

Café Internationaal became me. Laid-back, cradled in mesmeric rhythm, Dutch cozy with a communal spirit. I was always in the good company of others there, from near and far, also touched by its soul. There were times when the Café was so packed that I would just pass it by or hang outside for a smoke. I had to be there. Thought-provoking words, silent reflection worked into well-placed songs; perfect pours into precision glassware—the *fluitje and the vaasje*; the former, thinner and smaller, the latter, thicker and larger, also known as the *Amsterdammer*. Café Internationaal was where expression was democratic and alliances were kindred. It was where I would make lasting friendships, honestly play my saxophone and the story of "Al Basha" began to write itself.

Each morning my characters greet me with misty faces
willing, though chilled, to muster for another day's progress
through the dazzling quicksand the marsh of blank paper.

—JOHN UPDIKE

CHAPTER XIX

THE CREW

Good fellowship and friendship are lasting,
rational and manly pleasures.

—*William Wycherley*

Michel

Michel is the son of a spirited, live-wire mother, much like Ma, and a solid yet soft-spoken, iron craftsman father. Michel's left eye sports an ever-mended, weathered, black leather patch he had made in Scouting Nederland to replace the hospital-issued, scratchy Danish-made one. Michel presents himself with control and a skipper's swagger, as if a parrot were perched lovingly on his right shoulder. The only thing that seems to elude him is a woman capable of reeling him in.

Michel does not believe in generation gaps, classes, or rankings. "Young people will eventually figure out that most of the bullshit technology is...well...bullshit." He professed that "once they learn how to have really good sex, they will want to be on something other than their devices."

This has been his barkeeper philosophy. Michel pours and wields his hand-forged *bierschuim schraper* - with which to scalp the foam, with great conviction. When one particular discussion inevitably returned to the only topic, Michel proclaimed that good sex was the very lynchpin for creativity; the essential component of profound thoughts by which mankind has survived and thrived. This had nothing to do with the overrated miracle of procreation; it was all about making the naked connection, doing the dirty deed— communication through fornication – making love, not war – the honesty where the legs meet.

One day after ample *vazen* and reflective repose, Michel played the music of De Dijk, the soundtrack to his doctrine: "Yes, I am no lawyer and certainly no Superman, but I can make the case that sex is the true mother of invention."

Inside my empty bottle, I was constructing a lighthouse
while all the others were making ships.

—CHARLES SIMIC

Michel pointed out that the Wright brothers were only able to lift an airplane into the air after practicing- with pilot Wilbur assuming a prone position, mounting a mock "Flyer", played by Orville. "Man's success in flight was born from incest and sodomy. That's how the lift and the thrust that others failed to achieve was realized by the American bachelors. Orville and Wilbur were definitely getting it on."

"*Alstublieft!*" I blurted out, an interjection that I so often misused.

Michel had hardly rested his case, now turning to the telephone. According to his research, Alexander Graham Bell had lustful designs and was working on something else altogether, causing his own diaphragm to vibrate, spilling something other than battery acid when he called out, "Come here, Watson, I need you!" And that, Michel concluded, was the original phone sex.

"What of Thomas Edison?" I volleyed.

"It was for the purpose of illumination. Edison was a man of precision, and gas flames did could illuminate Mina's…filament.

One of the regulars made a point of clarification, noting that Edison's second marriage was years after he invented the lightbulb.

"I am mistaken. He made a movie of his second wedding night. It was the first porno. *Meneer Betweter!* [Mr. Know It All!]"

For the next hour, those in and out of the Café offered up inventors and inventions, spinning science into sex-driven tribulation. The lone dissenter, fully-engaged, insisted that the betterment of mankind was the true and noble inspiration of these greats and that Michel was corrupting us into "…disrespecting, and with such prurience."

Michel rebutted, "Oh, man. That's bullshit. You know perfectly well that you don't give a shit about the betterment of mankind when you are a man or women of great ideas. You just want to get laid."

My turn. "Michel has a point." I proclaimed.

"Quiet! The lawyer, Superman speaks", Michel heralded.

"*Bedankt* for intro, Michel…Consider, if you would, the greatest inventor the world has ever known: the man who was able to create a magnificent machine that could emulate a sultry human voice; one that has a hypnotic effect on many a man and women…"

"The Belgian!" a voice from the corner shouted.

"Yes. Of course," added another patron. "Adolf Sax."

Michel would always have the last word.

"His name was miswritten at birth. His real name is Adolf Sex. Franco here- he plays the Sexophone."

With that, Michel played Sonny Rollins, John Coltrane, Boots Randolph, Gene Ammons, Rasaan Roland Kirk, and Hans Dolfer well into the night. The bell sounded in rotation until the post-closing time last-last call, signifying that the next round was on him.

For all of his innuendo and play, Michel was all business when it came to hiring practices. He adopted the house hiring rules from Michelle:

First, he has to know you, personally so; Second, you must speak fluent Dutch. He has not let me fill out an application- not yet anyway...

Nicole

Endearing, adorably honest and unmistakably strong is she. All those who have sat at Nicole's meticulously kept bar have been drawn in by her alluring eyes. Nicole is a gifted and passionate schoolteacher, way out of most men's leagues. In time, I would fall in love with a woman who was every bit of Nicole's ways.

One year, a frumpy mother and her aloof late-teens son, with reservations in the Café's hotel, had somehow grabbed someone else's suitcase upon arriving at Centraal Station. Its contents were random and worthless. They were such easy marks - this was undoubtedly a 'switcheroo'.

Without missing a beat, Nicole re-gifted from Hotel Internationaal, a very high-end, Russian made, fully stocked "welcome back" toiletry kit courtesy of clunky Lithuanian bar fly, a guest of the Grand Hotel Krasnapolsky, who had tried to woo Nicole with it.

The foul played duo had sizable carry-on bags and the city of Amsterdam at their disposal. Yet they never left the Café, keeping their not-luggage oddly close by. It seemed as though they had never intended on leaving even if they hadn't been swindled.

For a moment, I wondered if they were conning all of us, working a "Pig in a Poke", the intricacies of that scam Nicole understood all too well. "They are too decent and obtuse to be part of such trickery. Although they would be good at it, all they are is very unique."

Just then, the mother pulled out a travel-sized Scrabble board from her frumpy sack, and the two of them began spirited play. This was no con. These two were insane.

Michel, Nicole, and I started our own virtual, visualized Scrabble game: I started with LUGGAGE. Nicole spelled [L]OST. Michel - VA[G] INA. Nicole played [S]I[N]NER, pointing her finger at Michel, who "accidentally" knocked over our board, apologizing for ending the game - declaring himself the winner.

I think as a woman it's in our nature to nurture someone else.
Sometimes at the expense of ourselves.

—EMILIA CLARKE

Casper

Casper is a cross between the very best Drenthe farmer and the serenest Huntington Beach surfer. Café Internationaal's even-keeled blues aficionado, Casper has an irrefutable way with exotic women and possesses tech savvy that is pure wizardry. Casper was the very first person I met by name in Amsterdam – and the first friend I made. Cool as a cucumber, crafty as a pitchman, kindly as a saint; freewheeling and self-confident as a high-priced gigolo - Casper.

He sports a gringo mustache that says "all business." Grown out years before - specifically for holiday in El Salvador. In many ways it was a hit with the Las Flores females. And so, it remained above his upper lip.

Casper is the Café's lawman, the *Wyatt Earp* persona to Michel's *Doc Holliday*. As if donning a six-shooter, Casper handily keeps smarmy hotel guests in check and can show dubious Café patrons the door with the machismo of a cowboy atop his broken-in saddle - belted to a dutiful horse.

Always after dispatching anyone untoward, Casper would usually accentuate the incident by stroking though the jungle of his upper lip without saying a word. Then, giving his patrons the hairy eyeball, Casper would line up the *borrelglaasjes* [shot glasses] and load dangerous con-coctions that no one dared refuse.

In his calculating fashion – for pure sport - Casper always seized the opportunity to play patrons against one another; or at least it seemed that way to me. He once eagerly introduced me to an elderly, seem-ingly stand-offish English gentleman. This was a setup for the conversation that followed - with Casper keen to see which of us could make the other squirm. Although I would always grant concession, buckle to ego, bow to bravado, even endure sharp nips without retaliation, Casper knew that if overly poked at, I would unlikely remain idle.

Before Casper could even fully introduce me, to my chagrin, Sir Snobbingham, as I had silently dubbed him, driveled, *"Who is this gorm-less soul you offer?"*

My very presence seemed to have offended him. Still, the stout, musty, would-be deep thinker made a generous gesture, offering to dumb down his vocabulary for my benefit.

Casper chuckled and then lowered the volume to the Ohio Player's "Fire" just enough for him to hear the heat about to rise.

"Truth be told that Texan cowhands embrace the Queen's English in better form than you British," I floated his way.

Tinhorn took the bait.

"My good boy, you must be joking."

"I should nary joke about the Queen's English, and neither should you," I scolded.

"That is simply chimerical!"

"The only 'chum miracle' I know is the ten-pound (American weight, not British price) Atlantic mackerel that the Miss Rye Harbor's first mate hauled in off of the Isles of Shoals in the Gulf of Maine... "- I quipped in my very best *Hawkeye Pierce*.

From his front-row seat, Casper presented *jenever*, neat, to my mark-in-the-making and a freshly poured *vaasje* to me.

"Fish tales, l-e, not a-i, aside," I explained, "in those glorious days of yore; You remember? Back when you had empire? A gentleman [I demonstrated] would bow and offer 'hallowed to thee.' Well – to this day- deep in the heart of Texas, a man's brim tips and he always offers a hearty, 'Howdy!'."

"Well played, chap."

"Chaps, you mean. That which they don at sunrise and doff at sunset."

"I do say, sir that you have me confounded."

With that, then, I offered you a draw – and I don't mean a gunfight – I mean in the form of a toast. Unless you would like to do shots?"

"...Long live the Queen and all her ships at sea!"

On one lazy Sunday afternoon, enjoying a *vaasje* with regulars, a white cargo van illegally turned and then awkwardly parked right on the Warmoesstraat, its front end wedged on the sidewalk framed by the Café's picture window. Two rather haggard, very fidgety Middle Easterners, donned in all white, quickly exited out and then whisked away from it.

Certain that I was about to die and with not a second to squander, I grabbed for the bell rope and rang it deafeningly loud, sounding the alarm. Casper saw what I did and was already there, simultaneously cranking out *fluitjes, vazen,* and *borrelglazen.* Just as I was getting ready to chug my Heineken, the soft-spoken New Zealander placed his hand on my drinking arm.

"Settle down, mate. Let's you and I and – let's all of us - enjoy this last one." We toasted and drank. Just then, our would-be murderers hurried back to their van, toting huge laundry bags, clutching claim receipts between their teeth.

One peered through the picture window, stopped in his tracks and apparently told his sidekick to do the same. He saw our terrorized looks. Everyone stood dead still. Then, he pointed to the van and said something to his sidekick. They both broke out laughing before he could finish his words. We broke out laughing as well, and we toasted them. Then, they nodded and pointed to us, as if to say, "We had the drop on you, but we have chosen to spare you." Casper played, "Nights in White Satin."

Pairing music with the moment has always been Casper's forte. A Dutch man and the girl he had just met, amazed with her fluency in both English and Cantonese, came in. When he told her that I was a lawyer, she looked at him and said "Loser." He was taken aback, yet impressed with her bold front.

"What can I say; it's a living."

Through her heavy belly laughs that followed, she explained that the word she had spoken was Cantonese for "lawyer." She then choked out, *"You are a loser."* loser."

"I love that part of languages," she said through her laugher. *"How about you, loser?* I lost it. Then everyone around us, even those who had not heard our conversation, started laughing. Someone rang the bell, and the laughter grew.

"Just so you know..." I added, "...I have a lot of close friends who are losers. I put in a lot of hard work and sleepless nights in order to become a loser. My Dad is so proud; Ma knew, from the time I was three, that I would become a loser. She tells everyone she meets about me, her loser son."

The bell rang once again. Just then, Casper pulled up then cranked the Beatles' "I'm a Loser." We celebrated.

> *The ultimate value of life depends upon awareness*
> *and the power of contemplation rather*
> *than upon mere survival.*

> *—ARISTOTLE*

Michelle

Under Michelle's ownership Café Internationaal had revitalized and would thrive in a new millennium. Decisive and self-confident, it was no wonder that Michelle sized me up from the moment we met. To have worked for her, I would have gladly given up being a *"loser"*. I offered up everything to show my gratitude to Michelle and her special place; constantly auditioning for busboy, bar back, bouncer (through the power of words, which generated the strength in numbers), Spanish interpreter, street sweeper, *advocaat* [loser] and on one occasion, plumber.

It was upon my tenth yearly visit when Michelle, into her mid-forties, turned the Café over to Michel and Casper so that she could give birth and take on motherhood.

Dutch-Illiterate, I would seize every opportunity to assume the role of Spanish/English translator, pretending to be Dutch. Shortly after the media-hyped Chilean mine rescue, a party of four of their countrymen checked into the Hotel Internationaal. I assisted Michelle by decreeing the house rules in my pidgin Spanish.

Michelle asked, "What else was that you were telling them?"

"I told them to walk about and enjoy the fresh air... below sea level..."

Tommy

Tommy, "Tommy Boy," is Dutch long and lanky with burnt-red hair. He is easy going has culinary acumen and is typically seen toting provisions for his next kitchen creation. Tommy was vehemently opposed to the smoking bans. The café's version of the UCLA-era Bill Walton, Tommy has precision, talent, and congeniality. He runs the bar like a pro and over time has developed, at least from from my vantage point, the very best pour.

When the Café Internationaal is open, smoking is forbidden. After officially closed, as the last meaty oak chair is propped up onto its heavy table top, smoking is full bore.

Art is the most intense mode of individualism
that the world has known.

—Oscar Wilde

Lieke and Nienke

Lieke and Nienke are virtual twin sisters—yet with alter egos. Lieke is tall and tough yet calm; nibbles at her food; Nienke is petite yet packs a punch and is not shy about throwing it. Keen with/kind to the bright and gentile, they give no quarter whatsoever to mean or meager. Either Lieke or Nienke can hold her beer better than most anyone. I was flattered to be the only person each of them so kindly forewarned to not attempt to keep up with them. And they have such beautiful singing voices. Lieke and Nienke are *Mijn Nederlandse Zusters.*

Nena

Nena swooped in from under the cloud cover and covertly converted Michel. She has the way of sporting her signature glittery burkas; Zeedijk is her runway when she struts her stuff - with her accessorized pet Chihuahua, "Draak", always three regal steps behind and reverently to her right. When she enters the room, it is mystical…

An illuminating and mesmerizing sense of fashion – and edgy superheroine look and swagger, Nena and 'Draak' were determined to reform Michel and his parrot. In the end, either they would be devoted -as one -or Michel would walk the plank.

> *In the early days, we just wore black onstage.*
> *When we introduced white, for variety,*
> *and it simply grew and grew.*

> —FREDDIE MERCURY

Of Note

On my first Amsterdam Monday, I was tooling around the *Spui* (a very Boston Back Bay—tranquil) section of Amsterdam. At high noon, a siren that I had heard many hundreds of times before—from the classic series *The World at War* and other manly war movies—started to wail. Instinctively, I broke into a run, overcome by utter fear and sheer panic at the thought of an air raid. I did not know where to go, so I just kept jittering about, too afraid to even passersby where the shelter was, let alone notice that no one was taking cover. I was shaking and on the verge of wetting myself.

Thankfully, an older family that had just exited a book store noticed me and calmed me down, explaining that it was merely a pre-scheduled, once-a-month test. I had survived my first and only blitzkrieg.

"What were you thinking?" their oldest son asked, obviously both amused and bewildered. I didn't say anything; I was still internally clutching my bladder and catching my racing breath. Instead, I pointed to the sky, and while still sucking air and freaking out, I used charades to demonstrate *Stukas* and *Messerschmitts*. From the small crowd that gathered around, I heard *Luftwaffe*. Someone put his hand on my back and said something in Dutch and then in English. "*You're safe. The war is over. Well. It least that one is.*" With that, the crowd dispersed, many of them turning back to look at me with bewilderment.

When I finally gathered myself, determining that it was time for me head to the Café, an elderly gentleman approached me and told me that while I was given a warning before a bombing that did not happen, it was important that I know how during the war, many small cities and towns were bombed without any warning—its most ancient, *Nijmegen*, tragically by mistake – from *American B-24 Liberators*.

These important Amsterdam moments and meaningful Dutch connections filled me with a sense of belonging – moved by the Dutch duality—tolerance vs. sensibility, kindness vs. frugality. Old ways vs. new ideas. It invigorated me and validated my views.

> *Much of the Netherlands lies considerably*
> *below sea level, as you well know…*
> *the country of the ingenious, resourceful, and doughty Dutch*
> *has literally been born of the sea.*
>
> —Joseph B. Wirthlin

On hump day of my trip, I traveled from Amsterdam to Baarle-Nassau, located in the Brabant Province in South of the Netherlands, to visit HAAGEN FTP (Fire Training Products). This small factory featured a state-of-the-art fire simulator, which I experienced. Donning full Dutch turnout gear, I walked in room in which insipient fire, a textbook rollover, a menacing flashover, and a blood-curdling, pre-backdraft were replicated. It was perfectly safe yet more real-life than many of the fire conditions I had encountered. Unlike "real" fire,

HAAGEN's superheated chamber could be rendered extinguished and completely ventilated into the countryside in fewer than five seconds. HAAGEN's fire-training equipment is the very best in the world.

The town that the factory surrounded is a cartologist's conundrum. While technically situated within the Netherlands, there are pockets of Belgian territory within. Depending upon one's nationality these are either Enclaves or Exclaves; and upon what side of the street, one would could be standing upon sovereign Belgian soil. In some houses, families eat their meals in Belgium, yet sleep in the Netherlands.

The very day I visited was the christening of HAAGEN FTP's soon-to-be completed addition. The boss, who reminded me of my fire chief, presided over the festivities. Warm but firm, "The Chief" was genuinely loved and highly respected. Thankfully I wore a suit. Embraced and treated like an honored guest, attending that special occasion was one of my proudest moments in the fire service and as an American.

One of the technicians pulled me aside and proudly said, "I'm pleased that you were able to experience our products. They are perfectly safe but when you train with them you will forget that. They teach you how to react 'life or death' way. I can tell your adrenaline is still up from "*de kachel*".

The greatest danger for most of us lies not in
setting our aim too high and falling short, but in
setting our aim low, and achieving our mark.

—MICHELANGELO

On my second to the last day of my trip. I met Lars, a poet from Rotterdam. Lars was a gangly, somewhat sickly type, much like David J. Gallant, who had been my collegiate counterbalance, roommate, and treasured friend. David had been raised in the Fall River area and was Portuguese/Italian American. Like Lars, he was a Beatles aficionado and a poetry man. If the similarly wan look weren't enough, Lars and Dave shared a deep passion for baseball and all of its nuances of perfection and symmetry, optimism, tension, and resolve.

They each had played the game at early ages - had good bats, great gloves and cannon arms. They each had a thing for showing photos from their Little League years, almost identically posed in batters' stances. Above everything, they exuded measures of self-confidence that were off-set by self-deprecation, yet often hard to tell whether it was lamentful or tongue-in-cheek. Like David, Lars had a long fuse and could handle himself in just about any situation without ever having to come to blows. Sitting with Lars took me back to my Back-Bay days with David.

Although David was usually under the weather, only once did I fear his death. It was early one spring morning, when I awoke to find his face contorted into a blood-soaked pillow. I freaked out and grabbed him by his hair. He awoke and flung the novel and red, felt-tip pen to which he had been clinging, catching me on the bridge of my nose, which of course began to bleed. The felt-tip had bled out onto his pillowcase, pillow, and mattress.

After things settled down, and just before someone on the dorm floor fired up a sunrise "doob", I professed, "*Better red and unread than dead.*" Through pasty sleep-breath, fanning the smoke seeping in from the hallway from his face, he fired back, "Okay, Joseph Comrade, bleeding heart of darkness." Just then, our dorm's daily alarm clock sounded. On a rooster's cue, our resident half-crazed, 'steroid-embalmed, Division III -College Football, (free) outside linebacker, in fortississimo{*fff*}, butchered the bridge to Billy Joel's "*Uptown Girl.*"

*Personalized beauty is about each woman
being able to create her own makeup routine
that complements her coloring and style.*

—Bobbi Brown

Lars was clutching an orange, worn, frayed, Italian leather-bound pocket notebook. I asked him about it and he told me that it contained the bulk of his poetry. He proudly added, "I am a writer, I am the Poet of Rotterdam." I pulled out my ninety-nine-cent, spiral mini-notepad onto the bar, removed the dog-eared sheaf of notes and slips and cards, and slid the orange Walgreens special over like an upturned ace, so close to the notebook, raising the ante; in a gesture that was three-quarters soli-darity and one-quarter satire, I professed, "I, too, am a writer – I came here to tell a story – So, I call dibs – I am the Poet of Amsterdam."

"Franco, you can be today's Poet of Amsterdam, but otherwise, Albert Verwey is the poet of Amsterdam." Michel concurred as he was double pouring.

Lars, barely above a whisper said, "I didn't want to spoil your excite-ment; but Michel is correct."

"Here, poets. These are on me." Michel quipped as he plopped down twee vazen.

"Never mind about all this trivia...." Lars now sidestepped as he twirled his glass a few times. "Proost!"

"Now, let's talk about your poetry."

With all of this, the cheeky bravado, side-stepping and refocus on the written word, I was clearly having a David J. Gallant, Dorm room Déjà vu...

"Have you asked yourself what is really compelling you to write 'Al Basha'? What are your motives, Franco? You are not the first person to come to this city in search of your words; you have the potential to be in great company. But you need to dig deep, just like John Locke did when he found refuge here. Otherwise, your story will consist of only those two words."

I told Lars about Umair and "Al Basha" and the edict/mandate. Lars gave me a true poet's take. "Writing histories only gets you so far; it will document the chaos but not much else. Maybe Umair is trying to get you past a certain point; my guess is beyond where he is now. If that is the case, you must appeal to your personal anthropology. Merely recounting the events in Umair's and your life will leave you adrift. You must be will-ing to go deeper and confront your human side."

Lars was right. Simply chronicling commonalities between my life and Umair's would not free my own years of self-created torment, untreated emotional wounds, and self-destructive personal life. Umair wanted more from – and for – me.

Through the rhythm of Café Internationaal, we drank and talked, and I wrote it all down. Lars asked, "Is all of this going in your book?"

"No, Lars, my book is going into all of this. You have opened my eyes and widened my view. I am no longer overwhelmed. I'm excited about this process..."

Many hours and *vazen* later, Lars confessed that he needed to apologize to me, that he had not been entirely open with me. With the click of my pen, I pushed my inked-up notepad aside, out of arm's reach, and then showed that my hands were empty.

I sounded this click many times before when criminally charged clients were about to honestly, truthfully confess their sins. Yet in most cases, those were the moments when they were about to retract lies that they had sworn on their mothers' lives or mothers' graves or their children; what was no longer "the God's honest truth." Throughout my years of taking confessions, the first version was usually garbage - and for sheer comedic, tension-relieving value, I would play it up as if I believed every line; with unclicked pen miming away, feverishly non-writing, nodding my head, and acknowledging its symmetry - all the while in anticipation of the trap tripping and the folly falling. Why waste the ink and paper on nonsensical yammer? Why rub it into those whose liberty was slipping away?

But this certainly was none of that. Had Lars transformed himself, through his own transformative advice to me?

Out of respect - not disbelief, what I was about to hear would not be memorialized. Summoning up my legal very best, I owed it to Lars to reciprocate with solid advice, get him out of his mess and form a plan to handle whatever harm he had caused. While I never drank on the clock, it was commonplace to meet up with my colleagues at a bar and talk about cases and trial strategy; I have handed out my business cards and even given consultations in many a men's bathroom, whilst either sitting and standing. Once, a cop happened to be sitting on the toilet between a prospective client and me. He agreed to pass my card, but groveled for a referral fee.

I was now in my comfort zone. Sensing that this was something that Lars had been holding on to for some time, I pressed him. "So, Lars, who did you kill?" I pondered whether it was over funny money that some decade-dead body in the Zeedijk Canal was now being dredged up.

Perhaps his dirty deed was not done? Was he running a sweat shop? Was it something that I would regret knowing? What was Lars's skeleton in the closet?

How strange that over my trip, although I had yet to meet anyone from Rotterdam, I formed a secondhand opinion - by adopting others' views. It seemed that Amsterdam stood in relation to Rotterdam how my cherished Boston stood to New York City.

Amsterdammers generally seemed to relish in and soak up their places in the world, enjoying their exalted status, among the cobblestone streets, footbridges, and canals in the very cradle of the Netherlands, much like Bostonians, who bounced around "Bean Town," the "Hub of the Universe." Not trying to be too big or bright, Bostonians were content to be down and dirty yet without the overbearingness that New Yorkers put out there. The Boston- Amsterdam vibe was for me: exuding self-confidence and when in doubt, charm.

Those from Rotterdam, so it seemed, carried chips on their shoulders with what I interpreted as Big Apple attitudes. Unlike New Yorkers, these Dutch got a pass from me. Rotterdam, after all, was horribly devastated during the war. Sheer terror rolled in from the Eastern skies and obliterated the city – primarily to make a point. In this sense, the City Amsterdam had it much less worse.

Lars was my client – and even I had not punched in, the one-word order of day- each day in Café Internationaal and around Amsterdam was *gezellig*. It was only proper that I grant Lars, the Poet of Rotterdam, safe passage -and *vaasje* on my tab - to confess in confidence.

Was it sexual deviance, Ponzi-style larceny, or, indeed, that dead body in the canal? Not that any of this would have fazed me. Such transgressions were my bread and butter, and rather routine. In fact, most criminal fact patterns had come to bore me.

There is the little-known enigma of the area probate and tax law. While dusty and dreary on the surface, the reality is that between the lines of many ledgers and wills are unspeakable crimes – exploitation – deprivation – connivery and cruelty, covered over by well-drafted papers; often committed by those who "seemed so normal". Which of his decrepit relatives had Lars swindled? Even after running through at least fifty scenarios – quasi covers of tunes I had already heard - my respect for Lars – and his mystique greatened. And he was in very good hands.

His silence finally broke.

Lars confided that during the war, his Aunt, then in her late teens, while riding her bicycle, encountered a German soldier; this appar-ently terrible thing happened on a misty, cool, pre-dawn morning. The patrolling German soldier detained Lars's Aunt and then searched her belongings. He eventually uncovered her contraband; she was distributing underground newspapers. Lars's Aunt was doomed. As Lars told me of this, I became paralyzed with her fear.

Then my mind wandered. I envisioned some old German war vet-eran, found dead with a newspaper rolled up and shoved into his slit throat; a seventy-years-late special delivery from Lars. The Rotterdam necktie. I was way off.

Lars described how that soldier set his terms for his dear Aunt's release: He would let her go in exchange for one kiss. Lars became emo-tional and asked for my forgiveness, as he then grew so very sad. He turned away and shook his head from side to side, clearly overwhelmed by this personal shame.

He took a deep breath and told me that his Aunt kissed the German soldier. Even worse, she had gone on to tell this to her family, of this "terrible thing" that she had done.

The lawyer emerged and summed up that Lars's Aunt was a lot stronger and more self-assured than that German soldier. And whether it was her first kiss, I was glad that it wasn't her last. My take was that the German soldier was likely more afraid and confused than Lars's Aunt. If he had been a heartless marauder, he would have turned her in or attempted worse. Of course, that move might have cost him - she might have slit his throat…

I re-ran the facts of the case and I just couldn't see this one Lars's way. For me, it was peanuts; if this was of some scarlet letter theme, its font was microscopic.

Lars looked at me and gestured for me to say something. Gezzelig and Lars's earlier advice to me dictated what I was about to say.

"Lars, your Aunt was very brave to fight with the underground. As for what she did? All I can tell you is that, had it been me in her shoes, who knows what I would have done. A dead-to-rites- spy? Jesus, Lars…. If had been in her shoes, to save my ass I would have bent over and offered it, and I mean it - and hope that doing so would spare the rest of me".

"This is what I believe, Lars. That German soldier probably had no intention of taking your Aunt in. He probably had only two things on his mind, just like any other soldier: getting back home and romance. Your Aunt betrayed no one; I consider it a war's version of a love story."

"And as for soldier boy - he either survived the war, in which case I am sure that he lived out his days thankful that he had not turned your Aunt in; or he did not - in which case hopefully his last thought was of that cool, misty morning and his warm embrace with an intrepid and determined Dutch woman, whose life he spared."

"That is the important human side of your family's war story. It's what really counts…and I trust I recounted it as you have taught me…Did I tell her story?

"So Lars, the poet and teacher of Rotterdam, let us drink to your Aunt, but first, you must kiss me."

Lars laughed through tears; I cried through my laughter.
Then Lars asked me, "Do you have any war stories you might share with me? Aside from yesterday's air raid?"

Somehow, my only World War II legacy, which I experienced when I was six years old, unhinged from my memory. It was one of the only times that I can remember going to Ma's home, where she and her twelve siblings were born and raised and where my Gramma Chiveta and two of Ma's siblings lived until their passing.

My Uncle Richard was at the kitchen table with a dusty glass of milk in front of him. It was warmed-over and scummy. He just sat there, with his left elbow on the table, palm cupping his chin, silently staring into space and acknowledging nothing. I remember stretching out my hand to shake his, and as I got closer, I could smell him. He was wearing his army fatigues, which had an unforgettable odor, it was dank and exuded thick danger. It stayed in my nose - and when I opened my mouth to breath, it went on my tongue. Every time I breathed it, bad, unrecognizable thoughts came into my head.

On the ride home, Ma answered the question I was too afraid to ask. She confided that her brother, Richard, whom I would never see again, had fought at Guadalcanal. Before the war, he had been a dancer and singer; he was "a live wire and quite the ladies' man." When I asked Ma how the war could take all of that from him and not give it back- at least after some time passed - Ma explained, "You're smart, but you may still be too young to understand this: It's because he saw horrible things. And what he saw - it broke his heart; and none of us around him could fix it."

Taking a page out of my "time-to-break-the-tension" playbook, Lars barbed: "On a happier note, What about you, Franco? Have you ever come close to dying?"

The First time: I was eleven, working on an upstate New Hampshire hay farm. The farm family's eldest, rather limited sophomore son, Michael and I took a break. I jumped atop and sat on the tractor's huge tire and tried to talk with him. But there was nothing we could talk about. He didn't understand a word I said and what came out of his mouth left me speechless. Without warning, he fired up the engine and popped the clutch. In his limited mind, he envisioned me being thrown off and away. Instead, Newton worked once again; I rolled down the tire and the tire rolled toward me. I distinctly recall making the choice to live rather than die, pushing against the treads as I tuck-rolled over my fat stomach out and away to safety. My nose scuffed by the tie's rubber and my knee bruised when it flopped onto a rock, I was too shaken up to say or do anything while he begged -and without waiting for me to stop shaking threatened me - not to tell on him.

The Second time: I was in high school. Two of my friends and I were sitting on top of our dopy friend's father's beater. Joe Clogham, the would-be grim-reaper, had just gotten his driver's license and was showing off his newfound freedom in the form of his Dad's boat of a car. My two fellow-doomed and I were camped out on the massive hood, playfully mocking this wood-panel doored hunk of junk.

Oblivious to its power and having also apparently no concept of basic physics, Joe decided to take off and run circles around the parking lot.

We hung on for dear life. Specifically, I hung on to the bases of the windshield wiper arms with all of my might, while the others stacked on top of me. Once again, it was gas engine against me; but this time, the "tuck and roll" was not the correct answer. We were too scared to scream out. As I clung to those nubs, my blubbery flesh endured four death grips. After three or four laps, he slammed on the brakes. I became their airbag, as they smashed my girth into the windshield. Master Clogham, finally realizing how close he had come to manslaughter times three, ran off...forgetting to put the death-jalopy into Park.

The Third time: I was in college, driving through Providence, Rhode Island, with the rest of our debate team during a horrendous snowstorm. Everyone but our designated driver, David, was feeling no pain. All of a sudden, his Olds Cutlass – gifted from his Uncle Nunzi – a Zero Mostel and Jack Benny hybrid - which required engaging both the foot and parking brake - in a "gate and feather" tandem, skidded out, spun, and corkscrewed into the path of a bucket-equipped public utility truck. The last thing I heard was its horn, playing Fanfare for Doppler. The next thing I saw was it sliding by our death trap, as we were both faced in the same direction. I could feel it - the pocket of air between it and us- somehow killed our engine, but not us. The only thing I could think of was that most famous iceberg eviscerating the Titanic's belly.

The four of us, our two university debate teams, finished first and sec-ond, 8–0 each, one point apart. My machine versus me record was now 3-0.

Denial ain't just a river in Egypt.

—MARK TWAIN

The Fourth time: I was atop a roof fighting my first of three consecutive New Year's Eve house fires. Our Truck Company was ordered to ventilate the roof. Just when we had finished our last cut, fire shot from the eaves, and the roof started to buckle. I flung the still-running Stihl saw down the roofline to the open ground. It stuck with its blade into a dormant tulip bed and then flopped onto its back, leaking and bleeding out oil and gas. Our other two crew members dove for the ladder, riding its side rails to the ground. I set my sights on an evergreen tree, springing myself up and out, using the corner gutter, and successfully landed on a canapé, with just the right give and take. Once we were all accounted for, we laughed our asses off. I had already pissed my bunker gear; the other two falsely denied crapping themselves.

12. Fully involved house— Limited visibility

The Fifth and most recent time: It was on a splendid midsummer Sunday afternoon, I was at home gardening, when my focus was shifted from basil to an arrestee - courtesy of the lockup keeper at the Calumet City Police Department. After gathering the necessary information, I called his hard-of-hearing, incomprehensible retired steel mill worker father from the number written into the dirt with my hand spade. I was to meet dear old dad, who sounded like he was half in the bag, at his home to secure my retainer then head to the station. I showered my precious herbs and then got myself ready.

In less than twenty minutes I arrived at a tucked-away, squalid, dilapidated, brick bungalow that had seen much better days. Just as I entered, the father, donning a frayed winter pajama top and decades-old, saggy Fruit of the Looms, apologizing for the odor of his fresh bowel movement, grabbed what I presume he thought was air freshener and hit the dust-caked dining room, just under the greasy, tilted-over ceiling fan. I squinted out "Black Flag" through the grimy air. Reverting to firefighter survival training, as my eyes and inner ears burned, I held my breath for a solid minute sticking my face into the armpit and my ripped open shirt, to receive a fistful of clammy tens and fives, which he insisted on counting.

When the sergeant met me at lock-up door, he took one look at me and said: "You look green - and smell like my jag-off know-it-all, brother-in-law the frickin' exterminator of the family...and boy do I hate that him...What a complete tool!"

Every strike brings me closer to the next home run.

—BABE RUTH

Lars remained speechless. After a healthy swig of his *vaasje*, he said, "You have much work to do, Phoenix.... or maybe you have cat blood..."

I retorted, "Well. I do like *Gato* Barbieri...You may be onto something, Doctor." With that we said our goodbyes.

The next morning, my last day in Amsterdam, I paid an obligatory visit.

Let parents bequeath to their children not riches,
but the spirit of reverence.

—PLATO

It had been years since I thought of Joey Lark, his quirky decency and good nature, his story of having fallen prey to betrayal and cruelty would come back to me at Anne Frank House.

Upon my arrival, a small group of us was attentively formed by the museum staff and then ushered in. We stayed together and grew close over our journey. At the ground floor, we gestured to the elders of our group, Ruk and Noshi - from Pakistan, to lead our way and set our pace; throughout our ascent, we extended the time and space for the young French parents to explain things to their children, whose image of hope the rest of us were so fortunate to have before us.

> *To us, the ashes of our ancestors are sacred*
> *and their resting place is hallowed ground.*
>
> —*Chief Seattle*

While on an upper floor, my raw eyes caught a framed black-and-white photograph hanging on the wall between two picture windows. I studied it; then, as my senses made the connection, yet before I could fully process it, I began to retch. That picture of the SS regiment marching down a cobblestone street had been taken from right where I was now standing. The stones in the picture were like a comparison print to the latent ones I could clearly see two stories right below.

Now thrown back-in-time, to bear witness to the perversion of the rule of law was more than I could handle. Pondering what I would have done and what I would have had the courage to do, left me vulnerable.

I was breaking apart.

Barely able to breathe, overcome with fear, I could not keep the strength in my legs. I slumped to the floor in terror and began to cry. Those children rushed over to rescue me and helped bring me back. They each took hold of one of my hands for the duration; my little fellow firefighters.

When our group's time came to an end, our elders wished all of us peace and happiness, and we, in turn, extended their wishes to each other and back to them. We started to walk away, rather awkwardly, then stopped, turned around, and embraced each other one last time.

As I returned to the Café for the final time before my return to Chicago, I recalled how Joey Lark, like Anne Frank, was always so perceptive when it came to other people's feelings. When he really wanted you to take his advice, he would soften his tone and preface his words with "Dis is what I just said to my udder friend; so I'm gonna tell you da same 'ting."

To be trusted is a greater compliment than being loved.

—GEORGE MACDONALD

I did not want to leave Amsterdam. I had said good-bye to all of my friends, except Casper with whom I stayed and helped shut down, with whom I smoked and drank until it was time. Casper finally said, "Franco, you have to go, for now."

We embraced and I left. I took in every step from the Café back to my hotel. This was no good-bye. This was "hello," "hold that thought," "I shall return," "you're coming with me," and so on.

I was overcome with good thoughts of how I would feel upon my return.

I kept it together until I got to the lobby of the hotel. My cab driver and the hotel staff waited. We all began to cry.

Under this whirl of emotions, I was eyes wide open at Schiphol with that same buzz that tingled me upon my arrival, which seemed so long before. Although completely out of it through passport inquiry, boarding, and flight, my dreams were swirling with real stories and a firm resolve, as Lars put it, to confront my human side.

Until I returned to Centraal Station, that would be my freshly swept, glistening cobblestone path.

CHAPTER XX

RETURNING THE FAVOR

You know capital is not patriotic.
Capital goes where it needs to go to get a return.

—Steve Stivers

After clearing customs, reacting with bitter-sweetness to the US Customs Agent's "Welcome Home," my flip-phone finally up and running, I had to reach out to Shawnee and tell him that he was my prophet. I had to tell him about Lars and "*Al Basha*" and how I had been touched by the City of Amsterdam and the Dutch ways.

He answered, "Counselor!" I told him that I was at O'Hare. With a smile in his voice, Shawnee replied, "What time does your flight leave, Counselor?"

"Funny how I feel like I'm still there, like I haven't left," I replied.

"You never will, Counselor. I know Amsterdam gave you the permission to find the person you want to be. And I know that you are going to see '*Al Basha*' through. You just keep writing, Counselor."

"I owe you, Shawnee."

"Hey, Counselor. You've always had my back, solid. And you trusted in me to have yours. I have always said what I meant and always meant what I said. You always respected that aspect of me. And that's what you and I are all about; trust and respect. Brother my brother."

Litigation: A machine which you go into as a pig and come out of as a sausage.

—Ambrose Bierce

As soon as I got to baggage claim, my flip-phone started ringing unmercifully. Using my upturned suitcase as a makeshift desk and my baggage claim tickets as my legal pad, I took a dozen calls, writing down names, inmate numbers, case numbers, and charge details. I made follow-up calls to lockups, loved ones, potential bail sureties, and clients in need. I was telephonically invoking rights and making appointments as my lonely suitcase circled like a roulette ball. I was all alone in an empty claim area, but for two circles by the drug-sniffing beagle.

This sudden gear-shifting and the overload of information produced the shakes. That carousel started to give me the spins. This deluge of potential cases, a wave of new clients, issues, court dates fees threw me around. I shook out of it by thinking like a Dutch merchant; the ledger showed that the following year's trip to Amsterdam had already been paid for.

Like clockwork, after every return from Amsterdam that followed, calls, texts, and e-mails, wire transfers and credit card payments would pour as the beagle and I exchanged warm, familiar greetings in baggage over every year.

As I lumbered my way down I-294, my body began to act like a passenger's and not a driver's. I was having a tough time holding myself together; only by hyper-focusing while employing vagal maneuvers [bearing down] did I make it home without incident. I should have pulled over. This would be the last time that the Amsterdam-bound I would drive myself to/ navigate the jet-lag squall from O'Hare. I hired Sir Isaac Dixon within a week after my return. He laughed with appreciation when I scheduled and paid for his services a year in advance. Sir Isaac Dixon would be a special part of every one of my yearly Amsterdam journeys to follow – and so many other special events...

With my ass now dragging, I was able to somehow stow myself away from Erin and into my cozy basement guest bed, embrace my excited children and our kitten, Dan, with big hugs and bigger kisses. I held them close until they wiggled away careful not wake me; giving me permission to finally pass out.

I had scheduled a trial for the morning after my return. It must have made sense at the time. Now working against me were three demons: confusing jet lag, slightly mitigated sleep deprivation and a lingering, synergistic-like effect. Too much of me was still in Amsterdam. For my body clock and squinty eyes, this was a midnight-in-Amsterdam trial. Otherwise routine, the trial commenced with an oddly intense morning sun, which drenched the courtroom. Exhausted, transformed, and enlightened, I could feel a convergence form, between my familiar, professional self and my thoughts of Amsterdam. Freed up from shallow inhibitions, through my story-telling perspective, I was determined not to let go of "*Al Basha*" or Amsterdam.

For the first time in over a week, I would be called into the adversarial process. My prepared trial outline dictated how to attack the witness, yet my gut told me, "Al Basha"/Amsterdam. Trusting my gut, I abandoned the outline. My cross-examination of the state's star witness, a seasoned police officer, would be unlike any of my thousands before. I chose not to confront him, not even brush against him. Instead, I engaged him in an unassuming, cozy manner, as if he and I had just met and were enjoying a *vaasje* at the café. Through this Dutch cross-examination method, that officer became an eager participant in the conversation. With each inviting question, cross-examination took the form of a cobblestoned, canal-bordered street. With the city of Amsterdam under his feet, he eagerly responded and just could not hold back.

Wanting to savor this spiritual moment, I slowed things down. He and I may as well have been outside of the Café having a smoke. Cross-examination was an open discussion, with his candid answers inviting the questions that followed; creating a highly usual record. In due time, we neared the inevitable—the irrefutable wall that was closing in. To have let him hit it would have been cheap and unkind *zonder*[without] *gezellig*. After all, this was our moment to share.

Under this Midwest pre-spring, summer-like sun, this trial was a validation of "*Al Basha*", the power of story-telling, the virtue of Amsterdam and the soul of Café Internationaal. It was one of the many good conversations about self-recognition, character, candor and redemption I had had over the previous week.

"Officer, what do you think about the case?"

PROSECUTOR: Wait a minute. Hold on a minute. This is crazy. I have to object.

JUDGE: It is crazy. Basis?

PROSECUTOR: It…it…it calls for a legal conclusion.

JUDGE: I think it calls for something more than just that; your objection is overruled… Officer?

WITNESS: Counselor. I think your client is not guilty. She is not innocent, but who is? With all due respect to the Court, I'm just a cop, I'm not a Judge, but I'm telling you, Your Honor, that the counselor here got it right. Again, with all due respect, Your Honor, you really should find the defendant not guilty.

The Judge rested both sides and waived all argument; bypassing – actually, taking out of the game- both the State and me.

This case would be the Judge's finest hour. In an otherwise routine matter, His Honor rendered a ruling hardly so – it was as profound and poetic as any United Supreme Court Justice's. Perhaps the Court had traveled to Amsterdam.

Though I could not be with my friends in Café Internationaal, this trial was just about the next best thing. Perhaps its spirit, personal connections and meaningful moments could be substituted for aggressive trial tactics and legal palliations after all?

As I walked out of the courthouse, familiar second-guessing started to kick in. Was this not another just verdict, rendered in that Midwest populist way? Had today not simply wooed me back into the good graces of my old, usual ways? Could I not find an Amsterdam right here?

The early March weather was unseasonably warm and dry. While I was driving under full control, the scatter from the day before began to creep in. I did not know what to hold on to and what to let go of. I tabled these questions, welcoming the distraction of my next order of business. There I would surly reacclimate – the buzz of "March Madness" would surely clear my head and reset my thoughts.

Contrast is what makes photography interesting.

—CONRAD HALL

My stop was a local watering hole, "The Fifth Quarter", my fire department's designated bar. I was to meet Kane and buy him lunch—liquid, solid, or a combination. Technically, this was a gesture of thanks for Kane's willingness to have "covered" any calls forwarded from my office while I was away in Amsterdam. It was a total of zero, not counting one wrong number. Not one call came in—not one arrestee, suspect, warrant surrender, offender—nothing.

Perhaps by running things down with Kane, friend and former fellow prosecutor, drawing on his prairie perspective, he would help me sort all of this out.

Kane had missed a list of callings: coach, farmer, professor, ballroom dancer, cop, or perhaps even Pacific Northwest pothead. He was one of the best basketball players I had ever played with (who never took it easy on me) and he was quite a tennis player (who took it very easy on me). Kane and I are from different upbringings. His cleverness is unassuming, with a twang on irony's sharpest edge. *Norman Rockwellian* raised, Kane is nonetheless street-smart and politically savvy with just the right touch of cynicism.

Contrasted with my blazing fire is Kane's carefully measured flame and steady fuel supply; particularly when faced with the stupidity of others. When I might scream, Kane always laughs. Only when crowded in on past his certain point, as if with basketball in hand, will Kane "take it into the paint" with ferocity. Once unleashed – no matter where or why, Kane's elbows will nip, he will draw the foolish foul and sink the toughest of shots, - ala John "Hondo" Havlicek.

This is no wonder, considering that Kane is a documented, direct descendant of William of Orange.

Kane's princely son, Max, proves how adversity builds character. Like his Dad, Max too missed his calling. Max is a throwback to a different time and place. He is the reincarnation of Robert Gould Shaw. He once said asked Kane, "Why did I come out of Mom's belly? I love you more than her."

While hanging with Max one day, waiting on Kane to saddle up for Court, I sat in the front room's easy chair, witnessing a battle unfolding atop an Oriental rug. I surely recognized this amphibious landing, with plastic pirates crushing the unsuspecting stuffed animals of various shapes and sizes. I watched Max circle the manned watercraft in and from the Persian rug sea and cut through the unsuspecting ranks on the fringed shore's edge. I remarked to myself, obviously loudly enough for Max to hear. "The Inchon Landing?"

Max got up from the floor, walked over to me, touched me, and said, "You are in the wrong war. This is the Battle of Roanoke Island. Burnside led his men." He pointed to the strewn about monkeys (the 'barrel full of' genus), adding, "Those Horses drowned. These are the battles that you must win. My Grampa was in the First Division."

Just before Kane and I left, Max decreed in a solemn way, far beyond his age: "Dad, when you die, I want to die too."

I looked to Kane and declared: "Max, if your Dad goes, we all will go." Max cheered: "Okay!"

I've got a great ambition to die of exhaustion rather than boredom.

—Thomas Carlyle

The closest thing I came to a forced march began exactly a year later, on the morning I was scheduled to return to Chicago from Amsterdam on what would be my early Christmas. As if heralding Santa in, I had been up all night, playing. On a shower, having meticulously pre-packed, by the time I got to Schiphol, I was ready for my visions of sugar plums - waiting the dance out, until I was in the air and leveled off over the Atlantic.

My fellow passengers kept me awake with their flight delay angst-filled, bitter chatter now into its third hour. I was determined to stay awake, certain that my self-discipline would deliver runway-to-runway deep sleep. While all of my fellow passenger's complaining turn to snores, I forced myself to stay awake, which turned into a state of sleep-deprived delirium. By the fourth hour, I was hearing voices and unable to keep any one skewed thought from its next or the one before.

Finally, we boarded the plane. I was back in economy, but when the business class flight attendant saw my tenor sax, she smiled and said, "Saxophone man, follow me." She brought me to a business class seat, offered to stow my tenor then set me up with two glasses of quite tasty midmorning champagne. I threw them back and poised myself for a transatlantic coma. Just as I licked my lips, slipped back and passed out to the new age boarding music soundtrack, the announcement was made: my flight had been canceled.

There I was, hardly able to control myself. All those around me reacted with outrage; I was the only passenger who was shuddering with uncontrollable joy.

They were immersed in panic - about logistics, ruined plans and missed connections. I could empathize with none of it. Instinctively, I grabbed my belongings, tossed back what was in random glasses from tray tables in my path. Rearmed with my tenor, I attached myself to the flight crew, playing the part of crew liaison and exited in lockstep. As I stayed a half step behind theirs, I said to the third pilot, "Thank you so much; you have no idea how happy you have made me."

With its newest member, our crew made its way out of the gate; the flight attendant/saxophone trustee grabbed my arm and insisted that I not wait in line at the hotel. She gave me some sort of pass code to present to the hotel's front desk personnel while pointing to the "flight crew" tag she had fixed to my Sax-Pak; She pulled out a pen, grabbed my hand and wrote the code on it. "The rest is up to you." It had the makings of something out of Penthouse Forum.

Own only what you can always carry with you:
know languages, know countries, and know
people. Let your memory be your travel bag.

—ALEKSANDR SOLZHENITSYN

I drifted back, needing a slow pace to process all of this. Finally geared up, I moved ahead through the terminal. Honing in on a Frenchman, stating his case for an upgrade from economy class to business class, because his Monte Carlo-bound flight, too, had been canceled, I stopped, looked and listened. He kept upping the ante, demanding and was granted more and more from the acquiescing customer service representative. Now fixated on his poker-play, I grabbed a pen and wrote on my clean hand every word of his pitch. After pushing the envelope to its bitter end, a higher up finally stepped in and said, "No more." He said not a word. Catching my gaze, he shot me a wink. I nodded, then bowed with praise.

Intent on redelivering his script, I shook off the bubbly's effects and made my way to my carrier's desk, making sure to show just enough of - but not too much of that flight crew sticker. I aped Frenchie's every move and then went over the top. Walking away with a return flight first class seat upgrade from my business class seat and free round-trip business class seat for next year's flight, I pre-booked the flight right then and there. With two confirmation codes now in hand, it was then off to the hotel, to grab a shower, find whatever wind I was on - then head to the city.

In response to my first year's departure day neurosis, I made a mental note to always prepare a to-do list and tape it to the inside of my hotel room door upon arriving. This would become ritual. The list began and ended with "PASSPORT." Ever the document hoarder, I had stuffed the handy treatise into my jacket pocket ten hours before after what was now my first of two Amsterdam hotel checkouts.

How lovely was reposting the tattered document, reusing its still-tacky tape, onto the inside door of my comped out, metro-swanky, hotel room. Once refreshed, I made my way to the elevator, encased in glass - ala the Jetsons - with an overhead view of the atrium banquet room below. As I descended, my recognizable fellow travelers, now waiting with number cards to dig into the conga-line-presented food trays, pointed up to me, as if I were a caged zoo animal about to be ceremoniously released to the wild. I beckoned them – any one of them - to join me back to the city. They all shook their heads and waived. As I exited the elevator, the dutiful flight attendant, who I later learned had secured that luxury suite for me, grabbed my arm and she said, "Hey. At least you can promise me that you will make it back and not miss your flight. Hmm?"

In reply to my nonverbal lack of commitment, she said, "You are still part of this crew. And I - we all- like you. All of us have to make the flight, in seventeen hours. And so will you."

And so would I.

With that, it was back to Amsterdam and back to Café Internationaal. When I had boarded the tram, I became overwhelmed when I noticed that I was the only passenger - and that it was the first time for me - to be Centraal Station bound, completely empty-handed. Free as a bird, I rejoined my friends at the Café to celebrate early Christmas and drink to Santa for the best gift I had ever received.

By the time I returned to Schiphol, sometime after four in the morning, the thread by which I had been hanging was about to disintegrate.

I do recall stopping in my tracks - on a dime- when I heard a distinctively authoritative whistle blow. I was approached by armed guards, who demanded that I account for my whereabouts. Slumping, all I could muster was a point to the hotel. They ordered me to produce my passport. I once again pointed. Unable to lift my head, I said, "Officers, are you familiar with the expression 'I hit the wall'?"

One of them asked, "Are you American?"

"Yes."

"Please continue."

I then explained what it meant and that I was there.

"When are you scheduled to depart Schiphol?" His opening gave me my sixth wind.

"Originally earlier today, which technically was yesterday, but that changed to tomorrow; which is technically today."

They lowered their weapons and laughed.

I now held the floor – so I thought- and continued on as to how I had had the remarkably good fortune of having my flight canceled. I then asked if they had encountered any of my fellow passengers in such a way. One of the guards commented in understandable Dutch that my fellow passengers had been swarming customer service, foolishly complaining, all afternoon – on full stomachs - but that was many hours ago, and all of them, all of whose requests and such were completely denied, were now sound asleep.

"They obviously don't celebrate early Christmas," I quipped, as I stumbled a bit.

The guard in charge offered one of his men to assist me back to my room. I replied, "Your generosity is appreciated, but assuredly unnecessary. I am 10-4."

"Well, then, Santa Claus. Please go to your room. Set your alarm. And do not, under any circumstances, miss your sleigh-ride back to Chicago.

It leaves in less than five hours. Be out of your room in a solid three. Are we 10-4?"

The last word was theirs.

I skulked my way back to the hotel, they bantered about "hit the wall" and "10-4", referencing American action movies.

When the blaring alarm clock sounded, I was laying back in a desk chair. I had no idea where I was. The bed was never touched. I went through my trusty punch list a dozen times. Now completely glazed over, I somehow made it to the gate. Sputtering on fumes and now unable to hold on, like the day before I simply refused to pass out. I was awakened by my angel flight attendant, who lifted my chin to make sure it was me. She lugged me onto the plane with my fellow crew members.

He was a wise man who invented beer.

—Plato

By the time I met Kane, he was already into his second pint of Guinness Stout, which was hardly his ilk of drink. On top of that, "The Fifth Quarter" was hardly known for dark anything, let alone stout. Kane's misplaced pint perfectly fit in with my lingering Amsterdam experience. Gazing at it took me back to another place and time in Europe. It drew up memories of the many cascading pints I caressed when in Ireland some fifteen years before.

**Whenever I think of the past,
it brings back so many memories.**

—Steven Wright

That wild trip featured two haggard, Russian flight crews; talking my way out of fisticuffs against local, inebriated rabble; and Erin's Dad unceremoniously, to put it diplomatically, coming out of the closet; not to mention the best rack of lamb, southern fried chicken, and Chinese food I have ever eaten. That slog across the Emerald Isle, with diverse cuisine, gay liberation and perfect pints – while a seeming lifetime before – set many standards. I played on the streets of Dublin with a bad-to-the-bone trio (equal parts *Average White Band* rhythm section and *Korn*) and in the city of Cork – Ireland's Pittsburgh -with a Beatles-esque blues band that at my insistence changed names from its trite/so blah "The Finnegan Three" to my fitting "Reckless Youth".

Cork was edgy; I almost learned the hard way not ask for a Guinness while there.

As if reading my mind, Kane declared: "My man, you are definitely going to like this," pointing to his pint glass. After ordering for us, Kane turned and quipped, *"Tell-eth unto thee, noble descendant of William of Orange, of ye wayfaring ways upon the Netherlands."*

It was a great opening. But I just could not find where and the words with which to begin. Like a well-placed life ring, the pint was delivered to my fingertips. This elixir was percolating, inviting, and alive. An unbelievably flawless, surgical pour, crafted by a frumpy Midwestern bar matron – a good starting point for whatever may come.

This was my first drink since leaving Amsterdam. It was mother's milk, succulent, invigorating, and encapsulating. It was Guinness I knew - in every good way. After I lowered the pint glass onto the bar, I felt a firm yet unimposing hand come to rest upon my shoulder. I turned around. My brain shifted through several gears and then finally accepted who was standing before me. Granted, he was out of uniform, but it was him: The very police officer, who a few hours ago - for him, quite a few pints ago— had proclaimed my client's innocence from the witness stand. I was speechless on every level.

He had the drop on me, and his grin confirmed that knew it. Now the floor was his. He raised his pint of Guinness as he handed a second to me. He said, loud enough for all to hear, "To innocence!" As the bar bottomed up, he disappeared into the crowd.

Kane turned to me and said, "Man, you haven't come back, have you?"

That pint, and the others that flowed were spirited and inviting. With the sounds of March Madness our background music, an envious Kane took in my life-changing Amsterdam experience.

Pints later, my body clock was telling me to call it an early night.

Water's never clumsy.

—Matthew McConaughey

CHAPTER XXI

IT'S A SMALL WORLD, AFTER ALL

Friendship at first sight, like love at first sight, is said to be the only truth.

—*Herman Melville*

As I headed to the exit, I spotted Mark Regal, a mutual friend of Erin and me and gave him a big hug. Mark hurt both for me and Erin in different but equally loyal ways. He was a buddy to my children. I had met him through Erin with whom he had worked and drank. Mark felt the pain of my marriage, my general dissatisfaction and yet he always stayed impartial; close and genuine with Erin.

Mark was a social worker's social worker, with a European athlete's frame and an even bigger capacity to overlook self-created shortcomings and see beyond poor performance with earnest sympathy and broad understanding—hardly my best qualities. Mark always found kind words and would complete thoughts in order to assure his students and his friends that things were good and sure to get even better.

Love at first sight is easy to understand; it's
when two people have been looking at each other
for a lifetime that it becomes a miracle.

—SAM LEVENSON

Mark said, "Franco, I want to hear all about your trip, but first let me introduce you…"

He had been right all those years. Things would get even better. Just as the sun was setting on my incredible day, body clock hay-wired, Mark gaff-hooked me and flopped me to True Love. Unquestionable, undeniable, without-a-doubt – Undeniable Love. This was Love At First Sight.

I looked into Melaura Lois Carattini's eyes and found my own soul. My heart was beating as if she had taken my hand for a walk over Amsterdam's cobblestone streets. At that moment, I unconditionally offered up everything, surrendered it all and borrowed against anything I could think of - and turned it all over to Melaura. She was my Amsterdam.

Before me I was certain was the most honest person I had ever met. For so many tumultuous years, I had blindly suffered self-created misery, shut myself in with a spouse and in a marriage that was a colossal failure. Now, in this revealing Amsterdam moment, I felt recharged. I found hope; I came alive.

I knew it from Melaura's eyes, honest and warm, discerning and vigilant. Her hair and wardrobe had a solid European look, cleverly accessorized with a touch of Latin flare. Her handshake was firm and unwavering. I had fallen in Love at first sight; there was no interference from any self-created fears or self-limiting reservations. Neither inhibitions nor technicalities of any kind would get in the way.

I wanted to spend the rest of my life with Melaura - and if she would have me, I would be hers. If she would not, I would still be hers. When I learned that she was a schoolteacher, I should have asked for her hand right then and there.

When Melaura confidently told me of her nomadic upbringing, bouncing around the globe, it was game over. When Melaura asked me about my lifetime travels, feeling like she and I were in Café Internationaal, I shared the story of my travel - from barber chair to barber chair.

CHAPTER XXII

BARBERS

Some guys will cheat on their girlfriends
and sleep like a baby at night
but feel guilty when they go to another barber.

—*Unknown*

Touched by Melaura's recount of her warm, rugged experiences speckled over the globe, I offered my world travel – through the barbers of my life - albeit by appointment only.

The first leg of my journey was a makeshift, three-chair barbershop built in a car garage, next to the tractor barn adjacent to a huge field. My Dad's grade through high school running buddy, Charlie Hampoian, employed with New England Bell, cut hair on the weekends. Everyone but the three-year-old me spoke Armenian. They called me "*Khelok*", which means "Quiet" (virtually identical in sound to the Dutch word for "Luck" – "*Geluk*").

My Dad ritualistically presented me to the shop's patriarch, Harry [Garo] Garabedian, who had two sons, Charlie [Garabed] and Harry [Haratud]. The shop overlooked the lush Truck farm, where succulent tomatoes, cucumbers and the sweetest corn flourished. For the Salem, New Hampshire, Armenian-Americans male community, it was Saturday haircut and Sunday church –always the big day…

When the twenty-minute drive became unworkable, my Dad took me to "Zona's Barbershop", saving Garabedian's for a few rare occasions. Over the rest of my single- digit years, I was perched atop a padded booster seat, inhaling the manly scent of that double-stitched cape and my uncontrollable drooling, while the bulky hair vacuum skidded over the base of my head, neck, and, especially, my ears. I remember not believing it when six-year-old Bahred cried in pain after a mole on the back of his neck was nicked at the hands of Mr. Zona. I sat perfectly still, and Joe, who I had unfairly marked, continued to work on me.

With self-confidence and swagger, Mr. Zona had all the answers. A "Jimmy the Greek" type, he spent more time talking book than paying attention to his patient. Joe, his much older and quieter associate, looked every bit like Jimmy Durante. He had extremely shaky hands. So, I did my best to work with him, learn his touch and anticipate each snip in between his wide tremors. Over time, I figured if he cut me, he cut me. Once I accepted my fate, Joe's straightedge neck shave grand finale was with hands as calm as sleeping caterpillars, leaving my little-boy neck as smooth as a baby's bottom.

During my high-school years, I decided to see a stylist. However, it was not just any stylist—rather, it was a woman of Portuguese descent, mother of teenage daughters. These girls were friends of mine, each about whom I fantasized at bedtime - on alternating nights. Yet I had always felt more than a spark for – and from - their mother; and not merely from my quips and anecdotes. She took a different liking to me. I became fully charged when she would get close to me while cutting my hair. I worked very hard not be afraid of these feelings. In time, she nudged her daughters out of the nightly rotation of worked up, heated thoughts, becoming the first "older woman' in my life.

In Boston, my Suffolk University's technically on-campus barber was located atop Beacon Hill. Tucked away just next to the Massachusetts State House, run by an Italian, his shop was decorated with Calcio Italiano regalia, alongside faded pictures of John F. Kennedy, former mayor Kevin White, Phil Esposito and an autographed Franco Harris football card. I made my introductions, having wisely ditched the jeans and backpack, dressing the part of who I needed to let him know I was - someone with smarts, raised to have class, and that my blood relatives were connected. When Luigi asked, I told him of my Merrimac Valley's mother's bloodline. I was allowed in. I knew to properly conduct myself or be sent packing with a kick in the ass.

Whenever someone walked in while Luigi was working on me, he would always look first to Luigi. Only if Luigi gave me the nod would I look up and offer a respectful greeting; otherwise I buttoned my lowered lip. Luigi was assured, in as few words as necessary, that no matter what, I would never, ever stick my nose into any conversation – because "my ears don't hear what they shouldn't."

Were words often exchanged that were hearable and notable? Absolutely not.

I always met Luigi with a tie on—under V-neck or cardigan sweater or an assuming elbow-patched sport coat and slacks, even on those hot fall-semester or sports-talk abound spring semester days.

After college, moving on to Law School and the far-north side of Chicago, Edgewater, I lived in a high-rise studio apartment. It was an area checkered - with safe and unsafe blocks. I spotted a place just under the Granville 'El" station called Bunny's Natural House. Bunny looked like an older, shorter, heavier, Jheri-curled "Refrigerator Perry", snaggle-toothed and all. My haircuts there were all-day affairs.

Patience is not simply the ability to wait –
it's how we behave while we're waiting.

—Joyce Meyer

I came to know the African-American barbershop pace/cadence during the summer of 1984, while living in Paterson, New Jersey, where Leon's Barber Shop held court. Leon was the brother of M. L. Carr, who was quite a character, a deceptively solid utility player with the Boston Celtics 1981 and the soon-to-be 1984 championship teams. M.L. played nasty, mind games amid his never overstated skill. This was the summer of Magic versus Bird; a seven-game saga. Leon and I were the only two Celtics fans in his shop. We joked how it felt like we were the only two Celtics fans in the City of Patterson.

From the first time Bunny and I met, he called me "Charlie." It stuck. When our many conversations became deep, he drove his intended message home by calling me "Charles." Later that year, one of my myriad street performance bands transformed from the rockabilly Black and Blue into a trio, consisting of two doo-wop vocals—one on upright bass, the other on guitar—and me on sax. I dubbed the group The Charlie Brothers. It stuck.

Any time after Bunny had heard terrible news over his WVON AM1450-tuned radio that involved someone "who was white" getting killed in the city, the next time Bunny saw me walking by his picture window - with my load of books, my sax or both, he would beckon me in, stop what he was doing and tell me how relieved he was to see me alive. This, sadly so, became our running, gallows-humor joke. My response would be that he actually wanted me "capped" because he just didn't like cutting my cracker hair. He would then retort, "You ain't no cracker, Charlie; you're a Melba Toast, topped with just the right touch of New Orleans olive salad."

"In that case, Bunny, I had better not get my sad, sorry ass killed."

The day before I moved from the edgier Edgewater to the posher Lincoln Park, Bunny looked out for me. He stepped out of the shop; it was the very first time I had seen him do that. He invited me to his home for a going-away, get-together. His castle was a lavish suite overlooking a rugged stretch of Chicago's Lake Michigan waterfront. He played rare, underground jazz videos, including Miles at the Plugged Nickel, recorded on eight-millimeter film, that he had converted to VHS. Bunny's wife was a sweetheart, and she had obviously heard of me. When she pulled me in for hug, she whispered in my ear, "So what's your real name, Charlie?" Just then, Bunny told me that I was the only "client" of his whom he had ever invited into their home. "Charles," I quipped. "Charles Franco Minasian."

Bunny was big-shouldered, gritty, and unambiguous. For me, he embodied Chicago's dual, often contradictory, sometimes neurotic nature. Bunny was tough, territorial, and stubborn yet carefree, genuine, and loyal—an enigma like his beloved '85 Bears. And he too was a huge Larry Bird fan.

Bunny always watched over me- and we both knew it.

Quality is not an act, it is a habit.

Aristotle

I found the Chicago/French version of Bunny and Luigi near my Lakeview two-bedroom apartment, which my roommate and I rented for $425/month – all utilities included. There I met Andre, a barber who loved WMAQ AM 670 talk/music radio and Dammam tea.

Andre sported short-sleeved barber coats, accented by ascots, even in the dead of winter. He was connected to his alderman and had an in with "Streetz and Sanz". Andre adored his dainty cups his tea, giving credit to the Dutch, not the British, for introducing it to France. "Coiffeur Andre" featured Parisian coziness, Chicago toughness with but a touch of Moroccan spice. In due time, I learned how Andre and his family had barely survived World War II. On the brink of starvation, tucked away into the damaged countryside, they survived on grass and stream water, just like my childhood idol, Bruno Sammartino. When I mentioned this to Andre, he said, "I knew Bruno's mentor, Édouard Carpentier."

After I moved from the city to the South Suburbs, I stayed with Andre through that rather mild winter, but over the spring and into summer that followed, that thirty-six-mile schlep became too much. On an apropos July 14, 1992, I bid a tearful au revoir to Andre, who responded, "*Bon chance, 'Francoise'...*"

I tooled around my town's business streets, searching for a new tonsorial parlor, eventually passing a hand-cranked barber pole. Across the adjacent picture window, hand-painted black and in baseball uniform cursive font, was scribed, "The World's Greatest Barbershop." My search had come to an end. How absolute. What bravado. All other barbershops were now literally second to mine.

For the next twenty years, Paul, Bridgeport [Daley enclave] South-Side Polish guy, defiant, Catholic-school student, Vietnam War combat veteran-turned-hippie, cut my hair. Paul loved *The Three Stooges* and was an avid lakefront smelt fisherman. This 1968-drafted Marine took great care of all of the older veterans. Both Rory and Mollie got their first haircuts from Paul. Polaroid pictures capturing his reverence and their booster seated glow hung on either side of a Columbia Pictures head shot of Curly.

The community which has neither poverty nor riches
will always have the noblest principles.

—Plato

Once waiting my turn, I heard a World War II veteran mention in passing how he had participated in the liberation of Dachau. Not wanting to intrude into his soul, I tried to confine my words to offering praise, as other patrons and Paul had done. But I just could not help myself. With a witness to the crime of all crimes and on the stand, I had to make my record. Paul saw my wheels turning, silenced his buzzing shears and said, "Get on down, man." With permission to approach, I examined him:

"Was it sight, sound, taste, or touch?"

As he and everyone pondered my question, I said:

"What I mean to ask, if you will permit me, is what did your instincts tell you - and when did you first know?"

"How odd that you should ask that. It was that smell. Unlike anything we had ever encountered over there. It was heavy and it was ugly and all about the air. We caught it a quarter-mile out. Everything went real quiet and anxiety crept in. To a man, we knew that we were headed into a hell worse than any action we had seen."

"It was so horrible and so unbelievably systematic. It had a strange effect. The bunk lizards, they really stepped up and found a high gear; the live wires, they didn't utter a peep; and it hit the toughest guys the hardest."

"What was it that hit you the hardest?"

"Their touch. Those poor damn people; they had taken on more shit than any of us; and even though they were so pitifully, physically drained, their hands gripped me and my buddies like a vise. They filled all of us with a real sense of why we fought and why so many of our other buddies had died. Somehow, they lifted our spirits and pulled us out from our own darkness. They taught us how precious our lives were."

"Listen here, Franco. I want to thank you. No one has ever asked the right questions and let me say what I have wanted to – for so long, what I really needed to. So, I thank Paul for cutting your hair, and I thank you. Give me one more question, like Colombo always does."

"What's the bottom line that all of us and everyone else needs to understand?"

"Here's the bottom line: We may have saved them, but they sure as shit saved all of us. Can you imagine? We were a bunch of young guys. And we were scared. And the German people? They were terrified...Our guys, we didn't know shit from Shinola. We just took orders and fought to try and stay alive so we could make it home. In many ways I survived because they survived. Those people we rescued? The truth is that they rescued us."

Paul said, "Right on, man. Semper fi."

This was the most important "direct examination" of my life, a survivor's story told in the finest courtroom of them all. An important and lasting public record was made - in the World's Greatest Barbershop.

In time, Paul began to wind things down, cutting his hours and setting an out date. I made a decision. I had always kept my hair tight, short, and clean. The last time I had used a comb was thirty-five years earlier. Now, I was about to do exactly what Paul did when he came home from Vietnam. I would let my hair grow out and get long.

Around this world of clippers, shears, scissors, and straight edged razors, I had so fortunately traveled; finding a landscape of disposable paper collars, capes, soaking combs, earnest talk oiled—and the good company of such decent people and their stories.

Melaura's journey, her global adventure, bestowed upon her an ability to be self-sufficient, frugal, and adaptable—a cross-cultural child. But having lived in so many places Melaura hadn't found her own; not until I took her to the shores of where the Gulf of Maine meets the Atlantic Ocean—my childhood backyard. It was that much closer to Amsterdam than our Midwest stakes.

CHAPTER XXIII

MELAURA

True love is like ghosts, which everyone
talks about and few have seen.

—Francois de La Rochefoucauld

Melaura Lois Carattini, the sum of Umair's mandate, Syd's vision, post-Amsterdam validation; she is the culmination of the most beautiful, considerate, stylish, warm, confident and direct ways of every person I have known.

When faced with any set of circumstances, from crises to mundane moments, Melaura has been endurable and hopeful, showing all sides of optimism and unyielding resolve. Melaura refuses to let me waiver, no matter what we face and will not allow me to deny my shortcomings, let alone hers.

From the first time I set eyes on her, Melaura has proven that all things are possible. Honest and principled, she is inclined to spend very little time on mediocre efforts and insufferably shallow matters. Courting her, I could feel the sun and cherish the moon, finally having the strength and balance to live openly and honestly - which is to say – no longer alone. We accept and trust in one another, by celebrating our imperfections and quirks and making peace with our frustrations and fears.

Such moments are the poetry of our story.

True love at first sight and my wonderful life with Melaura that would follow did not cancel out my past.

Instead, it would allow matters- that still mattered in ways I would finally comprehend - to come into the light. Now living life in an open way, there would be no quarter for what I had subconsciously sidestepped and outright repressed.

Love is our true destiny.
We do not find the meaning of life by ourselves
alone - we find it with another.

Thomas Merton

My first marriage, abounding in unhappiness and self-deception, tempered only by an overriding, unconditional love for my children, compounded my preexisting emotional confusion. When I fell in love with Melaura and found my partner for life, I would no longer live in denial. I would never again conjure up ways to mask true feelings, concoct false ones, or close off the path to true ones; no matter the cost.

Melaura's cross-cultural childhood, having lived in so many places – having never formed a sense of home, left her unsettled in sad way. How touching that she would finally find what she was missing, of all places, in my childhood backyard - on the edge of the Atlantic Ocean - atop New England's Great Boar's Head. The moment Melaura walked into our family's living room and emptied herself into our old easy chair, I could feel the weight of the world—her sense of rootlessness—lift away. Her long, unconnected journey had finally come to an end. Melaura had before her eyes and into her heart that which she had longed for.

Even though I never, ever thought about it, I had not yet made peace with my past. There remained, however subconscious and suppressed, unrealized, unfinished business that I could finally tend to and square away.

It isn't where you came from, it's where
you're going to that counts.

—*ELLA FITZGERALD*

During my sixth trip to the Netherlands, five years after Melaura came into my life and two years after we were married, a now thirty-year-old, untreated pain, so repressed that its story was subconsciously skipped over in early "*Al Basha*" drafts, finally resurfaced.

My first broken heart would be healed; of course, under "only-in-Amsterdam-could-this-happen-to-me" circumstances. Soon to be emotionally vulnerable once again, I would undergo yet another revision - and finally parole those whom I had falsely accused and unjustly punished for having allegedly hurt me or having somehow made me hurt them.

Three decades later, even after finding Melaura, my true love, I was still far from understanding how immature, unhealed, stubborn and aching my heart still was.

And so, I would face an old feeling—a love that had all but destroyed me. Café Internationaal never did take to cheap denial or shameful retreat. And so, neither would I.

Not even Melaura's power could conquer what was so deeply set: repressed wounds that were anchored, however rusty, to Miriam and our long-ago experience in Washington, DC.

Finding Melaura would give me everything - Finding Melaura would free up the space, perspective, and courage for me to understand my years of folly – and make peace with what otherwise could have been, perhaps should have been or what arguably would have been – then retake the path before me and move forward.

CHAPTER XXIV

INGAAR, THE RINGER

Remember that they [the French] are always
discouraged if they do not succeed immediately
in anything which they undertake.

—KING PHILIP

True to seven years before this year, my Amsterdam nights ended as my days began; at Café Internationaal. On this seminal night, I landed the only open barstool, facing the iconic beer tap, Germanic/Romantic-themed. To my right was a man who appeared to be in deep, tethering thought. To my left was the turned back of a Dutch girl, who was chatting it up with her pal. Her Dutch had a quirky, New York accent. As I cocked my ear and took that dialect in, the man asked me, "Do you come here often?"

"Not often enough," I replied, taking in with a smile how fortunate I was to be right there, right now.

Everything about him was French: his shave, his cologne, his fashion, and, of course, his accent. His engaging, not-quite telegraphed intentions were coaxed, as if on some cue. Luc and I had a friendly conversation that he kept turning into playful chat with grazes of sorts. After a few rounds, he politely - but stridently - moved in and propositioned me in my right ear.

In uncharted territory, wondering if I had led him on, I had to find the right words to turn him down. For his ears only, I informed *mon bonhomme* that I was married, straight, and therefore must decline his offer. As if I had reneged on a bet, he pressed, "Franco, whay nat?"

It's not that he wouldn't take no for answer, just that my first one was lacking. I took in a deep breath of the Café and said, "Look, Luc, it's definitely my loss, not yours, but I'm married, and I'm not gay. You and I; we just ain't gonna happen."

He said, "You break the heart," gesturing to his chiseled chest. Then, he put on his scarf, coat, and gloves; au revoir. He was gone. I muttered to myself, as if running calculations, with a smile on my face, feeling weirdly exceptional and undeniably flattered.

For the very first time that evening, I turned to my left and looked into the eyes of Ingaar Abraam. With a wide smile that reached her eyes and a gentle, confident laugh, she shook her head and said laughingly, "Hey heartbreaker…Who are you?"

In the wake of the Frenchman, I was thrown off – literally speechless - I was no match for Ingaar. My tacit fluster must have seemed self-assured. Before I could regroup, Nicole stepped in and as she slyly placed *vazen* in front of Ingaar and me, she spoke to Ingaar in Dutch, I recognized certain word to my short biography. Café Internationaal was in session.

> *A human being becomes human not through the casual*
> *convergence of certain biological conditions, but through*
> *an act of will and love on the part of other people.*

> —*Italo Calvino*

Nicole moved down the bar - Ingaar moved in. She wanted to talk and listen. At first, it was all about music; hers and mine. Not only had I obviously gotten over my break-up with Luc, I felt myself in some oddly recognizable, faintly familiar free-flow; unabashed as our conversation turned edgy and all-too-assuming, this was registering something from within. Our topic of conversation, jazz, tamed this uneasiness; for the moment, I was in safe haven. My vocabulary drew a sizzling, perplexing smile. Ingaar was taken in by every bit of what I had to say on the matter.

Nicole was watching from afar and passed me the Heineken logo-embossed scratch pad and pencil, *en twee vazen*, before I could ask.

How well Nicole had come to know my diet.

At Ingaar's request, I penned a pocket dictionary of music termi-nology, which included "vamp," "turnaround," "hook," "stank," "straight ahead," "take it out" and "in the pocket." Ingaar painstakingly and passionately pondered aloud and then repeated each of its entries until she could say them "accurately", which was in such a soulful, New York/Dutch accented way. She then said, "I'm so glad you turned him down."

Ingaar was gritty and very Dutch. While I may have impressed her, even touched her, what mattered more was that something was happen-ing to me. I had no fear of the connection that was developing between us. From deep inside, a sense of self was being drawn out, and I could feel that all of this was how it should be and that this was what was meant to be.

I had to be alone with Ingaar. I needed to be with her. My heart was not pounding; my mouth was not dry. I was not in heat, yet I was not in direct control. In the hours that followed, the energy grew, but what was fueling it I could not quite get.

With Ingaar's permission, we walked to my favorite view of Amsterdam. A stroll from the Café, in a serene, reflective spot, was the breadbasket of Amsterdam - the soft underbelly of Zeedijk.

Unlike the distant, pre-Melaura past, when this would have been the opening for me to make my move, this time I was being moved- by some inner force. There we were, in this very special, so inviting place, on the edge of a breathtaking canal – and more.

This moment would not let me go. Now I couldn't catch my breath, as something inside of me was consuming it.

We locked eyes. She smiled. I slid my hand under her field-of-wheat blond hair. With my right hand over her coat, I held her side. As the distant North Sea winds blew and the gulls crooned, I continued to hold her. It was as if we were kissing. When I released her, I stepped back a bit and once again looked into her eyes. Just then, it all came rushing in. All of those important, so long-ago lost pieces to my unfinished emotional puzzle had now finally fallen into where they fit; where they belonged:

The Frenchman - Barry Goldwater, wanting what he wanted. Café Internationaal - his Senate Chambers.... I was now back on the basketball court in Washington, DC, with Miriam, my first true love; but this time around, I took my still- lingering, broken heart.

After all these years, Ingaar and Amsterdam would make Miriam and DC – and me - right.

> *It is still an open question, however, as to what*
> *extent exposure really injures a performer.*
>
> —*Harry Houdini*

I had little time with Ingaar. Her train would depart Centraal Station in a few hours. True love and a redemptive rebirth were upon me. My thoughts were retelling my story; of a first marriage, which had begun in deceit and ended in divorce; of a father's heart pouring itself out his children, even as growing intolerance to their alcoholic mother darkened; how toward the twilight of a bitter marriage, lost time was made up for with a succulent, young woman, over a rapturously unforgettable night and into the morning.

My infidelity, which expended a decade of pent-up passion, left me so light on my feet, uncluttered and in pure delight. No disappointments, no strings and no regrets. I felt eternal gratitude for that sweet and fiery girl. Yet in the end, all that fiery night did was effectively treat a serious symptom.

I had no intentions of sleeping with the "10" Ingaar; and yet I could not be without her for our remaining hours together. There was no temptation; only the realization that I had to be with Ingaar until we would say goodbye. I had opened my heart and finally – after thirty years, it was time to deal with heartbreak – this time the right way.

Avoiding danger is no safer in the long run than outright exposure. The fearful are caught as often as the bold.

—HELEN KELLER

This nonnegotiable demand that I reclaim my heart, knowing that I was destined to expose it once again – here in Amsterdam - was clearly meant to be. I found myself back in that very first love – as with Miriam- innocent and honest, fearless and free.

The next four hours were warm and loving and recognizably predestined to soon come to an end. This Amsterdam experience, more than any other, gave me the strength to finally accept my humanity and take ownership of my human frailty.

I was given a second chance to rewrite my history. Amsterdam would clean up DC – and on many levels, set "Al Basha" free.

Liberation does not come from outside.

—GLORIA STEINEM

Ingaar had always gravitated, usually to a fault, to musicians. She had stellar pitch and rhythm, and her voice conveyed a rather peppery rage. She had sat in with and successfully fronted for punk rock and rave bands, all of which consisted of musicians with varying degrees of talent, but to a man were either needy, greedy or seedy.

In Ingaar's voice and from her look, all they saw was talent to exploit and a very desirable mark to conquer.

The time came for me to walk Ingaar to Centraal Station. My heart ached, just as it had decades before when my Greyhound Bus from Washington Deco to Boston's South Station was loading up.

As we approached the majestic façade over that familiar cobblestone path, we stopped along the water to embrace. Mindful of the fleeting time, I held Ingaar close - and felt her close to me, knowing that now was about to be nevermore.

When we got to the platform, Ingaar and I held each other for what seemed an eternity. Just then - the whistle blew - and I looked her in the eyes and told her that I loved her; she told me that she loved me. I kissed her as any decent Dutch man would kiss a Dutch woman - left cheek/right cheek/left cheek. I was so grateful that this beautiful woman had been there for me; as if she knew what I hadn't yet figured out.

For me, this was first love – second take. It was the way it should have been the first time.

Ingaar boarded the train, and our eyes locked as the train headed out and cleared the platform, and then she was gone. Tears began to fall as I stared at the utterly silent platform; even the wind stood still.

Centraal Station.

I felt yet another powerful transformation. This one - from hurt to comfort. Amsterdam once again delivered me a rebirth. This great city proved that the pieces of my life were retrievable; that I was salvageable. I was given permission to let go of what I shouldn't hold on to, so long as I picked up and never let go of what I shouldn't let go.

For so many years, I had repressed my DC past, thereby forging a rough trail of failed relationships, marked with my emotional stinginess and fraudulent role playing.

No longer assailed by my past, I would tell my story - and I would fulfill Umair's mandate in the way I now knew he meant.

Through this Amsterdam experience, my emotional life would never again be blundered through or neglected.

I walked back into the Café and rang the bell. Well over the oblivious cheers, Nicole looked at me and through her warm smile seemed gratified with what she had fostered.

Over the next vaasje, a clumsy melody and chord changes came into my head, the one that I had scribbled after returning to DC. I would finish what I had started after I returned from DC –then set aside: My very first composition, which I would tile "The Ringaar".

CHAPTER XXV

TRUUS

*In every shoot, between the actor and the
director, there is manipulation.
I'm not saying that negatively. It's healthy.*

—Adele Exarchopoulos

When Ingaar cleared the station, after one last look at the wounded me, she sank into the nearest seat, hugging herself and smiled through her own tears. Truus, a salty Dutch girl across from her, had taken in the entire platform scene. She looked up sheepishly and quipped: "What's the story?"

"For once in my life, I used a guy for the right reason, and I let him use me for the right reason."

"And for what was that?"

"To feel love."

"He did not hold back - and without any expectations – he was caring. No more 'apple and egg' jerks for me!"

"I will never again settle for anyone who doesn't hold me like he did. Even if I never find true love like him again."

"You will find it again, Ingaar."
"Why wouldn't you? After all, you have entire life to fall in love again."

Sin, guilt, neurosis; they are one and the same, the fruit of the tree of knowledge.

—HENRY MILLER

Just before Truus got to her stop, Ingaar said:

"Geertruida. You do know, we deserved each other, almost like we have been together for such a long time…"

"Ingaar. He will love with you forever."

Truus and Ingaar locked eyes and exchanged smiles as the train approached Truus's stop. Now standing alone on the platform, her left hand clutching her chin and her right hand hugging herself, processing it all. She hoped that Ingaar would find happiness and wondered if the time had come to break the stubborn old promise she had made to herself and finally agree to let the love of her life in.

As if Truus had been holding this moment back, waiting for this moment, the words of her favorite teacher took hold: "If there is no benefit, there will no damage, either."

Ingaar had now realized that she was much more than she had always dumbed herself down to be for the sake of approval; some pitifully cheap version of her truest self. She now found herself celebrating – having been with a decent someone and in a genuine way – and finally seeing herself as deserving no less. That the two of them shared something each had been denied, was special…

The only antidote to mental suffering is physical pain.

—KARL MARX

The next morning, while on my way to Schiphol, my guilty mind began to spill over, screaming in my ears how I had so selfishly wronged Melaura. I knew that she had every right to know of my infidelity. To claim that my night with Ingaar was technically not adulterous was cheap and smacked of my old ways; I would not resort to clever rationalizations upon trite technicalities – that would only compound my crime. I could not honestly deny that I had an extramarital affair. Ingaar had touched my so heart deeply. And while I was healed from an old wound, I felt like dog shit.

Was it now my fate to have traded in old, suppressed regret for a new, more complicated and fatal version? Had I sacrificed one old pain for a new worse one?

I struggled with this emotional hangover. My head was throbbing. How would I be able to confess my undeniable infidelity, to tell Melaura that I allowed myself – that I willed myself - to fall for another woman? Worse yet, that I did not regret it. DC closure aside, I had fucked up royally. I started to dry heave.

How I made it to Schiphol later that day remains a blank. I do remember that I was unable to clear the first tier of security and was subjected to a secondary screening. I barely passed, due to my frenetic, preoccupied look. My cryptic guilt-laden answers only made matters worse. Schiphol supervisors and Interpol were called in. They searched all of my belongings – unwrapping the gifts I had bought for Melaura. That was a rather cruel touch of irony that made me laugh with shame. When I did so, the authorities were all but certain that contraband was at hand.

With every book, you go back to school. You become a student.
You become an investigative reporter. You spend a little time
learning what it's like to live in someone else's shoes.

—*John Irving*

Eventually, I made it onto the plane, where I sank deeply into my seat. On my list of memorable unsettling flights over the years (bipolar Tibetans, freaky Chinese crime dramas, Charlie Trotter-level cuisine and twice assuming patient care in bona fide medical emergencies) was this number one- *numero uno.*

Sensing my uneasiness, the man next to me offered his hand, identifying himself as a Dutch newspaperman, a reporter. I was oblivious to his introductions, too engaged in an inner debate losing on both sides. Out of a sheer sense of flight (as in "fight or flight"), I started to get out of my seat during takeoff. He gently - but firmly- reached over, gripped my shirt sleeves, and shout/whispered *"Hoi. Rustig Maar..."* then calmly said *"I think you and I need to relax a bit."* We locked eyes; I nodded, and he let go. He whispered to the woman to his left, perhaps reassuring her that I was not some Armenian terrorist. She whispered back in Dutch. I recognized *"gek"*. I probably did look quite crazy.

Once things leveled off a bit, he turned toward me, squaring up, cupped my forearm firmly - without aggression – and said, *"So why don't you tell me what it is that troubles you? We have a little time to talk – if you wish."*

I confessed to him that I was certain that I had been unfaithful to my wife, whom I madly loved, in the worst way. *"I'm curious in that you seem to have doubts?"* he replied, "What is your wife's name?"

"Melaura. Melaura Lois Carattini."

The woman poked her head out, sneered at me – then sat back.

"I have to know how much damage I have done so that when I confess I am completely honest."

The woman now leaned into his ear and said something in Dutch to him, to which he replied to me, *"My* wife." While I could pick up very little, she said something to the effect of either "You had better let me help you with this one." or "You had better not let me get my hands on him."

Clearing my way to tell my story, with apologetic humility, he asked me if I could explain it all to his wife and him - so they could "...better understand my dilemma." As an attorney, I had been the one on the bitter end of such conversations over a thousand times, using interrogation methods - coaxing confessions; but this time, I had the guilty mind – and was putty in their hands.

For many years, newspaper reporters and cops were cut from the same cloth. They drank together, shared information, practically worked together, and, for the most part, did the same job— albeit one with a pen and pad on the street, the other with cuffs and a service six or belt-clipped .22 revolver. This man was cut from that cloth of an old school reporter.

After conferring with his wife for a moment, who appeared to concur with his approach, he called for the flight attendant and in Dutch asked - well before beverage service was underway - for three beers and three brandies. Until they arrived, he said nothing. Belted in at fifty thousand feet over the Atlantic, I was too weak to say or do anything.

The the beers and brandies were served before we leveled off. We touched plastic cups and drank to "the power of flight". Then, in a seemingly rehearsed way, we poured brandy onto the ice and raised our plastic cups. At least my basic functions were still intact.

Once I confessed my sin, he gathered his thoughts and told me that I had to tell Melaura because I had seemed to have actually done something right, not wrong. He assured me that I was everything to Melaura and was certain that Melaura was everything to me. He told me that I had somehow managed to simultaneously hold on and let go, when doing each so correctly mattered the most.

His wife said: "Hey. You put everything on the line. - and you didn't fuck it all up." He nodded and said to her, "*Het was vrij geweldig.*"- "It was quite splendid."

He then turned to me and said, "*No doubt, you are a survivor. In my business and probably in yours, being so is a rarity. For you to have found Melaura and the way you honor her - and now with you having rewritten the history of that pain in your heart to which you had so forlornly clung, is very special – so very rare.*"

"*Proost!*"

Ingaar had set my past free. Our time together, rapturous and painful, settled the unsettled and made things right. I would not regret. I would now be pleased to share this with Melaura. When our eyes met, it was far better than the first time – it was a celebration of our future and all of it possibilities.

"*Tell Melaura. Tell Melaura Lois Carattini of this – and leave nothing out. Tell her your story.*"

"Celebrate your love for her and what she means to you."

His wife added, *"...and make love to her."*

The two of them looked at each other with a sparkle.

When the time was right, I confessed to Melaura that for so very long in my life, I had been a child; a self-righteous, closed-off coward. The fear of opening my heart turned my very soul brittle and cold. Having found her counted for everything.

That she rekindled me, awakened my spirit and was the love of my life counted for even more than everything.

That without her, I would have never been able to come to complete terms with pain from so many years ago and take responsibility for repercussions over the decades that followed, which counted for so very much.

We held each other tightly, not wanting to ever let go. Melaura told me how happy she was that I had reclaimed my broken heart and so sorry that it had caused me such pain.

Melaura then looked me in the eye and asked me: "How were you able to fall in love me?" I told her that I had no choice in the matter.

"I had longed for you since the day I dropped out of kindergarten, self-confident - but so sad and alone. Every time I was stuck out in the cold on double-runners and against mean-spirited slap shots, I wanted to be inside and by the Sunny Glenwood, wood-burning kitchen stove and laugh with you. Before I ever met you, I missed you when we were apart. I have always pictured your eyes and your smile. I have always longed for your comfort, kind words, and your closeness. That is why each day with you as my wife feels like the first day I met you. I had no choice in the matter when it came to falling in love with you."

"As for Miriam and Ingaar. I fell in love with them, because I have always loved you."

"You need to take me to Amsterdam."

Melaura, ever-loving – the perfect schoolteacher, who encouraged self-expression and has always demanded honesty. I love her more and more with each new day. While at times I can be emotionally wobbly, I am evolving - into a stronger and more enlightened person.

Yet despite Melaura's following year's preflight "tongue-in-check" admonishment, another Dutch girl and I would find each other – stroll about Amsterdam's cobblestone streets of Amsterdam in yet another physically close, meaningful, and lasting way.

> *Well, when you come down to it, I don't see that a reporter could do much to a president, do you?*
>
> —Dwight D. Eisenhower

CHAPTER XXVI

CONFIRMATION

If you create an act, you create a habit. If you
create a habit, you create a character. If you
create a character, you create a destiny.

—Andre Maurois

Before leaving for Amsterdam, this time with both tenor and soprano saxophones in tow, Melaura sent me off, saying, "Play great. And no more falling in love!"

And yet upon my return from Amsterdam to her arms, I would be obliged to once again confess.

Over years long past, Café Internationaal had been a hot spot for live music. Its Latvian-built upright piano, ornately wood-trimmed was dusty, out of service, and woefully out of tune; pushed into the corner of the Café for my first few years. This French-wired, keyed, and hammered, a centerpiece for song and jam sessions was eventually sold off. I cannot say that Chet Baker played it or was accompanied by it, but I contend that he very well may have.

What a pity that live music at Café Internationaal was now a thing of the past. The room's acoustics were close to perfect – with high, decorative ceilings; a solid floor; ornate, wooden trim; large picture windows; and its sweetest acoustical feature: upper walls, upholstered in real leather. As to both sound quality and soulful vibe, Café Internationaal was Muscle Shoals. It was an ideal live recording venue - flowing sounds of European liquors and beers, Dutch cheer and such special human energy.

It is the nurse that the child first hears,
and her words that he will first attempt to imitate.

—QUINTILIAN

I had experienced this the year before, testing Café Internationaal's acoustics and reviving her stage, when I stopped by for my pre-gig hang. I was Schlepping my tenor sax, which became the conversation piece of the two young Germans who were sitting in "my" far corner of the bar, enjoying their *vazen*.

At the large back table on the opposite side was a bachelorette party of older, sultry, British babes. In the midst of their come-as-it-may walking tour of Amsterdam; their white uniforms, fishnet stockings, heavy makeup, and hotly contested game of "Spin the Dildo" gave them away.

No match for these nurses, I took a seat next to Max and Hans. As we began to bond, the two tallest of the giggly gaggle kept goose necking in our direction but not directly at me.

From the midst their giddy chatter, I detected one word, the only word that mattered: "saxophone." Nurses Long and Lanky stood up and deliberately strutted over to me. As if on cue, Max and Hans shifted their bar stools to create the opening. I did my part, gesturing to Michelle for *vijf vazen*. Without missing a beat, I asked, "Care to take my temperature?"

Michel, who had already moved in, quipped, "Sax Man—what confidence. Ladies. Please forgive him. He is a very sick man."

The taller one asked me, "Is your tongue hot?

The other, seemingly more subdued of the two said: "You have to play for us. And if you do a good job, I'll fiddle around in your bum."

Michel asked: "Sax Man?" Max and Hans answered his question for me, making it a unanimous decision.

I still had to think this one through. While I was known as "Sax Man", I had never played for anyone in my Café. Until now, it was all on the honor system. And however obliged I felt to deliver, I had no rhythm section and was not feeling very *a cappella*. On this occasion, technology and its disciples would save the day.

Still baffled by its capabilities, I had taken along my flywheel-controlled iPod for the train ride to and from my gig hour away. When fumbling around with it during this year's pre-Amsterdam preparations, I noticed that I somehow downloaded a slew of my *Jamey Aebersold* rhythm tracks.

And so, I did have a band; yet in order to make this performance work, I needed Max and Hans. I commandeered them to ply their trade and work some magic. "I have a trio on my iPod. I need you to set them up. Can you make what's in this play all around us?

Hans replied: *"We can play it and we can run it through my device and Hans can mix it for you...."*

"Well fiddle my bum!"

I chose the very tasty standard, "Scotch and Water." I broke out my horn and adjusted my mouthpiece.

As if on cue, Michelle stepped in as emcee. On her downbeat, this newly engineered band came to life. On her '" Take it away, SaxMan!", Hans and Max, faded in Jamie Aebersold's iconic "...One, two; one, two, three, four..."

I hit it – laying it way down and very dirty.

The sound was fat and full, as we were a live quartet. I had big sound - that filled the room with good volume. Since I had played over this track over and over again, I knew every kick and nuance, the last out and every rhythmic detail to its live-feel ending. I made it count. Max and Hans telepathically took my cue at the final turn and worked the iPod-turned-mixing-board. Rhythm and volume faded out with ease in the café, turned jazz club.

By the time that last tasty note floated away, the Café was full, and it seemed to have gone back in time. I was there and wanted to stay.

The nurses were all over me. Michel stepped out from the bar and said, "Man, you have to do another gig here. A real gig!"

I said, "On Sunday, a year from tomorrow, I will play here. And I will put it in writing. Shall we execute a promissory note?" Max and Hans entered the date into their calendars. They would show up at every gig that followed.

Now riled up by Michel, who told them that I was a criminal defense attorney, they chanted, "Speech! Speech! Speech!" The floor was mine.

I told them of Umair's story, as poetically as I could, revealing his broken dreams, his kind and gentle, but terminally wounded heart - and his mandate that I tell our stories.

Homage to Hans and Max, I recounted my years in the fire service, when having a solid crew meant survival. I told of the unique healing powers of the many other "hot and bothered" nurses, to whom I turned over patients after our crew rendered paramedic care.

I summed up my argument. "If only Umair were here, so that each and every one of you could...."

The meekest of the group, who the rest referred to as the "slapper" yelled "Shag him good and proper."

The cries of "Sax Man! Sax Man!" were aptly overtaken by what quickly swelled up a veracious cry: "Umair! U-mair OO-mair! OOO-mair! OOOO-Umair...OO...OO...OO...OO!"

I grabbed a fresh coaster, took out my pen: *"Note to self: 1. Keep alive what had just musically happened; 2. Find Umair and tell him of the night when eleven British nurses were gushing over him..."*

CHAPTER XXVII

KRUISPUNT

Music is…a higher revelation than
all wisdom and philosophy.

—Ludwig van Beethoven

A year and a day later, as per the contract with Michel, I would - pardon the legal parlance – *specifically perform*. While I was partial to the quintet, a quartet (with a drummer doubling on LP, Latin Percussion) seemed a perfect fit for Café Internationaal.

Two weeks prior to my KLM Royal Dutch Airlines flight, I had UPS'd charts to each member of the trio - compiled through the Internet, relying upon my local musician connections and just plain *Geluk*.

Opening/Closing night began with Casper, patrons and the trio creating our playing/listening space; we set up, individually warmed up- then kicked back – until the bassist pondered: "So what's our groove?" A five-minute, give-and-take, round-table about-everything followed- while the audience drank up and took in what was unfolding before them without a note even close to being played…

We talked about our lives and our music. This was music – the democratic way- and so the right moment would dictate what was to follow. I asked permission to name us "*Kruispunt*", or "Crossroads" – my tribute to the special intersection just outside and, as it turns out, our drummer's present station in his life.

Just as I counted out our opening tune – Scotch and Soda- Hans and Max walked into the Café. Over a two-hour set, *"Kruispunt"* delivered-fine harmonics, delicate and balanced- an organic, sincere sound that became the room.

The bassist and drummer, who had fit this gig in with just enough time to catch their train to Germany for a three-month tour with a show band, bid me farewell with "This night will sustain us. Thank you for making this special night happen for all of us."

When I walked back inside the Café, Casper handed me a note, which was given to him earlier in the night: "Must make train to Frankfurt –We miss the Dildo – How's Umair??? - See you next year - Hans and Max"

I hung out with guitarist Sanzo Fadgio, born and raised in Sicily. In the midst of us swapping gig stories, I shared mine about the eleven nurses. After that, he kept asking me about them. I pondered aloud whether he was sticking around hoping that they might return. While I knew they would not, in the best ways, they had never left.

Amsterdam's music-filled nights would always prove to be stories with unpredictable endings.

Neither Sanzo nor I had packed up our instruments. We just took in the night and enjoyed a smoke, with our number-one fan - a local girl named Leentje, who had joined us. She had a beaming smile and the body of a farmer's daughter. Sanzo had telegraphed designs, which were as bold as his sound.

Leentje liked to drink and loved to sing. She had a thing for "Autumn Leaves," but only its first four bars – which she crooned over and over again. Her voice was soulful and unpretentious – and naturally in-the-pocket - punctuated with an assertively, sexy twill. Leentje had very good pipes. Those first four bars were Leentje's sweet birdcall.

Sanzo and I reflected on the gig and what each of us had experienced. Leentje was taking in our conversation. One more set, one more night together, as *"Kruispunt"*, and it would have been even better than it was. We laughed at the tease of it all. "Shall I try and catch them?" I quipped, gesturing to Centraal Station. Always tantalizing is the thought of performing with great musicians.

Then Leentje piped in, "Why do you two keep talking about it? Stop talking about it. They are gone. You are here. *Play!*" Sanzo and I looked each other in the eye, laughed a bit, finished our smokes, and without a word, as if this interplay had been scripted, held the door for Leentje to enter.

Once inside, Leentje began to talk us up. We could feel the buzz outside. Just then, one of our guests, a Moroccan, came outside, to have a smoke, and ever so humbly suggested that we open our encore set with "Sugar."

We all smiled.

With the both the room and us ready, we left the *Kruispunt* – at least for the moment – ready to get to it – it was time to get down on it.

Without my asking, Sanzo tuned me and then laid down a deep, pocket bass line beneath dirty and fat overtone chords. "Sugary Sugar." We spoke not another word. Our set consisted of the song meant to fol-low the one just played. Something like this had happened only once, some twenty plus years before, on literally my last night in Boston - before leaving for good.

The only certain freedom's in departure.

- ROBERT FROST

During my last days and nights in the Back Bay, I was living it up, in anticipation of heading to Chicago for Michael Jordan and three years of law school. Out and about, our feeling-right group, on our way to who knows where, walked past a guitar player who was laying it down on the corner of Exeter and Boylston, just outside the Dunkin' Donuts. I stopped dead in my tracks.

He quoted a George Benson riff, then asked *"Do you play?"*

I had said, "Yeah, man, a little tenor, but not like the boys down the street." I was referring to the Berklee College of Music, where the real musicians could be found.

He set down a heavy, four-bar John McLaughlin-esque rhythm under *"Please- go- and get – your/Sax- then- come on- back/ a, one – two/ a, one-two-three- four, three, four..."*

I peeled off from my pals and trotted back to my dorm room; I scooped and returned. Without saying a word, he and I played for three hours straight to a huge crowd. It was my *au revoir* to my Back-Bay bastion, while the aroma of coffee and doughnuts filled the air.

We closed the extended set with "Blues March."

> *Nearly all the best things that came to me in life*
> *have been unexpected, unplanned by me.*
>
> —CARL SANDBURG

This Leentje-inspired after-set with Sanzo was in that special, Back Bay way.

The Cafe was still filled from the when the quartet had disbanded. The energy was penetrating; the groove was deep. The Café was gezellig. Sanzo and I played until we landed on a vamp that seemed to have a mind of its own, ready to take us out, on cue. I extended my gratitude; then, at the turn, Sanzo returned it and then the vamp called time. It was burning and beautiful. I was back in the Back Bay and in my Café. My saxophone had again so dutifully taken me here, there, and everywhere.

By the time Sanzo and I had packed up, buzzing from what we had laid down, Leentje was quite drunk and playful. Sanzo's Italian pedigree emerged with only the best intentions. Leentje nipped at him – playfully so - but when he did not correctly heed, she came in with a bite. It was that alluring duality of Dutch women; the will and ability to simultaneously embrace you and knock you to the ground - with equal precision.

Without warning, Leentje ditched her impeccable English and began speaking in her Dutch. Sanzo's vocabulary was limited; mine was better and always gained momentum during my Amsterdam nights.

Sanzo decided it was time to say goodnight. I helped him load his amp and equipment onto his bike. He assured me that in one year exactly, he and I would share the Café's stage. I bid him "Ciao Sanzo.!" He peddled away, ringing his Pat Metheny-sounding bell. "*Tot Siens Franco!*" he replied.

The trust of the innocent is the liar's most useful tool.

—STEPHEN KING

I was in good form and continued to quench my thirst. For the next hour, Leentje seemed just fine, then her switch flipped; she walked out of the Café as if under some spell. She explained that she had to find her bike so that she could ride home. Simple enough. I offered my assistance- after walking in circles for a few minutes, I finally realized that Leentje was totally hammered. I suggested that she come inside the Café so that Tommie could assist.

"She can't ride home." Tommie ruled. Without me catching it, he was selling her on the idea that I walk her home. I couldn't refuse Tommie, so I agreed to walk her home. Tommie would later – some time later - confess that he had forgotten to reserve a cab and was too tired to walk her home, and so dumped Leentje on me - knowing that she was in good hands.

Obviously oblivious to Tommie's "dump and run", yet how foolish was I – in retrospect - to feel the need to assure him, of all people. And yet I did: "Tommie. Listen. All joking aside. You don't have to worry; it's all *gezellig*".

Even worse, he kept up his ruse, by joking, *"Yes, Sax Man, but you are on holiday, and you seem to have a way with these Dutch women."*

Ha Ha, Tommie.

Dare to be honest and fear no labor.

—Robert Burns

And so, with my tenor and soprano as our chaperones, I would walk Leentje safely to *haar flaat* – her place. We navigated three street corners over those now fully resurrected first four bars of "Autumn Leaves," being sung with a repeat – one marked with the infinity sign. Leentje just would not let that classic go. I tried to get along - so I sang along, answering her on bars three and four - her one trick pony.

After a few storefronts, I grew weary. When—as an act of protest—I modulated the pitch up a half step, Leentje adjusted and changed key as well.

Keep walking.

We were now over seven street corners into our walk, with my ever-heavier horns. I broke a sweat. I thought to ask her in Dutch, *Ho vie feder* (further) *ees ut hui* (house), *en engles alstublief* (English, please).

She replied, "It's not really any of your business, but we are almost there. Just a little way."

"Bijna, [almost]? ja?"

"No lame Dutch from you. No English either. Silence!"

We kept walking. When we had well passed her "almost there," I started to get salty with skepticism.

Yes, lame Dutch from me.

"Slat ons maar links (left) *oof ons rehts* (right) *oof?"*

She replied in Dutch, *"Niemand* (Neither). *Mein flat ees en Leidseplein."*

Leidesplein! Leidesplein???

I fished out a La Fleur cigarette from the half-pack tucked into my soprano case that I had bartered from a French fan and his hot Indian date in exchange for a quarter-pack of Marlboros. How desperately I now needed a few pulls from Napoleonic tobacco to reconfigure my broken {cassé -*fr*} compass.

Although hardly straight or sober, I knew full well where I was, and I knew where Leidseplein was not. What I did not know was what now to do other than smoke. Those first four bars – like a bird call continued chiming in, now outright mocking me. I set my tenor and soprano on the cobblestone, leaned up against a bicycle, took its seat, and continued to smoke. Leentje asked for a taste. "It's French." I retorted. After a rookie puff, she started to get wobbly, uttered something in French, and turned away from me.

Damn it. What I saw about to unfold could not happen. Leentje was - in firefighter's parlance - "out of service." We were now where I knew Leidseplein was nowhere near, and we had already walked three canals away from my hotel, which was as far as our caravan could realistically make. Getting to Leidesplein for me alone with two saxophone chaperones would have taken everything out of me. Trying to put logic out of my mind, I lit up a second La Fleur from the nub of the first. It rebelled, becoming the preamble to my game plan.

I explained to Leentje that we simply could not make it on foot to Leidseplein. With no cabs in sight and no way to hail one, the only plausible solution… was that we about-face… and… she would stay with me and that it would be *gezellig*.

Leentje started looking around for her bike. How very strange that, from where we stood, in a city with as many bikes as people, there was only one bike in sight and other than its lock and chain was dilapidated.

I pulled out yet a third La Fleur (for which I was so thankful), stuck it in my mouth, lit it from my fresh one, and then passed it to her as I exhaled, dusting the air with hopes of French diplomacy, if not just a bit of Dutch perspicacity.

Leentje grabbed and dropped it. I fished it out of the cobblestone and inspected it and passed her mine, making sure she had it before I let go. We finished them silently, leaning into each other over the Beursplein cobblestone.

After its last, full pull, I called up all of the Dutch I could, hoping to get her to chillax. "*Nay slecht me* (no bad me); *Ik ben ut advocaat* (attorney); *u bent me niet blij* (you are me not happy); *niet blij reis* (not happy trip)."

Leentje tried to keep a straight face, but still burst out laughing at me.

I offered my arm and tried to pick up the pace. My trusty shortcuts were out of the question. All the while, my tenor and soprano were causing my unoffered arm to burn.

Finally, just outside the buzz-in door to the hotel lobby, wiping my sweaty face, I announced, "*Hoe blij* [happy] *ben ik* [I] *dat wie* [we] *zijn hier* [here]."

Leentje seemed caught off-guard and began to spin in some intoxication-laced panic, paranoia, confusion, thankfully tempered with cheeky curiosity. Whether fight or flight, she was clearly on the verge of charging. She said something that sounded like what the dawn hotel staff used to say to when I returned from my nights of playing, then began to slump. With no time to set down my horns, I desperately hoisted her to a rubbery, upright - with my knee posted under her admirable posterior. Shaking off the burn in my joints, I gazed into her wobbly eyes and said in my version of Cary Grant–laced Dutch, "*Niet meer gespreken en Nederlands; Engels, astublief, mijn mooi vrouw* (No more Dutch! English will have to do, my dear)."

This exclamation, more for my benefit than hers, got her attention, however blurry. Next, I shifted dialect gears to faux-John Cleese/ sarcasms for my own sake - I proclaimed, "*I am well respected in this manor and in this manner. I have earned a finest of fine reputation as being a gentleman's gentleman of civility, humility, propriety, and piety...*"

Pushing this, I pushed, *"Ye will not embarrass me. Taketh mine handeth. 'Here into, Lettuce head. Romaine!' Vamanos, Lechuga Degas, entramos nosotros into this hallowed place. So, scamper through the lobby; lumber to the lift. Uppy we goey, Missy – no woey. On a dime – to my quarters. Fully credentialed and credenza- executive—sovereign— veranda, Miranda…downwind from some Indonesian sweatshop, where Multatuli's mother-in-law…turns tricks and mends Muumuus…"*

Why I resorted to this gibberish, I cannot explain.

> **It takes many good deeds to build a good
> reputation, and only one bad one to lose it.**

—BENJAMIN FRANKLIN

My "sharp flat" situated over the Dam Plein, where flags of the Netherlands and Amsterdam fly from masts fixed to its open balcony was so very fine. Whenever I open its French doors the sensation of being aboard some docked Dutch sailing vessel has fed my lively imagination.

I literally pointed this feature of the Hotel Amsterdam's façade to Leentje, my last hope to prevent a bad scene from unfolding and being denied forever more this cherished room (let alone any other) at this magnificent iconic Hotel.

I fished out my second-to-last La Fleur, lit it up, and pulled. With a smoky, French underground air about me and now out of concocted character, with a tetchiness, I laid down the law.

"Showtime, Leentje. You are going to pull your shit together, girl, right now, and be the poster child for '*gezellig*'. I will count down from ten, and when we get to one, you'd better '*gezellig-up*', or we will both be lying in the street and then all bets will be off for both of us. And if you feel yourself starting to freak out, just sing 'Autumn Leaves'.

Leentje was swaying and listing and leaning, laughing and cleverly mocking my self-mockery. This was my hand and I was about to go all in. What would be the worst that could possibly happen?

I began my dreaded count. When it was at "one," Leentje turned my shaking arm loose, picked up her pace, strolled away from me into the lobby, said something apparently charming to the night desk clerk, smelled the flowers, grabbed two apples from the bowl, walked to the open elevator and while faking an apple toss, held it open for me. As my saxophones and I staggered in, she shifted one of the apples from her left hand to under her chin, casually pressed the button to the second floor, and then Sir Isaac Newtoned it to her right. When the elevator door opened, she said, "Go." With Leentje now getting pushy, I fumbled a bit - then finally keyed open the door to my room.

She stepped across me, pushed it open like a pro, heeled it for me, and then entered the room.

Once inside, however, like a Dutch "*Sybil*", she began to rekindle her squirrelly "find my bike" fixation. Now finally in my element, I called for the apples, and set them in a lined wicker basket and placed it atop a chic Euro-wooden coffee table, just under its spot light.

As gingerly as I could muster, I finally released my horns onto easy chairs and let out a guttural moan. Leentje sat back on the bed, arms outstretched, and then fell backward. I pushed up, dove across the pillows from the other side, latched my arms across her just before she bounced off. My heroics tensed her up and sent her to the verge of freaking out. I jumped off the bed nearly hitting the deck myself. She sat up propping the pillows behind her back as if to get comfy then began to stare at me in a pejorative way.

"Ohhh no you don't." I raised Leentje's gaze with a look that stated: "Don't kid yourself. That was no cheap feel. I don't do cheap feels. Whatever inadvertent contact was made – that's on you."

Leentje seemed to feel bad about having given me the "hairy eye-ball". Seizing the turning tide, I pointed to the chair and quietly asked for her permission to sit down. I silenced my moans as I slumped into this Italian leathered sanctuary.

After about two motionless, silent minutes, her eyes closed; mine were right behind...

I gently, surgically cautiously, took off her boots. She turned slightly and tucked her arm under her head. I rotated her out of her coat, rolled her with paramedic-trained panache, and then gingerly covered her. The broken record began to play – those first four bars of "Autumn Leaves". But this time, Leentje sang the bridge and took it the last refrain...then fell asleep.

Finally, I took off my overcoat, tossed it onto my tenor case, pried my shoes from two barking dogs and was ready to sleep in *La Poltronna Italiana*. All I needed was that last La Fleur - my Red Auerbach victory cigar. Tiptoeing out and onto the balcony, shamefully about to break yet another of my hotel's written rules, I proclaimed *"Vive la France,"* I and lit her up. As she burned down, an unfamiliar, faint noise from beyond Centraal Station crept in and then grew louder. I could not place it. I did not like it. It was something big—so with the general quarters alarm having sounded, I snuffed out the last La Fleur—half smoked—and carefully tippy-toed back inside to my station.

The next two hours, as the room's digital clock mockingly announced, I limped forward in time assailed by a noise that violated the Geneva Convention. It was a sonic sheer that some laborer's apprentice might have made by persistently misusing a jackhammer in a futile attempt to uncouple two wrecked freight train cars, one loaded with scrap metal – the other, rocking from the shift in its poorly-secured kitchen equipment.

Leentje's snore was an untapped crowd control device. What came out of her defied the very laws of sonics. My brain stem was being seismically ripped away with her every respiration. After what seemed to be my extended sentence to incomprehensible torture, a last sober thought crawled out until I somehow passed out:

What in the world will Melaura make of his?

Sometime around six in the morning, Leentje's silence startled me. I jumped up, completely disoriented, and assumed a fighting stance, ready to attack. I somehow managed to reset my bearings and self-issue a "stand down" while now sucking air through my all-over achiness.

Neither of us said a word. We just stood there. Leentje was fine, I was still gasping and disoriented. This would not be *"Goedemorgen"* or making her coffee or offering her breakfast. She gathered up her belongings, knocking over the makeshift, towel-draped puke bucket I fashioned. Shaking her head – mocking my scout effort - Leentje headed for the door and without looking back, muttered something to herself, followed by a thready *"tot siens."* She was gone. Her awkward departure reminded me of my young prosecutor early morning escapes.

For the very first time in my many, up-too-early Amsterdam mornings, I fell back asleep – resuming my place, over the covers on three-eighths of the bed. After I officially awakened three hours later and went through my morning ritual, I did question whether this had been but a dream. Two apples answered no.

> **If I take care of my character, my**
> **reputation will take care of me.**
>
> **—DWIGHT L. MOODY**

I meandered my way into brisk air to *Renee's* for my "to go" (*meene-men*) double espresso and a potato-sized baguette to take in on the steps of my Dam Square stage. In due time, still shaking my head, with my ears still ringing, I began my jittery walk to the Café. By time I made it into Zeedijk, I realized that my standing, my reputation, in the vibrant, inti-mate community in which I had always considered myself but an appre-ciated guest, had changed.

The details of what had transpired only hours before, and that I had already made up my mind I would keep under wraps, were already out there. The word, out on Zeedijk, caught up with me as I tried – ears still ringing - to commence with my daily routine. Throughout the day, I was flowered with expressions of gratitude for having watched over their beloved Leentje.

When asked what I thought of her, I responded with one word, "*Drilboor*," taught to me by my hotel's handyman, which so-accurately translated to "jackhammer". My precision trumped its intended humor. "*Eigenlijk, dat ees Leentje.*" Leentje, my exclusive slumber party invitee, could both sing it sweetly and with sway with her sultry croon – yet could shift the earth with her megaton master-blaster uvula. And that I tended to her as I should have, the earth shifted a bit for me.

It was an avouchment across the board. Leentje trusted me; I trusted her, and even better, we trusted each other – which is the essential com-ponent of any successful sleepover.

I was confident that Melaura would accept my impending confession in the same way as Leentje and our Dutch friends accepted that their otherwise-reserved Leentje and I bedded together.

Love has no age, no limit; and no death.

—JOHN GALSWORTHY

My rapturous return to Melaura, with us making up for lost time then exchanging barbs about my slumber party confession would give way to tears and be darkened with sadness.

On March 30, 2010, a vibrant, beaming young man was taken from everyone who loved him. While he and his crew were advancing an attack line into a single-family home to valiantly back up a rescue team that commenced a rescue search, Homewood Firefighter/Paramedic Brian Colin Carey, who was on the nozzle, gave his life.

Brian embraced life and its every kind of music; genial in a princely way, he was always so very eager to please others. A young man of good deeds and a calling for service to others, Brian loved to read, to travel, to run and to debate…With an irrefutable Irish charm, Brian had the old county gift of bringing out a big smile across the face of anyone in his presence - even bigger than his treasured one.

On the morning of Brian's funeral, current and former members of the Homewood Fire Department gathered at the station. As was done so many times before some of us and after many more of us, the Company Officer announced our apparatus assignments. From there, each crew self-designated an officer, engineer and firefighters to answer this call.

Brian's funeral was held at St. Bernadette's Church in Evergreen Park, a blue-collar South Suburb where his family had roots. Along the route from the Church to Holy Sepulchre Cemetery, sidewalks, town-homes, businesses, parking lots, apartment buildings, gas stations, houses of worship, bungalows and convenience stores, street corners, and porches were manned by ordinary citizens of every kind and the rank and file of every school along the way. Chicago police, fire, and streets and sanitation crews filled in. CTA buses stopped – passengers poured out to pay their respects. Catholic School Sports teams and their coaches and staff were in their uniforms- you could see on their faces how they were taking to heart the important meaning in all of this.

Fire Departments poured in from all over the region, the state and beyond – from far and wide - to be there as a company of one, to honor Brian Colin Carey and to comfort his family and friends. Along the parade route, I saw for the first time in so many years, fellow firefighters with whom I had worked shift - who had left Homewood to serve on other departments. They stood parade dress, donning their Class A's, backed by their spit-polished, black-bunted apparatus. One of Homewood Fire's former members, Ken Sterling ['Cy Sperling'] staged an engine that he alone manned, standing at attention until the very last of the procession filed by.

After Brian's funeral, family, friends, firefighters and other public safety personnel gathered to mourn and drink.

Just as our crew was about to depart, a young firefighter from a down-state department was having a medical emergency. One of the very best medics on our Department and I assumed patient care in Homewood 562. We stabilized him – then the three of us held each other and cried.

I returned to the station on Homewood 564, the ambulance in which my very first "save" was recorded almost a decade before. Seated backwards, I shared patient compartment with flowers gathered up from Brian's gravesite, reverently arranged from floor to the ceiling, which were to be delivered to and entrusted with churches, schools, and busi-nesses throughout our village.

I thought of my Grampa Vartan, who cheated death when he was young and lived to be very old and his beautiful, fragrant flowers... and for the first time since his passing, some thirty years before, I recalled Grampa Vartan's beaming smile, hearty laugh and clever wit.

As I drank in the bouquet from the delicate mountain of flowers, which gave me comfort, and reflected on the day's bittersweet story, I resolved to honor Brian Colin Carey evermore - to never forget this Prince of a Man - "Boo", to those who loved him the most, dearly cherished him and knew just how special he was. I would revere Brian's family by rededicating myself to living the kind of life and celebrating it in those ways, which shall forever define Brian Colin Carey's: Flowing with music... filled with laughter and charmed sentiments...and ever-donning a wide and warm Irish smile.

Brian Colin Carey.

**For life and death are one,
even as the river and the sea are one.**

—KHALIL GIBRAN

CHAPTER XXVIII

MUZIK

Music is medicine.

—Jason F. Danielian, Suffolk University Forensic Speech Team (1984)

Amsterdam bestowed music unto my soul - and bestowed my soul deeply onto Amsterdam. Playing there freed me from my doubts. When in Amsterdam, no permission or justification was needed to collaborate and play. The Amsterdam scene was all about sharing, passing it around and drawing the audience into the conversation.

I loved music for so long and it always seemed to reciprocate in greater measures. Kind and forgiving, always willing to hear me out, yet it would never hesitate to correct or even scold me. Music never left me out, put me down – and certainly would not let me off the hook.

Making the most of performing with other musicians took on greater meaning over the years. When I was much younger, "making the most" meant a failed attempt; one full of sour notes – "clams" - at best, eluding embarrassment. With time, honest assessment and greater determination, I make up my mind to not sloppily stab at what I was not ready to play. This honest resolve progressed into earnest effort, albeit with marginal success, to relay a decipherable message; this left me wanting more - and the willingness to actually work for it.

By playing more and committing to a relationship with my horn, I found greater confidence and achieved more proficiency. I accepted the fact that I liked playing more than practicing, which meant that my saxophony would only improve so much. And I was okay with that. Through the benevolence of others - much better musicians who appreciated my love for music, perhaps more for what I could hear than I could play, I was given opportunities to perform and the platform upon which to show whatever I had.

I grew increasingly at ease and self-confident when playing types of music I liked to play and in performance settings right for me. Yet when it came to music I either did not like or would not commit a proper effort, what came out of my bell was either stubborn or lacking. Given these and many other limitations, I clearly was not cut out to be a professional musician.

This hired-gun precision was necessary for an aspiring musician to both earn a living and build a reputation. I had neither the conviction nor the stamina to nail it, night after night, gig after gig, sometimes two a day; even if I did like the lead sheets or scores in front of me, I just did not want music in that way. I am forever grateful that professional musicians who recognized my limitations appreciated my taste in and love for music – and that I was so perfectly excited to play, I could lay it down with at least some measure of respectability.

> *What I have in mind is [a classroom] where [students] could sit around a table with a teacher who would talk with them, and instruct them by a sort of tutorial or conference method, where [each student] would feel encouraged to speak up. This would be a real revolution in methods.*
>
> —*EDWARD HARKNESS, PHILANTHROPIST*

In those moments, music delivered to me what nothing else in my life could. Not even my most impassioned trial advocacy, my finest cuisine, or feverishly running a full court offense; not even reducing stories to words – through the rhythm of Umair's mandate- could draw out from me what playing my saxophones can. And to the extent that my audience has been pleased, I chock it up to the lawyer in me; advocating their love of music, then resting my case.

Amsterdam would enhance my musical experience, bring out more from my saxophones and allow my soul to come out from hiding. No matter where I performed there and with whom I shared the stage, it was welcoming and endearing and I would be ushered in to make my mark. During these energized Amsterdam sessions, the other musicians - knowing that I had come all this way to be a part of their experience - made sure that my journey left me fulfilled, eager for the next year's round of sessions.

Music is the distillation of the spirit, the atmosphere,
and the soul of a place in sound.

—*Kurt Elling*

There was such giddiness and great joy during those Amsterdam sessions, with devotion and kinship abound. The sound was robust and groove was deep. From other wayfarers, I took note of and poached such great lines and phrases and learned how they viewed performance art both on the stage and in between sets.

Years later, during my first Dutch-speaking year, I learned that unlike the American English version of the word "hobby", which conjures up images of flying a kite on a Sunday afternoon, music was *mijn hobby* – my "passion" or "avocation".

The expectations of life depend upon diligence;
the mechanic that would perfect his work
must first sharpen his tools.

—*Confucius*

One late night (early morning) in Amsterdam, while sitting in with a Funk/Ska band, and a sax player walked in. He had the same case as mine, but carried his with the dual backpack straps – not the meatier, single sling over the right shoulder that I fancied. I was hoping he would sit in on this clearly announced last set. Instead, he inserted his case into side of the stage and hung back. After the colossal hit concluded, I introduced myself... to Maxime, a Belgian, now living and playing in Amsterdam. We sat and drank and talked. Maxime shared with me his struggle with the music; his elusive, dangerous quest – the one that I totally rejected many years ago. I sympathized, but thankfully could not empathize. Music and I had a cozy relationship.

Many Stella Artois later, I began to say my good-byes. I had already packed up my horn and had it set to back of the stage, under the upright piano. As I made my way to the door, Maxime became unhinged. My intoxication notwithstanding, I easily ran the numbers and tallied up - Maxime thought that I was stealing his horn.

13. Corpus delicti—Getting out of Hock

Seeing no other choice but to undercut and outright befuddle both the Judge and the appointed attorney of a pair of career criminals, I "recommended" their releases, but requested that their cases be held over to the next day. The complaining witness, victim of their crime, was sitting in the back of the court-room, unable to decipher any of this, let alone imagine what I was about to set in motion.

When the rag-tag pair's attorney questioned my posture, the Judge snapped:

"Hey! Would you prefer that your clients stay locked up for two weeks? He's agreeing to let them out! Defendants released; case held on call to tomorrow. Call the next case."

As the Judge and public defender continued to go at each other off the record, their clients stared at me until they passed back through the security door to the lock-up. When I turned toward the complainant, he was already gone.

I called in a favor so that the lockup keeper would push the paperwork through and expedite their out-processing. At the service entrance to the Area's loading dock/ lockup exit waited their arresting Officer and me. They shot me a look, as if certain that I had toyed with them and was about to rear-rested - and put some other case on them - just for good measure.

I told them, straight out, that if they would allow the police officer and me to violate their Fifth and Sixth Amendment rights, were willing to disclose the pawn shop where they hocked their victim's property and let us take them there and 'straighten this mis-understanding out', I would dismiss the case. The younger, mouthier of the two pushed back:

"What if we don't?"

"Then I will likely be fired from the State's Attorney's Office and face disbarment - probably lose my law license - because, as I told you, I have vio-lated your constitutional rights."

The worn and hardened, older of the duo finally spoke, pointing his finger in the face to his much younger, mouthier cohort: *"We gonna' do what he say. I told you that messin' with horns is wrong. This here cat, see he's trying to make all of this right. We doin' his thing…. But you guts to be straight with me, Mr. State's Attorney. You is trippin' cause it's a horn, ain't that so? Be straight with me man."*

"It's not just a horn, my good man. It's a 1968 Selmer Mark VI Tenor Saxophone. Gentlemen. Shall we go on a Freedom Ride?"

I bartered away the "$2,500" tag dangling from the neck of this thing of beauty with the pawnbroker, courtesy of my business card inscribed with *"No goods herein shall be subject to seizure - unless pursuant to a search warrant or an open investigation a crime of violence - without first contacting ASA Minasian."*

Once that vintage horn was in my care and custody, there remained but one last order of business. I asked the Officer to find the complainant and make sure that he got a ride to court the next morning.

Once the *corpus delicti* was in his hands, its owner said, "Hey, State's Attorney. You didn't fool me. I knew that you played the sax from the moment you stepped out in front of the Judge. Shit, you probably better than me. I could see that you made up your mind to get me my horn back. I appreciate what you did for me - and I appreciate what you did for the two guys who robbed me. I bought that horn brand new, when you was just a kid - a smart kid, I'll bet - and a handful too... That horn cost me just about everything I owned. And thanks to you, it's all good…

> *I think to the extent you die with money in
> the bank, you've miscalculated.*
>
> —GARY DAVID GOLDBERG

I started to explain the whole single strap/backpack thing to Maxime. Given his highly intoxicated state, reason, let alone my complex explanation, was not going to trump his set suspicions. So, I laid my case down onto the chair and told the story about what was inside.

I recounted how some twenty-five years before, I had participated in a high school speech competition, in preparation for which I wrote no speech; I memorized nothing. On the night before the big event, I worked – as a dishwasher. On Saturday morning I still stunk of sauté pans, steam trays and swill. As my dolled-up Ma and Dad drove, I slept. When I got to the clunky old American Legion Hall, scores of High Students were buzzing around practicing their obviously memorized speeches, changing words to their bound papers. When it was my turn, I told the audience "What Democracy Means to Me".

With the results of the contest being announced, considering who took third and second place, I was certain that I had won—but I did not. First place went to a buffoon whose words barely connected and who was shaking while preaching about the evils of communism and women's liberation. Whoever ghost wrote it for him was obviously senile.

I went home and then got ready for my double shift; Saturdays were always out of control. When I got home, sometime after midnight, slimy, stinking, and slumping, my Ma was having a warm talk and hot coffee with a gentleman.

He introduced himself as the speech contest's benefactor. He told me that a terrible mistake had been made and that I had won, head and shoulders above everyone else, and that, somehow, they thought my scorecard was part of the scoring rules. He told me that notwithstanding my perfect score, he could not ask for the money back from the "winner," but he insisted that I accept his personal check for half of the first prize (third-prize money), adding that it was a brilliant speech - "*It left all us stunned. It was certainly worth more than this check.*"

"With that money," I proclaimed to the crowd of bar patrons that had moved in close, "I purchased *this.*" I opened the case and revealed my 1927 Evette-Scheaffer, to the roar of the crowd and the laugher of Maxime, my accuser turned straight-man.

"May I play your saxophone?" The room went silent. I paused; then told him that I had never ever let anyone play my horn; paused, then said: "Maxime, it would be my honor."

I handed him my strap and even offered up my mouthpiece. He was a bit wobbly, so not wanting to create too many moving parts, I did not hand my horn over to him. Instead, I set it back into the case and let him get his feel for its weight and balance. I figured that if I tried to hand it to him, one of us just might miss the other's cue.

Maxime popped his vintage Otto-link mouthpiece onto it, took it for a walk - then a stroll - then a jog -then a run, - then a sprint -finally something that rivaled the Flash. He circled around the earth of my tenor, winding sound and technique like some massive spool of copper wire, forming a coil and generating a magnetic flow of pure energy.

Maxime was a superhero on my saxophone; the only one I played for almost three decades. My mouthpiece, nestled in my case, had recently replaced the only one I played for almost four decades.

I do not quite know what inspired me to look into mouthpieces. Until then, "mouthpiece" was slang for "lawyer." There just somehow came a time when mine did not seem right for my horn and did not feel right in my mouth. So, way out of the blue, I contacted a mouthpiece maker. I told him what I was looking for and why.

Dance must have a precision without fault.

—*Arielle Dombasle*

Jody Espina recognized my symptoms, offered up his time, advice, and rendered a delicate diagnosis. I asked him how buying a mouthpiece works; he said that he would ship it to me, and I could check it out. If I did not like it, I need only return it unscathed. When it arrived, it felt like an early Christmas – albeit on a sweltering August day. The windows were closed, with my recently replaced air conditioning unit cranking.

I pulled out and readied my tenor. Selected a reed from a rubber-banded group of ones set aside for special occasions; broken-in, proven predicable and smitten by my spit. I had even graded them so that I could call the right one into service for the right moment. Although I dreaded picking over boxes of reeds and breaking them in, it was a tedious task well worth it.

For this holiday performance, I conservatively opted for a B+. I fastened the reed onto this glistening mouthpiece then, more gently than usual, joined it to the neck; this shiny shank of precision metal fit like a glove. My hands were shaking and my heart was beating fast.

The first note I played rushed through the neck, carried deep into the horn, and eventually came out of the bell and around the room and into my ears. For the very first time, my horn seemed happy that I was playing it. This mouthpiece delivered a sound that had eluded me; now it was filling my horn and coloring the room.

There was a time in my life when I went so long without playing. My horn grew dust fell into utter disrepair. I looked at it – in such a decrepit state - and then asked myself aloud: *"Play or don't play? Call it a day and pack it away, or get on your horn and keep chasin' it? Make up your mind, Franco."*

I found a repairman in Jersey City, who gave my horn the same look Dr. Sceduri gave me during my skin and bones examination; although he was angrier with me than she was. I apologized and told him "We've been through a rough patch, but we've reconciled". He replied: "Don't ever let it happen it again."

My new mouthpiece was like our third honeymoon.

Maxime unstrapped my horn and handed it back to me, anatomically correct and protectively balanced. The crowd receded, knowing that this should a private moment. He looked me in the eyes and said, "I'm sorry, but you need a new horn; you are beyond this horn, Franco. It's holding you back. I heard you play. You know I did. I know you love this old girl, but it is time to say good-bye to her. You need a new horn. You have to believe me. And I know, I know - I thought you were a thief. But this, Franco, what I am telling you – it is doubtless."

There are no constraints on the human mind,
no walls around the human spirit,
and no barriers to our progress except
those we ourselves erect.

—*Ronald Reagan*

I was on my flight home, my horn overhead. Once I landed, still buzzing from this trip, I continued to ponder, and even lament, Maxime's edict. I was willing to trust in what he told me; after all, it rang as sincerely and with the conviction of Billy Quill's prophetic "Change is good" talk. But this was different. This was my horn of thirty years; my travel companion, my center stage partner and beloved showpiece.

One week to the day after having returned from Amsterdam, I received a call from Barry Sperti, saxophone repairman extraordinaire - who had tended to mine for over fifteen years. Barry, who I refer to as "my pediatrician" is a smooth and melodic player; a well-rounded singer with a tasty range and resonating sound.

I was always the one to call him; never the other way around. I would call in desperation, seeking Barry's services to fix a leak, stop a squeak, unstick the stuck, tune-ups and most importantly – to give them a pre-Amsterdam clean bill of health.

Barry's call to me was out of the blue.

Acknowledging how he had never really kept tabs on me, he figured that I settled back in from Amsterdam. Barry explained that "While you were doing your thing over there, I came into a great tenor sax - and - well, something told me to put it to the side, wait until you get back from Amsterdam and give you a call and – well, get this horn ready for you. I just feel that this is going to work out for you."

Maxime.

Before I picked it up, I had a long reassuring, appreciative, reminiscent talk with mine, sympathetically removing my strap and my mouthpiece; it was reminiscent of turning off the lights and tip-toing from my children's bedroom just after they fell asleep.

There were so many great things about "Barry's beauty". It was very demanding and rewarding, patient but uncompromising. But there was much about its mechanics, my clumsiness with its keys and a most troubling feeling of unfamiliarity that was now getting into my head and distracting me – and I could hear it in my playing.

Needing some sound advice, I reached out to Rodney Rosebird, a burning, bad-to-the-bone baritone sax player, with whom Melaura and I had pleasure of meeting after a Chicago Theatre gig [Royal Scam - Steely Dan]. As a conversationalist, he displayed the same measure of precision and conviction as in his playing; Rodney was a great listener and with a warm smile.

Out of the blue, I called him - and to my surprise, he picked up. I could hear NYC (New Amsterdam) in the background and sensed that he was on his way to a gig. I made my case succinctly, expressing my concerns. Rodney listened, then laid it all down:

"You can spend a lifetime searching for the perfect horn, letting some good ones get away. Therefore, this is what you must address: Is it giving you a platform over and above your old horn upon which to improve your sound and better your playing? Are you willing to work with this horn, get to know it and - if necessary - compromise or, at a minimum, consider changing some old ways? If the answer to those questions is yes, then buy the horn. Even if you are not sure, buy the horn. That you are calling, tells me something. Actually, it tells me everything. Look, if you can afford it, buy the horn. Even if you can't you should buy it. You need to buy that horn. I suspect that you already knew this. So, buy the horn. Enjoy."

14. Criminal Justice— Consideration and/or Kindness

As one old-timer, paddy-wagon cop told me when I had just started in the office - fresh out of law school, "Always Remember: Even when you can't make a buck, you can always make a friend. That's the way you should do business out here. And I don't mean shaking people down. What I mean is for as long as you stay in the office and then when you go out on your own — make sure you spend your money wisely and make friends whenever and with whomever you can."

I took his advice and befriended private attorneys, forensic chemists, PDs, hypes, court sergeants, loan sharks, clerks, beat cops, hookers, federal agents, bookies, doctors, car thieves, social workers, born killers, detectives, counterfeiters and everyone in between.

I would assist and at times enlist other local, state, federal, and diplomatic law enforcement personnel- at all hours of the day or night - with time typically being of the essence and with high stakes in play.

In so many ways, being a prosecutor was like my street musician days, except with a briefcase rather than my horns; the take-home pay, oddly enough, was comparable.

Building cases and working up files was invigorating. Sizing up the evidence and then making the call was like improvising over a jazz standard. Having the power to dispense justice with the will to exercise discretion and determination set things right defined my professional life. In any situation, be it a hotly contested jury trial or during long hours at a police lockup or while chasing down information out on the street, I never let go of the marching papers I was issued when hired as prosecutor with the Office: Always Do the Right Thing.

CHAPTER XXIX

TROUBADOUR

Wherever you go, go with all your heart.

—*Confucius*

During my fourth trip to Amsterdam, I struck up a conversation with a Hotel Amsterdam's receptionist about my Law School/ street-musician days. Both he and my fellow guests who joined in seemed perplexed by two realms: one – delving into the prim, arduous study of law; the other my saxophone escapades - in an almost fictional place.

*Chicago is constantly auditioning for the
world, determined that one day,
on the streets of Barcelona, in Berlin's cabarets,
in the coffee shops of Istanbul,
people will know and love us in our multidimensional glory,
dream of us the way they dream of San
Francisco and New York.*

—*Mary Schmich*

After grinding through my 1L classes before my virtually all-night studies, I would meet up with a street performance band and enter into Chicago's overland and underbelly—the CTA – with its lattice of elevated and subway trains and buses; musician-friendly conductors and drivers.

Years before becoming a prosecutor, I made friends with beat cops who loved our music and would clear the good spots for us; some of whom would – years later - be my trial witnesses; conductors who would slow things down - leave the doors open and peer their heads out from their cabins, taking in offering their riders a minute or two of soulful music.

On occasion, I would face mean-spirited patrons of a certain ilk who would tell me to "Get a real job." I would reply with my pat, overly apologetic, "I really don't have the time for a real job; with law school and all."

Once taken aback, I made them mine. "How much do you make an hour at your real job? I'm sure that like us, you are underpaid. You have a real job because those who underpay you like your work. And while this may not be a real job, we nonetheless invite those who like what we do to underpay us."

Once talk turned to soulful sounds, wallets would open and the money would flow.

I saw it all in the subway—drunkenness, sex, delirium, pickpockets, and even death. I am glad that this was pre-smart-phones, tweeting and streaming and viral and the rest.

Our band's cutting edge technologically consisted of our guitarist's state-of the art battery-powered amp. When either a guitar or a bass string would break, we would put on a light show for our crowds, tossing the "dearly departed" across and onto both the second and third rails, generating an arc with a firework-like fanfare; the Upright Bass's Low E string could rattle teeth from its immense sonic blast. We referred to it as a "Richter Scale in C...TA"

Malique Kohsan's scuffed and scratched, dinged and dented, pin-repaired cracks and splits, ancient upright bass had a sweet, assertive sound that would resonate through the subway tunnel (the hole) in a mighty way. True to Spinal Tap, our band went through drummers galore – the last was our sixth. The best of them was a heroin addict, to whom we would give a higher percentage of the cut; the worst was a brother who strutted like a real, hip hipster; his swagger and rap were unmatched, but his playing was oh so corny, in a very painful way.

The band's name changed as it transformed from R&B through Rockabilly to Straight Ahead. We were once hired on the spot at Washington and Dearborn stop to play at Northwestern Memorial Hospital, for a rich doll's husband - who had just undergone surgery and was recovering. It was his birthday.

Knowing that we could always cajole, sweet-talk or Bogart our way into any spot, we took the "gig".

In these situations, I would take charge, employing Moe's tactics to get through the door. And when I found myself and the band against the ropes, I waxed whatever legalese I had feverishly taken notes on that day; as if on cue, Malique would lay down a walking bass line under it. Once I stopped taking and we all started playing, we were in and owned the audience.

That hospital-room gig was as surreal as a San Francisco acid trip. We turned the ICU floor into a sock hop, jamming on tutti-frutti for fifteen minutes. It culminated with the birthday-boy patient lumbering out of his bed, IV, and catheter lines and all, with his ass hanging out, doing his postop version of "The Twist meets the Duck Walk." This was to the sheer delight of the nurses and other patients and their guests—and to the shock of the resident who made his way past the crowd to do his obligatory rounds. Just as he threated to call security, I reminded him of studies that had proven that music releases endorphins – and so he regard us an integral component of his patient's healing process. I then suggested that he take a break from his rounds and dance with which-ever nurse he had his sights on. The doctor took my advice, as we played [with a dirty bass intro] *"Fever"* ... For that hour's worth of madness, we made five hundred dollars, *"cayshhh"*.

There were times when, either before or after playing, the boys and I felt the urge to play for food. We would walk around, searching for the perfect spot, sniffing out the perfect cuisine to satisfy our palettes. We would then stroll into the chosen restaurant, pitch the maître d', and close the deal. We did this not because we had to; we could pay for any meal, albeit in small bills or handfuls of change. We did this because we knew we could - and somehow felt as though we were historically obliged. We set up, hit, and then feast. Troubadours of the highest order were we. Hoofing it around Chi-town, playing for food— it was so medieval. It would get my head right for the looming overnight case briefings and memoranda typing.

At each of these play-for-food gigs, the host or hostess in the front of the house was truly puzzled; he or she would be incredulous - but never refused our offer. The back of the house almost always produced a chef/percussionist, playing congas on an oversized, seasoned stockpot - or a breathtaking dishwasher/vocalist. From the front of the house's wait staff often came hand-clapping, an impromptu dance troupe, or background vocals; always with rhythm and in harmony. We would never ever, *ever* accept any money from the patrons. Instead, we asked them to pass their intended gratuities on – to the house.

This was bartering, arguably pure communism in the truest, highest form. That I was in the midst of the rigor and incongruity of law school made this all the more worthwhile and important. The drudgery of *Prosser and Keeton on Torts* and *The Bluebook: A Uniform System of Citation* and the *UCC* was always best served after these great meals.

As I recounted those law school moments, the faces of my listeners showed disbelief. It seemed I should back up my story and prove that it was hardly fictional.

"Please excuse me, just for a minute. I'll be right back."

I grabbed my tenor from my room, returned to the lobby and invited the guests to join me. One of the clerks said "Shake a leg." After which his coworker, with explanation in Dutch, corrected him and then she said, "Break a leg." Her co-worker remained perplexed by the phrase's contradiction.

But before I could leave, the Indonesian bellhop insisted that he carry my horn. The audience and I crossed the bike paths, tram tracks and car lanes to Dam Plein, where I chose a sweet, sunny, unassuming, acoustically optimal spot. The bellhop set case down with great care and then stepped back, authoritatively so, creating a stage and arranging the audience as if he had done all of this before.

I pulled out my tenor and began to play. This would be the fourth time in my life that I would play on the cobblestone: Boston, Dublin, Barcelona (via Amsterdam), and now, my beloved Amsterdam.

> *Your soul knows the geography of your*
> *destiny and the map of your future.*

> —*John O'Donohue*

The gig in Barcelona came at the end of a whirlwind day and night: Tapas, a bachelor party and a lively time in festive streets. I flew there from Amsterdam, during my third trip, just a few months after my second. I had learned about a special event that a 'friend of a friend' was to attend in Barcelona. The more I learned, the more I wanted in; after all, I could return to Amsterdam, peel away to Iberia, and then return to Amsterdam. My friend brokered me an in - I booked my four flights.

My Amsterdam night before heading to Barcelona was bursting with history, reverence, energy and fine music; which filled my soul with Dutch national pride. It was eve of the Queen's Day celebration. Taking it easy before my southbound Intracontinental flight, I ordered room service, which was specially prepared and delivered. The kitchen and staff knew that I had the best seat in the house.

With fine food and wine and an Orange Tulip before me, I opened the windows to my room overlooking Dam Square, to take in the sounds of the Netherlands National Symphony Orchestra. I felt like royalty. The energy in *Dam Plein* invigorated me; the spirit of the

Netherlands overwhelmed me. Amsterdam having become me, I nonetheless abdicated my fair city, seven hours later and made my way to Centraal Station to catch the train to Schiphol and abscond to Iberia.

Over that stretch from Dam Square to Centraal Station, I felt like a sax-schlepping salmon swimming upstream. I was the one and only per-son heading toward Centraal Station and out of the city. The further I went, the more people were heading toward me, each and every one clad in festive, cheeky, seductive, and regal orange. It was 5:00 a.m., and beer, cigarettes and weed abounded. The Schiphol bound trains were empty. By the time I arrived there, the scene was even livelier with Orange than Centraal Station – it was soon a total mad house. Everybody from everywhere was heading in or just hanging out there. I was the only person heading out on Iberia Airlines.

The flight attendants were *chevere*/lovely, whose aid I came when berated by some pompous Brits, whose arrogant accents I could only slightly understand. I translated, in my pidgin Spanish, what these utterly rude passengers were asking, peppering *mis palabras* with insulting inter-jections, directed at these tawdry turds.

I informed the very {'*muy*' – Spanish} lovely {'*mooi*' – Dutch} flight crew, in my version of Español, now was firing on all cylinders, that I was an attorney, firefighter, paramedic, and their very own saxophone player and requested that for the duration of the flight, they should direct all untoward inquiries to me. They took care of me and I took care of the ingrates. Upon our landing, the Captain learned of my assistance and thanked me. I shouldered my saxophone like an M-1 and saluted him.

In the heart of Catalonia – ¡Viva Barcelona! Fixed, by all technicali-ties, to crash a bachelor party. It was big food, big drink over a warm and vibrant night. I was all-in.

At one point in evening, after feasting on tapas, the tab for which I picked up, the boys and I were doing shots of this and that. By this point, I was well past my third wind and onto my fourth. My fellow cast of characters, who had now taken me in, signed me up for some ritual whereby the emptied shot glass had to be slammed down on the table.

It was a case of "When in Rome…" Somehow as I slammed my shot glass down, it torqued out of my fingers, spun around the table, clipped a coaster and then jumped back up to a righted position, like a pacifist battling top.

The boys went ape shit. I was their Duke. The groom offered to dump his best man for me; then his fiancé - he begged for my hand in marriage. That was my cue to saddle up my still-shouldered sax, peel off and find some music.

One member of their group, sensing something from my impending departure, persuaded the others that he must serve me and so leave and take up with me - or so it sounded to me. Walwyn spoke no Spanish but was on to something that I wasn't; he was giddy with this sense that a mystical thing was about to unfold. We made my good-byes, and the boys saluted us, as the by my side, Londonderry-born-and-raised Walwyn, whom I dubbed "Sancho Panza", and I, schlepping my tenor, set out on *El Camino*.

We walked through the town and took it all in. Then, as if it were destined, Sancho and I were beckoned by an old, frail, gimpy and very excited man; he insisted that we follow him, so, of course, we did. As we journeyed on, the old man was announcing us, building up a crowd. Our walk transformed to some ancient pilgrimage.

Then, suddenly, the old man stopped. There we were, at the edge of a long, dark, yet inviting alley. The old man broke into a dialect sermon - then an eastern dance over this seemingly sacred crossroad. The spirit moved him. Sancho and I were offered and gladly accepted drink and smoke of many kinds from those around us who knew way more than we did.

The old man wildly talked us up, as one of his friends who heard of this happening joined the group – made his way through - and escorted Sancho and me down the path, into darkness.

The end of the alley revealed a huge, enclosed, cobblestoned inner courtyard. The crowd that had gathered was now filing in behind Sancho, our guide, and me. Over one hundred people poured through the alley. Just as we reached the abyss, they parted to let the old man through. Sancho looked at me and said, "It seems we have been invited into the very heart of Barcelona. Please, Franco. Hand me your case." I passed it over to Sancho, just as the old man took my hand and walked us over a few paces and then motioned to us that we had arrived.

There I was, in a magnificent, mesmerizing inner square. This plaza, surrounded by buildings, was ornate and timeless. It was a sanctuary. The crowd quietly circled around us. Sancho laid down my case ever so gingerly. Either mystically or instinctively, Sancho had positioned the case in its correct, upright position and then opened it up for me like a pro. All I could then do was to quietly assemble my sax. I handed the rubber-banded reed and asked Sancho to "Would you be so kind as to remove and hand me A-? "

Not quite knowing what to play, and feeling the effects of everything I had, I decided to go uncharacteristically bold. I laid down a fat riff, mind you, just to warm up my well-traveled, but two-day dormant tenor.

Once I let it that one riff out, Sancho and I watched it bounce off the four walls of this plaza and overdub in its center. I was an ensemble of one, capable of projecting, folding and thickening sound, my tribute to the sound of the symphony I had taken from another public square.

The acoustics were most perfect. Many other musicians would have never left here – or at least not strayed too far. After all, this was Red Rocks meets Muscle Shoals, tucked into the belly of Barcelona.

For the next hour or so, I accompanied myself, sending out heavy, bass pedal notes and then midrange triads, followed by upper register riffs. I played recognizable songs—standards from my pop, funk, and soul mental library—songs that I had only thought I knew, only to rediscover them and reconsider the very heart of each of them. It was clear to me then, as never before, why they had been written. It was my first-ever music theory class. And I could see and hear every chord.

Life finds its purpose and fulfillment in
the expansion of happiness.

—Maharishi Mahesh Yogi

When the church bell rang and my chops were gone, I faded out the last note, open middle C#. The crowd smiled and paid their parting respects to the old man. By the time I had finished, my case was full of money. I am glad that I did not notice it pouring in, because my insistence against payment might have disrupted the moment and deprive me of the one to follow.

I offered it to the old man. "Gracias, *gato, pero, por favor...*" He graciously countered, gesturing to Sancho and me as if to indicate a three-way cut. Sancho piped in with a British accent, "*Esta bien.*" Sancho cut it; it was over one hundred fifty euro - per man.

We were packed up and paid. The lingering sound was fading out. We stood there, silent, taking it all in, peering about the plaza and the sky above.

I kissed the hand of that special, delectate old man. "*Gato,*" he replied. He then said to Sancho, "And you are a good boy." It was time to leave this Promised Land, the place where my music had wildly blossomed and seemed to have seeped into the plaza forever.

Sancho offered me a smoke and said, "That jam was jammy." We smoked, and pondered, peering at the sky and looking about the plaza. When we finished our smokes and made eye contact, we started laughing. It was Barcelona.

CHAPTER XXX

DAM PLEIN GIG

Do you wish to rise? Begin by descending. You plan a tower
that will pierce the clouds? Lay first
the foundation of humility.

—SAINT AUGUSTINE

Showtime. "Live from the Dam." I opened with "Tequila," working Glen Campbell's kick-off rhythmic riff, then jumping on the melody, filling in every part. When I got to the response, I did a two-bar turnaround, then repeated it, then repeated that, until from afar, its cue was finally caught. It was an older Dutch couple, riding by on their bicycles who shouted back in unison, "Tequila!" then dismounted and began to dance.

Mindful not to stray too far from the melody, I kept my solo clean and the rhythm tight. Hand-clapping helped. Euros poured into my case.

During "Our Day Will Come", the audience's attention was being drawn backstage, behind me, those instincts I gained from my Chicago days kicked in. I kept playing, did not overreact, making a subtle, rhythmic turn. Behind me familiarly positioned on the steps of the National Monument, were over thirty, cheerfully dressed, bright-eyed high-school students and teacher.

It was time to turn the stage over to them, so I vamped, modulated down a half step then faded out. They cheered. I bowed first to the audience, then to them.

It seemed that they were scheduled to give an outdoor performance in the Dam, which was my cue to pack it up. When the kids turned a bit restless, their director, a professorial hippie type, gestured to me then came over and introduced himself as Franz von Chossy.

"My students and I, were, on a sightseeing tour. You inspired them, us, to sing. But we must insist that you join us on your stage. How is your sight-reading?"

Sight-reading presumed that I could read music. Twenty-five years before this, in my clarinet days, I could read and respectably sight-read. Since then, that skill was rarely employed; and it is not like riding a bike. On those rare occasions when sheet music was involved, either the score was easy enough or I had to practice it to the point of committing it to memory. As for sight-reading, I may as well have been as blind as *"Vanderbilt"*, the comical sentry from *"F-Troop"*.

There was, however, no – freakin – way that I would not spot-read and, if necessary, even spot-transpose whatever it was that Franz might put in front of my face.

"Well, I am not wearing glasses; of course, I don't wear glasses..."

"Franco, you will do just fine. Allow me, please." With a school teacher's assurance, Hans summoned one of his baritones - by whistling - to be my human music stand. Young Karl offered his hand. I shook it and said, "It's you and me, Karl. I got dibs on shaking like a leaf; that means you have to be rock-steady."

Karl replied, "Perhaps we should shake in unison, like a pair of maracas?"

We laughed, followed by Franz and the group, none of whom had caught a word of our discussion. Comedic catharsis, complete; it was now all business.

This was a supreme score; the choir was clean and sweet. It filled the air and kissed the square. It was so lovely. Hans asked me if I could simply play along with the rest of their set. He said, "You called for us—we were on our way to a museum, but I believe that that these songs, all Dutch compositions, are calling for you."

They sang into, around, and out from the square. It was magnificent. The sun and the wind and the trains and taxis and the bicycles all took to our found rhythm. In this incredible moment, that Queen's Day Eve revisited, we were the voice of Amsterdam. They would sing; it was superlative—this German high-school choir, visiting Amsterdam, and me. When the music came to its end, Franz asked me how long I have been living and playing in Amsterdam.

"I'm not a musician; I'm a lawyer from Chicago."

He easily (by American standards) got the attention of this class and told them, in German, what I had just said. They laughed, almost on cue, and then applauded me.

Curtains.

The audience went about with its day. Patrons at the outdoor cafés raised their glasses. The waiters waved at us. The *Politze* presence was huge.

The last order of business was to gift them the heaping contents of my case, easily three hundred euros. "The Pizza is on me." Franz and I hugged as the worked-up students resumed their applause.

I packed up and strolled back to the hotel, taking it all in. The receptionist, my fellow guests, and their cab drivers were all standing outside of the hotel, as if to welcome me home.

They were shaking their heads in warm disbelief. The receptionist told me that when he was young, his uncle – who played the trombone - told him about a time when music filled the Dam. He added, "I know you are at home here in Amsterdam; so, maestro, make it our pleasure to have you come home to us every year. My uncle would have insisted upon it."

Faith is an oasis in the heart which will never
be reached by the caravan of thinking.

—*Khalil Gibran*

So many of my Amsterdam saxophone experiences seemed predestined.

I found out about a club named "*Blijburg*" (a cheeky play on Ijburg, the name of the town where it's located - and the word *blij*, meaning "happy") from an alto sax player I had met years before. I was walking around *Spui*, when I saw a tall, red-headed, bearded man riding his bike, backpacking an alto.

Instinctively and impulsively, I let out my Ma's whistle, a loud-as-hell "fwee-oo-weeet!" He stopped. I approached him. We struck up a hearty conversation. He turned me on to a hip place that I should check out, but forewarned me that it involved both a train ride and a long walk. The last words he left me with were "Just keep walking straight; you won't know if you haven't found it - but will know when you do." I was headed to Blijburg. I found, and then boarded, the 26 train.

There were many non-English-speaking Dutch people on the train. We struck up a "conversation." They seemed to know where I was going and what I had set out to do. Well past where the Ajax lays it out on the "soccer" field, the train was approaching the *Bimhuis*, Amsterdam's posh, big-name jazz venue. In Dutch, of which I then spoke not one lick, they "told" me that my station was the next one. I was certain not, given what the alto-cyclist had told me. The train stopped. I shook my head. They insisted that this was my destination and that I should exit.

After a minute or so of back-and-forth, the cashier/conductor came out from his booth and asked me in English: "Are you not playing here?"

"No, man, I'm sitting in at Blijburg."

He chuckled and then explained to my guardians where I was correctly headed. It apparently did not click at first, but one of my caretakers made the connection and filled the others in. In that contemplative, Dutch-accented English, he said to me, "*Blijburg has very much soul. That is going to be a good place for you, actually better than here. I would come to hear you, but I have to host my in-laws and endure their criticism of me—well, actu-ally, endure everything they have to say about everything.*"

"I will play some blues for you."

I neglected to ask him how far of a walk it was…so once I got to the stop, the very last stop (the 180-degree bite in the tracks gave it away), I started to make my way. The stop itself was desolate, but, being from the New England seacoast, I could feel the water, and I started to walk. I walked, walked, and walked.

Finally, I saw life. I got closer. It was a loft warehouse, and I just happened to see two of its residents heading inside. I stopped there; I needed to take a break. I lit up a smoke to ponder things. I repeated, out loud, "Just keep walking." I readjusted my sax-pack straps, hiked up my pants, mounted up, and just kept walking.

At the very moment that serious, legitimate doubts started to creep in, I heard, far-off into the distance, both water and music. In an effort to listen, I dropped my head and noticed sand over the cobblestone. I cinched up my sax-pack and moved toward what my ears were so elated to hear.

Two giant Buddha statues stood guard and invited me in. It was a bow-arched building, strewn with festive lights. The waft of good food drifted toward me.

This Eastern-adorned, 'fish shack' and 'hippy crash pad' themed, French Bistro featured an open fireplace and a Persian rug. It was mystic.

The band, the music, the sound, and the vibe were so heartwarming. The only thing that cut against the night was the train schedule. My very last train was at 1:00 a.m. I had to catch that train.

That session was in-the-pocket cool. The pianist told me, "I like that you play only that which is necessary... You are a man of few but very good words. I can't believe that you are a lawyer - or maybe I can; you must be a different kind of lawyer. Please come back next year, but in the meanwhile, please do not miss your train."

I missed my train. Plan B: I ventured toward what felt like the main street, lit up a smoke, and considered my options. Just as I finished it, a car—what I thought to be the only car—approached from the distance. I flagged it down, using a combination of "Taxi!" and "Hey! Remember me?"

It stopped. As I stepped toward the passenger window, not knowing how to gesture "Don't take off – Give me one sec" in Dutch, I held up my hand in a combination wave off/ halt/ unscrew a lightbulb. He looked at me with utter confusion. I begged him for a ride. He said: "Where are you going? Because I'm on my way to Amsterdam."

MY MAN!

With that, he gestured me into his car. He was playing Miles Davis - "So What."

We talked very little over our cozy journey; instead we hung on every solo, which my benefactor knew, verbatim. He got me to the quiet *Jordaan* [like Boston's Beacon Hill, but flat] side of Centraal Station. I thanked him for the ride. He thanked me for the company.

> *Art is a collaboration between God and the artist,*
> *and the less the artist does, the better.*

> —ANDRE GIDE

The next year, on a night that followed a very long day, I made that last train from Blijburg. It took everything in me to hump it to catch the train. The conductor saw me running and waited. I limped on – on my second try.

"Thank - you - Grif – ith – ugggh..."

Somewhere between finally taking a seat and Centraal Station, I fell asleep. Thankfully, the Surinamese conductor, came out from his booth and gently woke me up. "Sax man. Sax man. SAX MAN. We are here! We are at Centraal Station!" I jumped off, unregistered, still officially asleep, I looked back - my arm decided to raise my fist and gesture 'Black Power', as I yelled, "My Man, Griffith!"

He waved back and smiled and rang the bell.

CHAPTER XXXI

ON TOUR—OP TOURNEE

If you come to a fork in the road, take it.

—*Yogi Berra*

On my return to Amsterdam after the very un-European smoking restrictions had been implemented, changing—for better or worse—the climates and tones of most clubs and cafés, I sat in at a nifty little blues bar, called "Malo Meloe". Off the beaten path, right in front of a canal, and near the Amsterdam Fire Department Headquarters, a building resembled a modern-day American city jail. Across the canal from Malo Meloe was a neon Texaco sign, which might otherwise seem out of place, but for me, it pleasantly conjured Kenmore Square's similar neon icon and also seemingly out-of-place Fenway Park's beacon—the Citgo sign.

I had a smoke (outside, of course) and then I walked in and was greeted by both the waft of cigarette smoke and the hostess, a small, pound-for-pound rugged, earthy-hot, Goth matron. Defiant Dutch? Hardly. When I gently inquired, the hostess boldly and proudly explained to me that everyone in the bar (she made it a point to declare that it was Greek-owned) was provably blood-related. They were all cousins, uncles, and so forth. Since the recently enacted "no smoking" law was intended to protect workers, these were family members, and the law did not apply. It was the classic contrarian response to any regulation, its loophole.

Pulling out a smoke, I asked, "Where does that leave me?"

Without missing a beat, she replied, "As one of my ex-husbands, which according to the regulation also technically counts. We were divorced because of...your mistress." She gestured to my sax as the source of the alienation of our apparent former affections. Aleithea was clearly an edgy, business-minded descendant of Socrates himself. And very easy on the eyes.

This Café was Greek to the bone, and I was there to stay. Yet the only musician there was a tall, rather imposing, lion of a guitarist, working over his steel guitar. Not a steel guitar, mind you, but a guitar made of steel. It was Hammond B-3 dirty. He was a trio of one.

When he took a break, Joep VanLeeuw and I instinctively embraced. He was pleased to have my company. "How about a real, book-referenced, rockabilly, jazz-rock jam?" In an instant, we crafted a set list.

He smoked some very blond and giddy Moroccan hashish. Outside, of course. Then, we played and played. The room was filled with energy and smoke but with nary another musician. It was meant to be us; we played the night – then the wee hours of the morning- away with a Memphis-flavored, deep-pocket, dirty-street sound.

Joep's upper register rhythm riffs had high-hat all over them. When the session finally ended, on "Groovin' High," my Greek family invited Joep and me to their makeshift dinner table. *Opa!*

My "ex-wife" and I were now squarely, apparently on talking terms; for once in my life, my spouse could outcook me. Her food was defeatingly delicious, succulently oiled, and seasoned with just the right amount of tang and spice.

Around five in the morning, I was out on Amsterdam's Jordaan, reminiscent of when I had also been on Boston's Kenmore Square at five o'clock on many occasions. I hoofed it back to my hotel, just as the sun was rising up from over Germany.

Trust this side of yourself. It will take
you where you need to go.
But it will also teach you a kindness
of rhythm in your journey.

—JOHN O'DONOHUE

The music of the year-two Café Internationaal gig was of such beauty. Not only did I now receive the great fortune of performing with Sanzo once again, but this time, I performed with a trio of brilliant musicians whom he handpicked.

Sanzo seized upon what he and I had begun exactly one year before; unfinished business we spoke of during last year's ("Autumn Leaves") post-gig/pre-encore set conversation. He craved the perfect trio to take us to another level.

Unbeknown to me, he had lined up and booked them almost a year in advance.

They were killin' players: Tavius Nieboer, standing tall like Big Bird, worked the fingerboard and neck of his upright bass, funky, fat and with fluidity. Deep in the pocket, gliding straight ahead, Tavius located the room's sweet spot and aimed his notes at it, just as Malique had in CTA subways and on its platforms- the most memorable being the post-Cubs games Addison Inbound party porch. Kappar Crudeko, the drummer from Latvia, was surgically utilitarian and mean-and-nasty funky.

Equal parts clean and dirty, yet a minimalist/light packer, Kappar developed every conceivable rhythmic sound and color through just a floor tom, a snare-turned-tom, and a high hat-turned-ride. With just these three components, Kappar produced an infinite, full spectrum. He expressed himself like a pianist, anticipating, creating space and setting the time in an organic way. We were in his house now; as the Café itself became his fourth piece.

If this weren't more than enough - and it was - things got shaken up a bit. Our pianist, a tall, baby-faced Brit, who dressed like a rapper and wore a crisp Yankees cap, strolled on over. I had learned that sporting my beloved Red Sox's enemy's brim meant no offense or curse; it was simply Euro-chic.

He was more excited to play my set list selections than me, genuinely gracious for the gig and smitten by the room and the Café's vibe. Before Dominique Marshon's first solo hit the bridge, I was ready to renounce the Red Sox. Under that cap that Ruth once donned, was pure power. I took inventory of every piano player I had played with, seen and listened to: Dominique was the Big Bambino. One of the most meticulous, yet unassuming musicians I have ever known, on this night, Dominique Marshon reigned supreme; his was a hauntingly magnificent piano performance.

I was in the company of the finest musicians. I had the best seat in the house of these all-stars—what a masterful rhythm section Sanzo built! He and filled it out with his savory, often hauntingly rich playing...

Knowing that I had much on my mind, they built me a platform, stood by my side then ushered me to the lectern. The packed house was moved by their commitment to draw me up and take me on my journey.

It was so pleasing, truly orgasmic; although not my first Amsterdam music/orgasm achievement.

> *It is not by muscle, speed, or physical*
> *dexterity that great things*
> *are achieved, but by reflection, force*
> *of character, and judgment.*

> —Marcus Tullius Cicero

I had never put in even the fraction of the effort and disciplined nose-to-the-grindstone, balls-to-the-wall commitment and shedding that Bahred has. He is a true musician, a gifted player; who can recite the changes from memory to most any standard and whose arrangements are Quincy Jones-like in their powerful message.

In response to my self-pity, he would often say: *"Do you like to play? When you play with other musicians, do they like your playing? The people you're playing for, do they like your playing? Do they listen or do they leave?*

When it comes down to it, you need to only consider two things: Do you like to play, and does playing like you back?"

"It's that simple, unless you want to - and are willing to- complicate things. Then, you are talking about a whole other set of rules; and you must be willing to surrender what you have for what you don't. And if you are, then we are having an entirely different conversation on a different level and on different terms, which involves you studying musical theory, playing a little less and practicing much more."

"I think you have a good thing, not worth spoiling. Your playing will get better on its own; you won't even know it 'till you hear it come out. There are plenty of cats out there who wish they could get from the horn what you do and as easily as you seem to. They have a love-hate relationship with the horn; yours is really quite envious. For as - no disrespect - lazy as you are, you have a lot going on. I wouldn't mess with that. What I would do, though, is get a lesson with a pro. Pay him to be honest with you. Then you will get even more answers."

I took Bahred's advice and got a lesson with working, teaching tenor player. I met with him a week before I had left for Amsterdam.

He fixed a lot of my mechanical problems - quite easily, and sensing my aversion to practicing, gave me some enjoyable, quickie exercises to 'shed'. Above all else, he offered sage advice: In order to get better, if I wanted to get better, I had to feel comfortable with the way I sound. While he was pleased that I did not like the way I sounded, he cautioned me not to punish myself.

"Whether you care to admit it, your sound is quite good; maybe that's why you can't stand it. Guys who like the way they sound have always worried me, and for good cause. That's an honest sound coming out your bell; just accept it. Surrender to it - but negotiate your terms. You need to feel comfortable with the way you sound; that way you can nurture it and stop arguing with it. Once you do this, you will start playing less notes and stop playing those 'scaredy-cat' runs and phrases, which are intended – the way I'm hearing it – for you to hide your sound.

"And since you don't have to worry about paying the bills, play when you want to and what you want to; keeping all of this in mind, of course."

"I envy you and I really dig your sound and your phrasing. It's like some cross between Tom Scott and Chaka Khan. Am I hearing that right?"
Was I hearing him right?

> **Put off thy cares with thy clothes; so shall**
> **thy rest strengthen thy labor,**
> **and so thy labor sweeten thy rest.**

—FRANCIS QUARLES

During that post-lesson trip, after sitting in at Bourbon Street with a seventies Rock/ Jazz meets R-and-B band, a young, feisty girl from Ireland seemed anxious or eager, so I noticed, to approach me.

Raw-boned, shapely, cleverly dressed and in her early-thirties, she was on holiday with her friends, one of whom was soon to be wed. After I had packed up my horns and was ready to join the post-set chill, she came up to me, and in a sultry Irish brogue and said:

"I heft a tally ya...I low-ved year playin'...you gave me an orgasm...It was ay real one - I wasn't fee-kin it...I was gooshin' and evra-tin...Year goot on tat sax...Tiu fockin goot...Christ, I'm soaked down to me knees."
I cried. Lesson learned.

> **Real love is the love that sometimes arises after sensual**
> **pleasure: if it does, it is immortal; the other kind**
> **inevitably goes stale, for it lies in mere fantasy.**

—GIACOMO CASANOVA

CHAPTER XXXII

JACK NICHOLSON

One language sets you in a corridor for life.
Two languages open every door along the way.

—*Frank Smith*

My seminal "lost in Dutch-to-English translation" moment came during my third trip to Amsterdam. I decided to take in a stage performance at a charming and quaint theater, which showcased some great musicians who also played bit parts in the show. It was in Dutch. At first, I was totally lost, searching for words that sounded like English. I started to fall behind the snappy and well-received lines. Giving up on English, I eventually found some sort of rhythm in the show, admittedly by borrowing from those around me and faking: I laughed when the audience did, commented softly to myself when others did and turned pensive on their cue. And by the third scene, I had actually convinced myself that I was now fluent in Dutch.

Late in the show, I heard two words that I clearly understood: "Jack" and "Nicholson." I heard those words more than once; tuning my ear in, even shifting in my seat into this heavy monologue. Just then, the stage darkened, and the vibe turned somber and quiet. I was now struggling, in my new-found Dutch dialect, to come to grips with the reality that Jack Nicholson had died. So reverent were the cast, crew and band in paying such meaningful tribute to him.

My sentiments drifted away from the show, as I recounted all of the many great, inspiring, stellar roles that Jack Nicholson had played and those important honest messages his characters had conveyed with such grit. Now that he was gone - I grew sad and was brought to grief.

When the show ended, the cast, band, and audience gathered for food and drink. The lead actress and I exchanged glances. I went over to her and dropping my pretense let her know, apologetically so, that I did not speak Dutch. In English, she asked me how I liked the show. I complimented her and then ramped it up, as if some Screen Actors Guild emissary from the States, thanking her for paying such a heartfelt tribute to Jack Nicholson.

She replied in kind, yet spoke of him in the present tense, which I attributed to limited English skills – and that was completely fine with me.

Then, in some weird, gratuitous attempt to clean it all up and tie up my hurt with her awkward verb conjugation, admittedly patting myself on the back for pulling it in nicely, I commented on how, even though he was gone, it was poignant that she should think and speak of him in the present tense.

"What the fuck are you talking about? You speak like he's dead!"

I gasped. My lip quivered, and as I reached out for her, I yelped, "He's not dead?"

She started to laugh. She got everyone's attention and shared this moment with them in Dutch.

Their saxophone player moved through the cast, somehow sensing that I, too, played the saxophone and proclaimed, "He was dead, but you somehow brought him back to life, without playing a note." The lead actress surmised, "We will have to work this mad bit into the show, no?"

I did not leave the theater until the next morning.

Franco Minasian

Worry does not empty tomorrow of its sorrow,
it empties today of its strength.

—Corrie ten Boom

What I did not tell them is that during the show, side by side with my frenetic translating through their first act, I had finally paroled myself from past misjudgments—determined to replace constantly reliving them with regretting them - but then allowing them to 'rest in peace'.

I wanted to use new math; isolate my old ways on one side of the equation and find the sum of all good things yet to come one the other. For so long, I had exhausted myself, compounding the past, safekeeping grudges against others and, worse yet, against myself. When Jack Nicholson had died, I willed myself, in his memory, to take a new and healthier look at my own life.

I finally accepted that practicing law had been a comforting distraction for me and by focusing on the misdeeds and consequences of others, constantly applying legal concepts, offering mitigation, exposing the malice in motives gone bad and all the rest, I was simply substituting my professional world of conflict resolution for what I could not in the vital realm of my personal life.

Amsterdam theater – culminating in a premature eulogy - somehow called out and exposed my predictable behaviors, the constant fear-driven hyper-focus and the rest of the tired act that I had been putting on and performing for too long. It was time to say goodbye.

They would almost throw the cops in jail
when they tried to arrest me.

—Lawrence Taylor

As Jack Nicholson, back from the dead, had begun filming "*The Departed*", I went to work. Inspired by his resurrection, I put my resolve into practice- during yet another trial that I had set to the morning after returning from Amsterdam.

Over my twelve years a prosecutor, I had called thousands of police officers to the stand. Dusting my old hat, I referred to my client, underlining "the defendant" or "that guy," with a pejorative sneer. By sheer luck, there was a frumpy PD sitting at our oversized counsel table, working on a stack of files. Rather than gather up his things, he asked if he could stay and work. He was the perfect prop for my setup; through which I would fool that police officer on the stand into thinking that I was the prosecutor—and that the frumpy public defender was my client's attorney.

As the officer entered the courtroom, I had already positioned myself at the state's counsel table, putting my notes down next to theirs, inveigling an awkward half-smile from the young, jittery prosecutor. I began with straightforward, open-ended, standard questions. His responses were routine. Once he had gone through his lines, with my hook now set, I took it from the top, but this time around, I formed my questions in a way that forced him to articulate, rather than merely affirm. He responded by ad-libbing; it was all sloppily contrived.

I nodded with reassuring approval when he finished, as if to say, 'Keep going; you're doing great.' And he did. He spun the story around and around again.

Granted, there was no question pending, but I talked over the state's thready objection, which resulted in an 'Overruled' from Judge – who was now thoroughly confused and questioning his own scorecard.

The courtroom was now mine. "Officer, you seem to be having some trouble with my questions."

Before he could finish his desperate "Well...I'm having a hard time recalling...", the Judge got in on my action and asked: "*Could you explain what you mean by 'hard time recalling'?*"

The Officer shrugged his shoulders, lowered his head and muttered, "I don't know. I guess I really can't..."

"...I have no idea. I really don't know much about this case. Just what I've been telling the state here."

The Judge did a double-take, then barked: *"He's not the state. He's the defendant's attorney. That's all I need to hear. Motion granted. Case dismissed."*

As the officer left the witness stand, he did a double take on me, as if he still believed that I was the prosecutor—that is, until the frumpy public defender got up and exposed his frayed, stained suit and worn-down shoes and an armful of "Office of the Public Defender"–stamped files, skulking into the lockup to talk to his dozen clients. The officer shook his head, smiled, and winked. It felt like I was back in the Office, controlling the proper outcome; all the while, those young gun prosecutors were shooting blanks.

It was no Scorsese; but then again, I am no Jack Nicholson.

Whatever you are, be a good one.

—ABRAHAM LINCOLN

Over my cherished years in Amsterdam, I have often been questioned about the morality in representing those who I knew were guilty. "Guilty {*Schuldig*}...", I have many a time said: "It is but a legal term of art. Whether the accused actually committed the crime is but a distraction; hardly dispositive. The only thing that should matter in a Court of Law is the evidence and what it proves – after all, aren't we all *Schuldid?*"

Many would say, "You sound like a lawyer." To that, I would retort: "Well then. I rest my case."

The language of friendship is not words but meanings.

—HENRY DAVID THOREAU

I marvel at Amsterdam cops. Daunting in stature, they seem to have this knack for taking control of and closing out most situations on the canal-bordered cobblestone, with a show of force and a pragmatic application of diplomacy. Every *politze/burger* encounter I witnessed on the streets of Amsterdam displayed that now-forsaken, old-school CPD way known as a "street adjustment." What I saw in the Amsterdam Politze furthered my sense that the Amsterdam way of life was for me.

An Amsterdam trip years later would end with my obligation – established from my promise. In the years before, my good-bye was in simple, tearful words: "I have to go now." I would then slip out the Café and head back to my room, stopping along the way to cry.

Aside from my basic guidebook phrases and cheesy "here and there" words, I spoke no Dutch. And it seemed not to matter that much. Everyone around me spoke such tasteful English. On those rarest of occasions, when my friends could not come up with the English word and would ask, "How do you say...?" I would have fun with it, serving up fringe phrases, extreme or hyper-interpretive answers, which they enjoyed.

Such wordy conversations would typically divert, sometimes never to return to the basic phrase originally sought after. It was like some linguistic illumination of a Hieronymus Bosch masterpiece. When the intended word or phrase was finally uttered, it would bring laugher and a celebration of an end to our mad, wordy journey. For me, the highest compliment was when someone would ask: *"Would you mind, please? I'd really like to translate all of what just happened into Dutch - for the others?"*

Growth is the only evidence of life.

—JOHN HENRY NEWMAN

I confess that I felt left out when my 'Hello' or 'Good Morning' or, as a last resort, my tip my hat to a passerby pedestrian, would be passed over. When I offered to open a door or help someone, particularly a woman, I was routinely shut down. When I would move up or in, however chivalrous or gentlemanly, Dutch men would always take the better, sometimes protective, angle.

When any of them would say anything in Dutch that I really wanted to be in on, I would throw up lame prayer hands and say:

"Shame on me, but I speak no Dutch...*Habla Espanol?*

> *"Why would you tell me that in English, then ask me something in Spanish. Porque?*

"Because I feel terrible—left out—that I don't speak Dutch."

> *"Do you live here?"*

"No."

> *"Then that is a very kind gesture. A very decent thing for you to say. And you said that you an American? Hoe interessant!*

This is why - when in Amsterdam - Spanish (rattle-trap and with a New England snap) was my first language; always when in the midst of showy Americans or clunky Canadians. My fallback was feigning muteness or speaking in tongues, peppered with letters from the [38 letter] Armenian Alphabet.

On my 'year of the commitment' trip, I had started playing around with a new invention: The "App" - courtesy of Casper, who had installed it on my cell phone—to my astonishment, without a computer, or a disc, let alone tools. My new travel companion could translate English to Dutch or Dutch to English - in a snap.

Incapable of correctly pronouncing most of the Dutch that it churned out, I would resort to showing the resulting words and phrases to the poor targeted listener, adding over-the-top mime for emphasis. For the most part, however, the App was a flop. Many times, its answer was received with bad reviews: "That doesn't mean anything." or "Nobody really says that." or "Just tell me what the hell you are trying to say, in English."

If you risk nothing, then you risk everything.

—GEENA DAVIS

During my last night – my last time at the Café until the next year- there was not one familiar face in the crowd. The Café was filled to the brim with those who had just returned from a hard-fought *Ajax* match. Nicole's protégé, Lieke, who had a knack for cleverly aping the quirks and ticks of Michel, Casper, and Tommy, had no trouble holding this crowd down - but understandably had no time for me. Lieke was rau- cously pouring and presenting scores of vaasje with her cherished endearment, warm words and bright smile. So there I was, counting my dreaded hours down in my post-match, packed-to-the-gills café.

Content just to take in this final night's vibe. I helped clear tables - no writing - no deep thought. I was already packed for my morning's flight and feeling no pain.

As things developed, I kept hearing this one word, from so many voices, so I started to hark for it. It kept coming and seemed worth know- ing. When I finally landed it, I said it to myself and then just loud enough for my ears only, readying to summon up its English translation from my cell phone, for I clumsily searched, practically groping myself.

Lieke yelled out, "Sax Man!" and then gestured toward what I could not see. My cell phone was neither on me nor in my coat nor atop the bar next to my vaasje. It was in my hand.

She poured me a second vaasje- "This one's on me." While enjoying Lieke's perfect pour, I resumed repeating the word then plopped off my bar stool over to the doorway, struggling to keep my balance, reciting that elusive word while attempting to resuscitate the unresponsive App, damning both it and my now overheating cell phone.

The Café was loud with obvious post-match bravado, yet for some reason, I did not think to simply step outside to the quieter street, mere paces away, to perform this situationally difficult task.

Instead, admittedly unsober, I barked the word louder and louder, straight into my cell phone. It would none of this, either unable or unwilling to decipher what I was preaching, arguably replying "Speak clearly, you drunken asshole!"

Under the swirl of Dutch conversation all around me, I stood resolved and undaunted, determined not to be denied my desired translation. I cleared my throat, squared my hips and bent my knees, as if I were some Armenian Olympic weightlifter about to clean-and-jerk.

With all of my might, I belted out that elusive, but not to be denied word, deep into the gears of my defiant cell phone as if my life were on the line.

The entire Café snapped into dead silence.

I looked up, bewildered, and then looked down to my phone, which read "Translating" for what seemed an eternity. I saw smiling, silent, awaiting faces. Lieke and two of the Café's regulars and always a sight for sore eyes – the Jack-of-all-trades, Southern Gentleman, Milan and the Van Gogh double, human slide rule, Scotland-born Matt – who had slipped in unnoticed by me, had come to my defense and were desperately trying to temper the now worked-up pack, while trying not laugh.

Meanwhile, which seemed a lifetime, that dreaded, damned, dooming "Translating" prompt was still slow-roasting.

Finally, out popped the English translation: "&$#@% (profanity)." I hung my head as they all finally had their laugh. Only Lieke and the ever-thoughtful bar-back Koon came to my rescue, shrugging off my apology as unnecessary and my lame "*Ik ben Niet gezellig!*" contrition with "It's okay, Sax Man; it's all right." Koon then jumped ship with "That's a terrible word you said." Lieke shoved him into the coffee machine.

Now sobered up and decimated with shame, with my head hung, I made my way to the bell, reached up, and as I did – I was overcome with an epiphany. I grabbed the rope and gave it a yank of determination. The patrons cheered or jeered but then quieted when I called for the floor. Lieke cut the music. You could hear a pin drop. A group that had just walked in stopped in its tracks.

"*I give each and every one of you my word that by the time I return, next year, I will speak your language. Then, if I should choose to utter that terrible word, it shall be properly declinated and conjugated in context. I give all of you my word, that I will somehow learn to speak Dutch and regain 'mijn gezellig'.*"

They all nodded; Lieke embraced me and I began to cry. I rang the bell yet again. "*Dat maakt twee,* on my tab." We all drank.

The night went on into the morning- until I had to go.

I returned to Melaura from Amsterdam, once again on a mission - not that I needed to conjure up a reason or some motivation to think about Amsterdam let alone return. But this was destiny's way- to keep Amsterdam close to me until my return. Over that year, I made time, using books, CDs, the internet, and foreign channels and films to learn the Dutch language. Doing so was important and necessary in so many good ways. I would keep my promise.

> *The nice thing about doing a crossword puzzle*
> *is, you know there is a solution.*

—STEPHEN SONDHEIM

The Dutch word for "time" is by far the best translation: *tijd*, which is pronounced like the English "tight," with a slight snap at the end of the last consonant, in equal parts *D* and *T. Tijd.*

For musicians, "tight" is a term of bestowment, as it is a most desirable quality. A "tight" musician is one with time and rhythm and punch; who can find the pocket and fall into the groove— one who is clean, smooth and recognizably rhythmic using both sound and space.

The next year in Amsterdam was all about *tijd:* The presentment of many changes. Nicole was gone. Tommy was on the move, having taken up work as a pastry chef's mate aboard a cruise ship. My photographer friend, Jos, never made it to the Café to share his clever work and profound thoughts. The corner sandwich shop, where I gave birth to the *schoenlepel,* was closed for remodeling.

Located at "Prince and Zee", was a spot that I had frequented for lunch after my midmorning coffee was ready to give way to my midday vaasje at the Café.

This happened on my first trip, go figure. The first time I walked in, rather late for lunch, in between rushes, the short-order cook/owner served my food with a cloth napkin draped over his arm. I could not fathom if he was making fun of me or thought I was somebody else. Either way, his food was impeccable – and I kept coming back.

I hit it off with his so sweet, tough daughter and the rest of the staff and I hit it off, which included the other cook - a Justin Timberlake look-alike with the pipes to back it up, as I discovered on a post-Blijburg night. Once I stepped off the '26', I decided to walk to my hotel - via Warmoesstraat, which was a matter of habit. It was well after the kitchen was closed and the doors were locked. But on this particular night, the lights were on and there were people inside. I was welcomed in for a late-night karaoke crazy extravaganza. I requested - and they jumped on - "*Brown Eyed Girl,*" the only karaoke song I had ever sang (at a fellow fire-man's bachelor party).

My concocted sandwich, the sustenance by which I transitioned from late morning to midday, consisted of smoked salmon, tomato, lettuce, a touch of red onion, salt, pepper, and a thin drizzle of olive oil, nestled in a triangle-shaped baguette. I named it the '*het schoenlapel*' (the shoe horn). Once asked by an elderly, Dutch man, who had pressed the owner about why it was not on the menu, why I had named it this, I explained that it was an essential means in order for me take up the day. And since every day for me in Amsterdam was special, it was only fitting that a special sandwich with a special name should usher it in.

He held up his cup of coffee and said "*Proost!*"- then told the owner that he would be having a *schoenlapel* with his scrambled eggs—cut in half to share with his lovely, intrigued wife.

I was so unabashed and eager to write my story - with a growing excitement to express myself in pidgin Dutch, confident that my last year's promise was both a blessing and a sign. I had found my rhythm, albeit a clunky one; speaking, riding the tide of a new language and the drive to understand. Honing in and focus on swirls of Dutch conversations, at times I looked like I had imbibed mushrooms. I just couldn't get enough of this cannily beautiful and unassumingly assertive language.

As I made my way about the city, I listened then repeated aloud the words Amsterdammers walking, bicycling, and tramming about. I was moving in the right direction.

Although one particular group I came upon, gathered about Zeedijk, seemed out of place. They were not tourists, yet they traveled in a pack, making frequent stops – though not to take pictures. They were donned in vests and seemed unconcerned with time; over three hours, they remained in place. While everyone else was trekking across the *Kruispunt*, they confined their activity to bumming and sharing smokes, foraging for weed, and picking over cheap street-food leftovers. They had the air Seattle's homeless teens. I became mesmerized, curious about this secret society of midday squatters, marking Zeedijk as their territory.

Michelle broke my trance: "Ach…taakstaffen."

"Wat is dat?", I inquired.

Taakstraf, she explained, *is* the Dutch version of Cook County's SWAP, a "put criminals to work" program. They were racking up community service hours by simply hanging out. This left me more jealous than offended. What nonviolent crime, I pondered, could I could miscarry in order to join their ranks?

The Dutch language was swirling around my days and nights - and even in my dreams. I even took a stab at telling my story in Dutch.

One an otherwise uneventful midday (*gewoon midag*), Michel was chatting it up with his friend (*met zijn vriend*), Rolus, a tall redhead with a scanty beard and rosy skin. Rolus had the contemplative look and calm demeanor of *Saving Private Ryan*'s Corporal Henderson. He sat at the other end of the bar - holding court - telling Michel about his wild night out. Once Rolus finished telling his story, I replied with "*Toch veel, hoe kan dat waar?*" the closest thing I could piece togeteher as "You can't be for real!"

> *Translation is like a woman. If it is*
> *beautiful, it is not faithful.*
> *If it is faithful, it is most certainly not beautiful.*
>
> —YEVGENY YEVTUSHENKO

Michel [in English] asked: "You understood all of that, Superman? You need to tell me what he said - and please – in English!"

I replied, "*Zoals jij het wil* (as you wish)," and then recounted Rolus's journey.

"Rolus made reservations at a trendy combination bistro/participation theater. Upon arriving at the venue, the host, as part of the restaurant's shtick, unabashedly verbally abused dinner guests and practically bullied them to their tables. It was all in jest. Guests were encouraged, even egged on, to reason and deadpan with their servers, expectedly to no avail...."

"...There was even some scripted, pratfall violence, which included a good-looking girl who would administer borderline, distasteful verbal abuse and then fake-spit on the most milquetoast guest, likely a shill...."

"...By the end of the night, the guests were noticeably physically and emotionally exhausted; they felt amazingly refreshed once they paid their bills, and they were preyed upon one last time. As a parting gift, they were gruffly ordered to leave the restaurant and crudely shown the door. The patrons enjoyed its overall therapeutic, cathartic effect. In fact, once outside, they expressed they wanted to return; that some eerie, seductive force was beckoning them to return. But for Rolus here, this one time was quite enough. Vowing never to partake in this again, he went home - and enjoyed a restful night's sleep..."

"*Corrigeren?*"

And so, having delivered my spot-on translation, I finished my *vaasje*, and – in an admittedly cocky way - rang the bell and pushed it, by asking: "*Ho vie doen?*" ready for my deserved complement. After all, I had nailed it – and quite well - given how Michel and Rolus gestured with approval to one another.

Michel then burst my bubble. "*Superman, I appreciate that you are trying. I love that you want to speak and understand Dutch. What you recounted was a magnificent story...*

...but you got it all wrong."

Apparently, Rolus saw it otherwise and came to my rescue. For about five minutes, Rolus and Michel were now going at it.

As I figured, Michel apologized - with a tributary *vaasje* to boot. I had nailed it. Ha!

Then Rolus took the floor: *"My linguist friend, I am impressed. You told of my experience, so more real than mine, but in a parallel universe, which makes you a Dutch mystic."*

I didn't nail anything. Michel started to laugh.

May I suggest, however, that your Dutch dialect might appreciate an alternative translation?"

Placation. Michel laughed harder.

With impeccable English—and a Mark Twain folksiness to boot—Rolus corrected the parts of his story that I had mistranslated; correction - made mystic.

"My best friend, Odulf, and I were arrested last night for having thrown a bar stool through a picture window of the Café where he and I had been drinking – drinking too much. This happened right after he told me of his successful proposal to the girl of his dreams. You must understand that she, Karin is her name, is his living nightmare. She is poison. When he proposed a toast, I went complete ape-shit. Two years of yoga classes—out the fucking window. I let it all come out. We were Screaming, crying; there was violence; then the property damage…abusing those around us who were trying to reason with us and shield their families from our ugliness. Then, the police arrived.

"They were very disappointed and were naturally quite aggressive. We were hauled away and thrown into a cell with some small-time thieves. They were Dutchman, who had learned their trade from eastern drug-smugglers—which is a very dangerous combination. All of us were served day-old jail food; then we were moved into a big cage, surrounded by all types from all places. There were Americans puking their guts out. Do you have any idea how being jailed totally disrupts the bodily functions?

"Our cellmates considered the food we were served to be quite tasty. Odulf and I, we languished in hunger for two days. On the morning of the third, Odulf's family put together the money to pay for the window and secure our release."

"I can't believe that Odulf is going to marry Karin. She is evil."

I said, "I liked my version better than yours. I am tempted to crash their wedding."

Michel offered to be my date.

"To linguistic license, liberation and self-imposed incarceration", we drank.

> *There is no such thing as the pursuit of*
> *happiness, but there is the discovery of joy.*
>
> —*JOYCE GRENFELL*

The Dutch Language is a difficult one; you can't get discouraged by the initial discomfort, but if you tough out the initiation, properly nurse your beginner's sore throat, your *bier*-soothed gullet will become pliable and the language will roll up and out from the guttural lowlands of the larynx - with ease. It is a Dutch national treasure – that its proprietors will always gladly share with those who show it proper respect.

I picked up an Amsterdam catchphrase, *ouwehoeren*, which is the equivalent of bullshitting, jibber-jabbering, or making idle chatter. The phrase literally translates to "old prostitutes." – homage to/an image of haggard, veteran, Red Light mainstays, stepping out from their windows and onto the street to talk to one another about nothing important - simply passing the time away in between would-be patrons.

Over my time in Amsterdam, I let my limited Dutch carry the day, resorting to English only when absolutely necessary. I kept my ears open, learning what I could from the conversations around me, determined on some level to comprehend every conversation. Each moment became a Dutch language lesson: television and radio, over my morning coffee, my enlightening midmornings and over my afternoon; into the evening and well into the night and late night/early morning. I would dream in Dutch – talk to myself in Dutch - notice when those around me were not speaking in Dutch. I was getting there...

Language is a process of free creation; its laws and principles
are fixed, but the manner in which
the principles of generation
are used is free and infinitely varied. Even the interpretation
and use of words involves a process of free creation.

—NOAM CHOMSKY

CHAPTER XXXIII

OUT OF LEFT FIELD

Through training, they quickly realize
that anger is a waste of energy;
that it has only negative effects on the self and others.

—*Jigoro Kano, educator, athlete, and founder of judo*

A few weeks after returning from Amsterdam, I litigated a murder case, pleased with how, through a *"Judgement at Nuremburg"* inspired cross-examination I simultaneously weakened the State's case and bolstered my defense of Cephas Moss. My closing argument meticulously recounted each piece of evidence and witness's testimony, all of which weighed heavily against the State. My adversary's rebuttal seemed almost desperate; sidestepping my schematic, blowing off the gaping holes in its own case – it focused on personally attacking me. I let it roll off - then bit down on my tongue - until the state falsely accused me of calling their witnesses "liars" and accusing the police of "framing" my client. These were cheap, crummy attacks, intended to bully me, belittle the trial and con the Court.

I demanded redress, telling the Judge that there were two occasions in my professional career when I made personal attacks against police officers: one, an undercover officer I prosecuted, who was part of a drug-money-tipoff scheme that almost cost an honest cop his life; the other, a lockup keeper who demanded fellatio from detained prostitutes in exchange for their freedom - a used condom his last victim turned over to the Illinois State Police rightfully sealed his fate.

To my utter shock, the Judge let those personal attacks – and the ones that followed - stand. Rather than render a ruling right then, the Judge oddly continued the case for the verdict. I figured that the Judge wanted to read the trial transcript, and that it irrefutably verified my claims, thought it wise to prepare a written ruling so that the inevitable 'not guilty' finding would withstand any criticism. The continuance was a good sign.

I shared my take on the continuance with Cephas's family. His step-father, Rod Doraunt, took me aside. A tech consultant who had come up the hard way, he had attended every court date and served as my other set of eyes and ears throughout the trial.

After assuring me that I had done everything - and more - to defend the young man he so loved, Rob then broke a promise he made to me when we first met – he was about to tell me my business.

"Franco, you are going lose. The Judge is going to find Cephas guilty..."

You cannot shake hands with a clenched fist.

—INDIRA GANDHI

"...I say this this because there is the story of someone dear to me that I have wanted to tell you about since you took on Cephas's case, but I did not want it get in your way. Now that your work is done and you have given it your all for him, you need to hear this, so you can prepare yourself like I already have..."

"...There were twelve of us - Kev, the other ten and me. Somehow, we ended up on the same baseball teams, from Pee Wee ball all the way through high school. The twelve of us stayed tight. Even after we graduated, we pledged to keep the team together. So, we formed a twelve-inch softball team and stayed together for eight years..."

"...Kev was a left field fielder, quick and tall. He robbed teams of home runs; he went for everything. When the ball dropped, he would get mad and charge at it; and the way he fired it back - forget about the cut-off; runners were held cold..."

"...We had a game set for 2:00pm. Kev never showed up. We couldn't get a hold of him, his family—not anyone. There were no cell phones, no Internet then. We all tried to find him, even tried to make out a missing person report..."

"...The next time I saw him was twelve years later. I was riding my motorcycle and saw him drive by in the opposite direction, and I nearly dumped my Harley - almost killed myself. I finally caught up with him. When Kev got out of this truck and saw that it was me, we both stopped in our tracks. It was as if he had arrived for the game, just twelve years late..."

"...Kev asked me if we won. I told him that we had lost the game, played one more without him, and got crushed. The other team, those guys cried with us. After that, the team broke up, and we all went on our separate ways. Nobody wanted to talk about it. We all thought Kev was dead..."

"Kev replied, That's on me. I'm sorry. Listen. I owe you an explanation..."

"Kev had been released from prison a year before after serving ten years of a thirty-year sentence for a murder that he did not commit..."

"...He was arrested by the local police three days after the murder, on his way to the 7-Eleven to get some milk for his stepchildren who lived in Indiana. Since he matched the description of one of the suspects—tall, male, black—he was taken in. He was convicted because the police strong-armed their witnesses into identifying him, and because the Judge ruled that the 00.001 percent chance that the DNA found at the crime scene could have matched his was more than enough to find him guilty. The 99.999 percent chance that the DNA was not his did - not – matter..."

"...In time, the Innocence Project learned of and took up his case. The DNA was positively matched to a man serving time for a murder he committed after Kev already was behind bars..."

"...I wanted to take him out. Do something. He said that he couldn't. He explained how he got up at a certain time, ate at a certain time, took a shit at a certain time, went to work at a certain time, came home at a certain time, and went to bed at a certain time. He had become institutionalized..."

"...I had to do something. The only thing I could think of was that I had a vacation plan completely paid for. I did what I had to do; I did it for me. I gave him a seven-day cruise and covered his airfare. I took him to the airport and had to practically force him to go. When he got back, he was deinstitutionalized. He moved to Wilmington, North Carolina..."

After taking it all I said, "You saved his life by getting him aboard ship and out to the sea. The inimitable sensation the ocean's vastness that you provided him—gave him perspective and let him 'return to port', so to say." "Kev is a prince. He is 'Al Basha'. I have a friend, Umair, who would want me tell Kev's story. May I?"

"Tell it just like you told of Cephas's innocence: fair and real - and how you paid tribute to the young man who was murdered."

"Has Kev forgiven those who wronged him?"

"I asked him that same thing. He has...and so will Cephas."

> **All of us have in our veins the exact same percentage of salt in our blood that exists in the ocean, and, therefore, we have salt in our blood, in our sweat, in our tears. We are tied to the ocean. And when we go back to the sea—whether it is to sail or to watch it—we are going back from whence we came.**
>
> **—JOHN F. KENNEDY**

On my last night of that trip to Amsterdam, I began to ponder whether I was becoming unhealthily obsessed with Café Internationaal, behaving like one of my "frequent flier" stalker clients. As if Michel had not only read my mind but scheduled my moment of question, he interrupted my turbulent thoughts and introduced me to Captain Steve.

Captain Steve - a Minnesotan and Delta pilot, like me had been drawn into the Café many years ago. Clean-shaven and snappily dressed in business casual, Captain Steve would make it a point to visit the Café after every landing at Schiphol, be it for coffee or a perfectly measured and properly paced *vaasje*.

"You and I are so lucky that Café Internationaal chose us...I stick every landing at Schiphol, every time. And just as I lay the bird down, I think of this place - sitting at this table - taking all of this in...I'll bet you don't stray far from here when you're in Amsterdam. I'm surprised we haven't met before now, but I know that we will either see each other here again...or just miss each other..."

To die is landing on some distant shore.

—JOHN DRYDEN

CHAPTER XXXIV

SUPERMAN

*All journeys have secret destinations of
which the traveler is unaware.*

—*Martin Buber*

One's street name is quite essentially the unchangeable title to his defining moment's short story. Not all attorneys have street names; most are known by their often-butchered last names; in some cases, by their first names and trite.

Every attorney's street name that I knew of was unflattering, if not totally insulting. As for mine? I cannot refute it. Not because I earned it; but rather how it came to be. It is a story worth retelling.

My street name was decreed during an unpredictable winter, just after my return from Amsterdam. Still thinking in – and trying to speak in – the Dutch language, I had to shift focus and prepare for litigation. I would contend with two gang-related shooting trials, with incongruous facts and variant legal issues, both to be litigated in the same week. The first began on Monday and concluded on Wednesday morning with an acquittal. The second began two hours later. The closing arguments for the second were made on Friday morning, resulting in a happy-hour acquittal.

My respective clients were released from the County along with only those whose nickel and dime cases either were thrown out or who copped to pleas in exchange for 'time served'; all of whom were now focused on getting their liberated grooves on and party. As for the two notches in my belt, they and their respective entourages, from rival gangs, some-how ended up celebrating "their" victories at the same spot: "*Mandingo's Aqua Blue Room*", a rugged bar that was nothing but trouble before they were born. The look and feel of that bar, accented with bullet holes, was that of a Blaxploitation film set. At least a dozen people are to have dis-appeared from there.

The "You're a free man!" cheer went on and the victory tale of each of my client's trials swirled around the room. There was a buzz in the air – and the buzz was me. Patrons on the periphery of the fray were recounting what they heard and through the osmosis the urban legend in the making, things started to get confusing.

This was 'Chinese Secret', in the hood, with the attendees retelling their respective second-, third-, and even fourth-hand accounts of my courtroom handwork. A synergy of converging, escalating smack-talk began to heat up, eventually making its way back to each of the liberated honorees - my respective clients.

As the story goes, their pride and allegiance to me were at the brink of getting the best of them. Simultaneously goose-necking for one another, they very dangerously made eye contact from Mandingo's opposite, grimy corners. Being true to what had got them in trouble in the first place, they wanted a piece of each other. On the dingy, dilapi-dated dance floor, they went from face-to-face to nose-to-nose, ready to throw down with the real possibility that someone from the entourages would "up" (draw handguns) then start "busting caps" (open fire).

Abandoning their common good fortune, my freshly former clients made it all about pride, but not self-pride. This was about lawyer pride: who had the baddest lawyer, whose lawyer "shut the state's shit down".

After a few rounds of "Your lawyer, he ain't shit!", territorial instincts kicked in. Each of them—and every person around them—was now salivating for a turf war to break out. Just as rounds were racked and fists were ready to fly, one of them just happened to finally mention my name. He butchered it, someone corrected him, albeit with his own mispronounced version.

They realized that they had hired and had been successfully represented by the same lawyer: Franco Minasian. With adrenaline about to get the best of them, they and theirs were in kill-or-be-killed mode, ready to "jump off" (engage in gun play).

Not a moment too soon, a tall, dark, slim, sweet thing, with a Donna Summers look and a huge Afro, clunked in her platform shoes to the center of the ring and uttered what became the street legend and lock in my reputation: "*You all's ain't had no lawyer; the man who done saved your sad, sorry asses? He ain't no mother fuckin lawyer—and he sure as shit ain't either of y'all's daddys neither. You all's almost kill't each other for him…Both y'all's had Superman.*"

And so, from the gallery of many a courtroom, "Superman" has been called out, followed by requests for my business card. I have gotten calls during all hours of the day and night, from the street, during in-progress traffic stops and police lockups; from those jammed up, their desperate loved ones, even by curious cops—all asking for "Superman." That the story of my life is literally a comic book tale is irrefutable.

> *I busted a mirror and got seven years' bad luck,*
> *but my lawyer thinks he can get me five.*
>
> —STEVEN WRIGHT

CHAPTER XXXV

UMAIR REVISITED

A thought…asked for words to set it free…
But this thought is a feeling…you live with it.

—*Javed Akhtar*

During that pre-Superman time in Amsterdam, daylight hours were spent writing "*Al Basha*". Once settled in [post-trials], Melaura told me how important it was to her that I put that "Amsterdam energy" into finishing what Umair and I had started, no matter what it might take. And even though she had yet to be in Amsterdam with me, she felt that we should pull stakes from the Midwest and find a way to re-spike them both on Great Boar's Head and there. She was geared up to plan a huge yard sale, to extend our thank-you/goodbyes then leave the Midwest.

Melaura said, "You like lists. So, why don't you make a list. And I think yours should start with 'See Umair.'"

Melaura was right. It had been too long since we had spoken, let alone met. I realized that the last time Umair and I had talked was on the day I had left for Amsterdam – the year before.

We like lists because we don't want to die.

True to his ways, Umair buried his obvious sadness, turning our conversation to celebrating my adventure; he was happy for me and pleased that I was making good on "Al Basha". It pleased him that I was making good on his mandate and honoring his vision: *"I wish I could go with you, so I could watch you be happy."*

"You're here with me right now," I replied. "You have boarded the flight with me every time, Umair. Please don't tell me you have forgotten about the nurses???"

One night – actually around 3:30 in the morning, I snapped out of my sleep – Melaura was already awake. We were both thinking about Umair.

Later that morning, while heading to Court, with the sun slicing through the storm clouds on their way to Detroit and Sonny Rollins filling my trusty Acura, I scrolled through my contacts, found Umair's old number, and called him. That I had awaked him out of a sound sleep, considering that he was an early riser, was troubling.

> "Umair."
>> *"Who is this?"*
> "Franco."
>> *"Franco?"*
> "Franco. Umair, it's me, Franco."
>> *"Franco?"*
> "Umair. It's Franco Minasian."
>> *"Franco! I was just thinking about you! What time is—the power went out…Did you do that?*
> He broke into a familiar laughter; on cue, mine followed.
>> *"Seriously. How did you do that?"*

We agreed to meet for lunch at Al Basha. Its aroma, ambiance, and menu were the same, but years of wear, tear and outdated décor mat-tered not, as the cuisine was even better than the first time.

Umair reluctantly told me of his life - of Loona's inexorable tor-menting. Having once again seized the upper hand, she now ran with a "born-again Muslim" angle, which she modified, by hooking up with men in uniform; cops and firemen. Loona used religion to cajole their youngest daughter and pull her away from Umair's 'strict' influence, applying her methodology of enticements, passive-aggressive innuendo and intimidation.

Loona then set her hooks into second oldest daughter, pressuring her into marrying a total slug who was marginally educated and mini-mally skilled. He lacked any potential and was void of any worthy future. His Americanized -Saudi family had a reputation as being swindlers.

Umair's younger children would not leave him - and clung to his nurturing ways. He saw to it that they were well-read and good Muslims. He stressed the virtue of self-respect and the importance of self-restraint, especially when answering to their mother.

His oldest daughter had already broken free of the dysfunction, moved to Los Angeles and was enjoying a successful career and healthy friends.

That Umair and Loona were still legally married – albeit living under separate roofs - soured me. When Umair offered his words of regret over my having withdrawn from his case, I let it roll off. He picked it back up.

"I wish you had stayed on the case," Umair now mealy-mouthed.
"You fired me. After I withdrew, you stopped returning my calls."
"I didn't want to bother you."
"That's such bullshit. You sound like my ex-wife Erin."
"You sound like my wife Loona."
"I rest my case. Second thought, I don't. I sound like her because just like her, I have balls. Remind me to order two falafels, To Go, for you to tuck two into your two-sizes-too-big, pleated chinos."

We busted out laughing. After it finally subsided, Umair gave his rebuttal:

"You told me I was about to make the biggest mistake of my life, and yet I would have none of it. You were right. I should have listened."

There was no way that I would let this be the last word. Considering all the goodness that my storytelling perspective had provided me since our last meal and how much I owed to Umair's mandate to write "*Al Basha*", a surrebuttal was plainly in order:

"Umair. Loona needed you in her life all of these years—and me totally out of it. You know that is so. That's why you never returned my calls. She had to have you all to herself - so she could torment you." "Your children had you there to take the brunt of her madness. As for your daughters who sided with her—they did so out of loyalty to you. Your children are survivors, just like you. They showed the fortitude that you taught them."
"Umair, you made the right decision. Had we pushed your divorce case forward, Loona would have succeeded in destroying you. At some point, either she or some unstable cop, or emotionally stunted young fireman, would have whacked you and then me. Loona would have testified for them and flimflammed the jury. You and I would be dead – our children fatherless; and her hit men would have beaten the rap on a double-murder. That's something I - just – could - not – live – with...."

We busted out laughing.
After it subsided, Umair asked:

"I don't understand why has she tried to destroy any relationship that I have tried to form? I made friends with a Polish woman. She was easygoing and of few words, but she was loads of fun. Loona somehow got a hold of her. It was over. I later met and began to strike up a very nice relationship with a Mexican woman. Same thing. Why?"

That required some thought and more information. I asked Umair why he had described these women by their ethnicities.

> "Because they are true to their culture - and they have values. The way that each of them was raised - in positive ways; they shared that with me and it was special. Loona is not true to Islam, certainly not to her cul...ture..."

Umair went slack-jawed and stared.

Delay is the deadliest form of denial.

—C. NORTHCOTE PARKINSON

Thinking that a 'lick' [armed robbery] was about to go down, I palmed the closest knife -fortuitously it had a meaty, serrated blade- slowly pushed the table toward Umair then eased my phone over to my unarmed hand. Ever so slowly, I dipped my shoulder and turned my head around slowly, like a rusty owl.

I exhaled and tabled the blade, while feasting my eyes on a late-thirties, perfectly postured, full-figured beaming woman, wearing a glittery hijab and speaking pristine Arabic. She was light-skinned, with those distinctively quirky Eastern European features.

Umair whispered and covered his face.

> _"I know her; she used to work for me, years ago, just after my youngest was born. She was always so fascinated by Arabic culture. She would ask me about Islam and its tenets; she was overjoyed to learn about Islam from me."_

He clumsily ducked and twisted toward the wall, overly pretending to be looking for something he dropped. It was a very unslick move.

"We began to grow closer, like a father and daughter, more like a good teacher and an eager student. Over time she would want to discuss the nature of and distribution of power in marriage under Islam".

"Eventually she challenged me, demanding that I justify my role partake in a 'fraudulent marriage,' one patently untrue to its vows and 'void' of what our faith decrees".

"Finally, she charged me with having compromised all that I knew and with being a coward, unwilling to express righteous indignation, reluctant to hold Loona to any values, so willing to defend an unholy marriage- one so fraught with fraud"

"As she grew stronger, I became weaker. Her quest to understand our faith and her commitment to undertake its tenets exposed me. It was a failed intervention. I retreated from her reason and she, in turn, backed away from my cheap excuses".

"The very last time we spoke was before she turned in her resignation. I held hands and said, in Arabic, 'Do as I say, not as I do.' I thought I would never see her again."

This two-for-the-price-of-one reunion was clearly too much for Umair. In a pale whisper, but in exaggerated charades, Umair pleaded with me to close out our check and begged me to cover his escape, in the same way as when we would leave the courtroom, with Loona always primed and ready to pounce. I gestured toward the exit. With a schmear of baba ghanoush globbed into his pleated lap, Umair and his oversized chinos, limped out of Al Basha.

To cover him, I picked up a menu, then let it slip out of my hand to the floor, muttering as I got up to retrieve it.

A burly grill chef falsely made us as up to no good. I quickly pulled out my wallet and flashed cash, letting him know this was no "dine and dash."

Now I saw what this was all about. This woman was so self-assured, an apple of the restaurant's patrons' eyes and a joy for her fellow workers,

Umair's long lost protégé was so full of happiness and generously shared it with everyone around her.

Once outside, I suggested to Umair that he gather himself then go back inside and talk to her. And if not right then and now, on some other day. I said, "I can tell you that this girl has found her way. She did what you said and not what you did. And, Umair, I did what you said and not what you did. And for that, 'Al Basha', I shall do right by your mandate, continue to tell our story and be forever grateful to you."

We stood in the parking lot for over two hours, joking and laughing – commiserating about our lives and our struggles- old and new.

Learning of Loona's cruel behaviors had saddened me in very close ways. During the month just prior to this reunion with Umair, Erin had washed out of an outpatient alcohol treatment program. She had broken promises to Molly, now sixteen, to whom Melaura was giving unconditional love. For Erin, the bottle was in charge and was all that mattered. Everyone else was relegated.

Erin had long since "resigned" from her well-paying, upwardly mobile, position as an education administrator to take a "much better job" as a part-time teacher's aide. Something bad, undoubtedly alcohol-related, had broken - and swept her professional future away.

Among all of the toxic tirades, Erin took to sending suicide-tinged e-mails and text messages to both Molly and Rory. It is no wonder that by this time, they began guarding themselves from the lies, deception, folly, cajoling, disappointments, and incongruous manifestations of their mother's disease—and, to no lesser extent, from my legacy of angry outbursts, expressions of despair, and nagging frustrations; my mishandlings and bad behaviors and wrong responses.

Rory turned away from me and rejected Melaura, rather than take sides against his mother. It was valiant, yet so heartbreaking. Mollie would eventually follow suit, choosing to move out, leave Melaura and me, and live under her dysfunctional mother's roof. Mollie's decision was the culmination of the despair in her tender years, witnessing her parents' marriage wither, enduring a farcical, overspun divorce, knowing that

I had found true love and seeing how I foolishly responded to Rory's escape. Just as Rory did, Mollie took one for the team and over her last year of high school opted for self- compromise; to a place of refuge, to watch over and on occasion get over on her unstable mother.

After all, now complicating the effects from their turbulent past was their seeing me happy and no longer reacting to their mother in negative ways; instead constantly, perhaps too constantly, expressing regret over my having done so.

Rory and Mollie have come back around; as young adults who are looking forward rather than backward, which is a mixed blessing. I know that in time, they will tell their story and not let their turbulent upbringing – and my mistakes - assail them. I hope that they will find their Amsterdam – that place in the world where they can tell their story and not be afraid to face their pain and show their sorrow and accept my forgiveness for the follies and frailties that I displayed; and not be burdened by that over which they have no control.

All I can do is continue to encourage them, by my honest words and through my sincere actions, to tell their story - so that they too can reorient themselves and make sense of the chaos of their young lives, much of which was the outgrowth of their mother's disease and my self-created suffering.

> *Destiny is not a matter of chance, it is a matter of choice;*
> *it is not a thing to be waited for, it*
> *is a thing to be achieved.*

—*WILLIAM JENNINGS BRYAN*

Loona and Erin were in many ways cut from the same cloth. Each had demons, were manipulative, quick to shift the blame; trying to keep their plethora of lies straight would result in unpredictable, angry outbursts. They would leave their messes for others to clean up, yet belittle those who did and scold the honest and concerned as being cruel and judgmental and wholly lacking their compassion and fairness.

Loona had duped the Mosque's Imam, twisting him into believing that Umair was oppressive, unmanly, and immorally cruel. Erin sold her family and friends that I had fooled her, oppressed her, set the bar too high – all of which drove her to drink. There is much truth to that.

Loona's ploys had sapped Umair. He was losing both his grip on to his own sense decency and his focus on the children's best interests.

If it were not for Umair, for Shawnee, for Melaura – for Amsterdam - I might have broken apart. By recounting the story of my life and Umair's, "Al Basha"- through the love from others, I survived and began to thrive.

Umair had found some measure of solace in pursuing a PhD, collaborating with a professor who nurtured his talent and intellect. How sad that Umair's past would come calling, clamp down, and kinked up this promising path.

His brother Sadiq had taken ill and was spiraling downward in chaos and into the darkness of Alzheimer's disease. Umair would not turn his back on Sadiq - and so once again he would surrender his passion, abandon a decent path; bogging himself down in his brother's inexorable misery.

However emotionally battered he was, Umair's big heart and warmth had stayed with him. He expressed how happy he was for me and all that I had come to find from heeding his words. Umair was eternally grateful to Loona for having given him children. And so, I too would be eternally grateful to Erin.

By the time Umair and I said goodbye, the baba ghanoush had crusted over. "Write our book, honey." he urged, then poetically proclaimed: "Hold on to your Melaura each and every day - To Amsterdam – The two of you - Make your way…"

The opposite of love is not hate; it's indifference.

—Elie Wiesel

CHAPTER XXXVI

LENNIE BRECZKO

Litigation solves everything.

—Jon Cryer

It seems that the component of our lives most conducive to swapping stories and identifying with the plight of others is the weather. December 2013 delivered an unforgiving, biting cold to Chicagoland. Its viciousness winter broke equipment, shut down businesses, and killed people. It forced strange changes in routine and bullied a grim perspective onto everyone's outlook. That winter's 'Hawk' (the Native American-coined word for such Lower Lake Michigan-driven, brutal cold snaps) made global warming seem a farce, albeit a welcome one.

That winter's weather personified the case of all of my cases and how it impacted upon me. Both were so bitter, utterly uncontrollable, and gravely life-altering. Just when I thought the cold snap could get no worse, as if imported from Siberia, its temperature plunged.

This evil winter also delivered a desperate client.

Lennie Breczko is best described as a fireman's fireman. He has a middle-aged, Peter Fonda-like demeanor. Born and raised in the Chicago suburb where he joined the fire service, Lennie rose up in the ranks from a young, reliable firefighter to a mature, trusted lieutenant to highly-respected deputy chief. Admired by anyone he met, Lennie lived up to his reputation throughout the suburbs of Cook County as an officer who could get any job safely done and then get back in service, 'ready-freddie' for the next one. Lennie would jump in and help anyone on the fire ground who needed it. He got antsy when hanging back with incident command; while he was white-shirt material, he preferred to be in the heat to see to it that fire did not win the fight.

Everyone knew Lennie was someone who was deservedly destined for a Chief's position. His chief, who was 'old school'/nuts and bolts, was very close to retiring, his sights set on sturgeon, pike, and bass filled lakes and rivers. Only a matter of time stood between Lennie's trusting chief passing command for Lennie to assume.

I knew of Lennie and his reputation, but first met him during my tenth and last year in the fire service—through our mutual friend, Kane, from whose similar folksy, Midwest populist cloth, Lennie was cut. Lennie was always earnest, compassionate and genuine. His reputation had been built not by self-promoting, but by what truly interested him: any person in his presence and history. Lennie displayed an outward calm and the curious, quirky nature of a prep school social studies teacher. How could he and not hit it off?

We became once-a-year golf partners, joining forces at one particular patrolmen's association late summer golf outing. Just before its cer-emonial 'shotgun start', I would be sure to call out, "I'm officer; you're engineer!", leaving Lennie to cart me around. We would engage in dis-cussions about golf and its nuances - nature, instinct, pressure, consis-tency, and self-determination - even though we could not play the game that well, we could talk about in epidictic terms.

Lennie and I would always give each shot our very best, hoping to land the ball in play. In that neither of us had the time for or interest in lessons, what we could offer was our commitment to each swing then leave the rest to the Gods of golf and Mother Nature.

Holding at solid one hundred degrees colder than any cart path over which Lennie and I had ever rambled over, Lennie's world was now about to break apart. On one bone-chilling, gusty, sunless afternoon, Lennie called me.

"Franco. I need your help."

"What's wrong, Lennie?"

"I need your help. My wife is in trouble."

Lennie had confronted her with the swirl of accusations that had made their way to him. In the fire service, every secret will inevitably turn from kept, to divulged, and then rumor. As the ranks say, acknowledging this way of things, "Tell a phone, tell a friend, tell a fireman." In this one regard, firefighters show like insecure high school, freshman cheerleaders. Any scandal-laden story was destined to make the rounds—to other departments, even to other districts.

This was a bombshell. Rumor had it that Lennie's wife, whom his Dad had pitched for a part-time bookkeeping job at a neighboring fire department, had stolen from its account.

Lennie confronted her.

At first, she projected righteous indignation and malingered hurt from having been so disparaged. That she averted her eyes and did not deny any wrongdoing when he asked her point-blank told Lennie other-wise. He was rapidly engulfed in fear, knowing that everything was about to change. When Lennie started to back away from her, an hour into their conversation, she caved in and admitted that she had stolen "some" money.

Lennie asked her how much, foolishly "starting the bidding" with one hundred dollars.

She said, "More."
"One thousand dollars?"
"More."
"Ten thousand dollars?"

"More."

"Don't tell me that it's one hundred thousand dollars."

"I think a little more."

She was off by over $250,000.

"What do I do?", he panicked. A panicking Lennie was a very bad sign. To calm both of us down, I kept the line tight and mechanical. I asked him if he was calling me as a friend or an attorney. He said, "Both." I said, "Lennie, there is no both. You need a good lawyer and lawyerly, not friendly, advice. And here it is: I'm telling you right now, as your friend, that you need me as your lawyer."

Given his public official status, holding brass in the fire service, no less, he had a duty to report his wife's wrongdoing. Lennie agreed that he had no other choice. It was settled. I would be his lawyer and find one for his wife.

That Lennie was duty-bound made him feel better, as he was so desperate to make things right. He had been blindsided; by not only his wife having committed a crime and that she had stolen, but that she had stolen so much money, of which he saw not a penny.

He began to ponder casinos, cocaine, or some smooth-talking gigolo.

Lennie Breczko was a throwback, a dying breed, the type to hand off his paycheck to his wife. He brought home the bacon; she paid the bills. I asked Lennie what he did for money. When he would ask his wife for some money, she would give him what she gave him. That explained why the stolen funds were right under his nose the whole time.

I had to make light of what just hit me. I shook my head and said, "Is that why I always paid for the beers and took care of the beer cart girls?" "You were told not spend your allowance?" We chuckled, as I pondered how deep Lennie's wife had sunk him.

Lennie formally waived his attorney-client privilege so that I could divulge our conversation to colleagues of mine in the public integrity unit of the Office. I reached out and asked bring Lennie in so that his thieving wife's third-party confession could be documented and his own statement could be memorialized.

I let Mickey O'Reilly, the public integrity/financial crimes prosecutor, assigned to the case, in on what I knew, assuring him that Lennie had no reservations about speaking to him or his investigators and that he would sign any "consent to a search" for whatever records or documents or other tangibles they might need. I suggested that Lennie could assist them in bringing his wife in to be arrested and processed into the system – so as to avoid any havoc and undue pain for their three children. Mickey was a straight-shooter. Raised in Beverly [Hills], a South-side Irish neighborhood; he was a bulldog framed; a decent high-school wrestler.

I was crystal clear with Mickey that Lennie felt duty-bound and mor-ally obligated to offer full cooperation and was still in shock – physically sickened - by his wife's larceny.

Then things went silent. I knew what that would otherwise have meant. But from Mickey? With Lennie?

"Mickey, come on. Nobody's looking at Lennie, are they?"
I received the scariest, most-feared response a prosecutor could ever make.

> "Listen, Franco. I have bosses to answer to. You know how the Office works. I gotta to do what I gotta do."

I assured Mickey that Lennie was clean and that he had no idea what she had done. Then I got scared: "Are you serious? You don't think he was involved in what his wife did? If I thought he was involved, I would tell you. And I wouldn't be bringing him in to make a statement. I would be bringing him in to give a confession."

Silence.

I offered to "*throw him in the lie box* (polygraph)."

Silence.

I pledged his presence before the grand jury for open season examination, waiving all of his rights, even his right to counsel. I offered to draft then have Lennie sign an across-the-board consent to search his home, his Office, his phone, his e-mail account, and even his body cavities—everything.

Silence.

I made it clear that I was looking for no deals or promises.

Silence.

I told him that Lennie was innocent.

Silence.

I gave professional assurances, staking my reputation.

Silence.

I got woozy from the suggestion that Lennie was being looked at for any of this. I began to beg: "As a matter of professional courtesy and personal favor to me. Please. Let me surrender him. You can't arrest him. Please."

"I have bosses to answer to. Franco, I'm sorry. I shouldn't even be talking to you. They know he's your guy and everybody knows how you operate. But they are not budging on this, so neither can I. Franco, we're done talking. And don't even think about going over my

head. You're too smart for that. I shouldn't
even be talking to you."

I tried to choke out, "Hey Mickey. Listen, I appreci—"

He hung up.

No snowflake in an avalanche ever feels responsible.

—Stanislaw Jerzy Lec

I started to get queasy, began to gag and keeled over; alarms were
sounding for me to puke, cry and pass out. Injustice was about to be
served, and there was nothing I could do to stop it.

On December 19, 2013, police officers from three law-enforce-
ment agencies -a makeshift task force -executed a search warrant on
Lennie's house and an arrest warrant against his person.

Somehow, his children's school schedules either were not passed
along, or worse yet, not even preplanned before over fifteen armed officers marauded into this residential, middle-class neighborhood to execute their totally unnecessary felony arrest warrant. They hit the house
after the two eldest children, high school and junior high students, had
left, but Lennie's youngest, a third grader was still in the house, all bun-
dled up, clutching her backpack and lunch bag. The CERT
armored vehicles rolled up instead of her school bus.

His young daughter was secured by a female officer while Lennie and
his wife were led out in handcuffs. Excessively armed, amped-up officers
overran and cleared the home – as if someone had tipped them off that
"public enemy number one" had been seen there. The media had been
cheaply called in to this sensationally over-the-top, truly lousy raid.

Both the local rag and the once-mighty Chicago Tribune dispatched
staff writers to spin out good stuff for its readers. Their crews took pictures and video from hobbyist's cameras, braving the cold to get in on

the fray. Cozying up to the press were quasi-media, soccer mom turned busy-bodies from "The Patch," an online local newsletter, another internet advent for those with too much time on their hands. Just as, in the words of Tip O'Neill, "all politics is local," most journalism had become both all political and all local.

I had gotten a heads-up, but given the weather, it was short notice. I received a call that came in as "pay phone", from a cop who said he owed me one. To this day, I do not know from whom this warning came.

"Minasian. Listen up. They are hitting your golf partner's house in twenty minutes, and they're going to hook your guy up. This shit's way so out of control. You'd better beat feet. You ain't got time to warm up your car. I'll call you back in fifteen sharp to make it turned over. If you're good, just let it ring. Christ, it's cold."

I had to scramble for coverage from other attorneys, calling in owed favors. My brethren of the bar came through. In less than ten minutes, I got coverage for five cases in three courthouses - through this bitter, blustery Arctic blast.

> *Driving is a spectacular form of amnesia.*
> *Everything is to be discovered, everything to be obliterated.*

—*Jean Baudrillard*

Tossing the freeze-dried blankets and tarps I had bungeed to my hood overnight, neither showering nor shaving, I put on what I had worn the day before, from atop my dry-cleaning pile then put the pedal to the metal. It first, I couldn't get above thirty...Once it finally registered a temperature, I pushed – triple digits on I-294, I was pulled over by a State Trooper. I got out, with no overcoat or gloves, leaned into the wind to get to his window. I told him who I was and where I was headed. *"Oh shit. I heard all about this clusterfuck. Get moving."*

When I arrived at the police station, just up the street from Matt Walsh's Office, I was told that Lennie and his wife were in the lockup. After fumbling out my credentials with my numb fingers, I was led in by the desk sergeant to Mickey then and a room full of investigators and big brass from at least five other agencies. For the very first (and the very last time), I resigned myself to the fact that there had to be some clear evidence linking Lennie to his wife's thievery. Selfishly, I was hoping that the smoking gun would be thrown in my face. Then, I could stare down Lennie through the bars of the lockup, shake my head and leave his co-conspirator lying ass for good.

There was no smoking gun and no such evidence. In vain, I offered Lennie up to show them that he was clean. My request was denied. I clarified that my offer was not hitched with any deals, promises, or demands; I was not asking for immunity or leniency.

I was so sure. I ran, then reran, every number, and every time, I came up with "innocent."

I waived Lennie's right to my counsel, agreeing to walk out of the station and only come back when they were done with him and their upside-down view of him as a suspect.

I was completely shut down.

When one of the investigators quipped, "It's the old head-in-the-sand defense.", I shot back. "If you think his head is in the sand, then why not interrogate him so that you can push it further down? Why not go at him and tie up your case? If you rush to judgment without hearing him out, then it is you who are holding his head in the sand. Right next to yours. Can you not grow a pair, Sally? Question him! Interrogate your suspect! Weigh his credibility, for Christ's sake! Is this not your case? It's your case! It's your call!! Do your jobs!!! We all know Lennie's kids are doomed to be motherless; she's going down, six to thirty. But you shouldn't play hide the ball, especially if you think – using that verb loosely - that he was on this. Breczko is innocent. You're totally wrong on this one. He has children —and you owe it to them to do your damn jobs. Otherwise, you're running a con on them—You hags are worse than their corrupt mother...

That one really pissed them off. I tried to take it back...

Too late.

Mickey got his Irish up and came in: "You're done. We're done. Get the f- Leave!"

> *The idea of redemption is always good news,*
> *even if it means sacrifice or some difficult times.*

> —*Patti Smith*

I stepped out into the hallway to cool off. I was met by a detective from the police department whose only job was to process Lennie and his wife and place them in cells. He whispered to me that he had no doubt that Lennie was innocent and that even after Lennie's wife's attorney invoked her right to remain silent, she pleaded with him to let everyone know that Lennie was innocent.

I pointed toward the cell-monitoring screens. He and I watched on one screen - Lennie pacing, crying, and obviously distraught; on the other - his wife was sleeping like a baby, her knees pulled up and in, her hands tucked under her cheek, like some angel:

"See. She's wired for this kinda' shit. Lennie is a train wreck. I'd better sneak his Mom and Dad in here for a visit, before he does something stupid... This is Fubar. I don't even know you from Adam, but I've known Lennie since we were in grade school and now he is in the freaking worst place he could be: hooked up for his wife's shit—and now you, mystery man - have to prove that he's innocent. Those yahoos in there are running something on him that I would never run on anyone – even a ruthless prick who I knew was good for it."

The detective then looked me in the eye and said: *"Listen to me. I'm begging you. You've got to help him. Their minds are made up. Someone mentioned that you worked for Matthew P. Walsh. If that's so then I know you know your shit. Most importantly, I know that you believe in Lennie just like I do. You're the only son of a bitch who can get him out of this, because I don't count for shit around here anymore. I'm a detective and they practically have me scrubbing the latrines. By the way, we're standing in a blind spot from camera.*

If anyone asks, I have been motherfucking your client and you this whole time. Got it?"

Before I could nod, he leaned in and mouthed—barely pushing air—poking me in the chest, *"It's on you to get Lennie out of this. And you God-damn-well better do it. That cold fucking bitch, thief-ass wife of his. I knew she was wrong from Jump Street."*

> *There is no greater feeling than when in the midst of battle, what you have envisioned is about to be achieved...The chess player announces, "Checkmate." The litigator says, "No further questions."*

> —JASON F. DANIELIAN, CRIMINAL PROSECUTOR
> AND DEFENSE ATTORNEY

15. System overloaded—Shoveling manure against the tide

The kryptonite of sensible prosecution has always been media sensationalism. From the Lindbergh baby to Patty Hearst to O. J. to Duke Lacrosse, big press and big cases never mix well. The press can hurt right-thinking prosecutors and seduce those without a spine.

A prosecutor's Office is bound to fail if poorly investigated and reviewed cases are rubber-stamped, dolled up and paraded into the system. My old Office was in disarray, having abandoned what worked so well: maximum efficiency, critical decision-making uncluttered case analysis - doing the right thing.

These were the marching papers carried out in every felony courtroom, manned by a unit of three prosecutors: the third chair, the second chair, and the first chair. The third chair was the grunt who, if able to keep the court docket and case discovery flowing and organized and master fetching, would be rewarded by working up trying serious cases with either the first or second chair.

The second chair was in charge of the bulk of the cases and would oversee and orchestrate the courtroom's day-to-day operations, field questions, resolve most issues and maintain the trial/motion calendar.

The first chair's job was to handle everything else; manage the murders and viciously violent crimes. The first chair was paid to assume the ultimate responsibility over the Courtroom, to protect its record and see to it that everyone played by the rules. Above all else, the first chair was to take the heat and back up his or her second and third chairs.

In my day, each courtroom actively worked up twenty-plus murder cases, with a dozen or so others awaiting trial or plea. Each courtroom handled about thirty serious or sensitive non-murders. As for any other case on the call, standing marching orders were: "Get rid of it!"; "Work it out"; "Deal it away"; "Reduce it down"; and "Lose it"— or otherwise dispose of it.

Twenty years later, I was invited back into my work space to discuss an armed robbery case with the second chair.

His office was overrun with files, strewn about to the point of nauseating me. By rough count, in my old file cabinet behind my old desk, there were at least sixty murders, stacks of unopened non-murder files, evidence, reports and junk jammed in everywhere.

It added up to too many cases for the system to handle. Files showed thick with dust; unmanaged, untried, and unresolved - with more on the way. What once moved cases like Hartsfield-Jackson Atlanta International Airport had become an overburdened refugee camp for displaced justice. The prosecutor said, "Isn't this sickening? It's a freakin' fire hazard in here. The other rooms are even worse. They look like homes on that screwy "*Hoarder*" show..."

My very best advocacy had failed. Lennie was in the system; fair game and fresh meat. Mickey was under pressure from those above him, which would put us at odds with one another; it would be "gloves off "in the courtroom.

The next morning, I appeared in the Preliminary Hearing Courtroom, before the Judge presiding over Lennie's bond hearing, the Honorable Kip Caradine; the first of many to follow. I made no bones, proffering for the record that Lennie Breczko was an innocent man. "The Law prohibits me from vouching for my client, and so I am prohibited, by law, from vouching for my client; but I hereby do..."

Judge Caradine did not care for Mickey's "head in the sand" company line. Judge Caradine knew where I was coming from; a former public defender, he had seen it all. And although Lennie's bond hearing was neither the time nor the place my absolutes, Judge Caradine was well aware of what the Office had become and how it had lost its way.

It is always good to be underestimated.

—*Donald Trump*

To Mickey's credit, although his bosses wanted him to publicly go for the throat, tempered his recitation, showing self-confident/cocky restraint. After all, he had Lennie's wife dead-to-rights and the stakes were huge for Lennie. If they both went down, his children would be without parents for a minimum of six years. Mickey's plan was to hold off on Lennie until his wife pleaded then pitch an offer of probation.

Mickey's bosses had other ideas. They wanted to pressure Lennie into pleading by keeping him locked up.

Judge Caradine set bond at one hundred thousand dollars, which meant ten thousand dollars had to be posted. Given the allegation and charges and the media coverage, I could not find fault. Lennie's accounts were frozen, so his friends and family passed the hat and put it together. Even better, an old family friend of Lennie's, Aiden Casey, a bank executive, offered to post the full amount on the spot.

I informed Judge Caradine and Mickey, finally feeling ahead. I was shoved back. Mickey, following strict orders from above, filed a motion to challenge any source of the bond money posted to secure his release, to ensure that funds were not proceeds from the crime. Such a motion was restricted to drug cases, where cinder blocked sized rubber banded tens and twenties were going to be posted by unemployed 'friends' of the accused.

Aiden's funds and her life were obviously worlds away from anything even remotely criminal— or Lennie's rogue wife and her financial high crimes. That Aiden never cared much for Lennie's wife was an understatement.

That frivolous motion coupled with worsening weather that shut the Courthouse down would hold up Lennie's bond hearing for over a week.

In the middle of Mickey's "dog and pony" examination, an annoyed Judge Caradine cut him off and ruled that Aiden could post Lennie's ten-thousand-dollar bond. Aiden, shaken up by all of this entire ordeal, pulled out her checkbook and began to cut the check right then and there.

Judge Caradine said, "Aiden. Excuse me, Ms. Casey. Slow down. It doesn't work that way." She replied, "Judge I can wire funds and give you cash, if that's how I'm supposed to pay you."

Everyone, including me gasped.

"Counsel! COUNSEL!"

"Your Honor, she is a businesswoman. This is unfamiliar territory."

"Just a minute. The Court is very displeased with so much of this. Not with you, Ms. Casey. Mr. Minasian will explain what you need to do."

I was grateful for Judge Caradine's puissance. While intrigued by my claims of innocence against the full brunt of the Office, Judge Caradine was grateful that having set bond, this "press case" was now out of his Preliminary Hearing Courtroom.

"Counsel, you had better get settled in and ready for some heat."

"Your Honor, heat is the one thing my client and I have trained to ready be for."

"That's fine. But you the two of you had better check who is operating the hydrants. All I can say is that it is good thing the two you have each other. Because the way I see — Wait! That's all I'm gonna say. Clerk. Clerk! Call the next case!!"

For another week, waiting for the wired funds to processed, Lennie would remain in custody at the Cook County Jail. Calls came in from by police officers, fire-service big brass, and politicians, asking that Lennie be looked after.

At the same time, Mickey's bosses were blowing in the "no special treatment" calls. Alert not to flag anything, corrections officers were sure to make paper and cover their tracks so that the jail records showed that Lennie was being handled professionally—nothing more, nothing less. Anything to help get Lennie through this was done so with a staged, bold front - that only his most seasoned fellow inmates could see through.

After playing four days of catch up my other cases and with the funds not yet cleared to secure Lennie's release, I went to see him. The weather was even worse than the week before. The deputies who were assigned to Lennie told me that, given his rapid weight loss and fatigue, they moved him to 'medical'. The physician's assistant, a retired CFD paramedic, freed up an examination room so Lennie and I could be face-to-face. Before he left, the guard held me back and said, "Give them a second or two"; they hugged and cried.

Before letting me in, the guard assured me that everyone was taking care of Lennie and that first they made sure that the other inmates knew that he wasn't a child molester. Word eventually got in, like it always does, about how Lennie's wife had totally screwed him—and his kids. After that, everybody, even the hard-core dudes, took good care of him. They gave him a corner and let him be when he would cry.

"Lennie's had a tough time, but it would have been a lot tougher if we hadn't ignored our brass – who got an earful from 'the Office'. Christ, that place has gone to hell in a handbasket..."

"Lennie's been a bit unhinged today, so I would play it cool if I were you, no offense, counselor," the guard forewarned.

Lennie looked like ten miles of dirt road. His gaunt eyes were raw from tears and unrest. Lennie was twitching, and he stunk of the jail. With the bitter cold outside, the heat was cranking; the room was stuffy and boiling hot. My thoughts started to swirl.

- Tom Hanks' *Philadelphia* role.
- Closet junky in withdrawal.
- His wife, Mickey and I are as good as dead.

I took a deep breath through my mouth, a technique I had mastered in college, when playing four-on-four on a Back-Bay basketball court, a subterranean heap at the rear of a closed-down, run-down grade school. Its right baseline was smeared with excrement, left behind by the homeless, who illegally squatted in its classrooms and physically squatted over the very spot from which I never missed. I tried to lighten things up with some "yuckety yuk": "My compliments, Lennie: You blend. You know, you should be grateful; this a wonderful learning experience- on how the other half lives."

With battery acid breath, that burned my nares, Lennie retorted, "Listen Franco. We aren't the other half. The other half is the other half. You and everyone else out there is the other half."

Lennie began to tell me how he felt like he was in a huge firehouse, where the inmates operated like firefighters and the guards were like lieutenants.

"The guards have been great, but the guys on my tier have been..." He began to cry.

"...like brothers..."

Lennie said that if it weren't for them, he would have broken. But they took him in, made him one of their own and cared of him. Feeling safer with them than the outside was starting to destabilize him.

Lennie told me he did not talk about the case, as his fellow inmates had told him from the beginning: "Do not talk about your case!"

The word had already gotten out got that Lennie was being screwed.

"They feel bad for me; especially because I am white, for Christ's sake. Can you imagine? Please, Franco - get me out of here. These guys are rock solid, but this place is not right. Even the guards know it."

Three days later, finally out of custody and back living under his elderly parent's roof, Lennie honored my demand that he not step foot in his house, not communicate with his wife about anything other than their children and that he must assume full, exclusive responsibility of the family's' finances. Not quite hearing me, Lennie told me how at night he could hear the tier. Lennie had been institutionalized.

At our next court appearance before the felony court Judge to whom his case was assigned, just two days after his release, Lennie started to get sweaty and woozy. Just about to hit the deck. My paramedic training kicked in; I clamped onto his upper torso from behind him and eased him to a sitting, recovery position. When Judge Jim Hayes called for medical attention, I said, "Please, Your Honor, that won't be necessary. Both my client and I are paramedics - we can handle this." My quip pepped Lennie up.

And that was the way it would continue to be for Lennie and me.

He regained his senses; his color came back and he carefully, but as assertively as he could, got back to his feet. True to who I knew Lennie Breczko to be, he apologized to the Judge Hayes for causing a disruption. My adrenaline still pumped jacked; I gestured to Lennie as I locked eyes with the Judge then to Mickey, my head pejoratively shaking and my face displaying disgust, as if to say, "Do you seriously think that he played any part in his wife's three-year-long rip-off?"

A year to that day later, her attorney requested the mandatory minimum sentence of six years in the penitentiary. Mickey asked for twelve. The Judge settled on nine years.

Her family then put into works a restitution repayment, a buy-down from the proposed sentence. Namely, in exchange for one hundred thousand dollars paid to the Fire Protection District from which she stole, they, through her attorney, brokered a sentence reduction. To my perplexity, it was for only one year.

I could not comprehend why her family would plunk down all of this money and not sock it away for her children. Why not start a college fund or invest in long-term money market account? Plenty of my criminal-minded clients, let alone my law-abiding friends, would have agreed to serve a year in the joint for that kind of money, even if it were not tax free.

Lennie's wife pled guilty and took nine minus one years in the peni-tentiary and the one hundred thousand dollars was handed over.

She insisted her guilty plea stipulate that she was the sole perpetrator, refusing to affirm, state, or swear to anything that even remotely alleged that Lennie knew of, let alone participated in, her deviance. I did not like it. It was as if she was trying to overstate the truth so that it might not be believed.

Later, I learned that Judge Hayes had actually agreed to a three-year sentence reduction, but between the time that she agreed and her plea/surrender, Lennie's wife forged a Court Order that had allow her limited freedom of movement from her house arrest for necessary, designated matters.

In a font, with language and ink obviously different from the Judge Hayes's, she was somehow allowed to "attend a candle party." Her deceptive ways, without any consideration for those who would be impacted by her dishonesty, had not changed one bit.

The secret to humor is surprise.

—*Aristotle*

Right after the "candle party plea," Judge Hayes retired. The Judge assigned to fill the vacant courtroom was none other than the Honorable Kip Caradine.

Just as Lennie's trial was finally about to begin, Mickey's partner, John Lyndon, a quippy, soft-spoken, frustrated playwright moved to cor-rect a typographical error contained in the fourteen-count indictment. It read, "Palos Heights Fire *Prevention* District," rather than *Protection*. I did not to object this form-over-substance, quite correct amendment to the indictment. How I had not caught this seemingly obviously typo was perplexing.

Just as Mickey began to deliver his opening statement—the official bell of this long-awaited trial—I just happened to glance down at the first count of the indictment. It flashed out at me. And there it was: a fiery gem. I quickly flipped through the remaining counts of the indict-ment, in awe that it appeared only once, licking out only from Count One. This was the quintessential moment of the trial. To my chagrin, it marked the no-nonsense, unabashed, and self-assured tone by which I would commence my counterattack to follow.

I cut Mickey off, rose up from my seat, and addressed the Court.

"Your Honor, while I am truly reluctant to move the Court as I'm about to, I have no choice. Over my own objection, given how truly magnificent this pun is…it's so brilliant."

"What is it, Mr. Minasian?"

"Your Honor, I must seek leave of Court to amend Count One of the indictment to reflect Palos 'Heights' Fire Protection District and not Palos 'Heist' Fire Protection District, as it so reads…"

With that, Judge Caradine, Mickey, John and I busted out laughing, followed by the entire courtroom, less one.

Under the roar, a tearful Lennie said, "You have no idea how important that was for me. This is our sign."

True to His penchant for the clever, Judge Caradine added, *"Mr. Minasian, I'm almost inclined to deny your motion."*

I was now poised to dictate the trial's tempo and tone and temper; and Mickey knew it. His bosses were nowhere to be found - and thus would not witness what they never should have let happen finally be undone.

His opening statement was 'safe'; it was predictably, sufficiently pejorative, parading around the courtroom the enormous amounts of money Lennie's wife had stolen and spent. It was hardly his finest hour. As if Mickey were trying to convince himself, he pondered about - rather than proclaiming with fervor - how Lennie 'must have' benefited from his wife's crime and 'likely' partook in this dishonest wealth. By the time he fizzled out, it was clear to me that Mickey finally realized that he too had been fooled by Lennie's wife.

He may as well have claimed reasonable doubt for himself.

Judge Caradine responded to this two-bit can of corn with a sour, perplexed look. Not willing to leave the lame alone, as if picking a fight,

Mickey poked that although Lennie may not have committed theft, given the number of fraudulent transactions his wife had made and the money their household benefited from, he 'that he could not have not known, was questionable'.

Judge Caradine went slack-jawed.

Mickey ended his opening statement, asserting that Lennie certainly failed as a husband by not knowing or attempting to know of his wife's criminality.

Judge Caradine lowered His head.

I then delivered my fifteen-second opening statement, referencing my "Answer to Discovery," a formal document which, prior to trial, the defense is required to file, noting its unorthodox proclamation: "My client will not rest on the presumption of innocence. I intend to prove his innocence, beyond a reasonable doubt…"

I told Judge Caradine that I would do so during my cross-examination of any witness the state chose to call to the stand. It was a 'check-raise', made so that Judge Caradine would give me free rein - to either build my case or fall on my face.

Judge Caradine now knew that before this trial's end, I would likely go all-in: "I must admit, Mr. Minasian, that I hadn't read your answer before now. I can't believe you did that. I am both shocked and impressed. State. Call your first witness."

The state's direct examination of its witnesses was polished, yet predictable; relevant, yet boring. Most of it led to Lennie's wife; other than through innuendo, none of touched Lennie.

During cross-examination of the Fire Protection District's Fire Chief, Lennie's wife's boss, I trapped him as to how he was certain that Lennie's wife hadn't gotten into his accounts.

"Because I checked. As a matter of fact, ever since this mess, I check my own wife's family book-keeping. I trust my wife and all, but after what happened to L…let's just say that I double-check. Did I answer your question?"

The lead detective conceded that he could not conclude that Lennie knew what was going on or not; he could only conclude that Lennie had not participated in her crime or partaken in any of her ill-gotten gained funds. I pushed the envelope and asked if she had perhaps set Lennie up. He answered, *"The way I see it, he may have himself up by trusting her."*

Each witness granted me every concession and ate every item on my pre-fix 'investigation's shortcomings and flaws' menu. By asking non-leading questions and letting them talk - it was just a matter of syllables before each witness either contradicted the State's case or bolstered mine.

When either Mickey or John, through redirect examination, attempted to rehabilitate each of their witnesses, the resulting answers sank their scuttling case even deeper.

After each witness limped off the stand, Lennie regained his old composure and weaned himself off of his two years of madness. Lennie and I were finally back on the fairway. The state was deep in the sand up against the edge of steep, overgrown bunker.

Just before resting the People's Case in Chief, Mickey moved a bucket-load of financial records of all sorts into evidence. But by that point, it was clear that Lennie's wife's outrageous thievery and frenetic spending spree was of her making and her doing – and carried out in such a way to keep it from Lennie.

The truth of the matter- as those on Lennie's jail tier, likely still there, had told him: He was guilty of having trusted his wife.

Once Mickey rested then slumped into his chair, I moved for a directed finding and then asked if I should argue. Judge Caradine replied, "No. Motion denied." He then asked both sides to approach.

Courage is almost a contradiction in terms. It means a
strong desire to live, taking the form of readiness to die.

—GILBERT K. CHESTERTON

Now at the bench, Judge Caradine asked me if I intended to call Lennie's wife in my case, letting me know that she was in the lockup and under guard guarded by the Department of Corrections personnel, who had transported her to the Courthouse from the downstate prison where she had begun serving her time.

"That's swell," I sneered. "Can't wait to see her."

He asked me if I wished to speak with her.

"No, Your Honor."

He asked me if I had prepared her for her testimony.

"Your Honor, I have never spoken with that...pardon me, with her. I care not to speak with her. I'm going to examine her. Cold."

Judge Caradine now understood that she was to be my adverse witness. I was 'pin high' and determined to tee her up and crush her with my trusty driver. The one Lennie always recommended I use, figuratively speaking of course. I was salivating at the chance to prosecute Lennie's wife for what she had done to my dear friend.

"Counsel, are you sure you want to do this?"

I replied, "I don't know, Your Honor; am I sure I want to do this?"

Judge Caradine, for the very first time I could ever recall, would not telegraph anything as to the matter at hand.

I then had turned to Mickey. "State, am I sure I want to do this? Should I call her?"

Mickey replied, gesturing to the Judge – in all schmooze - retorted, "I'm not tipping my hand, either."

I then squared off between the two of them and put it all on the table:

"Listen, the two of you. I just tipped my hand. And so now one of the two of you, if not both of you, had better tip yours. Otherwise, get my witness up here and have her sworn; although her oath ain't worth a plugged nickel – correction – 'a piss hole in the snow'... But at least everybody in this Courtroom will get to see who the real criminal is. That's the way I see it, with all due respect to the Court and all due deference to the State…"

Judge Caradine raised His head up and snickered; looking to the courtroom door, and began to ponder out loud and "remind" me of the obvious. Mickey turned ashen. Judge Caradine further reminded me that while I may not have met my burden as to the motion for directed finding, the State – and only the State - now bore the ultimate burden to prove Lennie guilty beyond a reasonable doubt:

> "Mr. Minasian. You don't have to prove his innocence, as much I know you want to."

Judge Caradine then asked me what I wished to do. I told Him that the defense was prepared to rest. He asked me if I needed some time to talk with Lennie. I said no.

> "Counsel. Court is in recess. Go talk to him."

I went back to the counsel table and asked Lennie to follow me out-side. He knew where we were headed. Since his first court appearance after being released from custody, my makeshift office was a scissor-levered, articulating platform that the courthouse maintenance crew used to clean the inside of the upper, exterior windows and the outside of the glass, knee-wall walkway overlooking the first floor. Lennie and I had always set up shop there. I would put my files out on its deck; he would grab on to the rails and put his foot up on the wheel. He now knew that this might well be the very last time we would meet there. And it time it was for all the marbles.

I told Lennie that we must rest and not call any of the thirteen character witnesses I had subpoenaed, let alone his despicable his wife. Lennie then asked me if I trusted the Judge.

I put it back on him:

"Did the Judge not prove himself to be trustworthy? Did He see not see things our way from the very beginning? Did He not sustain every one of my objections and overrule every one of theirs? Did He not correct me when I was wrong? Did He shut me down - or did He clear my path? Lennie, whether I trust the Judge or not, you and I know one thing. We have no choice but to trust Him. Because if we do not trust Him now, we will lose His trust forever."

"Lennie, we've attacked the fire and knocked it down. I know that you have the courage to push on and chase it. If I saw all of this as fire, I would do the same. With you as my officer, I would chase any fire, on any day of the week, especially with you by my side. We have talked about this for years. But this ain't fire. This is the law. We don't have to drown what we have put out. You're my friend, Lennie. But more importantly, I'm your lawyer. It is my advice to you, my client, that we rest.

Lennie said: "Sound the horn. Strike the fire. Let's pull out."

We went back into the courtroom and sat down. Just before Judge Caradine was in the hallway about to reenter the courtroom, Lennie reached over and put his hand on my forearm. Now under the threshold to the courtroom, seeing this, Judge Caradine held back. Lennie looked me in the eye and said: "Franco, I'm very sorry. I know it's not right. But I have to ask you this: If I were your son, what would you tell me to do?"

For the first time in the trial, I had to slow things down and ponder, deeply so. I looked to the ceiling and then looked to floor for the answer to a question that was way out of line; turning and twisting my head; my respirations picked up. Meanwhile, for what seemed a lifetime, Judge Caradine patiently waited, taking all of this in.

"It's an unfair question, Lennie. It's out of line. You know it is. But since you asked, I'll answer: Lennie. If you were my son, I would tell you rest."

Seeing Lennie's response, Judge Caradine announced that Court was back in session.

And with that, I rested our case. But this trial was hardly over. I needed to lay out what I had promised and leave not one iota of doubt that my client was not proven guilty.

Mickey's opening statement cleverly theorized that while Lennie may have surrendered his role as the household bookkeeper, he only did so after he knew that his wife had begun to steal. There was no evidence to support this. It was purely anecdotal. Mickey's argument consisted of grandiose claims, which the record belied. Nonetheless, it was a rugged one - that forced me to move in and put his case down for good.

...Just as his children unwittingly partook in consumption of items purchased with ill-gotten gains, I argued, so had Lennie. Loving and living with the secret purveyor of stolen funds was no crime. I insisted that the state's case failed to tie Lennie to any transactions; that the detailed investigation of his wife's wrongdoing showed him as having played no part whatever in her lone-wolf wife's crime, other than having trusted her...I commended Mickey for the earnest integrity and professionalism that he had extended to both Lennie and me throughout the case. Drawing upon my prosecutor years, I extolled the state's mission: its obligation to earnestly and vigorously prosecute any betrayal of the public trust...Yet in this case, I asserted, the truest victim of this cold and destructive crime was not Mickey's "general public," a small portion of whose tax dollars had been lifted. The victims of his wife's crime were the rank and file of the fire department, but certainly not from a measly budgetary sense of the matter...I pushed it forward, illustrating how police officers, on any given each shift, rely on themselves first; when fixing their Kevlar vests, asserting their authority, drawing their weapons, and most importantly when making split-second, life or death decisions. And how they often must do so alone, without the benefit of communication, command or a partner...The essence of what separates police work from fire service is one component: trust in others. When on the fire ground, crews armed with attack lines find then fight fire, with an engineer feeding them water, while truck companies raise ladders to ventilate the massive heat and smoke. All of them rely on whomever -first thing in the morning- checked and then rechecked their Air Bottles/Packs/ PASS devices then started up every cutting tool first. The very quintessence of fire service operations is, in a word: Trust...Lennie's wife betrayed his trust, by betraying the trust of fire-fighters by stealing their department's money...Lennie's wife's acts were nothing short of treasonous...She desecrated the fire service, which was her husband's life. If betraying her husband and what he stood for was not bad enough, what she did to their children was diabolical...Since that state failed to present any evidence whatsoever of Lennie's overt or covert participation in any part of his wife's crime, let alone any motive to have attached himself to anything so contrary to what he stood for, I asked the Court to find him not guilty...I reminded the Court that everyone directly or indirectly connected to her crime, including the rank and file, officers, chiefs, and trustees of the Fire Protection District, had been blindsided by her conduct...Lennie's wife fooled everybody who trusted her. They were all betrayed. Therefore, I concluded, if Lennie was guilty, then so was everyone else who she duped..

.

I'm every woman's dream and every man's nightmare.

—*Ric Flair*

Judge Caradine issued a brilliant but subtle, no winners or losers rul-ing. Reasonable doubt and the presumption innocence carried the day, by which His just and proper verdict was soundly rendered. That long and cruel, cold winter had finally ended.

Lennie was found not guilty on all thirteen counts.

Lennie was uncontrollably shaking with relief. His family left the courtroom and gathered in the hallway, where the press was waiting to spin a story. Lennie remained in the courtroom. Mickey, John, and I shook hands for a long time, saying nothing. We had some warm, hatchet-burying words, leaving things on good terms - then we said our good-byes. I turned around, and Lennie was just standing there, waiting for me, still numb and unable to hold himself steady.

So abruptly out from under the system, Lennie did not know what to do and simply could not leave my side. I gave him a big hug and whis-pered in his ear to leave the courtroom to be with his family and friends.

I then looked him in the eye and said, "Lennie, my work is done. I'm out of here. I'm sneaking out the back..."

I watched Lennie walk out of the courtroom for the very last time. Judge Caradine hadn't left the bench; He was gathering His things up and taking it all in. As I turned around from Lennie, my plan was to slip away, unnoticed. I was noticed- yet I did not break stride; as I passed by the bench, I asked "Your Honor?" while pointing toward the "Authorized Personnel Only" exit. Judge Caradine gave me the nod. Once back into the secured chambers corridor, I snaked my way toward the courthouse doors, determined to leave the thankful, the curious and press in the wind.

There, waiting for me in the back, was Rob Koch, a deputy sheriff - top notch -and with a heart of gold -who had been assigned to my court-room some sixteen years before, when I was its lead prosecutor. "I've been waiting for you kid. I know you never liked the limelight. I'm here to escort you the hell out of here. I knew you would get the job done. You always did, kid."

With Rob blocking for me, we slid past the crowd, into the vestibule, out the door, and down the walkway. "You're probably all clear from here. But just in case, I radioed ahead." I shook hands with Rob (we always shook hands), headed down the ramp with my two large files and my brief bag that I dumped into the back seat of a squad car manned by the Sergeant who Rob had radioed for assistance.

"Rob told us to leave you be and just get you to your car. But we gotta tell you; the word is out. What you did for Lennie Breczko and his kids was freekin' huge."

Redemption is not perfection.
The redeemed must realize their imperfections.

—JOHN PIPER

Lennie had expected the case to take up the entire afternoon and likely not to conclude until well into the next day. He knew the system - so had made arrangements with someone to get his grade-school daughter to her softball game. He had no clue as to whether it was home or away, let alone what team hers was playing.

When he found out. He began to cry.

It was an away game. Lennie pulled up to the parking lot at the ball-park, fighting to keep his composure so that he could take in this poetic moment. The ball field where his daughter was playing – with her game well underway - was right behind the very police station where he had been taken in after his arrest.

As Lennie approached the field, his daughter, playing third, with a go-ahead runner, her new friend, playing tough and crowding her, saw him from afar. The two of them sprinted in tandem off of the field. The home plate umpire called time.

Her team members all began to scream for joy. The opposing team joined in the celebration of this storybook moment. They all knew what this was about; word gets out in girls' softball. Then all of the parents from both teams let loose. The other team's cheering parents, ironically, were residents of the fire district whose tax dollars Lennie's wife had stolen. The field erupted in a wave of joy.

Goodness had been restored to Lennie's life. He could handle being a single parent, considering everything that he had endured. Word even got back to the jail. Those on his old tier cheered...

That Lennie was innocent, and yet that I had to fight so hard against the system so it would not fail him, took its toll on Melaura and me. We knew that it was time for me to take down my shingle and wean myself from the practice of law.

The key to this – the proper way to transition out – demanded that I think in an Amsterdam, story-telling way - and do my very best to conduct my daily affairs accordingly.

> *Anger is an acid that can do more harm to the vessel in which it is stored than to anything on which it is poured.*
>
> *—Mark Twain*

CHAPTER XXXVII

PULLING STAKES

Capital punishment is as fundamentally wrong
as a cure for crime
as charity is wrong as a cure for poverty.

—Henry Ford

I finally came to terms that the practice of law called up too many of the same behaviors and neuroses that had cluttered up my personal life for so long. I no longer took to arguing points of law or assuming any position on such matters. Those who called me, still got my time and my ear, but their problems would now remain theirs exclusively.

My legal career and the world of criminal defense, rolling up my sleeves and toiling in the adversarial process, simply no longer felt good. In many ways, the modern day American way of life of which the American Criminal Justice system was so much a part, was also losing its appeal - when compared to my Amsterdam identity.

The first time I pondered this reality was after my Anne Frank House experience, while participating in a poll offered up to patrons who had finished their journey. Emotionally rattled, I was in hardly good shape to weigh in on much of anything.

Nonetheless, I joined in on an opinion poll; its medium was a video presentation designed to generate responses from us participants. Direct questions followed short video vignettes that displayed various types of expression. The inquiry: Whether or not the depicted expression should be forbidden, or even punished. Not seeing any criminal or overtly riotous behavior, no clear and present danger, I hit what I presumed to be the "no" button.

When the results were in, it was a unanimous vote, minus one.

Panicking, thinking that I did not correctly read or closely listen, I was embarrassed that I had foolishly skewed the intended unanimous vote, having pressed the wrong button.

The second time, I paid very close attention to both the form of the question and the button instruction. This time, I got it right—that is until the results came in. Once again, it was all, less one. The others looked at me. They knew I was the lone dissenter - the rabble-rouser, shamefully upon this reverent ground.

I chastised myself for having confused "no" for "yes" and that I had once again blown it by casting my vote for in favor of deprivation and against expressive freedom. Now even more embarrassed, I reran my bad math. After doing so, however, it became clear that I was the *only* one endorsing the depicted speech. Everyone else had voted to shut it down.

"Freedom of speech? For even heinous forms of expression, no?"

"*Yes. That's right,*" an elderly German man said. "*It's ordained in the First Amendment of your Constitution. But right-thinking European people will never again give such hatred any safe haven.*"

"But the way we see it, unless you protect all opinions, even the most wretched, hatred will creep in in other ways."

"*And the way we see it, America saved our country. Good Americans gave their lives to fight against THAT,*" his wife replied, pointing to the vignette's frozen framed, spitting, ranting skinhead.

For the very first time in my life, I began to question whether the First Amendment's protection of free speech was all that it was cracked up to be. After all, why should educated environmentalists and tax-paying, hard-working tea-party members be lumped in with NAMBLA perverts and Ku Klux Klan bullies? Yet in the eyes of the highest law of my land, they held equal privilege and were fully vested with the law's protection.

That experience now remerged in the form of my conflicting views of law enforcement and its place to society, which raised two questions: "What am I doing?" and "Why am I here?"

16. The Beat Reporter

American law enforcement was under fire. Accounts of cops being shot at while processing blood-soaked, shell-casing-strewn crime scenes was now common place in Chicagoland. It was a dark throwback to the coordinated mayhem of the seventies and underground rebellion. Basic canvassing was no longer the once-efficient norm. Even the overflowing pool of trusty snitches, who had been worth their weight in gold and could be counted on for generating or dis-seminating valuable information, had now dried up.

For police officers working the beat, having the last word by getting to the accurate account of what had gone down was almost impossible; the good guys no longer held the streets. Well-meaning cops who tried to work up cases in ways they had learned from old timers were viewed as naïve, by both a new breed of officers who kept their heads low - and the criminals who con-trolled most street corners and kept their mouths shut, even when the truly innocent had been gunned down.

Back in my days as a prosecutor, most crimes were solved 'yesterday'. The cops I worked with knew when

and why and how to look the other way on minor infractions, so-called "petty shit" - willing to invest on
future returns—by forming alliances with people whose
eyes and ears would come in handy when it really
counted. Before all of this, open-minded cops would
not think twice about leaning on anyone who needed
it, and the community could stand by them and
their well-meaning decisions. This was a time when
not all- but enough - gangbangers, fences, dealers
and pimps would back a cop they could trust, even
if one of their own might end up roughed up or
collared. Such practices, rooted in common sense and
streets smarts, seemed no longer workable.

When one young reporter, a rogue throwback who had
taken up the archaic "overnight beat," followed up
on all after-dark, violent crime stories, was asked
what the people wanted, without any hesitation, he

replied that most people stuck in rough
neighborhoods - particularly the old-timers -
lamented how the battle of the streets was no
longer a fair fight. As one old woman put it, he
read verbatim: "Court don't ever work right anymore.
Not for us, not for the police, not for no one."
The residents he talked to, shocked that he was
even out there, were open and candid. They just
want CPD out there, on the streets. They missed
the days when they knew beat cops and 'tac'
officers by name and could offer them coffee,
food, a nip - even a few bucks for their trouble.

For this now ignored constituency, the grassroots
police work they could always count on and
generally stood by was ancient history. As one
retired steel-worker, an Englewood two-flat owner
put it: "The cops I knew would not think twice about

putting the boots to these punk-ass, disrespectful motherfuckers. Back in the day, many, many cops – hell, even the white guys – was the role model half of these dumb asses ever had. Young guys would actually shut up and lis-ten – and they at least tried not to fuck up. And when they did, they would fess up. Nowadays, you can't get close to cops with anything. They will shoot you, 'cause their hands are tied. It's fucked up. And I do not put all the blame on them neither. I just keep my ass away from trouble and keep tellin' my children that when the police are around, you keep you hands out of your pockets and way above my head – and do as they say – stay clear of all the rest of this crazy-ass shit goin' on out here go."

Though my new-found storytelling perspective, I found the way to stop futilely mitigating life's imperfections, let alone aggravating my own. It felt so much better to accept what I could not change and just keep writing my story. Operating under Umair's mandate, I could finally ponder in good ways my regrets and judiciously weigh my follies and mistakes. Those years of having obsessed over or excused away my blunders, with the ugly half-apologies and sour repentances, just about did me in.

By writing – telling my story and the story of those connected to me, the more principled and harmonious my view of everything else, certainly my law practice, was becoming. I was able to do my best, accept the system's limitations – hence my own to change it - then let it all go.

Melaura and I had a sense that doing business as usual – and our lives in the States – were both coming to a close. After all, my best professional days and worst personal ones were squarely behind me. While I was blessed that my stock and trade continued to provide my family and me with a comfortable standard of living, I had arrived at a place in my life – from my story telling perspective, beyond which I was now certain there was an even better story yet to be told – and in an even better place for it to unfold.

It was time to clean out the closets, clear things away, have a yard sale, give stuff away, pack it up the essentials, scoop Melaura and carry her to Amsterdam.

Efforts and courage are not enough
without purpose and direction.

- JOHN F. KENNEDY

CHAPTER XXXVIII

THE
CADENCE—WRITING

Writing is an exploration. You start from
nothing and learn as you go.

—*E. L. DOCTOROW*

Many Amsterdam-based musicians with whom I had performed over my years asked me why I had not tried to recapture the musical moments from my weeks in Amsterdam back to Chicagoland for the fifty-one weeks in between.

Melaura agreed – and encouraged me to perform live. It was Scott Pazera, a killin' bassist who put together "The Amsterdam Connection Quintet", comprised of the finest Chicago-based musicians from all over the world, who were touched by the idea – eager to recreate my Amsterdam live performance experience.

And why limit it to music? I pondered. If I could play Amsterdam here, why not write Amsterdam here?

The medium and methodology by which I was now reducing "Al Basha" to words varied: Handheld cassette recorder, manually percussed/

typewritten sheets, scraps of paper, coasters and e-mail/text reminders in all hours of the day and night.

During my next trip to Amsterdam, I finally decided it was time to do some writing there. I requested and was given permission to work at it in Café Internationaal.

Michel was elated; excited to have the creative energy of 'an aspiring writer' in the Café to titillate him, titivate the cafe and welcome in patrons. I tucked myself deep into a corner, at a round two-seater, swapping out its leather stool for one of the brawny oak-armed chairs from the larger, rectangle tables. From that nook was my vantage point to watch guests be drawn in and my friends to pour in, eager to recount for me their perspectives on my many celebrated times there over the years. Verse, laughter and tears would flow.

I believe the target of anything in life
should be to do it so well that it becomes an art.

—ARSENE WENGER

I pulled up thoughts and refined written recounts - some penned over Chicago-bound flights, many of which I hadn't looked at in years, from a mishmash pile of notebooks, notecards, back sides of legal forms, hotel stationery, coasters, placemats, and airline papers; margins scribbled with narratives: the log of my long, continuing journey.

Having packed my saxophones away, my pushed-to-the-limit chops now recuperating, for me to be there and write, sparing no intimacy and recounting it all in the Café, was what I believe Umair had in mind when we broke bread; which now seemed like a lifetime ago.

Solitude is creativity's best friend, and
solitude is refreshment for our souls.

NAOMI JUDD

At first, I sought inaccessibility and distance, finding it at Indiana and Michigan lakesides - over three-day weekends; leaving cases and clients and the courthouse behind. Then Melaura suggested a setting closer to home, where I could keep at it, without the travel time/hour change.

I set out to find a suburban-Chicago version of Café Internationaal. It was like I was looking for a barber. True to form, I found what I was looking for – at a location a mere five-minute drive, three minute / bicycle ride from our home.

I found "Grape and Grain" and Rami ("Ron"), Palestinian American entrepreneur; proprietor to a bar from which locally micro-brewed beers of all kinds flowed and where the sounds of "the Amsterdam Connection Quintet" would eventually fill. Endearing, worldly, and accommodating, Rami encouraged my writing. In Michel's way, he gave me privilege, put me in my place when warranted and most importantly, offered me the solace to carry forth.

Amid its revolving door of nutty, quirky, adrift barkeeps, "The G" presented so many clever twists that it often teased me into thinking I somehow was back in Café Internationaal; the words flowed.

One afternoon, Rami, as if out of the blue, asked me the title of my novel. After I told him, he replied, "*Oh. This is about some sinister syndicate client of yours? Murder?*"

"Why would you think that?", I asked.
To Rami - and by the Saudi meaning with which he was familiar, "Al Basha" took on a pernicious air. It was an underhanded compliment; an insult best whispered. Anyone referred to as "Al Basha" was loathed and feared; one who was heir to corrupt wealth, dirty money, big clout and connected power. As Rami put it, "*When I think of 'Al Basha', I think of Kim Jong-Il when he was a bratty kid.*"

Weighing in on our conversation was a tiny, straight-talking, Ponce-born New Yorican. Sasha was so perfectly both quite approachable and highly risky. The way she saw it, "Al Basha" was short for "I'll bash ya frickin' head in if you don't cut the crap."

Forming this impromptu International quorum were Dave, a populist type - much in Kane's way - and his *Nederlanse* wife, Joka - who never refused to indulge – and warmly (*gezellig*) correct - my Pidgeon Dutch. A school teacher, Joka did so with kindness - slow pronunciations and impeccably penned translations. She got a kick out of my twisted pneumonic devices – or *ezelsbruggetje* (donkey over the bridge) method.

Both Yoka and Dave – whose Dutch put mine to shame – jokingly kicked it around between themselves - then weighed in with their take – "*Uil Baasje*' – expressing their excitement to someday read my proletarian novel about 'a man and his beloved wise bird' -*Uil Baasje* [Owl Pet Owner].

Rami and I nodded with a grin, acknowledging that a linguistic consensus had been diplomatically brokered. With that, I announced a ring of the bell, which Dave and Yoka understood and explined to Ron and Sonya. With my acted-out clang, a round of microbrew was abound - on me.

Over the next ten months, I wasted not one second in the Courthouse; I developed great impatience with the dreary pace of "Court Time". The Courtroom environment had generally become so unbearable. I wanted to write or play my saxophones and be with Melaura.

17. The People vs. Me

An unimpressive prosecutor could not stop dilly-dallying, meandering in and out of the courtroom; so unsure of himself but for being doggedly unwilling to communicate with me or appeal to my experience.

My client's case was set for trial. My impatience now expired, my unchecked body language and facial expressions met with the Judge's consternation. In the middle of addressing another defendant, represented by a friend of mine, the Judge, now focused on me, queried: *Mr. Minasian, do you have somewhere else more important to be than here?*

"Yes, Your Honor. I most certainly do, your Honor."

The court reporter, my friend, the clerk and the deputies smiled. The baffled prosecutor just could not help himself:

"Your Honor, we object. This case is set for trial, and while we are not in a position to determine if we are going to be ready for trial, and at the moment we are not answering 'ready', we are not answering 'not ready'. Additionally, there are other matters that are also set for trial as well, but as to those, we are not either answering 'ready' or 'not ready', as well - not at this particular time."

"Your Honor, I rest my case."

The Judge stared down the state and ruled:

> *"Justice delayed, justice denied. Continuance denied. Case dismissed. Mr. Minasian. Your client is now free to leave. You, however, are ordered to tend to your business…There is a novel I am waiting to read…"*

My client and I exited the courtroom and he said, "I was hoping that you would beat this case. I am so glad that I hired you, Superman. Here's your money I owe you for this one - and here's some extra. I'm gonna need your help - it's on something that's gonna get me any day now. But that's a whole other story - and I don't wanna jam you up- with the Judge putting you on some much deeper shit and all…"

The Art of Communication is the language of leadership

—JAMES HUMES, AMERICAN LAWYER

I was fortunate to have "the G", and its kindred cousins, Hailstorm Brewing Company and Blue Island Beer Company – each with the feel and briny waft of a Dutch cheese factory and the look and spit-polish of my beloved Homewood Fire Department's bay floor. As Melaura seemed to know all along, these localities would get me by, summon up good thoughts of my dear friends from Café Internationaal and create the needed space for me to write.

As if vying with my writing sensation, "the G" would also prove to be an incredible venue for the live music. A former recording studio, its floor, walls and ceiling shared Café Internationaal's sweet sound quality, acumen, soul, and *gezellig*.

I was making the most of my time away from Amsterdam and balancing my glee as some upstart writer against my resolve to be a closing-shop lawyer.

An ambassador is not simply an agent;
an ambassador is also a spectacle.

—WALTER BAGEHO

CHAPTER XXXIX

THE CODA

Faith is to believe what you do not see;
the reward of this faith is to see what you believe.

—*Saint Augustine*

For therapeutic purposes, I mindset myself back to Amsterdam, with constant self-imposed visions of Dutch cobblestone. In order to endure the dread of practicing Law, I never let my thoughts stray too far from this fanaticized canal's edge. This view of my world now became me, identified me and would navigate me through the bad times and the worse, wholly unnecessary ones.

Writer Ben Okari was correct: "From to the moment of our birth - from before our birth - to the moment of death - after our death, we live in a constant sea of stories."

And whether my story was, as Prosser [on Torts] described, "a mere convergence of time and place" or something predestined and willingly interconnected – I did not need to determine.

Committed to Umair's mandate and my destiny, I would continue to put to words the story of us, "Al Bashawat", and those of so many others: Our stories. Doing so had taken me across the Atlantic and brought me to Amsterdam – the place where I came to honest terms with my failures and weaknesses, found redemption and could 'reach out to inner peace'. Amsterdam embraced Umair's mandate and granted me permission to be human – to be the real me.

A rebirth out of spiritual adversity causes us to become new creatures.

—JAMES E. FAUST

My much-anticipated return to Amsterdam was a month away. I began to think about Lennie, from whom I hadn't heard since after his acquittal. After the trial, we both needed some space. He needed to reconfigure his life as a single parent and spouse to in inmate. I felt the urge to talk to him; and yet, my calls went unanswered. I resorted to sending him a text, which he and I disdained and so always avoided. After days of one-side communication, I shamefully quipped to myself, "Now that you're a free man, I'm chopped liver…"

The day before my flight, Lennie called. He sounded terrible – and did not say but a few skewed words.

"Lennie. What's wrong?"

He began to sob: *"Half of me wanted to call you, the other half didn't… half of me was afraid that if I did, I was going to be re-arrested and charged… and the other half – if you can believe it – was hoping I would…Franco. I can't seem to break free from the case – our case."*

"Lennie. Listen to me. You need to drop everything. Get on line. Find a last-minute cruise from wherever to wherever and get your ass out over the middle of the ocean. Trust me on this one – as your lawyer and as your friend. You do this and you will recover. Ask me, once again - If you were my son, would I tell you to do this? Yes. And if you need the funds, I'll spot you. You must heed my advice. There is precedent – someone like you who was falsely accused and run through the system. If you do not take my advice, you will never free yourself from the system's grip. If you do not promise me that you will do this, I'm cancelling my trip to Amsterdam.

> *"Franco. You go – and I'll go. I've always wanted to pass through the Panama Canal. My Great Uncle helped build it. I once made good friends with a Boca Raton Fireman, who has a Master's Degree in History from Notre Dame. I'll stay with him. My folks and my kids will be glad to have me out of their hair… Thank you Franco. I'm sorry we lost touch…"*

"So, I don't need to cancel my trip?"

Upon my arrival at Schiphol, after clearing my passport with spot-on Dutch, giddy with anticipation, waiting out my luggage with equally eager fellow wayfarers, I headed for my traditional jump-start, aromatic coffee at the kiosk I had been drawn to on every visit since my first.

The gentleman serving up coffee, tea and sweet treats, with a bright eyed and meticulous, college professor's way, made eye contact with me- through the crisscrossing wayfarers- from twenty-five feet. He reminded me of a leaner, self-confident Umair.

He shouted over out into Schiphol Airport's so alive atrium: "*Khosh-aw-ma-deed beh khaw-neh!*" ("Welcome home!")

Dreaming, after all, is a form of planning.

—GLORIA STEINEM

From my perplexed reaction to words I could not make out, he beckoned me to the counter. Dolling up a cappuccino, in impeccable English, he told me that he remembered me from many years ago, to the day. Those in line closed in and perked up their ears, as if I held some celebrity musician status, my tenor sax slung over my right shoulder.

Was I still over the Atlantic dreaming all of this?

That certainly made sense, given the many Chicago to Amsterdam in-flight dreams that crept into my transatlantic anticipation.

These mental, short films -and the one I seemed to be in-never holding the lead role-nurtured me - in such stark contrast to angry dreams of my troubled past; ones that threw multi-sensory conflicts and clashes of all kinds at me, inevitably startling me awake, leaving me to triage my throbbing, almost-audible pulse, over the aimless sleepless hours to fol-low; those horrible witching hours fraught with fretting and revved-up uncertainty.

But when over the Atlantic, in my Amsterdam-bound deep sleep, I felt safe and free; as if under the covers with Melaura, serenated by her quirky, polyphonic snore - soothed by her dynamic body heat. When by her nighttime side, I could always fall back asleep to the anticipation of our morning pillow talk, her school teacher prose; amidst my love at first sight pitter-patter and our first cup of coffee.

Upon each landing at Schiphol that followed my first, I could feel Melaura's love waking me up and ushering me onto my journey to follow.

But this was no dream. I had landed. I was in Schiphol.

It is better to be prepared for an opportunity and not have one than to have an opportunity and not be prepared.

—WHITNEY M. YOUNG JR.

I remember you from so many years ago! You were right here - and you are right here now - both times - just before Norooz (the Persian New Year), which is so incredible. Norooz is rooted in Zoroastrianism; it is the holy way approach springtime and celebrate its arrival as the rejuvenation of Mother Nature. It is that gentle reminder for each and every one of us to cleanse our bodies, minds, souls, and, of course, our hearts."

"Persians firmly hold that the present is what matters the most; we stay with and are mindful the present - each and every moment - and do our very best to treasure it. The present is the most precious time we have; it sets our past free and determines our future. It is not some cheap commodity. And over a decade ago – I saw this way, the Persian way, in you."

"We are all susceptible to make mistakes, regardless of who we are or how knowledgeable we may be. And so, one of the most important sayings from Zoroastrianism goes "All we need to be conscious, which means to live and love, is to have good thoughts, good words, and good deeds."

"This saying? It was beaming out from you. When you and I first met – and we did meet - it felt like we were family, celebrating Norooz. In fact, I have included a paper coffee cup in our haft seen, our holiday display of hope, inspired by your journey's powerful awr-maan-how (dreams). I knew then that you were beginning an important journey."

"As you went to find what was yours, with your musical instrument, luggage, and my coffee, I shouted out, 'Baa-beh-ta-re-aw-zoo-haa!' (Best of luck!)"

"Yes. I knew why you had come to this place - the City of Amsterdam; to fulfill your spirit. I was certain then that the City of Amsterdam had been waiting for you - even more than for me - and that it would take you in and never let you go. I know of this feeling and to know that it would be yours made my cry with joy."

"Now, with such great fortune, I see you here once again. I feel like a man who found his long-lost brother."

A growing crowd, many with their cell phones recording, closed our circle in, as others about its periphery gathered. Overwhelmed, all I could offer up was the universal sign of peace and, "Peace brother. Peace…Anoushirvan [as his nametag read]. Isn't that something? My grandmother's name was Anoush. She escaped from Armenia to Cyprus, where she and her young child were given refuge by a Persian family…"

"It is everything."

To my two fingers, Anoushirvan held up three, in response to which I felt obliged to respond with four. Chuckling, he said, *"Four is a very good number, but please, my long-lost brother. Let me explain…"*

Those in line, there ranks already closed ranks, gathered even closer in, surrounded by an even larger, like-minded gathering- Dutch and wayward travelers they joined in this welcoming and very special moment. It was one of those collective, *gezellig* experiences.

Anoushirvan now held the floor.

"Many Iranians - Persian people - they know this context. I have bid you – and I will always bid you - Se Paas. Se is the number three, and Paas means 'to value.' And so, I offer all of you what the spirit of this moment we all share offers us: Three great things in life - good thoughts, good words, and good deeds."

Anoushirvan reached over the counter, put each hand on either side of my head, drew me in, and then touched the top of my forehead to his, a most perfect, across-the-counter hug. Then, upon his gentle release, he said, *"Go to your place, brother. And until next year, if not sooner, Se Paas."*

"Se Paas", Anoushirvan, and Se Paas to all of you. Welcome to Amsterdam!"

The crowd lifted up and extended their hands—be it with three fingers or two and a thumb—in unison and with tears of anticipation we offered to each other *"Se Paas"*.

Now my way to Centraal Station- fueled by Melaura's love, with good thoughts of Umair, gratitude for everyone who touched my life; with "Al Basha", stories written and yet to be written, my good fortune from Umair's mandate – inspiring music and dear friends awaiting me, *gezellig* ways and the Dutch Language - over the cobblestone, flowing with great beer and succulent food – and so much more.

I, "Al Basha" had returned to the City of Amsterdam, where - I was more certain now than ever before - Melaura and I were meant to be.

As I exited Central Station, facing the morning sun, that familiar voice resonated:

"In each day and in every moment, it is the path before you that marks your story yet to be told."

Pro-capitalist power existed through an individualistic sensibility…this combination, which seems in many other places to be a contradiction, becomes an essential part of [Amsterdam's] identity.

—RUSSELL SHORTO

Acknowledgments

In recognizing the humanity of our fellow beings,
we pay ourselves the highest tribute.

—*Thurgood Marshall*

Motivator

Bryan Burrough: While on Aruba's tranquil breezy Eagle Beagle, at the Bucuti and Tara beach resort, I cracked open some light reading: 'Days of Rage'. In the beginning of his riveting work, it is written: "Without a doubt, this book is the single most difficult project I have ever attempted. During more than five years of research, I thought of quitting any number of times."

Bryan Burrough's words became my mantra; over the last year of writing "*Al Basha*", got me past uncertain points; demanding that I see it all through.

Editor

Dorothy Elliot: My dearest Dottie, who taught me that less is more, the reader is owed the right to make his or her own way -and that red ink is always on your side and means well. You are masterful and kind.

Writing Places

- Colon, Michigan: My very first stateside writer's retreat. Amish country; a great fire department; decent rowboat; on the serene Sturgeon Lake, but for that Sunday morning, when a massive fire-truck-red powerboat ripped through water, scampering waterfowl while cranking "Beat It."
- Lake Papakeechie, Indiana: Along the same longitudinal line, I found a slice of New England; bird watcher's paradise; a lake house fortuitously stocked with every conceivable writing supply; a knotty-pine bathroom with a psychedelic toilet seat.
- Stevensville, Lake Michigan: Perched over the underbelly of mighty Lake Michigan, where dear friend Mike Cassidy teamed up with Nick Liguras to transform a frumpy summer cottage into a swank, metro condo. A huge picture window buttressing the ever-shifting winds and climates; displaying dancing waters and an occasional wolverine; with an extraordinary shower and a buoyant sound system to boot.

Sounding Boards

John Eannace: My endearing kindred spirit; a gifted, humble and amazingly-talented lawyer who conducts himself in any Courtroom with poise, measure, and dignity; in ways that I can only imitate. John, Mary, Johnny and Colleen and Michelle – The Eannace's are family – and have always been there for Melaura and me.

Mike Bell: Equal parts mystery and open book, who does not take to cutting corners or mincing words. Mike is ever the safety-minded one. He missed his calling in performance art/stage production. We agree on most things; yet it is when we disagree that our friendship truly shines.

Kevin and Linda {and Strauss} Bewley: Good fences make good neighbors, but good drinks and kinship make better ones...

Official Court Reporters: One and all are equally stately and romantic. They encouraged me to write, to write and to write. After all, by trade they are the epitome of story tellers.

Official Court Interpreters: The unrecognized bastions of due process; along with Court Clerks, they assist those "in the system" and in their cross-cultural, no-nonsense way, have a handle on it all and see to it that the record is pure - and that at least one person at the bench gets it.

Problem Solvers

David J. Gallant: The resource for resources, the finest would be cross-examiner; he always has given me enough rope, while making sure I did not wind up dancing on its noosed end.

Linette's anonymous 'sister sledge': *F5. Select All* and so many other-wise elusive nuances of *Word*.

George and Kathy Jasinski: Pouring the finest wine and flowing with warmth and cheer. They are always in celebration of life and its succulence; ever-glowing with fellowship - and so therapeutic. George and Kathy are vigilant to their faith, loyal to their teams; and enjoy such a healthy connection to their affable children to whom I have always felt like a cousin when in their company...

Power Source Martial Arts: Sensei Andre Campos, his ever-supportive wife Georgia, Instructor Jonathan Hernandez and my fellow Judo players- who taught me the 'gentle way' – made me a better husband, father, musician, attorney and tennis player.

JK Consulting: Save. Don't panic. Save. Take a deep breath. Save. Justin and his team of NASA-like technicians- the Alfreds to me, their frantic Batman. Whenever I sent out the distress signaled for their tech support, I received it – at all hours of the day and night.

Morgan Carattini: Laughingly, lovingly and learnedly; the inspiration to my creation of a time line. Equally sensitive and sanely seasoned, her observations and expressions are how any proper Chef utilizes garlic - judicious and without overly mincing.

Ahmad Ben Sabet: He enlightened me as to how clever is the Persian language; and how optimistic are its traditions; and important is the Persian way of life.

John Tryneski: He got me down to the business of writing; by invest-ing his time, candor and invaluable perspective on my rookie-writer business model. John gave me the out to cut, reassuring me that my cull "...will make a great short story...trust me..."

Beth Ann Rodriguez: Her work on the Al Basha's cover and descrip-tive texts -top notch. Beth came through for me when perspective was sorely needed. It is no wonder. After all, Beth is Melaura's very best friend...

Of all life's treasuries /One is most preciously/
Kept in my heart/And that's the loyalty of friends
— BOBBY MCFERRIN

Sarah McMahan: When I was stuck on third base, she graciously offered to read "Al Basha". With the ivy flowing and the pennants flapping in the Lake Shore breeze, Sarah laid down the perfect bunt - with meticulousness and great care - and got me to home plate [with an arms-first slide]...Thank You!

Vendors

FedEx Kinko's, Homewood: Splendid equipment, hours and attitudes.

Jeff Fair: The wizard of Word. It was quicker for him to do it himself than teach me his tricks. When my keyboard went haywire, he installed a new one – even adding some action, which duplicated the feel of my soprano sax. "What would Jeff do?"

Contemporary Sushi by Chef Soon: The very best cuisine; Chef Soon's sushi is most clever and highly reverent. A young Korean whose skill and creativity is old-school Japanese. A great host with such panache, who puts his guests and his ingredients on equal first footing.

Family Liquors: Butch and sons, a throwback to the frontier general store, where cash is king, opinions are welcome and politeness abounds.

Dr. Henry Finn & his Weiss Hospital miracle workers – Gary Matthews/Physical [and Mental]Therapist: New Hip, New Hope.

Ryan Brothers Coffee/San Diego: Indeed- Life is too short to be bitter. Your beans are sweet...

Create Space/Charleston, SC: My Dream Team - So clever, caring and kind....

Café Internationaal's Morning Glory

Glenis: Hotel Internationaal's time-tested, toiling housekeeper. White wine regally becomes her. She speaks not one lick of Dutch- and you would never know it; sassy, self-deprecating, quippy and kind, and oddly lovable. Glenis and Michel constantly barb, like a living Leroy and Loretta of *The Lockhorns* comic strip. As a tribute to her, I promised a free copy of "*Al Basha*".

"Honestly, Franco, I'm relieved that you did; it's truly the only way I might read it - or perhaps I'll just hang on to it, and if it's any good, because I probably won't read it, I'll just sell it. That would be quite nice for both of us."

**He who receives a benefit should never forget it;
he who bestows it should never remember it.**

—PIERRE CHARRON